Splintered Light

Nova Sapiens Book III

By Lee Denning

D1738218

Twilight Times Books
Kingsport Tennessee

Splintered Light

Paladin Timeless Books, an imprint of
Twilight Times Books
P O Box 3340
Kingsport, TN 37664
www.twilighttimesbooks.com/

First Edition, July 2012

Library of Congress Control Number: 2012911328

ISBN: 978-1-60619-020-3

Pastel sketches by Heather Rosenberry

Published in the United States of America

Dedication

A very long time ago, groups of primitive humans fortified by a common belief system prevailed over other groups not so fortified. Epigenetics kicked in, and religion became a species-survival enhancer: natural selection. Then not so long ago came the Renaissance and an age of enlightenment: natural philosophers became scientists. Baruch Spinoza studied religious intolerance in a reasoned way, even though his Portuguese Jewish community excommunicated him for it. His contemporary John Locke came to hold Spinoza's view that the authority of government comes not from clerics alleging their words to be those of God, but from the consent of the governed. Thomas Jefferson later wrote those thoughtful words into our Constitution. So there's a clear trend line from our past to our present, and its name is reason. This third book of the *Nova sapiens* trilogy is dedicated to all its practitioners — of any race, creed, color, sex or other human variable — and to the hope that they continue that trend line into the future.

Acknowledgments

A number of people provided thoughtful reviews and opinions on various drafts of *Splintered Light*: Kathi Chiaruzzi, teacher and skeptic and novelist; Malo Forde, an Irish humorist both on and off the tennis court; Bob Silvestri, a true sci-fi fanatic; Don Berry, a writer and multi-talented entrepreneur; Dorrie Brass, a writer with a keen sense of humanity; Gail Gentle and Sean Haggerty, proofreaders extraordinaire; Phyllis Yu, a sanity-checker for our adaptations of human microbiology. All these wonderful folks helped us in developing a good story or in tidying it up, and we appreciate their kindness.

Ginger James, cheerleader and confidante, kick-started the whole writing process. Lida Quillen at Twilight Times Books saw the potential in the trilogy, and adopted it. Jan Kafka's editorial skills made this third book more readable. We offer them our profound thanks.

Seed concepts from the Institute of Noetic Sciences' various publications, as well as from Roger Nelson's Global Consciousness Project, underpin many of the speculations in this novel as well as its predecessors. We have taken great liberties in extrapolating these concepts to fit our fiction, and apologize if any seem off the mark. Any errors or omissions of course are completely our own. We encourage curious readers to visit the Institute's website at *www.noetic.org*, and Dr. Nelson's website at *www.teilhard.global-mind.org*. Fascinating stuff!

Chapter 1

The girl pounded down the forest path into deepening darkness. The bottom of the cloud ahead had lowered almost to ground level. A part of her mind sensed its moisture condense, its droplets form and gather and grow heavier. Rain would slicken the trail, slow her down. The storm was coming on so fast it seemed unnatural.

Did he make it happen? How?

Another part of her mind ranged outward, seeking the dark thing in pursuit, calculating distance and direction, estimating his intercept time.

He's gaining!

She picked up the pace, running flat out on the uneven ground, feet finding purchase with the instinct of a mountain goat. Her mind made another reflex calculation as lungs and heart edged into the anaerobic zone.

I can't keep this up. He's too damn fast.

The cloud bottom ruptured then and the rain came, torrents so heavy they hammered through the triple canopy as if it were tissue paper. The mental radar that let her detect him went chaotic, its signal degraded by the rain. But that would work both ways: *he can't pinpoint me either.*

The girl skidded on a wet stone and slammed against a tree, ripping her shirt on the rough bark, scraping skin off her shoulder. She swore with a hard grimace and spun off the trail.

Yes! A little fork... maybe... if he'll just buy it...

She ripped a second piece of sleeve, broke a branch and snagged the cloth on it, stepping on rocks and tree roots to avoid leaving footprints. She edged down the side of the trail, wet feet in the streams of water that would erase signs of her passage, then took flight again. The rain came down harder. Sudden torrential downpours were common enough on this part of the island, but this one? *Just too incredible.*

Lightning flashed. The compression wave followed instantly, slamming branches and debris into her back, knocking her down. She rolled as she hit the mud, then flipped upright and staggered onward. Her cheek was numb and she spat blood.

Did he cause the lightning? Could he have that kind of power? Here, of all places? How?

Fruitless questions now. The cards had been dealt, the dice rolled.

Too much power!

Fear began to build on that possibility.

And I'm totally turned around! How can I be lost in my own forest?

The fear rushed toward panic. She forced it down by reaching out to feel the forest with her whole mind. The interconnectedness flowed through her, its unity triggering commands from her mind to her body. Glands reacted, neurochemicals flowing into her brain's blood, a complex orchestrated balance of pain suppressants and stimulants.

Adrenaline-laced strength flooded back into her wobbly legs. She resumed running down the trail, feet again anticipating each unevenness and adjusting instinctively. Her mind filled with the confidence that she was truly a creature of this forest: adaptable, resourceful, agile, powerful. Calmness returned.

The rain stopped abruptly as she ran out of its shaft into sunlight and onto a dry trail. Yet the joy and calm proved fleeting; with the rain behind she sensed the distance between them had been halved. He was following her like a homing missile.

How can he do that? Through that downpour!

Panic flared again and she almost tripped.

Think! Make a trap? No, that would take too much time; he hadn't bought into the decoyed path, so he'd be on her before she could fashion anything damaging.

Sisters, help me!

Images of white-robed women flashed across part of her consciousness as she ran. *Face your fear, child*, stern voices invoked, *stop running. Turn and fight.*

Thunder roared behind her, as if the storm would spin on its heels and drag her back. She ran toward the late-day sun. A familiar tree flashed by, and she was no longer lost; the trail dead-ended not far ahead on a volcanic headland overlooking the bay.

I will face my fear. But on my battleground, not his.

Seconds later, without slowing her headlong pace, young Eva Connard hurled herself off the cliff and arrowed down toward the sun-speckled waves of Waimanu Bay a thousand feet below. A vortex formed in the bay as she plunged toward it, and spun a waterspout upward to greet her.

Merauke, Irian Jaya | Monday 1303 JYT

A gaunt face stared back at him in the mirror, a face he hadn't seen in eight long years. *The lines are deeper. The hair is shot with gray.*

Slowly, he realized the time in captivity had enhanced his appeal rather than diminished it. He smiled at his reflection. *Yes, that will do nicely. The very image of a prophet.*

A man entered the washroom behind him, froze, and stared into the mirror.

"Mahdi!" the man gasped. He went down on one knee, head bowed.

"Yes," Muhammad Zurvan answered. He ran an admiring finger down the harshly handsome plane of his own cheek, but suppressed elation. *I must appear humble.* Zurvan turned away from the mirror and let the old skills rearrange his expression accordingly.

"We thought you were dead," the man glanced up, a sidelong frightened look, then lowered his eyes again. "Seven years, Mahdi..." he murmured.

Zurvan studied the man. *The myth is being re-born. I must choose my words carefully, my actions as well.*

He spoke to the man almost in a whisper. "Long years. I wandered the wilderness. Now I return."

"Praise Allah!" The man quivered, gave another sidelong glance.

"I sought enlightenment."

"Mahdi!"

"I have spoken with the Prophet."

The man dropped his other knee, prostrating himself in the prayer position, gasping. Zurvan smiled at the top of the man's turbaned head. *I have him now.*

"I have met the Christ."

The man moaned.

"He is with us. He will pray with us, with the Mahdi. Speak it now."

The man began to sob, reciting the proper prayer. Zurvan stroked his beard, listening acutely, parsing the complex intonations. *Excellent! Years with no contact and they still remember the code, and the al-Mahama al-Kubra. Their discipline remains intact.* He erased elation from his face, making it thoughtful, humble, caring. Then he spoke.

"I have wrestled with Shaitan, in the wilderness."

The man jerked back up on his knees, shocked, and just stared.

"By Allah's grace, I overcame him."

"Praise Allah!" The man pulled off his belt and began to whip his back, weeping with joy, working himself into ecstasy. Zurvan watched for a bit, keeping his expression fixed.

Not too bright. But faithful; he stayed in place for years. He retained the code and came when I called.

Zurvan grabbed the man's flailing hand. "Peace, my son. What is your name?"

"Ahmed, Mahdi."

"Ahmed. Yes, I remember now. You were a boy when I entered the wilderness. You are a man now. And you remembered the code."

"I am your servant! As before. As always."

Zurvan reached out to grasp the man's shoulder. *If you can get me off this island you are. If not, I'll kill you.* He smiled at the thought. *So many years a prisoner of those wretched little creatures. I'm overdue for some killing.*

"Good. Ahmed, there must be no word of my return. Not a hint."

Ahmed's eyes widened, disappointment clear on his face.

"I overcame Shaitan once, Ahmed, but the devil is strong. His infidel armies are in the West. They have ears and eyes, all over the world, especially here."

Ahmed straightened, puffing out his chest proudly. "Islam will conquer all, Mahdi! It is foretold! The end time!"

"Yes, Ahmed. And that time is nearly on us. But Shaitan is clever, so we must be too. Clever and quiet, and building our strength unheard and unseen until we are ready. Do you understand?"

Ahmed nodded, silent, but Zurvan read the expressions fleeting over the man's face. *You crave to announce it, the great war. So stupid. Do I kill you now, Ahmed?*

"You must hold your joy close to your heart, Ahmed. No word of my return."

The man nodded.

"Not until my time has arrived."

"The faithful, Mahdi... your *Jaesh*..."

"Of course, my friend. A few must know. But very few; cell rules apply. And first you must get me off this island, to a safe place beyond the reach of the Indonesian government. It collaborates with the infidel."

Ahmed stroked his own beard. "There is a place... East Timor, in the highlands, a Muslim retreat. You will be safe, and welcomed."

One of my old ones, in the safety net. Yes! Zurvan kept his expression bland. *Well isolated, but... so many years? Are they compromised now?*

"The United Nations? Australian peacekeepers?"

"Not in the highlands, Mahdi."

And that country is no friend to the Indonesian government.

"Good. Then arrange it, Ahmed. Quickly! And when you return, bring me clothing. And scissors."

Waimanu Bay, HI | Sunday 1704HST

Eva Connard sucked in air as she fell, driving it into her lungs, commanding them to supersaturate her blood with oxygen. The waterspout caught and gently cradled her body as she'd intended, bleeding off momentum as they fell together toward the water surface. Her mind's radar sensed her dark pursuer launch from the cliff top, then the water closed over and she lost contact.

She smiled grimly. *He can't match my skill. He'll have a much harder landing. And then we'll see...*

As she dropped through the water she framed a second intention, a safety valve: *Attend me, my friends! I may need your help.* She sensed their instantaneous alertness as they forsook their game, turned as one and sped toward her from the deeper waters offshore.

How far out? She couldn't tell; water diminished her ranging ability almost to zero. *But they're coming if I need them. Good!*

Eva flipped and landed on the bay bottom, feet kicking up coarse black volcanic sand mixed with organic sediment. Fish flashed away, startled. The water was not as clear as it sometimes was, but neither was it murky. *No advantage either way,* she decided, but edged into the partial concealment of a rock outcrop anyway. A reflexive twist of her mind adjusted local gravity enough to counter buoyancy as she anchored herself to the rock. *Let him come to me; let him use up his oxygen and energy.*

Almost on cue, a pressure wave told her he'd hit the water surface ten meters above. She smiled. *Ouch! That must've hurt.*

And there the thing was, a formless shadow, almost invisible except for the distortion it caused in the water and the flickering around its edges. It twisted as it sank down.

Eva pulled a null field over herself and watched her body fade into just a hint of waviness in the water, a wraith against the rock and sand. *Find me if you can.* Then she slowed her racing pulse, reducing oxygen consumption. *Let's see who runs out of air first, bozo.*

The amorphous nothingness drove through the water and splashed up a wave of sand and sediment as it smacked into the bottom twenty meters away. *Ouch, that hurt, too, I bet. Or...*

It was, in theory, possible to project a gravitational field outward from the body. A higher skill level than she'd yet achieved, but... maybe not beyond that of her pursuer. The possibilities flashed across her mind and converged: drive a gravity wedge ahead of you to decelerate, push it down through the water into the bottom. *Did I see what I saw?* Her mind played it back. The distortion in the water could have been a null field around his body, or it could have been a gravity wave. *Deception, a decoy. He's very smart. And he's not where I think!*

Eva's legs reacted instantly on the thought, pushing her away from the rock just as his energy blade slashed down on it from behind. She spun, her own hands flaring ovals of indigo light, and parried a sweep from his foot. Coruscations erupted where their energies met. She sprang backwards into the cloud of sediment his decoy had raised, and snapped off her blades. *I can deceive, too.*

Eva blinked away the searing afterimages on her retinas, turned at right angles and swam across the bottom to flank his position. Fear rose again but adrenaline and anger drove it down. *Dammit! I'm going to win this battle!*

But her determination wavered as she emerged from the sediment cloud and found him standing in front of her. If he had been stunned by impact with the water, or was running short of oxygen, he didn't show it. In fact — she studied the flickering black nimbus around the emptiness of his null field — *he's laughing! He's laughing at me!*

Teasingly, tiny energy blades grew from his hands, making figure eights in the water. More laughter, mocking.

Anger shook Eva and her hands reflexively flared energy blades, but then her training imposed the coolness of reason. *I can deceive, too.* She waved blades to mimic her enemy's, slicing bigger figure eights, the water hissing and vanishing into the planes of pure energy. *Just watch my hands.*

He did, crabbing sideways with lightning quickness, his blades elongating to match hers, but not engaging. He danced across the bay bottom, studying her hand motions, hesitating.

Now Eva laughed at him. *Cautious. As well you should be. But it's too late now, sucker!*

The dolphin slammed into his back, driving him hard against the rock outcrop. Another one caught him from the side as he bounced off the rock; it knocked him onto the bay floor. A third hit him again, on a downward trajectory, driving him into the sand and muck.

Enough! Her mind screamed the command and the rest of the school broke off their attack and gathered around her, chirping. Eva Connard petted the alpha female on her nose and framed the intention that they should return to their own dolphin games. *Thank you, my friends. Well played.*

Senate Office Building, Washington, DC | Sunday 2210 EST

The Capitol dome gleamed white under its lights. The Senator contemplated it for a few silent moments through the window of his corner office in the Russell Senate Office Building. Then he raised his hand off his considerable paunch, gesturing toward the dome and the flag flying off to its side.

"Power."

He's getting right to it tonight, the younger man thought as he suppressed a fidget. "I'm aware of that, Senator."

"But not enough, son. Not enough power for what's comin' at us."

"I'm aware of that, too, Senator." *He'll lead off with patriotism.*

The Senator examined him, then glanced back out the window. He spoke sonorously. "We need to control this new species, boy. Adopt 'em, make 'em our own. It's the only way America will be safe."

"A way to make America safe; yes, Senator."

"I hear a 'but' in there, boy."

"Control is the issue. I don't believe it's possible."

"You wet behind the ears, son? It's always possible; just need the right leverage."

"Right. A judicious application of power. So you've said, Senator. And I've heard."

"I worry about you, boy. Seems like you hear, but you don't listen."

The younger man placed his hands flat on the desk, spread them apart then turned the palms up expressively. His ring clicked against the desktop. "I don't know what more I can do at this point, Senator."

The older man's gesture invited him to explain.

"Where's our leverage?" he continued. "The world is quiet. The Mideast is peaceful for a change. Mainstream Islamics are clamping down on their radical cousins. No other big conflicts in the world. The economy's good, the market's up. There's just nothing we can create an issue around. Nothing we can spin onto *Nova sapiens* and then come to their rescue, bring them into our camp... no opening wedge."

The Senator tilted his chair back and inspected him.

Like a bug under a microscope, the younger man thought, but went on anyway.

"And, Senator, their own strategy is working beautifully. Those young incipient *Novas* are flying completely below the radar. No publicity, no hint of what evolution is about to do to the human race. None."

The Senator's inspection continued, but he pressed on.

"And we can't expose them. You said it yourself: too much downside risk. All our projections agree on the chaos that exposure would cause."

The Senator gave a reluctant nod. "They'd be up for grabs by anyone, if we disclose their existence. Yeah. Still..."

The younger man watched him consider that, and reject it yet again. *You should see what I see running across your face, Senator. Greed. Lust. I recognize them all too well. Patriotism is just your cover.* The Senator blinked and rearranged his expression before he spoke.

"Access is the first step. Trust is the second." The older man turned aside and contemplated the Capitol dome again. "I'm lookin' for the third step here, boy," he added softly, "the one that gives us control."

"They make their own decisions at that enclave in Hawaii, Senator. Control isn't possible."

"Um. Direct control... maybe not, son. But you're smarter than that. I've seen you in action. You're slick."

"I've been working toward getting control, Senator."

"Work on it harder, son."

The Senator stared at him.

I have to do whatever he wants. I know it. He knows it. But he still toys with me. Ah, power.

"You gonna do it, boy; for the good of our country, you gonna get control..." The Senator gave him a toothy grin, crocodilian beneath empty eyes and coiffed silvery hair. "Whatever, however, you gonna deliver those *Nova sapiens* kids to us, so we control their power." He paused, then slammed his palm down hard on the desk.

"Or you gonna be fucked six ways from Sunday!" he shouted. "So go figure it out, boy! And God bless America!"

Waimanu Bay, HI | Sunday 1711 HST

Her blood-oxygen nearly depleted, Eva Connard strode across the bay floor, grabbed the flickering darkness out of the muck and threw it ahead of her to the surface. She shot upward and out of the water, gasping in buckets of cool clean air, and swam over to him as the null field decayed and his body became visible.

"Josh! You okay?"

Her big brother bobbed on the waves, paddling weakly and coughing out water. *Shit! Hope I didn't crack another rib. He hates that.*

Joshua O'Donnell groaned and vomited.

Eva swam under him and added some buoyancy as he spasmed and vomited again. She held him around the chest, feeling his pain and easing it. *No ribs broken. No lung perforations. Good.*

"Thanks, kiddo," he gasped, "I needed that."

"Hang on, Josh. Don't be the tough guy. Let me finish."

As they floated on the cool waves, Eva ran her hand over his back, sensing.

He took some nasty hits; especially that last one. But... liver... kidneys... yeah, good. All good. He really is incredibly tough. Relief poured out of her. She wrapped a healing intention around it and let it flow from her hands into his body. His gasping eased. He sucked in seawater to rinse his mouth and spat it out. Then he turned and smiled, his turquoise eyes the same color as the sunlit water. She watched those eyes flicker bright with a mix of pride and amusement.

"Nice improvisation, kiddo. Thought I had you there for a minute. Great ambush; never saw it coming."

"That's three times, Josh... in a row. Can we quit now?"

"I know, Sis. And I'm proud of you. But all three were close games. Too close. So we keep practicing. Sorry."

"Live fire exercises are dangerous," she objected. "Even with the safeguards of this place. With my mind locked into the gaming I might hurt you beyond my healing capacity."

"Life's dangerous, Eva. Especially yours. Or it will be shortly. You said that yourself, remember?"

Yes I remember that, Joshua. The waves rocked her soothingly as she contemplated him. *And I know this is just the calm before the storm. I'm grateful we're preparing for it together, and for the love that makes you risk yourself to prepare me.*

Her brother continued. "So every damn thing I can think up to throw at you, I will. Every Sunday."

"You're the deadliest creature on the planet, Josh. Who out there is going to throw something worse at me than you can?"

"Remember Lao Tsu, Eva."

She smiled at him. "Those who have knowledge, don't predict. Those who predict don't have knowledge. That one?"

"Exactly. Especially around the edges of chaos."

Edges of chaos. Yes, you're probably right; the attack will come out of nowhere. Something we can't prepare for no matter what. She sighed, splashed him, then popped out of the water to stand on its surface. *Still, he's right; we have to prepare all we can.*

"Come on, let's go have dinner," she said, laughing.

Eva Connard bent down, grabbed her big brother's hand and yanked him up to stand with her on the water's surface. Together they ran across the top of the gravity-flattened waves and up the black sand beach toward their enclave deep in the Big Island's volcanic rock.

Chapter 2

O'Donnell Enclave, Waimanu, HI | Sunday 1727 HST

"Well. No emergency medical for Joshua this time, it would appear," Dr. Sarah Kruse observed with more calm than she felt, "so I'll go check on my lasagna." She smiled at the images of Eva and her brother on the monitor as they passed the enclave's outer checkpoint. Her hand found the shoulder of the young woman seated at the monitor, felt its tension, rubbed it soothingly. *Let it go, Elia; the terror is over for another week.*

"You know how erratic her control is," Elia Baradei O'Donnell whispered as she drew her fingers across the monitor screen, touching the moving images as they started up the cliff. "She could have killed him."

"But she didn't. And her control *is* getting better."

"Not fast enough. Not for me."

"Nothing we can do about that, Elia. The first *Nova* to hit puberty, in a new evolutionary process... all we can do is watch."

"And hope."

"That too."

"I love Joshua. I love Eva."

"I know."

"It hurts, watching their... games. Their deadly games."

"We all agreed the training was necessary, both to accelerate the gene expression and to refine her control. It was unanimous. You agreed, too."

Elia sighed. "I know, Sarah, I know."

"But...?"

"My mind understands. My heart aches."

Sarah put both hands on Elia's tense shoulders, willing them to relax. *So young. She has yet to discover how much pain a heart can have.* "We have to go down this road, Elia. Eva has to be prepared. Joshua is right."

Elia let out a long breath and her shoulders slumped.

Sarah felt the knotted muscles release. *Yes, good, Elia. Use your Sisterhood training; ease your mind, even if not your heart.* She spoke calm reason. "And Eva herself senses the chaos is gathering faster than we thought. She knows she has to be prepared."

Elia let out another long breath. She reached up and squeezed the hands on her shoulders.

"I'm scared."

"As are we all." Sarah squeezed back. *Acceptance, child. It will be what it will.*

On the monitor, the view switched as a different camera automatically picked up the two approaching the middle checkpoint beside the waterfall and pool, on a ledge part way up the cliff.

"What, no blood this time?" boomed TC Demuzzio cheerfully as he walked into the Security Center. Mr. Bojangles, a large tiger-striped tomcat, slid through the door after him. It meowed, jumped onto the long console holding the monitor banks and stalked toward Elia.

"I thought for a minute I'd have to toss Bo here off the cliff in his scuba gear to haul 'em out of the water..."

Mr. Bojangles sniffed dismissively at Demuzzio and jumped off the console into Elia's lap.

"What the hell good is a freakin' security chief when Eva blows right through the perimeter and... goes underwater, for Crissakes? Where I can't pick her up on camera? That's goddamn dangerous. I gotta have a word with that kid. I gotta..."

Sarah shot him a warning glance and watched Demuzzio's expression change as the man belatedly noted Elia's trembling shoulder and the cat staring at him over it. His cheeriness evaporated.

"Oops. You guys were really worried, huh?"

"Eva's still a wild card at this point, Thomas," Sarah responded, "late puberty, and *Nova* genes just starting to be expressed... a lot of raw power in this locus for a young mind to control. You know it's dicey."

"Yeah... yeah, I guess." Demuzzio rubbed a big hand across his buzz-cut hair. The cat dropped back down into Elia's lap, and the four of them turned their attention to the monitor.

Eva and her big brother had clambered up on the ledge and now stood in the waterfall.

"Rinsing off the salt?" Demuzzio guessed.

"Rinsing off sins." Elia said softly.

"Say what?"

Sarah squeezed Elia's shoulder and clarified. "Thomas, the waters of a power locus are sort of a... spiritual crèche, we think, for *Novas*. We don't understand why."

"A crèche." Demuzzio studied the two forms in the waterfall, and reached down to the joystick on the console to zoom the camera on them. The fading daylight played an indigo glow around Eva and bubbled out to include her brother. "Spiritual, huh?" He rubbed the top of his head again.

Brother and sister walked out of the waterfall, through the pool and toward the camera. As they got closer, Demuzzio thumbed up the audio volume, but there was too much background noise from the falls. Joshua was gesturing, Eva laughing.

"What's that about?" Demuzzio muttered.

Sarah squeezed Elia's shoulder a last time and smiled at Demuzzio as she left.

"We'll hear about it at dinner, I'm sure. I've got to check how my lasagna is doing. They'll both be starved out of their minds."

O'Donnell Enclave, Waimanu, HI | Sunday 1730 HST

"You went outside the game parameters, Eva," Joshua gestured at the bay below them, "outside the power locus. You broke the rules." *I'm not angry with her, exactly,* he thought, *and it was a decent solution. But...*

"Josh! You're the one who said there are no rules! Just survival!" She poked a finger in his still-tender right kidney and he winced. "I survived this game, bro. You didn't." She laughed.

They climbed up the cliff path as he pondered that. *Her laughter is relief for me. So...* The insight came suddenly. He stopped and looked back at her.

"They pulled their punches, didn't they? Your dolphin buddies."

Eva smiled. "You're not sore enough?"

Finesse? So these training games are working? Their intensity is honing her control like we hoped? His logic ran off on a tangent. "The game reality... you buy into it even though your rational mind knows it's artificial..."

"I can do that, Josh. I have to do it, really — if I don't feel a threat right down to my core, the stress of the game isn't enough to accelerate the gene incipience."

Joshua nodded. *Force-feeding her own development. She believes the clock is ticking down on us and she's probably right.* "So how do you do that? Fool yourself?"

Eva moved past him on the cliff path as she answered.

"Rationality for my mind is not pure reasoning, like it is for yours. And my reality is more fluid, it can be more of what I want to make it, less of what the outside world wants to make it..."

She glanced back over her shoulder.

"...when I'm in the game, Josh, I have to be totally convinced that I could be killed."

"But not necessarily that you have to kill your opponent? Thus the dolphins." He sighed. "There will come a time, Eva, when you have to kill someone to save yourself. It's almost inevitable. Will you be able to do that?"

Eva shrugged as they climbed toward the cameras around the inner checkpoint.

"I don't know. But I'm not going to find out on my own brother."

I should be grateful for that. Joshua's logic shifted back to the main track. "So you *are* getting more control of this... fluidity of reality? You didn't tell me."

"I wasn't sure."

"Until now?"

"Well... last Sunday's game gave me a hint."

"You could have told me."

"I didn't want to influence your design for this week's game." She shrugged again, apologetically, not glancing back. "Wouldn't be a valid test."

"And today's game? Any hints from this outcome?"

Now she did glance back, and her eyes flashed in the fading light. "Today... was good. It feels like something has flipped over inside, some kind of genetic switch."

"So the psychic effect of these games, their intensity, their reality to you... it's honing your control of the power locus?" *Please confirm that for me, little sister.*

"I'm... I think so. I'm still processing the feeling."

"What does it feel like?"

"Like I'm bigger than my body. Like I'm not in one single place at a time anymore."

"Can you relate the feeling to Ireland, or Irian Jaya, years ago?"

"Well... back then it was like I was riding a horse. This is... more like I'm my own horse."

In the bay just now, you went outside the enclave's power locus... or were you in two places at once? He smiled at her uncertainly. Her response read his mind.

"I wasn't even close to being outside the locus, Joshua. I pulled it along with me, I think."

"You think?"

"All right. I feel. I sense. I guess. Whatever." She looked puzzled for a moment. "Or maybe I just know."

Good. That agrees with theory. As the changes manifest, she'll be able to carry a power locus with her. Or create her own. Maybe that'll happen pretty soon. Hallelujah!

Eva leapt onto the shelf and put her hand on the concealed pad. The camouflaged rock face of the O'Donnell Enclave rear entrance split apart to admit them. Joshua followed her in.

O'Donnell Enclave, Waimanu, HI | Sunday 1735 HST

"Lasagna's out of the oven and cooling down," Sarah announced as she re-entered the Security Center. "And I suspect you're going to be right about Lara's recipe, Elia. Smells like world-class stuff to me." She looked at Elia's face then at the video paused on the monitor. *Uh, oh; arguing again.* She smiled at Demuzzio. "Another debate, Thomas?"

The man grinned crookedly. "C'mon, I'm not that bad; I just like to get Elia jazzed up so she makes trouble for Josh."

Elia held up a finger then dropped it down onto the console keyboard. The video replayed Joshua's question to his little sister about killing to defend herself, then paused again at Eva's ambiguous answer. The camera captured the girl's face, looking directly at her brother.

"Well... that's good, Elia," Sarah observed, "she's not going to kill Josh. See how she's looking at him! Feel better now?"

"I do, actually. A lot better, especially if one of Eva's genetic incipiencies has kicked in. We'll hear about it at dinner, I guess. But..."

"Our debate," Demuzzio returned them to the argument, "is the usual..."

"The boundaries of power," Elia added.

"It always comes down to that, doesn't it?" Demuzzio rasped.

Sarah rolled her eyes. *They want to go at it. And I'm the referee again, like it or not. Ah well, it's probably healthy.*

Demuzzio snorted and picked up the thread, frustration in his voice. "Josh is right, Elia. The bad guys won't have any qualms about using power. Or abusing it. So neither can Eva."

"We don't even know who the bad guys will be, TC."

"Doesn't matter, dear. We know *what* they will be."

She hates that condescending tone. Sarah intervened, smiling at them both in turn. "Is this a male-female thing? You and Josh the testosterone hard-cases, Elia and I the pacifiers?"

"Nowhere near that simple, Sarah, as you know better than anyone. Except maybe Eva herself." Demuzzio rubbed the top of his head again.

I think he rubs clockwise when he's impatient, counterclockwise when he's frustrated. Sarah stifled the humorous urge to start a small research project.

"Self-defense is one thing, TC," Elia continued, "that's survival. It's your anticipatory concepts, how you and Josh have been talking to Eva about pre-emptive strikes. That's what worries me. How can you possibly know whom to pre-empt?"

"Eva will know... if our projections about her capabilities are right."

"Maybe. But we don't know how fast she'll move through *Nova* puberty and develop those capabilities."

Demuzzio shrugged. "So in the meantime... both of them together... Josh's rationality and logic, Eva's empathy and insight..."

"Even so, her judgment can't possibly be perfect. Neither can Joshua's. And, TC..." Elia struggled for a way to breach Demuzzio's stubbornness.

The man shrugged again, dismissively. "So mistakes will be made. It's inevitable. Collateral damage. Happens in war all the time."

"We don't want this to be a war," Elia said gently. And..."

Sarah saw doubt flicker across the man's face. *Hit him with his own practicality, Elia. He's too rigid for your moral arguments.* She glanced at Elia, watched her parse Demuzzio's expression and come to the same insight.

"...and collateral damage can come back to haunt you, TC, especially in today's interconnected world. Truth flies almost as fast as rumors on the internet. Might actually bring on a war."

Demuzzio conceded. "Might."

Sarah studied him. *Thomas! You're uncertain, but willing to gamble? That's new.* "Another of Joshua's projections?" She put reproach into her tone. "You and Josh haven't shared, Thomas?"

"Sorry. Hot off the computers just this afternoon. Got it while you guys were busy prepping Eva. Josh was planning to go over it at dinner. Wanted me to have it in case he was... umm... laid up."

Sarah saw Elia's shoulders slump. *Undercut by her husband, ouch. Dinner will be interesting.*

Demuzzio continued. "The projection says whack-a-mole really is the best way. If we take out key people, one at a time, organized opposition can't get started. The wraps stay on *Nova* development that way, until more kids come of age, until we have more of a critical mass."

"And if we can't keep it under wraps, Thomas?" Sarah asked.

"Hey. Different ballgame." Demuzzio shrugged and rubbed his head clockwise. "Josh is working on projections for that." He rubbed counter-clockwise. "As you know."

Arafura Sea, South of Irian Jaya | *Monday 1811 JYT*

Two men stood in the stern of the fishing boat. Ahmed watched the island of Irian Jaya recede slowly toward the horizon, framed by the boat's wake bisecting a flat glassy sea. Zurvan studied the young man's profile, debating the options. *He is faithful, yes, and useful. But he is young and stupid and a zealot. A two-edged sword.*

"Thank you for the scissors to trim my beard, Ahmed, and the clothing. And especially this computer. Were there any questions? Any hesitancy?"

"They obeyed instantly when I spoke the code, Mahdi. They provided all you requested. No questions."

Seven years, possibly eight for some. No degradation of discipline. Religious conditioning is a remarkable tool. Zurvan stroked the open laptop, watching it spin through its startup.

"I think the technology has advanced, Ahmed."

"I do not know these things, Mahdi. I am a simple man." He looked distrustfully at the windows unfolding on the laptop's screen.

"Ah, yes." Zurvan smiled at the young man. "As I was, in the wilderness. But now I'm back in the modern world."

"To conquer the infidel!" Ahmed quivered with excitement.

"We must use the tools of the enemy, Ahmed." Zurvan patted the laptop. "Turn their technological strength against them. This computer links to such tools. Do you understand?"

"As you say, Mahdi. Allah be praised!"

The laptop beeped and confirmed encrypted satellite communication. *Even more remarkable! That infernal O'Donnell boy didn't find my backup control center.* He keyed in the command to boot it up from its dormant state, and watched it come online. *This will cut years off developing a new strategy. Lovely!*

Zurvan studied the screen in the deepening twilight, keying through status messages as they appeared. The contact net was at least eight years old. *But if all the sleeper cells followed their instructions as well as Ahmed's, and went to ground awaiting the recall signal...*

"We will see, Ahmed, whether my *Jaesh* has been faithful, like you."

Ahmed began whispering the appropriate prayer. Zurvan let its cadence wash over him, feeling the power of the ancient symbolism, reveling in it as he considered his extraordinary good fortune. Finally satisfied with the laptop's reports, he shut it down, stretched his back and contemplated the crescent moon above the boat's running lights.

"How long to East Timor, Ahmed?"

"The captain says almost four days, Mahdi."

"The captain is to be trusted?"

"He is one of us, Mahdi; only the third circle, like me, but one of us. You spoke with him; he greeted you with the ritual."

"So he did, Ahmed, and his crewmate. But another opinion never hurts. Do you trust both of them to keep my return a secret?" *Third circle... do they have the discipline?*

"With my life!"

"As you have kept the secret?" he asked casually.

"Yes, Mahdi." The man's eyes flickered.

So. You haven't leaked yet. But you will. The news is too great for a zealot like you to keep to yourself. Well... you can serve me now in another way. Feed my hunger.

"Thank you, Ahmed. Kneel, and for your faithful service I will bestow the Prophet's blessing upon you."

"Mahdi! I am unworthy!"

"Nonsense. You have been faithful. Kneel."

As Zurvan held one hand on Ahmed's curly head, his other silently slipped one of the boat's fish-gutting knives out of its holder. The blessing completed, he plunged the blade into the back of the young man's neck, angled up under the skull, quick and paralyzing.

In one smooth motion he pulled the head up and slashed across the carotid artery, then lifted the body quickly away and over the stern. A few drops of blood splattered the rail. He bent over the railing in simulated prayer, presenting only his robed back to the shocked captain, concealing a near-orgasmic expression of pent-up relief. His forefinger rubbed a spot of blood off the rail. He licked the finger and smiled. *The sharks will enjoy you, Ahmed.*

Then Zurvan turned and walked to the white-faced captain and mate. "Ahmed would betray us." He arranged a sorrowful expression. "It was necessary. He died in the grace and mercy of Allah."

O'Donnell Enclave, Waimanu, HI | Sunday 2231 HST

Eva Connard winced, her hand flying to her neck. *What was that?* She pulled her hand away and looked at it.

Elia caught the motion from the corner of her eye and turned to look. "Eva? What? You've gone pale."

"I... oh, nothing." She felt the color return to her face. *That was weird.*

Elia studied her. "Nothing? You sure?"

"Well... *Nova* hormones, maybe. I'm changing." *Two realities at the same time? But that wasn't one of mine... was it?*

"So we noticed. You okay now?"

"I'm fine. Come on, let's get these dishes cleaned up. I'm ready for more dessert."

"I think you and Josh already cleaned it out, with your post-game metabolisms."

The two carried dishes into the kitchen. Conversation drifted in from the deck past the partially open glass sliders, the familiar sound of an ongoing debate. They grimaced at each other, listening.

"Eva's power of love versus the world's love of power," Demuzzio was saying, "Yeah, yeah, Sarah, I've heard that before. I know what you mean, but..."

Joshua jumped in. "It's a fantasy. Compassion is fine, but it has to be reserved for those *not* trying to kill you."

"Aside from that thing three years ago, the world's been very quiet, Joshua. And that was an attempt on you, not Eva." Sarah's voice went soft.

"Eva was the real target, Sarah. I was just an inconvenient obstacle. And from our own government, for crying out loud."

"Rogue elements, Joshua."

"Sure, but some of them probably are still out there. TC's right. Whack-a-mole is the best strategy."

"Do unto others before they do unto you?" Sarah's voice developed an edge.

"Yes. Before word about the *Nova* development leaks out."

"Best defense is a good offense." Demuzzio jumped into reinforce Joshua. "And I am your security chief, you know." His voice went flat.

Sarah's tone hardened. "Spare me the platitudes, Thomas. You know it's not that simple. And you certainly do, Joshua, with all your logic, all the probabilistic projections of your array of supercomputers."

Silence for a long moment then Sarah continued.

"And forgetting the moral dimension for a moment, you know Eva has trouble even swatting a fly."

"The games are conditioning her," Joshua replied.

He sounds uncertain, Eva thought. *Well... so am I, brother. But I'm trying it your way. We'll see.*

"Is that what these games are really about? Conditioning?" Sarah's voice went softer. "Joshua, you can't turn Eva into an executioner. She's not a soldier like you."

Silence lasted for another long moment on the deck outside, then her brother spoke in grudging acknowledgment.

"So give us an alternative, Sarah. To neutralize those who want to either destroy or control the new species."

"Empathy. Compassion."

Demuzzio barked a response. "He means a *viable* alternative."

Sarah's long sigh was audible, wafted into the kitchen by an errant night breeze off the bay. "Thomas, there's historical precedent. Jesus turned the other cheek."

"Yeah? You remember what happened to him?"

Inside the kitchen, out of view of the darkened deck, Elia and Eva exchanged glances. Eva yelled out through the sliders into the suddenly contemplative silence outside. "Hey, anybody want more dessert? We found some macadamia nut pie!"

Mr. Bojangles stalked in from the darkened deck and meowed at them. Eva crouched down and picked up the big tomcat. "Some dessert for you, Bo?"

He nuzzled her cheek and purred. She nuzzled him back.

"Or did you want to tell me about the Jesus alternative?" she whispered into the soft fur of the cat's neck.

Chapter 3

Retreat House, East Timor | Thursday 2117 PHT

Four days in transit on the fishing boat to East Timor had passed slowly for Muhammad Zurvan. *But not unproductively,* he thought as he gazed out over the moonlit jungle below.

The three men seated across the table waited out his decision nervously. He let silence build before he turned his attention back to them. When he spoke, it was a calm considered tone.

"The captain and his mate are a liability. Do you understand?"

"It will be done, Mahdi."

"At sea, preferably. An accident. Can you manage that?"

"Yes, Mahdi."

"Good." He nodded their dismissal.

Zurvan walked to the balcony and watched as they exited below and moved to their SUV. It drove quietly out of the retreat's walled entrance and turned down the dirt road toward the lowlands and the port. He laughed to the half moon hanging in the night sky. *Amazing. Many years with no word, and my Jaesh is still faithful. The power of the myth!* He shook his head in wonder and walked back inside to open his laptop and resume the review he'd started on the boat.

He sat down and scrolled again through the summaries his re-booted software and isolated server had created for him during the four days on the fishing boat. The sense of destiny flooded him: *I am chosen.* So much could have gone wrong, yet it hadn't. His ultimate failsafe had worked. That infernal O'Donnell boy, or possibly his surrogates at the US National Security Agency, had triggered the self-destruct at the Mecca control center, and clearly the boy had destroyed his first and second backups in Irian Jaya and Somalia.

But when Zurvan was taken captive and didn't issue the daily continuance order, the third backup center — his failsafe buried deep in an isolated corner of the Libyan desert — had automatically dropped its links to the outside world. Totally offline, the O'Donnell boy had no way to find it. And the zealots who physically guarded the installation had maintained the solar collectors and the infrastructure flawlessly: after all those years it booted up cleanly, and immediately started gathering information from the outside world. *And now it's almost updated.*

Zurvan stood and stretched, then paced restlessly across the darkened room, black robes soaking up the moonbeam as he crossed its path. He thought about Joshua O'Donnell. *You cost me seven years of my life, boy! With those primitive forest pygmies who tried to re-shape my mind.* He shuddered at the pain, all too clearly remembered, of their unrelenting efforts. *Playing back my sins in my mind, making me the recipient of all the suffering I dealt. Trying to brainwash me into morality, even trying to change my neural networks.*

He'd lost weight, nearly died, but the little people wouldn't let him, forcing food and water into his body and some kind of psychic manna into his mind until he recovered. Then they started all over again, months-long cycles that had blurred into years. He told them it was torture. They replied it was therapy, and laughed among themselves. He developed a grudging admiration for their persistence and skill, but he didn't break. Probably, he came to realize, because while his own sadism reflected back onto him was agony, it was also pleasurable. So that became his defense, a refuge his captors ultimately couldn't penetrate.

In the recovery part of each cycle, when he was strong enough to walk, their psychic fences somehow had kept him from straying far from the village, wandering in a circle until he returned. *Maddening.*

But then a week ago those little green men with their strange violet eyes had simply disappeared, along with their control over him. Their psychic fences had vanished. *And why was that?* The question still worried him.

Did they think me helpless? Neutralized? Or did their brainwashing work? But no, his pleasure at the dispatch of the hapless Ahmed showed his old self was intact.

The ping of the laptop brought him out of his reverie and overrode more analysis. He scrolled down the update list anxiously, then stopped. Intense relief flooded him.

"So, Prentiss! You finished it after all!"

He read the scientist's notes, recalling their discussion in his Mecca control center many years ago. *A Doomsday option. But it isn't, I see here. You cured the instability.* Amazement followed on the heels of the relief. *And the K'Shmar source cannot be detected because the internet is the carrier for its wave? Oh, Prentiss! Such a legacy you leave me!* The man clearly had to be dead: if not, the O'Donnell boy would have had the secret out of him and the control center in remote south Libya would not exist. He chuckled.

"I would pray for your soul, Prentiss... if only you'd had one."

Zurvan's long bony fingers paused over the keyboard, twitching. *A clever trap left by the O'Donnell boy?* His mind ran down the myriad pathways, weighing probabilities, finally concluding: *No. They believe me dead. The world has calmed. Things are going their way. They've grown complacent.*

He came to the decision quickly. *My destiny calls.*

A few keystrokes, and the monitor flashed: *K'Shmar activated.*

More keystrokes, and another message: *Mahdi myth activated.*

Final keystrokes, and a last message: *Nova sapiens disclosed.*

Muhammad Zurvan backed away from the machine, hugging himself, giggling.

"Chaos is descending on you now, boy. You and your devil-spawned sister Eva and the rest of your infant race. And I *own* chaos."

He turned toward the open balcony and raised his black-robed arms to the moon exultantly.

O'Donnell Enclave, Waimanu, HI | Sunday 1426 HST

Joshua entered the enclave's Security Center, Mr. Bojangles at his heels.

"So you're not running the game this afternoon after all?" TC Demuzzio looked up to study the young man's troubled face.

"No. Eva doesn't think she's... stable enough."

"Stable? That's a new one."

"Got her period again, she says."

"Well... second time, that's a good thing isn't it? Years late, we were getting nervous, right?"

"Third time. I was getting nervous, they've been erratic. But Sarah always thought a new species would be slower to mature physically. Looks like she was right."

"And so... okay... but what's this stability thing? Because puberty took so long to arrive for Eva, it's tougher on her? Bigger mood swings or something? Still seems like my usual happy-go-lucky god-daughter to me. A little... preoccupied, maybe."

"She puts a good face on it. But I don't think the usual physiological stuff — the hormonal changes, her body's development — is much of a factor, TC. It's the new growth going on in her brain; that's the tough part." He rubbed his head tiredly. "It's a helluva growth spurt, just over the past couple of days. And likely triggered by our current crisis."

"She's unstable from what? The growth or the crisis?"

"Too much brain plasticity right now, is all she'll say. She's worried she could kill me, if she really buries herself in the game like she should."

Demuzzio nodded. "And nobody's gone through this before, so nobody can help her balance it out?"

"Elia has some sense of it. She's a near-Nova, and she's been through some of it, so she helps Eva a bit. Sarah has a good intuition for it, so she helps more. And Sarah's knowledge of brain function and the fMRI results we're getting... those are useful markers... objective information from outside."

"But...?"

"But ultimately Eva has to work all this through herself."

"And nobody can truly appreciate what's going on in my god-daughter's cute little head?"

"Right. So we have to trust her to call the shots. There's nobody else qualified."

"That bothers you, doesn't it, Josh? As her guardian for so long now."

Joshua sighed heavily. "Her becoming a *Nova* carries risks I don't know about, TC. Can't know about. All I can do is guess. Scares me."

Demuzzio sighed in return. "Yeah. Me too."

Mr. Bojangles meowed.

"Now it's unanimous," Joshua added. He rubbed the cat and changed the subject. "Ah, shit! Tell me what you've found with the new software, TC; give me some good news, would you?"

He sat, and both men swung toward the console.

"I wish I could, Josh, but it's all bad. Gone to hell in a big way, in just three days." Demuzzio worked his keyboard.

"You'd be lot more efficient if you'd dump the keyboard and go to my new controller, TC."

"Can't get the hang of that thing, Josh. The way I wave my hands around, probably I'd start World War 3. Best leave me be a dinosaur."

Joshua shrugged. Mr. Bojangles yawned.

Demuzzio tapped a final key and a display popped up on the screen as he voiced his thoughts. "First, it sure looks like that K'Shmar effect is operative again. More subtle, though; no identifiable source, symptoms spread out. May be a false positive, your software says."

"What does NSA think?"

"They think it's real. Some kind of variant of the old K'Shmar. No identifiable pathway either." Demuzzio rubbed his head and continued. "NSA's holding back, though. I'm pretty sure we're not getting their whole story."

Joshua studied the screen and said nothing, just watched the scrolling data. When it finished he nodded agreement at Demuzzio: the National Security Agency was notoriously cautious at times about disclosing information, and this clearly was one of those.

"Second, the nutcases in the Islamic community are back. They claim some kind of new savior is arriving. Or will shortly. Name of Mahdi."

Joshua's head snapped back to the monitor, scanning synopses of websites. *No! It can't be!* A sense of lurking darkness flooded his mind. The scrolled data dropped into his mind's lattice-work logic, and it churned with analysis so fast and urgent he felt dizzy for a moment.

"Not a name, TC. The Mahdi is a title. An Islamic myth. Literally it means 'the guide to the path of righteousness'." *How calm my voice sounds.* It was somehow decoupled from the raging torrent in his brain.

"Yeah, whatever. Anyway, Josh, NSA says there's a lot of shit going over the internet about this righteous asshole, and it's pretty well correlated with the K'Shmar hits. Here's some more synopses."

Joshua dropped his head in his hands, not even looking at the screen. The logic lattice popped out the most probable answer, with tight statistical confidence limits right on its heels.

Yes, it would be correlated. Cause and effect always are. Demuzzio patted him on the shoulder. *TC doesn't know what's happening,* Joshua realized as the man continued.

"Third, a couple of science websites, which NSA says are pretty well-respected..." Demuzzio keyed their synopses onto the screen, "have let our cat out of the bag. NSA predicts the *Nova* thing will blow wide open in a couple more days. Government won't be able to sit on it. Not our government. Not anybody's."

The two men stared at the last screen for a long moment.

No they won't, Joshua agreed, *they can't. Not this time.*

"I should have killed him, TC."

"Killed who?"

"Zurvan."

"Shit, Josh! Zurvan's dead. Drowned in that river, six... no, seven, years ago."

"The Indonesians never found a body, TC."

"The way that flood was running after the storm, his body probably washed twenty miles out to sea, Josh. Fed the sharks."

"No, TC. He's back. This stuff... all at once? That's his signature. The probability is this close to certainty." Joshua held thumb and forefinger close together. *He's had seven years to plan. God help us.*

Retreat House, East Timor | Wednesday 2329 PHT

Muhammad Zurvan grunted with satisfaction at the news feeds flowing across the screen of his laptop. Major financial markets were oscillating wildly, not knowing what to make of the possibility of a sudden evolutionary appearance of a new breed of human. Pundits were speculating, even more wildly. Governments were backing and filling, appealing for calm. *Chaos has started.* He laughed.

He flipped to a summary of opinions from fundamentalist Islamic websites. They were casting the new species as an experiment of the West, an abomination created by gene manipulation, modern science gone mad. *An affront to Allah!* Many of the sites also had escalated his planted seed about the coming of the Twelfth Imam, and conflated that with stories of the new species. He flipped back to the news feeds and read stories of children hunted down and murdered along with their families. *The K'Shmar effect is taking hold. Just as I hoped!* He laughed again. *All in less than a week!*

Two of the websites even made explicit connections to end-time hadiths: darkness descending on the world with the *Novas* as its agent, and the appearance of the Mahdi to bring about the new order. *I could not have scripted it better myself.* He pounded the table.

"Your Mahdi is coming," Zurvan said, laughing. A sudden tropical shower drove rain into the room and he ran to shut the balcony doors. *Yes! The myth will spread.* Mirth shook him. *And the fools will believe it!* He stared out through the glass into the wet blackness until a ping brought him back to the table and his laptop. The message said that the Nova entity detection software had been updated.

"So, how many of these children now?"

He keyed the command and stood astonished: a constellation of bright little specks sprinkled itself across a dimmed outline map of the world.

"So many?" He entered the command to verify. The screen re-painted the same picture and pinged at him. He sat and drummed his fingers on the table.

"Many more than the Witch predicted!" He keyed in the command to produce an equivalent plot for the status seven years ago. A few hundred tiny specks populated the screen. He flipped back to the present and ordered a computer count of the incipient *Nova sapiens* children represented by those bright specks. But he didn't really need a count to discern the meaning of what he was seeing: their birth rate was accelerating. The question was why, or possibly how. *The boy and his sister? They quieted the world? Made it more receptive, safer for the Novas? Or is it something more subtle, some psychic factor equivalent to critical mass in a nuclear reactor? Some sort of recognition of change in the global consciousness?*

He slammed the table with his hand, jittering the monitor screen.

My Witch. I need her. The only dark spot in his luck — no, his destiny, he corrected himself — was the loss of the old crone Hessa, his personal oracle with uncanny insights into *Nova* development. But his search of Indonesia's police and security services databases for the seven year period had turned up nothing; she'd fallen off the earth. *Dead, probably. By the boy's hand, there at the pool.*

With an effort, Zurvan pushed aside the thought of his Witch and studied the monitor screen. *A brighter dot than the others, there in the Pacific.*

"Is that you, child?" He punched keys to zoom in on the area, and the monitor homed in on Hawaii.

"Back in your enclave?" He punched again, and the image bracketed the northeast coast of the Big Island. A digital readout appeared and tagged itself to the brightest blip on the screen, giving its signal strength.

"Oho! You're not a child anymore, are you, Eva Connard?" He studied the screen, moving the tag, trying to read the considerably lesser strength of several other blips.

"And who are those? Younger *Novas*? Or partials, like your brother?" Zurvan flicked through the readout tags, thinking about the only person ever to defy and defeat him. He snarled at the laptop screen. *Joshua O'Donnell, you owe me seven years of exquisite pain. And I will have it from you, boy. Extracted through your sister.*

He stared eastward through the balcony's glass doors. Outside, the shower had blown over and cloud fragments sailed across a clearing night sky.

You thought you won, boy; you and your devil-spawned sister and her tiger and her little green friends. He stroked the laptop again, pleased by its performance. *But you didn't. You stopped me for a long time, but now I'm back.*

"And in that time, my myth has only grown!" He began to chuckle at the irony. "The Mahdi has come!" He barked a howling laugh and slapped the table. Startled birds that had sheltered from the downpour took off from the balcony rail and darkened the face of the gibbous moon.

O'Donnell Enclave, Waimanu, HI | *Friday 0917 HST*

The fMRI scanner hummed. Eva Connard lay quietly on the table, intent on the images flashing across the screen above her. The tingling sensation the magnetic resonance produced in her brain was by this time more comfort than intrusion. *That's interesting,* she suppressed the giggle and stayed still, *I wonder if guinea pigs get to like it too.*

Minutes later, the screen went dark and the lights came up in the enclave's medical research zone. The girl yawned as the tray slid her out of the machine, then sat up and pulled out her earplugs.

"So how'd your favorite guinea-pig do this time?"

Dr. Sarah Kruse smiled at her. "We're seeing significant step-changes in your brain as you move into puberty, Eva. They correlate with all the usual hormonal markers in your bloodstream. But this last step is a giant one; I pray your hormone levels don't track it linearly."

Eva giggled at the sudden image of herself as a wood nymph. She felt a certain urgency in her question, but asked it casually. "So... my unfolding empathy gene is going to make me a mind reader? When?"

"Not soon. At the moment, I think your biofield can pick up the resonance of what's going on in a subject brain's left inferior frontal gyrus, maybe the anterior insula."

The girl paused before answering. "Resonance isn't necessarily truth."

"Point. And I'm just guessing at it, based on my subjective observations of how you study and react to Joshua and Elia when they're having an argument. But now it looks like you also may be able to pick up elevated neural action in the anterior cingulate cortex."

"Where conflicts get resolved?"

Sarah smiled at her. "Precisely."

"Is that useful?"

"By itself, not very. But your brain is so plastic, Eva... it has so many new avenues for collecting information. Sooner or later you'll tighten down the correlation between what you're sensing with your mind and the behavior you're observing."

"I'll start to see patterns? Be able to generalize? Differentiate between a conflicted person and one who might be lying to me?"

"I suspect that's where the data point to. We can run some experiments if you like. I'll climb in the machine; you can ask some questions, I'll tell some lies. We'll correlate your subjective results with the objective data from the fMRI scans." Sarah looked at her keenly. "Why? You have some special interest in this area?"

Mind reading would be better than picking petals off a daisy. He loves me, he loves me not. Eva looked back at Sarah blandly. "Oh, just curious, I guess."

Sarah studied her for a moment then shrugged. "Fair enough. All right, I'll get Elia and Joshua and Thomas to climb in the machine, too. We'll start to develop a baseline for you. Maybe you can generalize from there."

"But it won't be that simple."

"No, of course not. What would a Neanderthal make of a Mozart symphony?"

"A more sophisticated — if that's the right word — interpretation of what's being sensed is required?"

"Exactly. It took... what... fifty thousand years of evolution to move from drums and chants to a violin concerto?"

Now that's a good analogy. She grinned at the older woman. "You're a symphony, Sarah."

"Thanks. I love you, too, Eva." Sarah hugged her tight. "Come on, we'll be late for the video conference."

They walked arms around each other out of the medical zone, past the enclosed waterwall which isolated that zone from the Waimanu locus. Eva felt the power of the locus slide into her mind to welcome her back. *I missed you too.*

O'Donnell Enclave, Waimanu, HI | Friday 0932 HST

Sarah Kruse followed Eva into the enclave's communication center, admiring how confidently the girl strode across the room. *She's nervous, but you'd never know it.* Eva picked her tomcat out of the center chair and sat down. *Ha! She took Joshua's seat like it's been hers all along. Or did Mr. Bo reserve it for her?*

Joshua gave his sister and the cat a sidelong glance, then took the chair to her right, Demuzzio the one to her left. *Now that's interesting. Nice adjustment, gentlemen.* Elia cocked a quizzical eyebrow and took the left flanking chair, so Sarah took the right. She hid her amusement. *A new configuration. Well, at least it's symmetrical.*

Seven people smiled at them from the holographic projection stage at the far wall of the room. An eighth was missing.

"Hi, everybody," Eva opened the conference cheerfully, "and where's my newest buddy Pastor Bob?"

The hologram of Earl Phillips, retired Director of NSA but still plugged into that Agency in mysterious ways, answered. "With the President, Eva. A press conference is coming up in a minute; I thought we should watch it before we start our strategy session." The man glanced off to his left. "I've got a network feed here, I'll stream it to you."

Joshua nodded, and his fingers made quick precise movements within the virtual control plane floating above the top of the table. The big monitor screen alongside the projection stage came to life, the cameraman panning across the briefing stage in the White House press room. "The press conference was scheduled for tonight, Earl; why'd they move it up?"

"Didn't want the market to close out the week in the crapper, is my guess. If they put out some good news now, maybe the selloffs will stop. The last thing they want to see is more automatic trading freezes kick in."

"So it's good news? You know where the President's coming out on this?" Demuzzio asked.

"Sure. Doctor Blake wrote the speech for him, and bounced a draft off me." Phillips grinned at them. "It's good. Damn good."

"But this President tends to leave the market alone..."

"Oh, it's not an economic speech, Josh. I slipped in a few fiscal sedatives for the traders, but it's primarily philosophical. Or maybe spiritual, a real gut appeal to the people." Phillips glanced down again. "I think that's exactly what the country needs. Here, he's coming on now."

A number of clerics of different denominations walked onto the stage and took up positions against the backdrop curtain. Then, "Ladies and gentlemen, the President of the United States..."

He's a gifted orator, Sarah conceded minutes later as the President worked his way toward the classic call for action. All her neuropsychological training could not detect even the slightest flaw in his delivery. *He really means it. He's finally in our camp. Thank God.* She looked at the rapt faces around the circular table. They all sat entranced at the power and cadence of the near-poetic speech, staring at the President. Except for one: Eva was focused on the tall handsome man on the far right in the background, the author of the speech: Robert Blake. His résumé flashed across Sarah's mind. *Doctor of Philosophy. Spiritual minister and confidant of the President, of other world leaders. Unofficial but undisputed leader of the modern Christian evangelical movement. A television and internet congregation of millions, maybe hundreds of millions. Children almost Eva's age. A tragic widower, not yet remarried.* And, more recently, the twelfth member to be added to their Nova Council.

As Sarah watched Eva watching Blake, the intuition crystallized. *Look at her! She's in love!* The thought was totally confusing. *A child becoming a woman becoming a god... and she has a crush on a man old enough to be her father.*

Chapter 4

Senate Office Building, Washington, DC | Friday 2143 EST

"Man gives a fine speech, don't he?" the Senator grunted as the big wall monitor froze on the presidential seal. He tapped the remote and the screen went black.

From across the big desk, the younger man shrugged. *Try to temper it with some good news,* he instructed himself.

"At least the market's back up, Senator. I'm not going broke anymore. You either, I trust."

"So I heard. Five hunnert points up in the Dow, from the speech til market close this afternoon. Couple hours; gotta be a new record, huh?" The Senator levered his bulk up from the chair, knuckling the small of his back to straighten his spine. He walked to the big window and stared at the lighted Capitol dome.

The younger man watched him in silence, trying to discern hints from the Senator's posture. *He's not as angry as I thought. And he's a sly old fox; he has to realize it's going to be a longer game. So... rationality?* The man turned from the window and rewarded his guess.

"The President's in their camp now, boy."

Tone's neutral, that's good. "Yes, sir. That's pretty clear. But he couldn't very well stay hands-off once the word got out."

"Makes our job more difficult, son. Your job."

What cards do I show him? I need to be careful here. He temporized with generalities. "Maybe, maybe not, Senator. Sure, the plan we had in mind seems iffy now, so we need to regroup. But the chaos also has upset the Nova Council's plans. They can't play ostrich any longer; they have to deal with the outside world now.

"They need a new strategy too, huh?"

"Exactly."

"So what's that gonna be, son?"

"I don't know, Senator. Not yet." *Whatever it is, though, I'm going to shape it so it takes you and your wacky Arlington Potomac Group right out of my life.* He squashed the burning anger and made himself smile innocently. "I'm working on it."

The Senator stared at him for a long moment. He fancied he could see the gears clicking away in the vacuum of the old man's eyes.

"Awright," the Senator finally conceded, "a new ball game. I'm pissed, son, but I ain't gonna take it out on you. This Mahdi asshole is the one that fucked us up."

"You up on the myth, Senator?"

"A gister from NSA briefed my Intelligence Committee on it yesterday. End-times comin', this Mahdi shows up, leads the way to a new order. Primitive bullshit. Armageddon."

"But bullshit that resonates; especially in times like this. Did NSA identify who the Mahdi is?"

"Why you need to know that, son?"

The younger man shrugged. "Curiosity. Some Islamic sects see the Mahdi as an actual person, some as a kind of spiritual entity."

The Senator drummed his fingers on the desktop. "Uh huh. Well, I don't think I can tell you that son, the briefing was top secret."

"The information might help my planning."

The Senator stared at him for a long evaluative moment. "Okay. They think there's a real person behind it, because it's so orchestrated, it happened so fast. But he's pretendin' to be some kinda spiritual entity."

"In the modern world, a spiritual entity would be a safer fit with the myth. More flexibility."

"Yeah. That's what the gister said, too. Also makes the fucker less of a target."

"You think we'd take him out if we could find him?"

"I sure as shit would, son; in a New York minute. We don't need any of them goddamn ayatollahs readin' us the Qur'an six times a day."

"You really think it would come to that?"

"By themselves? Nah, they're too stupid. Oil money's made 'em even stupider. But if they get control of the Novas, somehow..."

"Yes, I see that. So I take it you want us to align ourselves with the President? Calm, rational, accepting?" *I've already geared up to do that with my people, Senator; it was the only option that made sense. But if I let you tell me then you can take credit for it.*

"For now, son. For now."

Both men contemplated the spotlighted flag fluttering over the wing of the Capital for a moment, then the younger man spoke.

"The President was very careful in his speech not to denigrate any Islamic beliefs, Senator. Or any of the similar Christian fundamentalist beliefs in this country about the end times..."

The Senator nodded. "Of course, boy! He ain't gonna get anybody pissed this early in the game." He gave a barking laugh of approval. "I may not like the man, but I gotta admit he's slipperier than goose shit on a tin roof."

"So let me be sure I get this straight, Senator. For now, at least, we're going along with the President's position. Irrespective of how that might irritate your Christian fundamentalist colleagues? And mine?"

"You got it, son. We let this play out a bit, see what happens."

"All right, sir. I can do that."

"But find a way to get me some DNA samples of those Novas, son. We need an ace in the hole. I got a lab all lined up."

O'Donnell Enclave, Waimanu, HI | Friday 2322 HST

"Working late, Thomas?"

Demuzzio jumped at the soft voice. He'd been so absorbed in the information NSA was streaming to him that he hadn't heard Sarah slip into the Security Center.

"Sorry," she added, "didn't mean to startle you." She put her hand on his shoulder and looked over it at the monitors then cocked an eyebrow. "The government's loosening up?"

"Presidential directive, full collaboration."

"They're serious, then. What's the quid pro quo?"

"They feed us the information, Josh gives them back his synthesis."

"They've got plenty of analysts, bigger computers, Thomas."

"Yeah. But Josh still has the best brain on the planet for this sort of thing. Analysis is one thing, synthesis is another."

Demuzzio glanced at her hand on his shoulder then up at her face. Her dark eyes stared intently at the digested summaries scrolling down the monitor screen. *I wonder why the woman looks so sad when she thinks nobody's watching.*

Sarah's hand pulled away. "Yes, of course. They're synthesizing too, but they want an outside opinion."

Demuzzio shrugged. "Josh's mind is a wild card. They don't have one. At least not like that."

She straightened up and shifted her attention to him. "I know." An eyebrow quirked up, gentle smile beneath. "Something you're not telling me, Thomas?"

How the hell does she read me like that? He sighed and gave it up. "Josh's latest... synthesis?"

"Yes?"

"Zurvan's alive. He's this Mahdi character."

She dropped into a chair.

"Oh, God!"

"Yeah."

"How long have you known? Why didn't you say anything?"

"Josh guessed it last Sunday. Took most of this week to confirm."

"To confirm? I doubt it, Thomas." Her dark eyes probed his. "You and Josh were trying to hunt him down, weren't you? And you didn't tell Eva because you were worried she might interfere again?"

Demuzzio rubbed the back of his head. *How does she get there that fast?* "Yeah, basically. You got a problem with that?"

He watched Sarah take a breath to compose herself, admiring the tiny signs of control as her mind took charge of her face. *Elia and Eva do that too. Is it some kinda Zen thing, or a woman thing? Wonder if they could teach me?* She glanced at the monitor for a frozen moment before turning back to him.

"No, Thomas, not a problem for me," she half-whispered. "I'd go hunting with you." The classically beautiful planes of the woman's face tightened into something primitive and vicious.

He recoiled in his chair before he caught himself. *Rage, Sarah? From you? Holy shit!* But then her control clicked back into place and she ignored his reaction.

"But Eva needs to know," Sarah continued. "Yes, she's still a child in some ways, but she's becoming a *Nova*. So she's the only one of us qualified, ultimately, to decide what to do in this... situation. You can't keep information from her."

Demuzzio sighed. "Yeah. You're right, Sarah. Just takes some getting used to. I'm her godfather, for Chrissakes. I bounced that baby on my knee, burped her, even changed her diaper once."

Sarah smiled at that. "And Joshua has the same problem, in spades... a stand-in for parents still in a crazy coma... yes, Thomas, I understand all this. Still..."

Demuzzio sighed again. "Uh huh. I'll talk to Josh."

"Thank you, Thomas." She patted his hand, took a last distasteful glance at the monitor and walked away.

He watched her through the portal and down the hall, admiring the graceful stride, feminine yet powerful. *Reminds me of a lioness. They all walk like that, though, don't they? Elia and Eva too. Wonder if it's that Zen shit and yoga they do together. Wonder if they could teach me that too.* He arched in his chair, then curled his head and shoulders down and put his palms flat on the floor. *I could use some loosening up.*

Demuzzio straightened and scrolled the monitor back to what Sarah had seen, an artist's rendering of what Zurvan might look like now. He let his mind chase idle thoughts. *Wonder where that rage came from. Something like that shoulda left at least a few little blips in her profile.*

"Run it again? he asked his reflection in the screen, "even if she has been on the team for five years?"

He keyed out of the NSA's download and into his security files. "And while you're at it, run our newest buddy's profile through a tighter wringer?" He rubbed his head as he contemplated the work involved.

Nah, Eva's got good vibes off both of them. That's a better check than any suspicious old cop like me can do. Demuzzio shrugged, toggled back into the NSA's download and watched their data and analyses scroll down the screen. *More pressing needs for my time.*

O'Donnell Enclave, Waimanu, HI | Saturday 0648 HST

Light from the rising sun slanted in over the water and rainbowed the spray from the waterfall as it fell into the pool. Eva Connard sat in a lotus position, floating just above the wet surface of the rock ledge that embraced the pool. Her eyes looked north over Waimanu Bay and the open ocean. The sun warmed the right side of her face. She sensed each color of the rainbow behind her without looking back.

Twenty-five hundred miles of emptiness, then the Aleutians. Can I go there? Now? She closed her eyes and ranged her mind outward. The bay moved beneath her first, then open water, her dolphin friends playing in it. Then, through the eyes of a sea-bird, came the cold peninsula, low clouds pushing against its hilly spine. The urge to go there grew, but with it came the restraint.

Not yet, Little Mother. Eva opened her eyes and smiled at the white-robed figure floating in front of her. *Soon, though. Don't be so anxious... a few more twists of the genome, a few more crosslinks in your young corpus callosum.*

"You don't know how long?" She liked to speak aloud to the visions when alone; it made them seem more real. The security cameras might pick up her profile speaking, but the words would be lost in the white noise of falling water.

Even though the sunlight passed right through it, the figure's robe rippled in a wayward breeze; a playful response to her mind's need for a more tangible reality. Eva's ears began to hear along with her mind.

"No, child. We are the past. We can measure your present, but not predict your future. It is as new to us as it is to you."

"I'm in a terrible hurry."

"That's what Alice said in Wonderland. Patience, Little Mother, it will happen soon."

Eva nodded. She had not expected anything else. She changed the subject. "He loves me? Or he loves me not?"

"Your Pastor Bob? We see him only through your mind. We can have no objective opinion."

"I hope he does. Love me."

A shrug from the vision. "He is older. He has children almost your age. He may love you like one of them."

"I think maybe I love him. Romantically, I mean."

"We think maybe he just reminds you of your father, absent in a coma."

"Different skin color."

Another shrug from the vision. "Not relevant. His manner. How he listens, how he treats you, how he respects you. It is clear in your mind."

"Eva!" Elia's voice sounded over the speaker behind the hidden security camera, "breakfast in three minutes."

The vision faded from Eva's sight. She stood up, arched back to look at the rainbow above and behind, and shot up through it to land on another ledge a hundred meters up the cliff. The door of the concealed entrance slid open to welcome her. A fading thought followed her inside: *Elia has prepared you well, Little Mother. She is a credit to our Sisterhood. Your powers are evolving. Patience! You will be ready soon enough... for love or war, or both.*

Her brother greeted her halfway down the entry. "Eva, I'm sorry. I should have told you this earlier. Zurvan's alive. My probability assessment is close to certainty."

She simply nodded. He stared down at her in puzzlement as they walked toward the enclave's living quarters.

"No reaction, Eva?"

"How long have you known, Josh?"

"Suspected since Sunday. Confirmed since... maybe Tuesday."

"You wanted to hunt him down, so you didn't tell me, right?"

"I'm sorry. I just thought that would be best."

"But you couldn't find him."

"He's pretty smart."

"Smarter than you? Than you and NSA together?"

"Probably not; but close. And he's still got major resources, apparently. And a whole world to hide out in."

Eva put her arm around his waist and leaned her head on his shoulder as they walked. "I forgive you, Josh."

He gave a relieved laugh. "You're not mad at me?"

How can I be, brother? I knew our enemy was alive a full week before you did. I felt Zurvan's cold steel in that poor man's brain/my brain, the blade ripping his/my neck. The water closing over him/me. The terror and blackness, oblivion. And I could have told you, maybe should have. But I didn't.

"No, Josh. I'm not mad at you. You thought you were doing the right thing. Sparing me." She stopped outside the kitchen area, turning him toward her and searching his face. "Just don't do it again. Tell me these things as they come up, okay? We'll decide together what to do. Just like always. Okay?"

Her brother's turquoise eyes flared with his smile. "Okay."

O'Donnell Enclave, Waimanu, HI | Saturday 0828 HST

Joshua stared northward from the kitchen deck of the enclave, out over miles of blue water and an empty horizon. *That's a long damn way.* His mind toyed listlessly with the quantum equations of collapsing wave functions that would allow the transposition of a physical body from one location to another in an instant of no-time. *I'll probably never figure it out,* he conceded. *The twins might, or maybe some other* Nova; *but I don't think a human intellect can do it. Not even mine.* He felt his sister's eyes on him and turned to her.

"The Aleutians, huh? Why, Eva?"

"Oh, no special reason. Just a wild place. Rocks and water and wind and rain. Easy to..." she searched for the right word.

"Visualize? Or..." he smiled at her, "...conjure?"

Eva threw her head back and laughed merrily at that. Joshua felt a stab of pain. *Just like mom.* He sighed.

"Don't try it without me, kiddo. Okay? Please?"

She shrugged, grinning. "Okay, *kemo sabe.*"

"I'm serious."

"You think I can get lost?"

He pondered that. "No, probably not. But you won't always know what's waiting at your arrival point."

She shrugged again. "So I bug out if it isn't friendly. Appear..." she snapped her fingers, "...then disappear. Poof." She snapped them again. "We've done it here, lots of times."

"This power locus knows us; we're keyed to its resonance."

"Transposition worked about the same in Ireland, Josh. And in Irian Jaya, once we hit the right resonance. It should be the same when I get the ability to carry a locus with me. Your own predictions say so."

He sighed again. "Yeah, it should, but... Lao Tsu, honey. Edges of chaos. And now Zurvan's back. Please?"

"Okay, bro, okay! You can chaperone my coming-out party!"

"Thank you!" This time he grinned back at her. "And when will that be?"

"Anytime now, I..." Eva's indigo eyes flashed at him, a deeper blue than the sunlit water offshore. Her body flickered. *Did it?* He blinked. *Or was it sunlight reflected off a wave?*

"In fact, right now!" She gripped the rail of the deck, knuckles white. "Wow!" Her expression changed from confusion to wonder. "Amazing Grace!"

Joshua put his hand over hers on the rail. "What? I don't..."

"The song, Josh! 'Was blind, but now I see.' Wow! It's beautiful!"

"Elia, Sarah!" Joshua yelled into the kitchen, "Quick!"

The two women rushed onto the deck. Elia stared at Eva, blinked, then moved to the side for a different view. She put her hand to her mouth, but Sarah was immediately analytical: "E-5 on the sequence, Eva? Retrotransposons? What happened to E-4?"

They all watched the girl's expression change from wonder to curiosity as she answered, dreamily. "Parsing and binding... new neurons. The cacophony... is a melody..."

Eva's body seemed to ripple, as if a wave of heat passed through the air in front of her. Then it stabilized and she smiled at them.

"I don't think there is an E-4, Sarah. Or maybe it's just a minor transition into E-5."

"We need to get you into the MRI, see what's happening."

Eva took a deep breath. "Wow! Yeah, okay. In a minute; I need to... process this."

Joshua watched the wonder flood back over her face. She turned her hand palm up into his. It tingled. The hair on his forearm stood up.

"Don't let go, Josh."

"I won't." He slid his hand up her wrist. It felt reassuringly solid. "I've got you. You're not going anywhere."

"But *we* are." She giggled and suddenly they were standing on a stone parapet. A cold wind whipped around them in the darkness. He dropped her hand, reflexively spun around in a defensive crouch and almost fell off. She grabbed his shirt.

"This is a safe place, Josh."

As she spoke he recognized the castle, the ancestral home of the O'Donnell clan in Ireland, and the twilit Balledonegan Bay to its south.

"Goddammit, Eva!" he exploded. "Don't do that to me!"

Eva took his hand and instantly they were back on the enclave's deck, in the warm sun and gentle trade winds of the Hawaiian Islands.

"I think my brother is starting to lose his sense of humor about all this," she told Elia and Sarah with a straight face.

O'Donnell Enclave, Waimanu, HI | Saturday 1318 HST

"Because I can." Eva repeated into the contemplative silence around the table. "Before this morning, transposition was academic, but now I can actually do it." She glanced in turn at each of the faces arrayed in the circle, some physical, some holographic.

"And I should," she added, "because a personal touch matters."

Her gaze lingered on her brother. *They're all troubled, but him most.* She felt the beautiful crystalline form of his logic lattices engaging the problem. *Oh, your problem is that you know I'm right. You're just looking for an excuse not to do it.*

"Joshua?" She kept her voice carefully neutral. "The probability of success?"

"Reasonably good. Seventy percent, plus or minus five."

She stifled the smile that wanted to greet his begrudging tone. *You're so honest, Josh.*

The hologram of Earl Phillips spoke. "But are these people the right targets? Religious leaders? Only in a few countries do they have any significant clout on political issues. Why not go to the heads of state?"

Joshua responded. "Earl, the existence of the *Novas* is certainly a political issue. A cultural one, too. But at the moment the anxiety is mostly religiously-driven. So that's what we need to work on first. Eva's right."

"We quiet that down, the politics will settle out?"

"Not entirely, but if we can take religion off the table, we'll move into a more rational debate."

"Politics is rational?" Phillips chuckled. "News to me. But my buddy Adrienne at NSA claims pretty much the same thing..."

Eva's thoughts skittered off to Adrienne O'Meara. *I wonder how her son Abraham is doing. He's a just little older than Josh and Elia's twins. I'll have to drop in on him now that I can travel.*

"...so my gut reaction is go for it. I don't see any particular downside," Phillips finished.

"Security's my concern, Eva," TC Demuzzio said, "and that's a big downside." He looked at Joshua for support.

"Mine, too, TC." Joshua shrugged. "But as Eva points out, we can work around most of the risk. Avoid set schedules. Get CIA and NSA to pick out gatherings and just drop in on them."

"Up close and personal? Show them Eva doesn't have any horns?" Phillips winked at her. "You just pop in to visit them, like you popped into my office this morning?"

Eva chuckled at the memory of the varied reactions when she and her brother had appeared in front of her Council members, sometimes inside multiple layers of their security. "Sorry. We just didn't think you'd believe us without a demonstration first."

"Well, if a person didn't have religion, that'd sure be a good reason to get it," Phillips chuckled along with her.

"Speaking of religion..." the hologram of Robert Blake said as it was projected into the empty spot across the table from Eva, "sorry I'm late. I had to get the tone of tonight's address just right."

"Can we see it?" Eva hoped the excitement in her voice would be seen by the Council as for the impending speech, not the man. *Do you love me, Robert Blake?* She felt a little color rise into her cheeks and forced it back down.

"Sure. It'll air at nine PM Eastern. The late news shows will have time to pick it up. Some of the cable channels said they might run the whole thing. It's not long."

"Will you give us a preview?" This time Eva couldn't squelch the blush.

"Sure, let me just..." Blake turned and his hand left the camera view. Eva's heart thumped as she admired the man's handsome profile. *Oh... why does he do that to me?*

Blake turned back toward the camera. "Looks like it's streaming. You got it, Joshua?"

Her brother nodded and flicked his fingers within the virtual control plane. The big monitor on the conference room wall came to life.

When the speech concluded the room reverberated with appreciation. Joshua looked at Blake's hologram thoughtfully and nodded to Demuzzio.

Eva smiled at them both in turn. *Well, brother, that speech just might alienate a lot of his televangelist flock; he's taking a huge risk for us. For me.* She sighed. *You do love me, don't you, Pastor Bob?*

She watched the man's hologram carefully, but it was impossible to draw from it the nuanced interpretations she could from a physical face.

I need to find a reason to see him again soon. In the flesh.

Chapter 5

UMC Capitol Office, Washington, DC | Saturday 2215 EST

The traffic on K Street below had faded to a whisper; the busiest street in Washington during the workday was almost deserted on a late Saturday night. Robert Blake — Pastor Bob to his millions-strong congregation in the United Ministries of Christ — looked down on the street from his private suite in the UMC lobbying office. He twirled a pen idly then scratched words on his notepad. Then he scratched them out.

The secure phone line chimed and a verified caller identity code flashed on the wall screen across the room. He trotted to his desk and hit the accept key on his computer. The image of the young woman that came up on the screen stunned him, as always. *Lord she's lovely. Look at those eyes. I've never seen that deep a blue; violet almost. And the face, so exotic, but so... universal; all those different bloodlines.*

Eva Connard smiled hesitantly before she spoke. "We just finished watching the broadcast, Doctor Blake, and some of the talking heads afterwards. Apparently a bazillion people watched it; even more than the President's speech."

He smiled back at her. *What's that? Makeup? Doesn't the child know she's just gilding the lily?* "I think we got lucky, Eva; it was a slow news day. And you can call me Pastor Bob like everybody else does."

"Your speech was perfect. You're taking a big risk, and we owe you a lot... Pastor Bob. The Council knows this, but I wanted to thank you again." She lowered her eyes a moment then raised them to look directly into the camera. "Personally."

Is the girl blushing? What in God's name is she... can she be... His chaotic thoughts cut off automatically as the practiced easy smile and natural manner of a born preacher took over.

"No thanks necessary, Eva. I did what I thought was right, what I thought Christ would do in this situation."

"I can't tell you what an enormous help it is! When people hear it from you, Pastor Bob — you've always made so much sense to so many people; I mean, your ministry and your books and everything — they sit up and pay attention. Earl Phillips says this will soothe a lot of concerns. Josh agrees."

"Well... good! I'm glad to hear I hit the right tone, Eva. Because right now I'm trying to recast it a bit, so I can preach the same message tomorrow."

"Oh! That's right; you're doing the Sunday Forum, aren't you? At the National Cathedral?"

"Yep. With a sermon at the service afterwards."

"Great! I'll get up early and watch."

"Ha! That would be four AM your time. Five-fifteen for the sermon. You'd better sleep in, child; I'll stream you the video."

"Uh uh, I'm getting up for it," Eva affirmed. "And I'm not a child!"

Blake smiled at the set of her jaw. *She probably will. And she's probably right about not being a child.* "Okay." He shrugged. "And I'm sorry."

Eva grinned acceptance back at him and changed the subject. "You tuned in late to our Council meeting this afternoon, so I need to fill you in on the discussion you missed."

Blake opened his palms toward the camera.

"Does your computer verify transmission security?" she asked.

He looked down at the computer that had been supplied when he became a Council member. "Green across the board, Eva. Go ahead."

"This is going to shock you."

"Okay. I'm sitting down."

"I had a... well, let's call it a growth spurt."

"A *Nova* growth spurt?"

"Yeah. And now — you holding onto that chair?"

"I am."

"Now I can transpose."

"You mean...?"

"Yeah. Be any place I want to be. So long as I can... *sense* the place. I guess that's the only word that fits."

"Wow!"

"Yeah." She laughed. "I gave a demonstration to some of the Council."

"You... what? Put in a magical appearance?"

"Yep." She giggled. "With Josh. He wouldn't let me go alone."

"But you didn't drop in on me..."

"Nope, you were busy with the President. I thought that might be..."

"Tacky? With the Secret Service and all?"

She grinned. "Josh said... 'impolitic', I think."

Blake steepled his fingers under his chin. "Good thinking. But what's the issue with the Council?"

"I really want to visit some religious leaders around the world; selected rational ones, like you. There's some... concern that it's too risky. I'd like your support in the Council. Basically it's a question of whether the results would justify the risk."

"Your brother? TC? What do they think?"

"TC is dead-set against it; too dangerous, he says. Most of the other Council members including Elia and Sarah lean toward his position. But Earl is in favor. Josh is on the fence, I think. But he's so damn analytical it's hard to tell; his position varies almost as fast as the data coming in."

Ah. So that's what this is about. She's trying to charm me into supporting her position. For a moment there, I thought... He shook his head and watched her face droop.

"I'm sorry, Eva. I don't think it's a good idea. Security doesn't worry me particularly, but there are other aspects..." he began, letting a preacher's sadness at the human condition pervade his voice and expression.

O'Donnell Enclave, Waimanu, HI | *Sunday 0122 HST*

Eva tossed restlessly in the dimmed light of her quarters, and contemplated going out on the deck to sleep under the stars. Finally she rolled up on one elbow and nudged Mr. Bojangles with her toes.

"It's his own goddamn message, Bo."

The big tomcat raised his head and delivered a sleepy 'so what' look.

She glanced at the clock. "He's probably having breakfast now, putting the final touches on it."

The cat yawned at her.

"Let us practice what Jesus taught. Let us greet the *Novas* with acceptance, not prejudice. With hope, and not fear," she quoted.

The cat meowed.

"Good words, Bo; powerful words. They speak to the heart. So I take them, and substitute Mohammed or Buddha or whatever for Jesus, depending on the culture. It would work, Bo. I know it would."

The cat rose and stretched.

"But he says I don't have enough *gravitas*, enough *wa*. That I'm only fifteen and a female." Her irritation built. "That's bullshit, Bo. I'm the first of my species. I can do things people only dream about. Miracles."

The cat moved up the bed and rubbed his whiskers against her cheek, smearing the teardrop.

"I should have pointed out to Pastor Bob that Jesus was only twelve when he chatted up the Pharisees in the Temple courtyard."

A rumbling purr resonated in her ear as the big tomcat rubbed his head against it.

"Ah, shit. You're not going to calm me down that way. Not tonight; I'm too angry."

Eva grabbed her bedroll and futon from the corner of the room and walked through the little lanai to the open deck. "C'mon, I'm sleeping outside. Let the trade winds cool me off."

Hours later, the girl finally slept, but twitched uneasily in her communion with the visions of long-dead Sisters. They sat around her in a circle; some smiling, some solemn.

"I'm feeling rejected," she told them. "Dejected."

They nodded in unison.

"I don't think he loves me. Not really."

"Not in the way you want," one of them guessed. Eva tasted her amusement at the sexual undercurrents.

"It's not funny! It's painful."

They all nodded agreement.

"And he's wrong! So wrong! I know I should be doing this. Every instinct I have says it's time for me to go out to the world; to be open, be truthful, show them there's no danger from the *Novas.*"

"Again, Little Mother, we can make no independent judgments. We can see the man only through your perceptions," said one.

"Ask your living Sisters, Elia and Sarah," suggested another, "they are more objective."

"That's... difficult. I'm not really sure I can tell them how I feel about him. I don't think they'd approve."

"They probably know."

Eva pondered that, rotating slowly to take in all the faces.

"You seek to impress Pastor Bob; to flatter him by adopting his message," one of them said shrewdly.

"I have my own message!" Eva snapped.

The vision grinned at her. "As you wish."

Eva had to laugh at the amusement running around the circle.

"I think I should do it anyway; transpose and talk to religious leaders one-on-one. Answer their doubts, show them I don't have any horns."

A collective shrug greeted that. "You are the first, the *One* of our legends. You probably are the only person able to decide what is best for you and the *Novas.*"

Eva twitched in her sleep and gave a long sigh.

"I have to do it. I must."

Another collective shrug. "Always do what you feel you must, child."

Eva Connard stopped twitching and dropped down to a deeper stage of sleep, dreamless. The moon set, leaving only starlight to illuminate the portion of her face sticking out of the bedroll. Mr. Bojangles contemplated it from his perch on the deck rail. Then he jumped down, stalked over and circled her sleeping form three times.

The girl exhaled a long sigh. The cat burrowed into the bedroll and curled himself into her neck, purring. The appointed hour for the forum and sermon of Robert John Blake in the National Cathedral came and went long before the eastern sky began to brighten over the Hawaiian Islands.

O'Donnell Enclave, Waimanu, HI | Sunday 1011 HST

"My Dream-Sisters say it's up to me, Josh. I'm the only one qualified. Nobody else."

And they're probably right, Joshua thought, looking at the stubborn set of Eva's jaw across the table. *But oh, little sister, you worry me.* "You said they were only one input, Sis," he reminded her in the blandest tone he could muster. "The Council is another input. As am I and my probability assessments."

"I value all views, Josh. I truly do. But..."

"You have this sense..."

"Yeah."

"Stronger than intuition..."

"Yeah."

"Of necessity, of urgency, of immanency? What?"

"All of those. None of those. I don't know, Josh, I haven't got any words for it. But I'm here, and at the same time I'm in other places. Or will be, or need to be... it's all sort of... the same." She gazed absently at the blue expanse of bay and ocean off the deck.

"I'm confused, Eva."

"Yeah, me too. But the thing is, there's an... interconnectedness. I *feel* what I have to do."

"So this is going to solve all our problems? Popping in uninvited on religious leaders, and somehow getting them on our side?"

"No... I don't think so. Not by itself. No, what this will do is set the foundation for something... bigger... down the road." Eva smiled at him. "Maybe your first guess was the best, Josh. Necessity."

"So these visits are necessary... okay. For what bigger thing down the road?"

She sighed. "I don't know. I can't even guess; our reality is too chaotic. But if I just touch it here, and nudge it there," Eva's hands moved by themselves as her eyes lost focus and looked inward, "I get the sense I could improve the chances of a good outcome."

You've been nudging the edges of chaos for a while now, little sister. You started seven years ago, in Irian Jaya, I think. "If you could define it better, maybe I could game it out. Evaluate the probabilities of success of different pathways." He sounded so forlorn that he had to laugh at himself. Eva laughed with him.

"Hey. You did it yourself, Josh. You nudged probability when Mom and Dad were dying in the power plant, that morning when I was conceived sixteen years ago. But can your intellect, all your machines, your supercomputers... can they tell you how you did it? How you got it exactly right?"

He shook his head, still laughing. "Too many variables. And my memory is pretty hazy on it."

"And you've been trying to analyze it for how long now?"

"Sixteen years... off and on."

"Yeah. Well. You're going to have to trust me on this, big brother. I need to nudge the edges of this present chaos toward a better outcome for the *Novas*, and dropping in on religious leaders is the way to do it."

"But it's not the end point."

"No. And I don't know what the end point is, Josh. I can't foresee it; I think it depends too much on our own actions."

"But the visit thing is necessary to get to a better end point?"

"Well... as your logic would have it, it's a necessary condition, but not a sufficient condition; not by itself."

"Other conditions have to occur?"

Joshua watched his little sister's eyes go hooded as she probed inward again.

"Yes, absolutely. But I have no idea what they might be."

A shadow flickered over her face as a gull hovered momentarily above the deck. *I've got a bad feeling about this, kiddo. I think you do too. But we'll try it anyway, I guess; you're the boss here.*

Another shadow flickered in the dim far corner of the deck behind her. Joshua slapped his hand hard on the table.

"Gaelan! It is *not* polite to eavesdrop."

His six-year old son flashed into visibility, chagrined.

"Oh, Ibrahim," Eva stage-whispered, "come out, come out, wherever you are."

A rustle in a tree hanging over the deck, and Gaelan's twin dropped ten meters to land smoothly beside his brother.

Joshua looked at them sternly. "That's not polite, boys."

Ibrahim feigned innocence. "Just practicing, Dad. Like you told us."

He gave his father and aunt a winning smile and elbowed his brother for support.

"The locus let us come out here, Dad," Gaelan added.

Joshua suppressed irritation at the defensive logic that so neatly shifted blame to an unimpeachable source, gave the twins his raised eyebrow and pointed to the door into the kitchen. The boys scampered away. Eva laughed.

He looked out over the water and up at the cliff top above. *A safe place, a protective locus for us all... and now we have to step outside it. I pray you're right, little sister.*

Eva's laughter faded as she looked at him.

UMC Capitol Office, Washington, DC | Sunday 1840 EST

Robert Blake basked in the afterglow of the congratulations he'd received for what most analysts were calling a seminal sermon at the National Cathedral that morning. The glow faded as he looked over preliminary statistics compiled by his staff; emails flooding the website showed that — seminal or not — UMC probably would lose twenty percent of its flock.

Always a tradeoff in this business. He sighed and typed quick instructions to his public relations staff to spin the worst of the feedback and then check on whether any serious UMC donors showed signs of jumping ship. As he worked, his eyes flitted uncertainly toward the small icon on the monitor that would announce an incoming secure call on the Nova Council line.

"Still angry with me, Eva?" he asked the icon. It stayed dim. He worked absently through the statistics, writing an occasional note to his staff while he thought of her reaction when they spoke last night. He talked to the icon.

"My messages, my words, Eva... they were designed for my delivery alone. All the psychometrics are carefully tailored, measured... fitted to me, my style, my cadence." He paused to bang out a quick note to his chief of staff. "They wouldn't work for you." The icon on the monitor screen didn't blink.

"Yes, the words have power by themselves, but to think that they would work as well for a fifteen year-old girl as for me? Impossible. I spoke truly, as your Councilor should. New species or not, you simply haven't the moral authority." He banged out another note to the head of his client contact group for major donors.

"You're too much of a wild card to let loose in the world. The equilibrium is too delicate to risk. So I'm sorry for what I said, but it was honest, and it was necessary."

The icon didn't blink.

"Call me, will you please? Congratulate me on the Forum discussion, and my sermon afterwards? You were getting up early to watch it, you said."

More statistics rolled across the screen. He studied them absently.

"I can't call you, you know, Eva. That would be psychological bad form since you're seeing me as a father figure." He paused to reply to another email.

"I think you may have a childish crush on me, too, but... that's a subject I think neither of us can touch. Not now, anyway. Maybe later."

The icon finally blinked. He smiled, typed in the security code and watched the big screen across from his desk come to life abruptly.

"Jesus was only twelve when he caused all that consternation with the Pharisees in the Temple, Pastor Bob," Eva Connard announced without preamble, "and I'm three years older. And female. Wow! Think of all the trouble I'm gonna cause! I'll let you know how it works out." She blew a cheery kiss toward the camera and the screen went black.

"Eva!" Blake's fingers flew to the keyboard, but an X flashed over the icon before he could enter the callback command.

O'Donnell Enclave, Waimanu, HI | Sunday 1245 HST

"Eva!" Joshua reproached her, "the man just helped our cause enormously. Why the hell did you do that?"

Her brother's question seemed to float in the air between her flushed face and the Council chamber's big monitor screen that had just gone black. She tasted the irritation around the edges of his question.

"I have my reasons."

"They are?"

"He aggravated me."

"Oh, come on!"

"And he's too damn pious."

"He's a televangelist, for God's sake! He's entitled!"

"Not with me, he isn't!" she said hotly.

Joshua frowned. "He took a big leap, he came over to our side, publicly. He's with us now. And then you blow him off like this? What's going on, Eva?" He moved toward the control console.

Eva blocked his path. "He said those great words he's been generating wouldn't work for me. I was too young, just a girl. I didn't have the... *gravitas* to deliver them to religious leaders."

Joshua veered off and sat in a chair, studying her. "So? It's just an opinion. Why get irritated?"

"Because he practically forbade me to do it!"

Joshua just cocked an eyebrow. "Hmm. Aggravation, piety, then a presumption of superiority? Okay, I see your point. Anything else?"

"Yes!"

"What?"

"He's wrong."

"Yeah. I think so too, little sister." He smiled at her.

"You do?" *I love you, big brother.*

"I do. Pastor Bob has never seen you up close relating to people. All he's seen is images, just hints of the force of your personality. You can take any words you believe in and deliver them with enough *gravitas* to drop an elephant in its tracks."

"Thank you! I'm glad you see that."

Her brother hid a smile. "But there's something more than aggravation behind what you just did. You're infatuated with Pastor Bob, aren't you?"

Eva looked away, at the empty black screen. Her fingers flicked absently above the virtual control plane and the computer kicked the screen alive, but then she pulled her hand back and dropped in her chair.

"It's one of your more poorly kept secrets," Joshua added gently.

She looked at her feet, concentrating on suppressing the blush rising in her cheeks. Her brother's tone changed, along with the subject.

"Well... maybe we can talk about that later, Eva. If you want to. Right now, let's talk about a few practice runs before we hit the big-time, okay?"

"Practice? Why? Just tell me where you want to go, Josh, so I can get a fix on it. I can take us there. It's simple."

"Simple? Then how come you can't explain it to me?"

"How do you explain color to someone who's blind?"

"Ouch."

"I'm sorry."

"Actually... I've been to the castle and back, so I'm not worried about the transpositional mechanics, whatever they are. I'm worried about what we encounter when we get there."

"Hostiles?"

"Always a possibility."

"We're a formidable tag team, Josh."

"I know, Eva, but..."

"You're worried that I can't be tough, can't be..." she said it distastefully, "...deadly."

"Yeah."

"Call up the coordinates on a K'Shmar hotspot, Josh. Show me, and we'll go there."

"Likely nothing at those hotspots, sis. Maybe just a transceiver of some sort."

"So? If there's no one there then it's safe, right? And you want a practice run..."

Joshua shrugged and worked his fingers within the control plane. A map of the hotspots over the world displayed on the big monitor. "Here's a pretty good one..." he homed the cursor in on the Indian subcontinent, "... northwest India, near Pakistan." He homed in closer and entered commands on the keyboard. A satellite image slid in under the crosshairs over the putative K'Shmar source. Eva leaned forward to study it. Joshua consulted the data scrolling across his console monitor.

"It's northwest of the city — no, the town — of Bhilwara. It's in the Aravalla Range — old mountains, I think, like the Appalachians. The center of the disturbance is 26 degrees north, 76 degrees east, roughly."

She watched him finger more commands, talking more to the display than her. "Elevated terrain, but I'm not sure..."

Eva looked away from the satellite image and closed her eyes. *It's... there, got it!* She opened them on her brother. *He likes precision, so...*

"Fourteen hundred twenty-three point five meters above mean sea level," she said as she walked over to his chair and took his hand.

"Josh, close your eyes so they'll adjust quickly; it's not yet dawn over there. Now exhale and yawn. Your ears will pop. Okay, on three. One, two..."

Chapter 6

Aravalla Range, Northwest of Bhilwara, India | Monday 0458 IST

They materialized in wet darkness on the side of a hill.

Eva giggled. "Oops! Forgot to tell you it was raining."

Joshua swallowed and his ears popped. His eyes tried without success to adjust to the miniscule amount of ambient light. *Not good*, his mind warned and instinctively he yanked her down into a crouch with him.

"I can't see a thing, Eva."

"It's a tropical shower, Josh; moving off now. The moon will come out soon."

"Oh, suddenly you're a meteorologist? With built-in weather radar?"

Eva giggled again and stood up. "Everything's connected, Josh."

"Yeah. I see that. For you, anyway." *Damned if I don't sound jealous.* "You can project the future now? How far ahead?"

"No, no! I'm just sensing where the shower is going, how fast it's moving, where the trailing edge is, that's all. Radar actually is a good analogy. The shower cell is a little packet of organization in the air's chaos."

The rain moved away as if on cue, and in the fuzzy moonlight Joshua could make out a ridgeline above them. He did a slow 360, taking in their surroundings. A valley below them had a few lights, dim in the distance. *A village, a small one. Several klicks, maybe five.*

"We're at the epicenter? Where the computer projected it?"

Eva smiled at that. "No, Joshua. I'm being very careful, like you wanted. It's in the next valley, over the top of this hill. We can..." she mimed little mouse feet with her fingers, "sneak up on it."

He looked up at the ridge. "Good," he said sourly, "that's exactly what we'll do. Thank you."

Minutes later they lay on a ledge overlooking a small barren rock-strewn valley. The trailing edge of the shower drifted off, revealing an antenna tower on the opposite ridge.

"Highest point around, right, Eva?"

She closed her eyes for a moment. "Yeah. For a few hundred miles. There are some higher hills to the northeast, but not many; Himalayas after that."

He nodded. "Makes sense. There's a receiving dish too, and a shed there at the base, solar cells on the roof. This is one of those World Bank projects — cell phones and internet to the hinterlands."

"Hiding in plain sight? Good idea, but how..." Eva looked at the tower uncertainly.

Joshua felt the clues tumble through a logic lattice and produce a certainty. "Oh! Zurvan's new distribution method for the K'Shmar wave? He's not using the global power meridians as a carrier. That's why NSA's network can't pick up epicenters. They're looking in the wrong place."

"So what's he using?"

"The internet."

"You're sure? Josh, that's fiendish! Here?"

"Wi-Fi, that's why our detectors pick it up, probably. The carrier signal is over the air from here. If it were running down wires we probably wouldn't see it at all."

Joshua fed that logic outcome into another lattice and got an almost instantaneous response. "And he's orchestrating this; timing the effects, sequencing them for maximum damage."

Eva looked at him, wide-eyed with horror in the moonlight.

"And another thing," he muttered, "there's got to be some local control here, an operator. You sense anything?"

Eva squatted on the ledge and put her hands flat on the rock surface.

"Right below us. The rock's a little different. Primitive, but... camouflage? Yes, I think so. So recon drones or satellites wouldn't pick up anything unusual?"

"A cave entrance?"

"I think probably so."

"Yeah, I think you're probably right; a cave, with an operator. Has to be."

"And he's putting the K'Shmar on the broadband carrier?"

"Yeah. We see the epicenters cycling at what looks like random intervals, but they're not at all. Zurvan is directing this, like an orchestra conductor pointing to the string section, then the horns, making sure everything comes together just right."

His sister stared at him, pale in the moonlight.

"Okay, Josh, let's leave. Let the local police handle this problem."

"No. I want a few words with the operator."

"Why? He's probably just some low-level grunt; gets a phone message, types some commands into a computer."

"Likely. But intel on the ground is always valuable. Come on."

Joshua began picking his way down the slope, with Eva trailing.

"What are you going to do, Josh? Walk up and knock on the cave door?"

"Exactly."

"That's not a good idea."

"Why not?"

"I don't know."

He looked at her. *She has the power, I feel it in her.* He shrugged. "Just stand off to the side here, Eva. He'll focus on me. If he's armed, freeze him in a gravity field. You've got good control in this place?"

She opened her palm to a boulder ten meters away, lifted it and set it back down.

"Yeah. I guess." She frowned at him.

He didn't have to knock, the cave had no door. A shadowy blur moved inside. Light flashed. In instant reflex, Joshua started to drop and turn, but the pressure wave of the explosion never followed. He landed on the floor inside the Nova Council chamber, Eva holding his ankle in a death-grip. The wall monitor of satellite coverage of the hilltop showed a bloom of fire in the darkness half a world away and behind them.

O'Donnell Enclave, Waimanu, HI | Sunday 1705 HST

Raw emotions hammered through her, almost drowning out her brother's urgent questions.

"Eva! Are you all right?"

Joshua's voice was thin, distorted, coming from some echoic distance. *Am I?* she wondered. *Oh, God! He was only a boy, not even my age...*

"Eva! Look at me!"

...just doing what he was told. He didn't even know...

Now Joshua was in her face, eyes wide, worried. She gathered herself and his relief washed over her, a sensation warm and loving. It gave her a tiny bit of distance from the emotional agony.

"Can you hear me, kiddo?"

"Yes," she whispered.

"Good. Take your rock-climbing grip off my ankle."

She did. The release of pressure paradoxically let the agony back into her mind: *I didn't mean to...*

Joshua hugged her. She wailed, sobbed. He held her. They rocked together on the floor. Running feet slapped the hallway outside and skidded into the Council chamber. She felt his left hand go up, felt the strength of its command. His right arm held her tightly, patiently, as she spilled out the emotional torrent.

Finally her sobs wound down into hiccups. Joshua's voice ramped up from a dim echo into its normal timbre.

"It's okay, honey. A close one, but you're okay, I'm okay. A booby-trap. We'll have to be more careful, that's all."

He doesn't know... the agony clawed at her again, but more weakly. She rubbed her wet eyes against his shirt and pulled back a bit.

"Tell me what happened, Eva. There was a blast in the cave, but you must have frozen it. How?" His eyes had gone distant, glittering with that intense focus they got whenever his mind was ready to absorb massive inputs of information.

She swallowed hard. "Shaped charges, set to blow outward, take out anyone in front of the entrance, but..." she sniffled, "not hurt anyone around the corner inside."

"Okay. And you did what, Eva?"

"I... changed... its direction?" She felt her mind struggle for words to put to the concepts.

"Some kind of dimensional tensor for force reversal, a gravity-derivative?"

She shrugged. "Dunno. Something I had to hold in place, though, while I grabbed you and we transposed out." She felt the tears start again. Her brother's eyes lost their intensity and went soft.

"Eva? What is it, honey? The guard?"

"I killed him, Josh." The words burned her mouth when they came out. Joshua took her hands. She felt other hands on her shoulders, comforting. *Sarah. Elia. Thank you.* "I felt his mind, in the second he was jumping for the detonator button. Then it was gone."

He shrugged his shoulders helplessly. "He was trying to kill us, Eva. You acted in self-defense."

Two tears welled out. "He was just a boy, Josh. Younger than me, I think."

"Oh." He looked even more helpless. "I'm sorry." He dropped her hands and thumbed the tears from her cheeks.

Sarah and Elia sat down on the floor on either side of her; each took a hand but didn't speak.

"I should have..." her voice quivered and tailed off. Her brother's image froze then dissolved into amorphous light. A long line of white-robed Sisters floated forward from the light and spoke to her.

Eva. It will be... messy, child. Are you up to it? The woman's stern face studied her.

"I thought I was," she whispered.

And now, with the blood of an innocent on your hands? A softer face asked that.

"I don't know."

No guilt, objected another face, moving up from the background, *it was a reflex, purely defensive.*

"I had the instinct to get us out of there. I should have trusted it; overridden Josh. The boy's blood is on my hands."

So, the stern voice spoke again, *will you go on? You are the first of the Novas, the One of our legends.*

Eva sighed. *If not me, then who?*

The women's faces faded, but her question lingered in their eyes.

Isn't there a better way? Her mind wailed it as the women receded into the light, and she heard her own voice whisper it aloud. Joshua's image unfroze and slid back into focus.

"I wish there was a better way, too, Eva. We all do."

Her pain was mirrored in his face.

O'Donnell Enclave, Waimanu, HI | Sunday 2217 HST

"I'll try, TC. That's the best I can do." Adrienne O'Meara's troubled face stared out of the monitor screen at him.

TC Demuzzio measured his words carefully: the young woman was in a delicate position. Old images flashed across his mind. *You've grown even more beautiful over the years, Adrienne O'Meara. Do you know that? Is it the three children you and Aaron have had? All* Novas, *according to our tracking. That has to be a factor, doesn't it?*

"So... persuade him it's the least bad alternative, Adrienne," he offered.

"I can give it a shot, TC. But you know... the President makes up his own mind, always. Don't overestimate my influence."

"We're not going to risk Eva. Not after the fiasco in India this afternoon," he growled at her image on the monitor.

"I agree completely. Eva's too precious to be used as a tactical weapon, even if she's willing."

"But we need those K'Shmar relay stations taken out. Josh's projections say if we do that, a lot of the wind goes out of Zurvan's sails. We give sanity a chance to recover."

"I agree with that, too. And so does my interagency task force." She looked at him quietly for a long moment. "Our projections are very consistent with Joshua's."

Demuzzio arranged a hopeful look on his face. "So look, we're not asking for the world here. Just three or four locations where unfriendly governments won't take action themselves."

"Send in our special forces?"

"Nah. I mean, run your own projections, but Josh says that can't be done fast enough to help."

Adrienne O'Meara shrugged. "We already did. We agree."

Demuzzio nodded and rubbed the top of his head. "Hell, it should be easy for the Prez, Adrienne. Turn the satellite, tune the laser, fry the equipment on the ground. A couple minutes per site, maybe. That's not much to ask. Do it in the daytime, probably nobody will see the beam anyway, Josh says."

Adrienne smiled. "Then he knows more about the weapon than me, TC..." She let the question hang off her raised eyebrow as to why that might be.

He shrugged. "He probably thought you knew. We're not hiding anything, Adrienne. Ask me whatever you want."

She contemplated him then nodded. "Still, TC, we're risking disclosure of a space-based weapon we've claimed repeatedly that we don't have. And our credibility in the world is better than it used to be, but still isn't all that great."

He spread his hands. *I can't do any more, Adrienne. You have to decide. And then the President.*

Adrienne exhaled a long slow breath. "Okay. It's four in the morning here. I'll let the White House duty officer know. And I'll wake up the National Security Coordinator; Carol can probably wangle me a few minutes of the man's time before breakfast."

Demuzzio let out a long breath of his own.

"Thank you, Adrienne."

"This is tough for me, TC. I'm a public servant, an agent of a government I swore an oath to uphold. And yet I'm a member of the Nova Council. I really should quit one or the other, like you did."

"The President knows that, Adrienne; he's said he's okay with it. The man knows moral nuance. And I think he actually likes that you've got a foot in both camps."

"Maybe. But what he doesn't know is just how thoroughly Josh has analyzed the government's capabilities, how much more the Nova Council knows than his agencies know."

"So when he finds out he'll be pissed?"

"He doesn't like to be leveraged."

"That's what I hear."

"So, TC... you and Josh and Eva... you're absolutely sure you want me to tell the President of the United States to use a super-secret weapon that's been a successfully concealed defense of our national security for... ten years?"

"Nah. Don't tell him. Ask him. Politely. Just remind him that it *is* our national security we're talking about here. Probably the whole freakin' planet's security."

She spoke through a suppressed smile, Demuzzio saw. "You're tough, TC."

"Yeah, well. He needs to be, too."

O'Donnell Enclave, Waimanu, HI | Monday 0953 HST

The message came from Earl Phillips at the end of the Nova Council session. His holographic image smiled broadly as he took the paper from off-camera and announced it.

"Got a message from Adrienne here, folks. Sorry she can't be with us, et cetera, et cetera, but the President just approved using the space laser. DOD is targeting some installations now. She's got her task force helping them out. Strikes will be tomorrow and Wednesday, in the daytime."

Cheers ran around the table from both physical throats and holographic ones. Eva sighed in relief. *Good. I'm not sure I'm ready for more blood on my hands.*

"The President wasn't happy about it, but apparently Carol Violette talked him into it," Phillips continued. "Smart man; actually listens to his NSC."

Eva nodded. "I'll thank them both personally, Earl. Everybody... thanks for your ideas. I especially like the one about calming the markets. Josh and I will do something about that."

Joshua looked around the table at the holograms. "Same time tomorrow?" The images nodded and as Eva waved his fingers turned the comm link off.

"Give us a moment, please?" Eva asked.

Demuzzio, Sarah and Elia traded glances then stood up from the table as one and walked out of the Council chamber.

"Eva?" Her brother was quizzical. "They'd probably have some input to offer."

"Yeah. They wouldn't want me to go."

He smiled. "And you think I would?"

"I think you're a better judge of risk and reward."

"So... where to this time?"

She glanced at the time zone clock projected into the holographic space that Earl Phillips had vacated. "Almost closing time on the New York Stock Exchange, brother."

"I haven't done any predictive modeling yet on the kind of language that might calm the financial markets, kiddo."

"You don't need to, Josh. I've got a pretty good idea what to say." She watched him struggle with amusement before he spoke.

"You sure? The market hates uncertainty."

"The *Nova* development ultimately will bring stability to the market, Josh. You've projected that yourself."

"Yeah, true... but timing..."

She grabbed his arm. "Come on. I've always wanted to ring that bell." She felt her other eyes look elsewhere, eastward across an ocean and a continent.

Their two bodies materialized with an outrush of displaced air behind a small crowd on a podium. A smallish man stood with his finger poised above a button as the seconds counted down.

"Excuse me," Eva said, moving forward and nudging the man gently aside with a gravity field, "May I?" She pointed at the button. He nodded yes, dumbfounded. "Oh thank you, sir, I'd love to."

She felt Joshua position himself behind her at the stairs to the podium, a tall imposing guardian even in his shorts, sandals and Hawaiian shirt. *Oops. Maybe we should have dressed for the occasion. Oh well, from the floor they can only see the top of us.*

The clock wound down to four PM. Eva's finger stabbed the button and held it. On the trading floor of the Exchange, heads turned, did double-takes. *I wonder if they like my shirt.* She lifted her finger off the button and watched the hubbub start to die. *It's a nice contrast to all the blue pinstripes up here, anyway.* Traders jostled to get a clearer view. An alert cameraman scuttled sideways and raised a videocam. *Now that I have your attention...*

Eva picked up the microphone with her left hand and flicked it on. Her right arm went around the small man's shoulders. She drew him toward her and kissed his cheek. A camera flashed. He smiled uncertainly at her, then more uncertainly outward at the quieting crowd.

"Thank you for the privilege," she told him. Speakers echoed her soft words across the floor, silencing the crowd for a moment. *Ah, they realize who I am.* She smiled at them. More cameras flashed. Cell phones were held high. Eva brought the microphone closer.

"Aloha. I'm Eva Connard. One of those *Novas* you've been hearing about. I'm a nice person. I want you all to know that I'm not a threat. I mean you no harm. No *Nova* does, nor will; it's just not in our nature."

She gave the crowd her winningest smile. A few smiled back tentatively. A few frowned. The rest stared with mouths agape.

"Some of you may have worried that the *Nova* development will be a threat to free enterprise. It won't. The only ways it might affect the market should be very positive: less greed, more openness, a more natural distribution of wealth across economic classes. Good things."

A murmur ran through the crowd as she paused. Behind her, Joshua cleared his throat. *Yes, brother, I know, I know.* Part of her vision noted the worry on his face. *But my message really is for the broader world. This is just a convenient stage.* On the floor below, two more videocam operators moved in. In another part of her vision, white-robed Sisters circled, debating among themselves. Eva smiled at them, and then outward, looking directly at the biggest videocam. *A network camera. Excellent!* She went on, unscripted, speaking from a place that was neither heart nor mind nor soul but an integration of all. *Contrition for the death of the innocent Indian boy,* one of her multiple awarenesses intuited, lending her its strength.

"The moneychangers in the Temple charged exorbitant fees for sacrificial animals. And the faithful who couldn't afford to buy an animal believed they wouldn't be saved. A terrible thing." Her voice softened. *Will brokers understand allegory?*

"And you people deal in economic salvation," she clarified in a near-whisper. A tear rolled down each cheek, and Eva felt the flashes from cameras get trapped in them, tiny packets of energy. She fed them into her voice to strengthen it as she segued into the tapeworm analogy.

"A market that's more... symbiotic... less parasitic," she concluded a minute later, "that would be a truly good thing." Eva steepled her fingers around the microphone and bowed. "Thank you."

She set the microphone in its cradle. A long moment of dead silence erupted into shouted questions. She turned away, smiling at the suits on the podium as she brushed by.

Eva took Joshua's hand and transposed them directly into the waterfall outside their Hawaii enclave. *Calming the markets? He'll need cooling off.*

Senate Office Building, Washington, DC | Wednesday 2243 EST

The old Senator stared across the big desk, his bulbous eyes pools of angry dark vacuum. "The little bitch! Fourteen fuckin' percent in two days!"

The younger man tried to meet the stare levelly. He shrugged. "The market's been overdue for a correction anyway, Senator. I'm not sure we can blame it all on Eva Connard."

"Bullshit, son. She jabbers about a parasitic market, about redistributin' wealth, and four hours later when the Tokyo Exchange opens it drops like a fuckin' rock. And then the fire sale goes around the world. Like that snake eatin' itself."

The younger man kept his face straight. *Ouroboros? Senator? I wouldn't have suspected you of allegory.* But he held his tongue and let the man rant.

"Two fuckin' days! Automatic tradin' trips! You got any idea how much money I lost, son?" The old man wiped away a dribble of saliva escaping the corner of his mouth.

"The girl didn't say anything a lot of other people haven't been saying for years, Senator."

The man snorted. "Fuckin' arm-chair philosophers. Left-wing cocksuckers, all of 'em. Commies. Not a goddamn brain in the bunch."

Including the new Fed chairman your committee unanimously endorsed, Senator? he thought, but said instead, "What struck me was that green stocks didn't drop."

The Senator snorted dismissively. "Weapons, munitions, that's where the big margins are, boy; not that solar shit. And all my personal stocks took a bigger hit than the market did."

"Maybe you ought to diversify more, Senator."

"Fuck that. We gotta get control back, son. You understandin' me here? That's how you make real money. Control the markets." He hit the desk with a pudgy fist for emphasis.

The younger man looked down at his own hands folded in his lap. They were fit, strong, tanned. *I'd like them around your fat neck, Senator. And if I can find a way to destroy your files on me, that's exactly where they'll be.* He struggled to make his voice soothing.

"The market got nervous, Senator, that's all. It'll bounce back." *Or will it? The child spoke the truth about a parasitic relationship. She could almost have been talking about you, Senator. You and your cronies are one of the tapeworms, feeding off the organism...*

"It goddamn well better bounce back, son. I'm worried. Fuckin' socialists sing their song for the past ten years and nobody listens, and then this fifteen-year old little bitch spouts the same message and the public gobbles it up. Jesus!"

"I think we need to be prepared for some changes, Senator. Adapt."

"No, boy. A U.S. Senator don't adapt to no goddamn little girl."

He slapped the table.

"I want control back. And you gonna get it for me, boy."

Chapter 7

Castel Gandolfo, Italy | Thursday 0906 ITA

They materialized off the shallow end of the swimming pool at the *Residenza Papale*, the Pope's summer residence in the hills southeast of Rome. The single Swiss Guard, a stocky man in a plain business suit, faced outward at the other end. He didn't see them, nor did he hear the outrush of displaced air caused by their arrival.

The old man in the pool swam slowly but steadily toward their end. Eva smiled as she whispered at her brother.

"Think we should walk across the water and haul him out, Josh?"

"Eva!"

"Just kidding."

She studied the swimming motion as the Pope approached, focusing down tightly. *There's an imbalance. He's hurt.* Commanded by her other vision, white-robed women came and circled above the man, diagnosing and confirming. *Left hip, arthritis. Right shoulder, the biceps tendon long head is abrading, and the bursa is inflamed.* She nodded her understanding of the physiological impressions conveyed.

The Pope reached the edge of the pool and put a hand on it. Her brother whispered in her ear.

"At least he's not wearing Speedos."

"Josh!"

The Pope looked up at her exclamation, startled. The guard at the other end of the pool spun toward them, drawing a pistol. Joshua smiled and held out his hands, empty. The guard yelled quick commands into his lapel microphone as he ran toward them. As he rounded the pool corner, Joshua held up a hand and froze him in a gravity field, mid-stride.

Eva squatted down beside the pool edge and smiled as she addressed the man. "*Un'udienza privata, Sua Santità, per cortesia.*"

The Pope's eyes flicked to the frozen guard, then widened and flicked back to her with recognition in them. He smiled tentatively and answered in unaccented English.

"I admired your message to the stock exchange, Eva Connard."

"Thank you."

"Or was it a sermon?"

She laughed. "I'm not sure myself."

"Jesus with the moneychangers? In the Temple?"

"Well... maybe a little. But not so harsh; those guys are nowhere near as bad as the Sadducees."

"Some would disagree. They seem to have evaded your government's latest attempt to regulate their morality. Again."

Joshua laughed. "Hard to legislate human nature. But Eva's tapeworm analogy certainly got their attention."

"Honesty in commerce has its place," Eva said primly.

"So it does." The Pope studied her for a moment. "A private audience, yes, of course. Young man, could you release Sergio?"

Joshua looked at Eva. She nodded. Her brother relaxed the gravity field but spun the man's weapon into the pool. The guard dropped to his knees then bounced back up and charged.

"Sergio!" The Pope's sharp command stopped him short. "They mean no harm. We require privacy. This is not an attack. Not an... Alpha condition. Stand down the Guards."

Sergio studied them for a long moment, then looked at the Pope and nodded. He spoke into his lapel mike, backing away to his former position, out of earshot.

Eva translated that body dynamic, and winked relaxation at Josh. *We're cool here, bro.*

The Pope reached up his left hand. "Could you help me out of the pool?"

I like this man, Eva thought, *he's a scientist like Josh, logic lattices and parallel processing, checking to see if our effects are repeatable.* She suppressed a giggle, formed a gravity wave and popped the man, dripping, onto the tile beside the pool.

The Pope walked to a chair and donned a terrycloth robe.

"Ah, so it's true. It's all true. Your... visitation... to the stock exchange was not staged, not a magician's trick?" He looked at her thoughtfully. "Miracles?"

"Depends on your perspective," Joshua laughed this time, answering for her.

The Pope raised an eyebrow, sat down and made an inviting motion to the other chairs. Joshua pulled two of them close and they sat.

"We need your help, your support, *Santità*," Eva offered gently. "The birth of the *Novas* is an upsetting development to some of the more..."

"Tradition-bound religions?" he finished for her.

"Well..." she looked at her brother.

"Precisely," he said.

The old man smiled at the honesty. He reached to a table for his reading glasses and a loose-leaf binder, then flipped through its tabs.

"Perspective," he looked at Joshua over the top of his glasses, "yes, I suspect that would be the key."

He put the binder back on the table and shrugged. "My Vatican staff has provided some ideas. So your visit is timely, even if unannounced."

"We'd be happy to answer your questions," Joshua answered while looking toward the binder, "but the plain fact is something needs to happen very quickly to prevent — or at least dampen — mass hysteria."

"Have you a particular message in mind?" The Pope switched his gaze to Eva.

"No. Whatever you feel is appropriate, *Sua Santità*." She stood up, Joshua with her, and held out her hand. The Pope stood and offered his.

"You trust me to say the right things, Eva Connard?"

She nodded. "You are different than most of your predecessors."

Eva took his old hand in both her young ones, formed the intention, and ran its energy up to his right shoulder and down to his left hip. He shivered, then smiled and stood straighter. "Better. A gift? A miracle?" His grip trembled.

"Whatever you feel is appropriate," she repeated.

"I would dearly like to have some of my learned Jesuit scientist friends talk to you, Eva Connard; study your evolving nature. Don't you owe that to the world?"

"Possibly. But there's no time now." She smiled warmly at him. "I must be about our Mother's work."

He frowned at that, then started to laugh. Eva let go of his hand, took her brother's and transposed them back to the enclave in Hawaii. The Pope's laughter still rang in her ears and she parsed its undertones. *Joy and sorrow and fear and courage, all mixed.* She immersed her empathic sense in its complexities for a moment until her brother's voice brought her back.

"That was interesting, Eva. Any more visits you want to make tonight?"

"Well... no. It's late, almost eleven. Bed now. Then the morning Council conference. After that we'll visit the Dalai Lama."

"Why? He's already our friend."

That he is. "Courtesy call, Josh."

O'Donnell Enclave, Waimanu, HI | Wednesday 2357 HST

Sarah looked at the younger woman askance. "I really don't think we're there yet, Elia." *First Thomas and Joshua and their pre-emptive whack-a-mole strategy, and now Elia wants something almost as dangerous?*

"The threads of that plan are clear enough in the Sisterhood's evolutionary tapestry, Sarah."

Sarah studied her face. *Is she over-reacting? Or am I underestimating the danger?* "The Sisterhood never meant anything to be immutable. And those threads appear in the tapestry more as a contingency plan, not as the preferred strategy."

"The preferred strategy was keeping *Nova* evolution under wraps until a critical mass was reached... it no longer applies at this point."

"So it's time to kick in the contingency plan, Elia?" *The earth-goddess myth, the girl-child as the Messiah.* "The tapestry is a psychic thing, it's not fixed. And it's mutating as fast as Eva's genes now anyway."

"The seeds have been planted genetically for millennia, Sarah; they're cultural incipients, just below the surface, just waiting to be triggered. They haven't mutated."

She's right, of course. Women's cults would explode around Eva. "You want to pull the trigger."

"I do... sort of."

She gets that set in her jaw, Sara thought, almost amused, *I wonder how Joshua deals with it.* "Those incipients are mostly buried in female RNA, Elia. Much of the other half of humanity probably wouldn't like the idea. Men carry culturally embedded concepts in their genes, too."

"Joshua doesn't. Our twins don't. The male Council members don't."

"All extraordinary males, Elia; not typical at all."

"There are plenty more non-typical males in the world."

Sarah shrugged. "Maybe." *Why does she have this bee in her bonnet? Have things come to a crucial point that I'm not seeing?* "But anyway, why now? Getting religious leaders on our side seems like it may work reasonably well. The Pope..."

"An easy target. He was headed there anyway, from what Eva told us before she went to bed."

"All right, then. Robert Blake. He lost a third of his congregation with his positive message in our favor. He knew what would happen, but he didn't equivocate. Didn't even try to spin it much."

Elia sat and dropped her face in her hands. "I'm so tired."

"Honestly, Elia, I think the Sisterhood's earth-goddess Messiah myth should be saved for a last-ditch effort; it truly is a contingency plan. It would offend too many men."

"Maybe fewer than you think." Elia raised her head, her eyes moist.

"Maybe, maybe not. But Elia, think about it... the men most offended would be the men with the most to lose. The ones in the power structure:

of politics, religions, commerce, whatever. Didn't you see some of those testosterone-laden stock market talking heads tear into what Eva said?"

"I know, Sarah; I know how deeply their self-worth is rooted in their status. And fundamentalists in male-centric religions and cultures also would have a fit... in Christianity and Islam especially."

"And yet you want to purposely trigger a firestorm? You want to introduce Eva as the second coming, the new messiah, a Gaia goddess? Why?" *Please tell me Elia; you're not making much sense.* "And it would surely offend men like Blake and the Pope; embarrass them."

"Oh, Sarah! I'm not sure. Maybe I'm crazy. But it's a feeling that we should bring it out now; that if we don't we'll lay it on our children. Ibrahim, Gaelan. All the other young Novas." She dropped her head back in her hands.

Sarah knelt beside the chair and wrapped her arms around the young woman. *She fears for her children. Have you had a Sight, Elia?* "The threads of the Sisterhood tapestry are legend, Elia. Ancient, some of them, older than the Old Testament. How much relevance might they have in modern times? And they are changing. Rapidly now."

"Maybe our old Sisters were wiser than we knew," Elia whispered.

"They lived in harsher times," Sarah countered.

"Exactly. They knew life and death up close and personal."

"So? That would make them better judges of what to do in a more complex world than they ever could have envisioned?"

"I don't know..." Elia's whisper trailed off into a half-sob.

The big tomcat Mr. Bojangles stalked across the floor of the Council Chamber and rubbed up against Elia's ankles.

O'Donnell Enclave, Waimanu, HI | Thursday 0012 HST

"The ladies are having another heart-to-heart," Demuzzio reported as he entered the kitchen. "You wanna beer?"

Joshua took his arms down from the French doors onto the deck, from which he'd been staring at the moon. "Nightcap? Good idea, TC."

"Any preference?"

"Whatever you're having."

"Kona dark? Pipeline Porter?"

"Sure, good" Joshua agreed absently, "I probably need the extra calories."

"Yeah? I thought Eva did the heavy lifting on that transposition stuff?" *The kid sure as shit filled her hollow leg before she went to bed. I never ate like that even when I was playing linebacker.*

"It's weird, TC. I think it's mainly an energy drain from her, but being with her in transit is like fighting against a gravity well or something — a lot gets sucked out of me too. Actually... yeah, I'm starved. What else is in there?"

Demuzzio looked in the huge refrigerator and pulled out a tray of left-over lasagna along with two beers. He set the beers on the counter and shoved the lasagna in the microwave oven. When he turned back, Joshua had drained half a bottle. *Hollow leg number two.* He turned and pulled out another bottle.

Joshua belched. "What are Elia and Sarah talking about, TC, did you hear?"

"I think Elia's moving closer to our position, Josh."

"Pre-emptive strikes?"

"Naw. Not that far. But playing the mythical card — bringing all this religious shit head-to-head."

Joshua took the drained bottle from his mouth, surprised. "Really? She hasn't said anything to me."

"I shit you not."

"But it's a contingency plan, TC. A last-ditch thing. Eva doesn't like it."

"Sarah doesn't either, from what I overheard. She says it's obsolete thinking, from bygone times. Might not work today."

"Oh, it would work all right." Joshua belched again, popped the cap off the second bottle and pulled steaming lasagna out of the microwave. "Want some?"

Demuzzio shook his head no and watched in awe until Joshua slowed for another belch, then voiced his doubts. "Sounds like crazy mythical shit to me. Eva as an earth-goddess messiah. Why do you think would it work?"

Joshua looked at him a long moment, toying with a last piece of lasagna. He sighed, chewed and swallowed, and drained the second beer before he spoke. "It's a long story, TC."

"Yeah? Another one of those you never told me?" Demuzzio stared at the younger man. *Me, your security chief?* "I got time. Got all night."

"Yeah. One of those. But don't go righteous on me, okay?" Joshua pulled another pair of beers out of the refrigerator.

Demuzzio took a beer and smiled. *Righteous? I love you, boy. I love my god-daughter Eva. I love everybody in this screwball place. But you sure as shit do keep your secrets.* "I'm listening," he said as he pulled on the beer.

"It would work because of the Sisterhood."

"The SIO? Your dead uncle Hamilton's organization?"

"He's not dead, exactly, but that's another story."

"Ah... okay. Well. Whatever. Get on with the story."

"Just triggering the myth by itself... that might not be enough. Especially now, with the situation changing so rapidly. It's almost impossible to predict whether the myth would get enough traction with enough of the population. And it would run up against serious opposition from vested interests. Economic. Political. Religious."

"Yeah? So how's SIO gonna make it work?"

"The Sisterhood would remove key opposition to the propagation of the myth."

"Remove? As in how?"

Joshua smiled and his eyes seemed to flicker, a cross like a star sapphire flaring across their irises.

Scares the shit outta me when they do that, Demuzzio admitted to himself. "As in how?" he repeated, taking another pull on the bottle.

"As in terminate. Assassinate. Shoot. Knife. Blow up. Behead. Whatever it takes. Wet work."

Another glint in those goddamn crazy eyes. "The targets?"

"There's a list."

I was afraid of that. "Jesus!"

"He's not on the list." Joshua smiled and patted Demuzzio's hand.

"The doers?"

"SIO's. Sisters."

"Women."

"Wives, lovers, secretaries, employees. In place, serving the target, trusted, mostly."

"And when you pick up the phone, they're all gonna do whack jobs for you?"

"No. For Eva."

"How many targets? A couple hundred?"

"Close to thirteen thousand."

"No!"

"Yes. And the projected success rate is ninety four percent."

"You're shitting me!"

"Nope. There's a sort of... Valkyrie class... within the SIO. Soldier mentalities. Tough ladies. You know; you've met some of them. Been working with them on this contingency plan for years now."

"So, you take out key opposition. With them gone, then what? You spring the legend on the world? Trot out Eva as the new savior of mankind?"

"Basically. That bother you, TC? It's not fundamentally different than your whack-a-mole strategy. Which I like, by the way."

That forced a chuckle out of Demuzzio. "A question of scale, Josh."

Joshua clinked his bottle against Demuzzio's. "I know. I set it up, but I doubt if I could do it. Half those thirteen thousand aren't really evil. But it's moot, anyway, for me."

"Moot?"

"Yeah. At this point the Sisterhood wouldn't let me pull the trigger, I'm no longer in command. They'd ask Eva if she wants to pull it."

"And she won't."

"Well... ultimately? If it's a last resort? If everything turns to shit and all the *Novas* are getting slaughtered? If humanity is about to self-destruct? Maybe..."

"And maybe not."

"I don't know where she'd come out on this, TC. I doubt if she even knows I set up such a thing — I buried it pretty deep." Joshua clinked bottles again, and drained his. "The hell with it. I'm going to bed."

Demuzzio spoke as he walked away. "Nice talking to you, Josh. Let's do it again real soon."

Joshua smiled back over his shoulder at the irony. "The ladies don't know about my contingency plan either, by the way," he added as he passed through the kitchen doorway.

Demuzzio studied his beer bottle, turning it in his hand. *Yeah, you folks do keep your secrets.* He thought about how Joshua's eyes had glinted eerily from the dim hallway outside. *I understand why you sat on that one, son.*

O'Donnell Enclave, Waimanu, HI | Thursday 1012 HST

The morning meeting rolled to a conclusion, the optimists in the Council buoyed by anticipation of a favorable statement from the Pope, the pessimists cautioning that ultimately the man's rubric was too conservative to expect much from a statement. Pastor Robert Blake, seated at the table for the first time as a physical presence rather than as a hologram, watched how well Eva related to her advisors. *Only fifteen years old,* he marveled, spellbound, *where does she get that kind of presence?*

The last of the holograms clicked off. Blake smiled at her from across the table and Eva giggled, breaking the spell.

"You do that well, Eva Connard. Grace and tact yet staying in charge."

The girl's cheeks reddened, but the color faded quickly. *She can control a blush reaction. Interesting.*

Sarah, Elia and Demuzzio stood as one, smiled at him and walked out of the Chamber. Joshua and Eva remained.

"Thank you for coming, Pastor Bob," Eva said. "You didn't have to; the holographic meetings seem to be working well for everyone."

And there it was again, that aura, the sheer presence. *Not only do I hear her words, I actually feel the power of her emotions, her thankfulness.*

"And you must be tired, flying all night," Eva continued as she got up from the chair. Her indigo eyes seemed to flicker bright for an instant.

Blake stood up also, then blinked as a sensation of powerful sexuality wound itself around him. *Good Lord! Who is this child? What is she now?*

"Eva," her brother said softly. The girl turned away and the sensation snapped off.

Blake straightened his knees against their sudden weakness and spoke to distract himself from the beginning tumescence in his pants. "I, um, have a mini-break before I have to be back in California, Eva. And I'm the only Council member that hasn't actually visited your enclave before. Thought it was about time I dropped by."

Joshua sat watching their conversation, his face a bland mask. Blake turned to him and nodded what he hoped was a signal that he would do no harm, that he understood the situation. *Or do I? A love goddess in a child's body? This is strange!* He composed himself and spoke.

"Do you have time to give me a short tour? All I really saw was the surface entry."

Eva looked amused. "A tour? Well, sure. But later. Josh and I have another... visitation to make."

"Right!" Joshua snapped to his feet. "Better get ready, Eva." His arm stretched toward the door. "It'll take you longer than me."

She giggled, a child again, and addressed Blake. "You must be hungry, Pastor Bob. Kitchen's that way. Lots of good local stuff. You'll probably get ambushed by Gaelan or Ibrahim..." Eva got a distant look, turned and ran from the Council Chamber, yelling over her shoulder. "...ask the boys to show you around. We should be back in an hour or so."

Joshua gave him an indecipherable look, then turned and trotted after his sister.

Hazrat e Mazumeh, Qom, Iran | Friday 0431 IRT

"You're absolutely sure we're invited, Eva?" Josh had a worried expression, scanning the mosque from their materialized position under an arch on the other side of the courtyard. "As guests, we're protected, but if we're just intruders, we'll be off on the wrong foot in this culture."

"Trust me, Josh. It's been worked out." She smiled easily and rapped a code on the wall. *But keep those reflexes sharp just in case, big brother. This one is definitely dicier than the Pope.*

"What time is it here, anyway?"

"Um, over an hour before morning prayer. We have time."

"Time for what? You planning on giving them something to pray about? Doing something other than we agreed to?"

"Actually," her indigo eyes flashed at him over the veil she pulled across her face "we'll have to play that by ear..."

A concealed door opened in the wall. Joshua spun and slid partially in front of her. She felt the energy blades instantly coil into his hands and feet, and touched his elbow reassuringly.

"Sayyida!" The woman started to kneel. "Welcome to Qom," she spoke in English.

Eva spoke sharply. "You are a Sister. No Sister kneels to me."

The woman straightened then smiled. "So it is true. The One has come."

"The One has come. As was foretold," Eva agreed.

The woman backed away and made a sweeping motion. "Then welcome to the Imam's house, young Mother. And welcome to you, Protector of the One."

They followed the woman down a dim hallway. Eva felt her brother's energy vibrations go squirrelly and touched his elbow again. The glow around his hands and feet dimmed to invisibility as they walked into a larger room. A tall gray-bearded man stood up from a table and greeted them in English.

"Welcome to my house, Eva Connard. And welcome to you, Joshua O'Donnell."

Joshua nodded respectfully. "Imam."

Eva bowed. "Sayyid." *A western table? He's gone out of his way to make me feel welcome?*

The imam smiled slightly and waved a hand at the five others seated around the table. "My Shia colleagues."

The men stood, two smiling, three frowning, and spoke greetings in Persian. Eva parsed the state of their emotions easily. *Three friendly, two neutral, one hostile.* She raised a hand to her veil, her fingers conveying that information to Joshua in their battle code.

The Imam gestured to two empty place settings. "Will you break bread with us, Eva and Joshua?"

"Since we are welcome, yes, of course." Eva dropped her veil and sat, looking calmly around the table. Joshua put his hand on the chair but didn't sit.

"Fatima!" The imam breathed. Befuddlement and shock ran across his face and jumped to the other faces.

"No!" the hostile screamed, "these people are infidels!"

Eva looked at him, then at the other imams.

"I am not Fatima reborn. But the Prophet, peace be upon him, was my ancestor, from union with his third wife Ayesha..."

"You lie! Ayesha had no children!"

"...with whose spirit I speak from time to time," Eva continued calmly. "The Prophet blessed her with a son, just before he died."

"Heresy!" The hostile imam picked a knife off the table and lunged for her.

Time slowed for Eva. She felt the awful force of a gravity wave smashing outward from her brother's hand, reached out and stopped it. *No, Joshua. This I have to do myself.*

She waited until the lunging man floated closer, then flared an energy blade from her right hand, severing his arm above the wrist. Simultaneously she cast a gravity wave from her left hand, throwing him across the room, slamming him against the wall and pinning him there.

Time sped up. The knife dropped on the plate, the hand on top of it, bleeding and twitching. The energy blade collapsed into her hand, and she let the gravity wave drop her attacker to the floor.

"Get a tourniquet on him, quickly. Ice the stump and the hand. A good surgeon may possibly re-attach it." Eva spoke sharply to the five men.

"Sayyida!" The Imam exclaimed. "My apologies! You are our guest."

"We mean your people no harm, Sayyid. We mean your faith no harm. But we will defend ourselves."

Eva felt the power, restless inside her, and let her eyes walk around the shocked faces. *Glowing eyes, in the face of Muhammad's daughter Fatima, the one they call Sayyida Zahra. Yes, that's a good image to leave them with.*

"We wish no harm to anyone," Eva repeated, "but we will defend our-selves." *And a good message, too.*

She took her brother's hand and transposed them back to Hawaii.

Chapter 8

Jebel Uweinat, Libya | *Friday 0824 CAT*

The trip from the retreat house in East Timor had been arduous but necessary. He needed better isolation and more security for the next phase, and
the United Nations peacekeepers in that nation were Australians, Western
infidels. The clamor about the coming of the Twelfth Imam eventually
would have broken down even the tightest security about his physical location, had he stayed there.

Now, Muhammad Zurvan stood on a sandstone bluff in southeast Libya,
watching the dust trail of his transport vehicle disappear back southward.
I'm tired. We rode all night. He inhaled deeply of the dry northwest wind off
the Sahara and found it much more to his liking than the tropical humidity
of East Timor.

"Ah, this is better, Muammar," he told the grizzled zealot who had
greeted him and now acted as his guide and bodyguard.

"Mahdi?"

"Much better, this desert air." He spread his arms and turned in a circle.
The morning sun had climbed over the peak of Jebel Uweinat to the east.

"Better than the caves, Mahdi?"

Zurvan purposefully looked into the middle distance, silent while he
considered the question. *Caves? Oh. A literalist. One of the later prophe-
sies, thirteenth century. Do I have adequate knowledge of his Sanussi beliefs?
Probably not; the sects are so different. A non-specific answer then; a parable.*
He smiled at the man. "There are caves of the ground, my friend. But also
there are caves of the mind, and of the soul."

"I am confused, Mahdi. The hadith..."

"I am here now, Muammar, in the flesh as well as spirit. That is all that
is needed."

The man pondered that then nodded obediently.

Zurvan nodded with him, metronomically, subtly encouraging the man's
thinking, watched the allegory sink in. *Amazing how gullible they are, once a
myth is configured to their beliefs. They hear what they want to hear. My witch
knew them well when she scripted this moment.* He stifled a laugh and asked a
question, curious about how this gullible man might answer, what it might
tell him about his *Jaesh* in this part of Islamic Africa.

"When should I confirm to the world that I am a physical being as well
as a spiritual one, Muammar? Hmm? What do you think?"

"Mahdi! I am but a simple farmer. I tend goats."

"I too am a simple man, Muammar," Zurvan replied as he affected humility, "tending the souls of our brethren. In the wadi of our faith, amidst the desert of the infidel." He gestured broadly to the desert below them, and kept nodding. Muammar began to nod with him as that allegory sank in.

Zurvan dropped the question and changed the subject. "You have internet access in your village."

"We do, Mahdi. The computer informed me when your bunker came alive. And a week after, it gave me the coded message to prepare for your arrival."

"You have done well, my friend."

"Allah has directed us to prepare for your coming, Mahdi. It is foretold. We have done what we believed we should," the man ended on a querulous note.

Well, now. Initiative! Is that a good thing or a bad? Zurvan debated it internally for a moment. *Time will tell.* He answered Muammar's implied question.

"Yes, you have. And you will continue to do well, my friend. I see it in you. And in the people of your little village. You are my *Jaesh*, my army, my shield against the darkness the infidels bring in this end-time. Against this abomination they have created, this new species they call *Nova sapiens.*"

"Thank you, Mahdi! Thank you! We are your servants."

"As I am a servant of the Prophet, peace be upon him," Zurvan intoned.

"Peace be upon him," Muammar agreed.

"Take me to the bunker then, Muammar. Have you been inside?"

"No, Mahdi. The code said to await you." The man turned and started to walk uphill.

Good, their initiative is tempered by discipline. "Were you surprised when the bunker started up, Muammar?"

"We prayed to Allah that it would, Mahdi; that we would live to see an end to the afflictions of the modern world, a return to the old ways."

"And so you shall, my friend. So you shall. Tell me, did the military check in on their radio tower and solar arrays at the summit after the bunker started up?"

"No, Mahdi. Just the routine monthly helicopter, last month. Two technicians, a few hours. Libya is not having problems with Chad or Sudan at the moment."

Better yet. When I offered Khaddafi the installation for better border control he took it as a gift, and asked no questions. So... the secret died with him? "Do you speak with the technicians, Muammar?"

"With them, yes, and their pilot and copilot. We give them dates and goat milk."

"Have they ever asked why the solar arrays are so large?"

"Yes, but we showed them the buried cable that feeds the village. They were content with that."

So there still are no questions. And the bunker's electrical draw is unmetered. "Excellent, Muammar. Now take me to the gate."

As they walked up a ravine toward the sandstone cliff and its camouflaged cave entrance, Zurvan inhaled deeply of the desert air once more. *I believe it's time to publicly confirm the arrival of the Twelfth Imam, in my very own physical person.* He stifled a laugh.

O'Donnell Enclave, Waimanu, HI | Friday 1015 HST

The morning Council meeting had been interesting to say the least. It probably was just as well that Pastor Robert Blake was en route back to the mainland and couldn't participate, Joshua mused as he listened to Elia and Sarah debate with Eva. *That would have tested the man's adaptability and loyalty at the same time.*

Demuzzio had taken the twins down to the bay to play with the dolphins. *Smart move, TC.* The debate definitely was heating up.

"I know the messianic myth the Sisterhood has set up for this," Eva said patiently, "and I understand the reasons for it. But I'm just a new version of human. I'm not a god."

Both ladies started to speak, but Eva cut them off.

"And damned if I want to be one."

"As a practical matter..." Elia began.

"I know," Eva answered, "I'm close enough. And yes, I could easily walk into the role..."

"The cults have already started," Sarah observed gently, "and it may happen anyway."

"So why not take advantage?" Elia added. She looked to her husband for support.

Joshua shrugged and spread his hands. "It's one of the scenarios that has reasonably favorable projected *near-term* outcomes..."

Elia's scowl told him she wanted a stronger endorsement.

"...but it also has a lot of downsides, and the error bands are the biggest of all for that scenario..." he shrugged again and added "...especially in the long-term." *Sorry dear, I have to be honest.*

"But now that the *Nova* development is public, Joshua, it may be the safest course." Sarah continued. "Your projections are pretty clear about that. So why not just take control?"

Funny how our positions switch back and forth between hard line and soft sell. Just shows how complex this chaos really is. Joshua shrugged again. "True, Sarah; by the numbers it's safest for Eva, at least in the near-term. But I'm not comfortable with the numbers. And that particular scenario has some nasty potential pushback in the long-term."

Elia tried again. "The Sisterhood built the female messiah myth for exactly this end, Eva. The psychology is in place; predispositions have been driven into women's genes over millennia of cultural cues."

Eva sighed with frustration. "I know that. I talk to my ancestors just like you talk to yours, okay? Probably more, lately."

Joshua watched the complex interplay between them, and ignored their fleeting sidelong glances at him. *I'm not going to referee. I'm not qualified. I'm a male. No ghosts in my RNA to consult.*

It was Eva's turn to shrug. "I may do it. I may *have* to do it, Elia," she conceded. "But for the moment... it's not me."

To thine own self be true, little sister. That really is the ultimate safe course, I think. I'll take your instincts over my statistical projections — even with all the sociocultural research, even with my three supercomputers down in Level Six processing it all...

"Exactly why isn't it you?" Elia was irritated. "You're the first *Nova*. Compared to the rest of us, you *are* a god."

Aw, shit, now I have to chime in. Elia's going to be pissed at me again. "The long-term downside is intolerance, conflict, maybe war," Joshua interjected. "That's where the projections fall apart."

"The *Novas* won't be intolerant, they'll have the empathy gene, both male and female," Sarah countered.

"But *Novas* won't be any significant part of the world population for three or four generations, maybe ten or twenty." Joshua rebutted.

"With an outsized influence," Elia amended.

"Granted. But cults or religions quickly develop a life of their own. Before you know it, the '*Nova religion*'," Joshua made quotation marks in the air with his fingers, "will become the one true faith. No room for others."

"And what is so different about that? Does not the Judeo-Christian God of Abraham want heresy expunged? 'Stone him to death, he who would seduce you from Yahweh.' That's in Deuteronomy, I believe."

"So it is, Elia. But you can't want pogroms and jihads and the rest of the crazy stuff that comes with religious power struggles?"

"It won't come to that."

"Why not? It has before."

"Because evolution of cultures — especially in the past few centuries — has been driven by reason and evidence and science. So today religious barbarisms get ignored because they're not consistent with life in the modern world."

"Good point," Joshua conceded. "But many parts of the world aren't all that modern, Elia. And frequently beliefs in myths are immune to reason and evidence."

"Education. Knowledge moderates. The Sisterhood knows that better than anyone," Elia countered.

"Some of its internet outreach has been phenomenally successful, especially among younger women and girls, even in less enlightened cultures," Sarah added. "So we'll just do more of that. Temper the cult mentality."

"We can make this scenario work, Eva. Make you a god, but avoid the pitfalls," Elia seconded.

"Avoid pitfalls," Eva mused. "You mean like how adroitly Pastor Bob walks the line, for example?"

"A case in point. Thank you, Eva."

I don't think they fully appreciate the crazy power of the god-myth that would form around Eva, Joshua thought. But he forced his mouth shut and watched. Eva slowly shook her head and spoke.

"Become a god? Take the power and use it? Create another religion? When history tells us intolerance is intrinsic to every creed... to say nothing of the backlash from established religions? I'm sorry... it's too crazy. Another religion... becomes just another monkey trap."

My baby sister, Joshua mused, *is really growing up.* Then a second thought occurred to him and he studied her face intently. *Your arguments are pretty pro forma this morning, kiddo. Did you stumble across my carefully buried contingency plan? So maybe you know that one of the likelier outcomes of starting a religion is having to personally order thirteen thousand deaths?*

Eva stood up from the table, ending the discussion. "Maybe it's okay as a last resort... if everything goes to hell. Right now, though... I'm not desperate enough to do it."

But she delivered her decision with a smile so warm and brilliant that the tension in the Council Chamber immediately evaporated.

Jebel Uweinat, Libya | Friday 2345 CAT

Or is it the right time? The question was far from trivial, Zurvan knew, especially now, when chaos could as easily amplify a decision as dissolve it into randomness. The cursor hovered over the *Send* button. Finally he pushed the mouse away and stood up and stretched. He paced around the high tech control center burrowed cleverly into the sandstone caves of *Jebel Uweinat*, then walked to the entrance to watch the moon set in the western sky.

I miss my witch. And even Prentiss was a useful sounding board on occasion. The answer came on that very thought, as tendrils of high cirrus edged in front of the moon.

"Yes of course. I can have it both ways! The old and the new. Superstition and modernity. And... it even protects me!" He howled laughter at the moon. "Of course! Thank you, Hessa!"

One of his Sanussi guardians turned on the lip of the wadi a good distance downhill. *Sound travels in the desert at night.* Zurvan waved, choked the laughter back and turned inside.

An hour later, the re-scripted video had been filmed against his blue backdrop and edited for maximum emotional impact. His finger didn't hesitate over the *Send* button this time.

An hour after that, his two visitors arrived, escorted by Muammar to the central living quarters in the cave complex. They bowed respectfully but did not kneel. *Good, Muammar has briefed them on my humility.* He gestured toward the table where refreshments awaited, and broke bread with them in the oldest of ceremonies.

Finally, with a raised eyebrow and open expressive hand, Zurvan invited their report. "Your smiles tell me much, my brothers."

"Good news, Mahdi."

"Ah. The details, please."

"The weapons are in place."

"All three? Well concealed?"

The two men traded glances. "Well enough for now. A concerted search by the authorities would eventually find them, we believe. A few days, possibly a week if they correctly guess the target cities."

Zurvan studied their expressions. *They talked about this, they decided on absolute truthfulness.* "I appreciate your honesty, brothers. To lead properly in the chaos of these times I must always have the unvarnished facts, you understand?" The men nodded in concert, and Zurvan nodded along with them. "Excellent. Spread the word. Make sure your colleagues all appreciate that."

"As you command, Mahdi."

"What cities?"

"Los Angeles. Las Vegas. New York."

"And you will call yourselves the Sword of Islam?"

The men nodded. "A nuclear sword, Mahdi," one of them chuckled.

Zurvan frowned at him. "How long will it take to detonate after the command is given?"

"About 30 minutes, Mahdi."

Zurvan looked at them questioningly.

"There is a specific arming sequence, set by their Russian creators as a safeguard. Our technicians have not had time to work around it."

He nodded. "All right. Now... you understand... that after your demands are made for the Connard girl, I must disavow you? Distance myself from your 'Sword of Islam'?"

"It is a necessity if you say it is, Mahdi. And we obey as we would the Prophet himself, peace be upon him."

"Peace be upon him," Zurvan agreed, smiling. "You obey? Then you may proceed." He stood. They stood and bowed, and Muammar escorted them out.

Zurvan closed the cave gate behind them and went immediately to the control center and began dictating the outline of his next speech. By the time he finished, the outside cameras showed predawn light in the dark sky over the ridgeline of Jebel Uweinat to the east.

I must sleep before I record the speech, he decided. Then his mind turned to other less important matters and he scanned the monitor bank for updates. His K'Shmar transponder in Nagele had gone black.

First in Bhilwara, then the others, like dominoes. "Yes, you react very well, my young friends." *But it takes up your time, it distracts you. You may even realize the K'Shmar sites are diversions, yet you have no choice but to react.* Zurvan laughed, the sound echoic in the hard walls and floor of the control center.

"You are dancing very nicely to my tune, Joshua O'Donnell. As is your sister, little Eva." He laughed again, louder, harsher, as the phrasings of his speech decrying the Sword of Islam started to form themselves in his mind. *I will speak in the high language of the ancient poets, little Eva, with the cadence and scansion such a matter deserves. Soon the world will learn you are a false messiah.*

O'Donnell Enclave, Waimanu, HI | Friday 1917 HST

Eva pulled her brother into the Council Chamber and shut the door hard. *Sometimes being super-smart is a drawback, brother.*

"Time out?" he guessed ruefully.

"You were about to lose your temper with your wife," she scolded. "Not something we need right now."

"Yeah," he admitted, "You're right. Not over the dinner table anyway."

She put her hand on his arm. "Elia is coming from a different place, Josh. Her mothers and grandmothers, and back down the line, came from more primitive cultures. She carries RNA coding that has been less influenced by modern times. A lot."

"Still... peace through superior firepower? Quite a switch. Seems so out of character for Elia."

"It is. But right now she sees it as the safest course. For me, for you, for the *Novas*. And especially for the twins."

She watched him process that perspective down through a logic lattice. *Your mind sparkles like a diamond in the sun when you do that, Joshua.*

"Okay. A mother and her cubs. Got it."

"Not out of character at all, then?" She grinned at him.

"No." He grinned back. "And yes, I will apologize."

"We welcome all views here at Nova Central," Eva intoned piously, "even though we may not agree."

He laughed at her facetiousness. Then Demuzzio rapped on the door and opened it.

"We got a problem." He walked to the console and keyed in commands. "The asshole has gone public."

They watched it, Demuzzio muttering imprecations, Joshua absorbing the translation supplied by an NSA interpreter. Eva watched and parsed the mullah's facial expressions. *Still a psychopath.* She sighed. *All that time with my little forest friends didn't rearrange his poor brain, like it did for the Crone. I wonder why not?* But intuition followed hard on the question. *I guess I know.* As the video wound down, Demuzzio's curses changed to wonder. Joshua started splitting his attention between the monitor screen and Eva's face. Eva felt his attention, but focused on the screen image, absorbing the power and cadence of the words, even beginning to understand some of the language. *Like Pastor Bob when he gets on a roll. You just feel it, way down deep.*

When it ended, Demuzzio spoke first. "Son of a bitch got religion? He actually sounds reasonable."

Joshua raised an eyebrow. "And still unleashes his K'Shmar?"

Eva shook her head. "He's gotten worse, Uncle Tee. Smarter. Josh?"

"Yeah. Brilliant speech, I'm afraid."

"Poetic. I think it was in the old Persian high language. Like Rumi. Ask the NSA translator."

"You could tell?"

"I could feel it, Josh. It moved me."

"Shit!"

"Yeah."

"What!" Demuzzio shouted in frustration.

"The man essentially just made himself impregnable, TC," Joshua clarified. "Even if we can find him, we can't take him out. It would prove his point. He'd be a martyr to most of the Muslim world."

"We have to find some other way," Eva added, "one that shows him to the world for what he really is..."

She contemplated them thoughtfully for a moment, then gazed into the middle distance, seeking the wisdom of her long-dead Sisters.

O'Donnell Enclave, Waimanu, HI | Friday 2346 HST

They'd watched Zurvan's video three times, the last in company with the full assembled Nova Council, eight present by hologram. Now the five members physically present in the enclave sat exhausted, contemplating their counterattack.

"Didn't leave us much wiggle room," Joshua opined.

Heads nodded.

"Blog traffic is running two to one positive toward him," Sarah announced, looking at some printouts. "Thirty to one in the Muslim world."

Demuzzio just listened, a notepad under his hand. His assigned role was — from his former military and police perspective — to capture those ideas that could be delegated to NSA and other government agencies or to the military. *A full day, and I haven't heard anything new yet.* He drew another doodle on the paper, a cartoonish Zurvan, and drew crosshairs through his forehead. Elia saw it and smiled wanly.

"Maybe Elia's right, Eva," Demuzzio offered.

"Maybe, Uncle Tee. But I think Jesus had the same problem with the Zealots. That's what Mary says."

"Huh? I lost you there, Eva. Say what?"

"Never mind." She smiled at him. "I'm tired."

He blinked uncertainly at a child who so suddenly had such cryptic depths. *I'm outta my league.* He rubbed his head. *I say we use all resources to*

find the fucker and whack him. Take the fallout. It can't be any worse than this.
He listened to Eva and her brother rehash Elia's preference.

"So the Sisterhood's long-range plan of making the first *Nova* a god, a new messiah..." Eva began.

"To be fair, it's still more of an emergency plan at this point," Joshua noted, "and still very dangerous."

"...just replaces one problem with a new one," Eva finished.

"And to be fairer yet, the Sisterhood's coding into the female gene began back in more primitive times."

"When that would have been a reasonable solution... and yes, I appreciate that genetic inertia. Okay. So today?"

"Infinitely more dangerous, because your... messiahhood... has provable science and evolution behind it, requires much less blind faith."

"But a new religion ends up blind anyway? Distorts the truth?"

"The greater the power, the greater the temptation. And the *Novas* represent a kind of power the world has never seen."

"So I'm right, a new religion is just another monkey trap?"

"Yeah. I think so. You've got good instincts, Eva." Joshua spread his hands and shrugged apologetically at his wife.

Elia's shoulders slumped.

"The present traditional concepts for God or Yahweh or Allah would have to go, Josh," Sarah said, incorporating an earlier thread.

"Conceptual revolutions are possible. Inevitable, in fact. Zeus and Baal are gone. Ptolemaic astronomy is gone." Joshua shrugged. "But it takes time."

"There is no time. And the world's not ready anyway," Elia snapped.

"Then there's going to be trouble," Joshua said.

"I can preach tolerance," Eva countered.

"You should."

"But that's not the answer is it?"

"Probably not."

"Something more fundamental..."

"Yeah. Ecumenism is nice, but tolerance only treats the symptoms."

"The goodness gene? Our god within?" Eva's eyebrow demanded an analysis.

Joshua processed the probabilities. "That would be the best bet; it has the most... resonance. It really was the message of most belief systems before modern religions came along and screwed them up. The trick would be to make sure the world understands the message as it applies to all humans, not just to *Novas*."

"No exclusivity."

"Right. That's where religions and cultures and belief systems typically run into trouble."

"Okay. That's something." Eva's brilliant smile belied the circles under her eyes. "Let's sleep on it." She stood up.

Always close on a positive note, Demuzzio mused. *Took me years to learn that. And my fifteen-year-old god-daughter does it without even thinking.* He smiled at her back as they filed out the door.

Chapter 9

O'Donnell Enclave, Waimanu, HI | Saturday 0554 HST

Eva tossed restlessly, the bed sheet sweat-soaked even in the controlled coolness of the enclave. Her mouth twisted and she jerked up, tendrils of consciousness snapping back into her mind like broken rubber bands. They hurt. *Something's wrong. What?*

She slipped into a sweat suit and trotted down the hall, slapped twice on Joshua's door in passing, and slid into her chair in the Council Chamber. The monitor came to life as her fingers flew across the virtual control plane. Joshua walked in, yawning.

"Early, kiddo. What's up?"

"Don't know..." Eva muttered, focused on the monitor, "...something."

Joshua slid into the chair beside her and looked at the screen.

"Wow. Global consciousness is restless, huh?" He studied the screen. "Huge chi-square stat. Something bad happen?"

She felt the crystalline song of his logic lattices engaging, chasing sleepiness out of his mind as he studied the screen. Her fingers flicked within the control plane, tracing the path she knew his mind would want to follow. They waited as the enclave's supercomputer array updated and parsed more data.

"Not yet, I think."

"But it will?"

Eva nodded. *You never foresaw this technology, did you, Sisters? A machine that predicts reality. Or the probability of a reality.* The monitor blinked and repainted the screen. *Yet how could you? My present is so radically different from your past, even a single generation ago.* She felt the white-robed shapes gather, looking over her shoulder. One of them snorted dismissively. *You need no machine, Little Mother. Not anymore.*

"Eva?"

She glanced at her brother. He studied the flashing icons on the monitor and engaged the control plane in front of his own chair.

"This isn't going to be good news..."

The big screen on the opposite wall came alive with a feed from Al Jazeera in Beirut, English translation in subtitles... *nuclear devices... Sword of Islam... unless deliver Eva Connard... for Allah to judge...*

Eva felt the blood leave her face. Joshua's arm went around her shoulders.

"They're bluffing, honey," he said. "They haven't the technology. Nor the smarts to get nukes past Homeland Security."

She shivered and gestured at the screen. "They do. They did."

He stared at her. "You sure?"

"Josh, I agree with your algorithm's output, this time."

"Shit!" He squinted at the screen. "The scroll says the CD they're playing is only a couple hours old. It's... dinnertime in Beirut."

"That's where they want me to show up. Why?"

Her brother shrugged. "Zealots control that part of the city, I think. Certainly the mosque they named is a hotbed of fundamentalism."

"In three days," she mused. "Giving me airplane time? They must not be following the news."

"Or maybe they don't believe it."

"So maybe I'll show up there now, turn myself in, see what Allah has to say."

"No!"

"It could be powerful allegory, Josh. I could cite the Qur'an."

"What?"

"There's precedent, in their view... 'And to Solomon we made the wind obedient: its morning stride is a month's journey...' Hey, think about it. What is transposition but riding the wind? Allegorically."

She watched her brother's profile as his logic lattices absorbed the concept and processed it. The chi square statistic on the monitor nudged up as he turned and studied her.

"Yeah, religion is allegory. Different kind of wind though, Eva."

"So what? The parallel holds. The legend comes to life."

He shrugged. "And I'd be your Jinn, out in front of you, clearing your way with my 'blazing fire'... that's the Sura you're citing, right?"

She watched the points of the logic lattice flicker in his turquoise eyes. Though worry creased his eyes, he smiled.

"Eva! You've been talking to your Sisters again?"

"Powerful legends, Josh. And the fundamentalists are a superstitious lot. Look at how fast they bought into Zurvan as their Mahdi."

Joshua shook his head. "Still no. Dueling Mahdis? A nice concept. Might knock Zurvan off his stride. But Islam isn't ready for a fifteen-year-old infidel female as its messiah. Especially the fundamentalists."

"Even some of the fundamentalists see the Mahdi as a spiritual entity, not a human being, Josh."

"I suppose. But still no, Eva."

"Why?"

"Because Beirut is a trap. Now or three days from now, it's a trap."

"Well, sure."

"You crazy?"

"The literal meaning of Islam, Josh, is 'surrender'."

"I know that."

"You have a better way then? Thousands of lives; maybe millions."

"I sure hope so. My convergence code is running, Eva. I think in a few seconds the computers may have enough GC data to..." Joshua paused as the monitor in front of his own chair came to life. "Yes! Here's the location of the first bomb. LA harbor, it looks like." He punched keys and a satellite view of the harbor slid onto the screen.

"GPS data?"

"Yeah." He gave her the coordinates.

Eva stared at the aerial for a moment, ranging her mind outward.

"Got it. Amidships, on a freighter. Not too many people around, I think. Want to?"

Eva watched his mind process the question, saw it add in the element of surprise. *Your mind is such a beautiful machine, Joshua. I wish you could see it at work.*

She knew his answer before he grinned at her.

"Okay. A look-see. In and out."

"No. We take it with us."

His eyebrow shot up, startled. "Where?"

"Deep water. Southeast of here, a thousand miles."

He nodded. "Pacific Basin. Could work. Out of the shipping lanes... okay, we'll see."

She grinned back at him. "A blaze of glory?"

"Don't think so, kiddo. Those things have an arming sequence. So far as I know we'd have plenty of time, even if they wired it against interference."

"Well then?"

He sighed. "It is the best answer. Take away the threat, even before the world can get excited about it. Before the damn markets collapse again... But just send me? By myself?"

"I can't, Josh. Not yet. I don't know how." She granted his doubtful raised eyebrow a bland smile. "That's true, actually. I can take you with me, but I can't project you. That kind of ability is generations away, if ever." She reached out her hand and took his, cutting off the next question.

Suddenly they were standing on the deck of a freighter being tugged into a berth in the Port of Los Angeles.

Disoriented, Joshua banged his elbow on a pipe.

"Shh," Eva cautioned, "this way." She walked ten steps, through a bulkhead door and down a ladder well. She stopped at the first door. A rusty nameplate said Cabin 6. Her finger to the right of the door handle blazed briefly and nicked off the deadbolt. A metal suitcase sat on the unmade bunk.

"That it?"

"Yeah."

Joshua studied it. Then he lifted it, grunting. "Gotta be. Too heavy for underwear." He set it on the floor. "You can handle the mass?"

"Sure. I'll adjust. Take one handle, I'll take the other," Eva instructed. "Give me your free hand."

He did, smiling at her. "Sea-level, okay? A thousand miles southeast of Hawaii. We drop it and bounce back to the enclave, *tout de suite.* This thing makes me nervous."

Typhoon building there at the moment, brother, she thought, *but a bit further south won't make a difference.*

Eva closed her eyes and ranged her consciousness west and south over the blue Pacific and took them there. The suitcase sank out of sight and seconds later the two of them popped into existence in the Council Chamber. Eva was immediately all business.

"Go wake up TC, Josh. Tell him Cabin 6 on that freighter. And give him..." she said, scrawling on a sticky, "the drop coordinates."

Her brother nodded, looking at the monitor. "Computer puts the second one in Newark."

"I see it. Come back and we'll do that one." She closed her eyes, calming herself, and pulled her legs into a lotus in the chair.

Joshua stopped short at the Chamber door. "What are you doing? Don't go without me."

"Of course not. I'm just warning the whales away from the drop area. Hurry back."

Jebel Uweinat, Libya | Saturday 1820 CAT

The flashing icon on Zurvan's monitor caught his attention from across the room, an instant before the warning vibration of the beeper on his belt.

"Muammar," he said to the guardian he'd been sharing a meal with, "I suddenly require some privacy. If you would be so kind..."

"Another vision, Mahdi?"

You're beginning to get on my nerves, fool. He smiled at the man. "We'll see." He made a shooing motion. "Now, please. Wait outside. I will call if I need you."

Muammar rose from the rug, wonderment on his face. He bowed as he backed out of the room. "A vision," he whispered as the door shut.

Zurvan scowled after him then ran to the monitor. *More fools. If they broke discipline without a reason...* But a few keystrokes and the monitor told him that was unlikely. The incoming call showed as properly encrypted, and in burst mode. Security would not be compromised. *Maybe.* He waited for the icon to go green, then enabled the speakerphone and barked into it.

"Keep it brief."

"The transponder on Sword One is off-line." The voice was flat, tinny in its de-encryption. But there was panic in it, he thought, from the cadence of the words. *Any problem with the bombs is a reportable event.* He held his temper and replied.

"Your call is proper. Tell me why."

"We are checking..." the voice paused for a long moment and when it came back online the panic was clear. "It is gone. Sword One is gone!"

"Say that again," he snapped. "The device is missing?" *Can it be? How could she have found it?*

"Gone, Mahdi!"

"Gone where?"

"We do not know. There is no signal from the transponder. It just stopped."

The little bitch! And her infernal brother! Zurvan willed calm into his voice before asking the question.

"The other two are in place?"

"They are close, Mahdi."

"Good. Send the signal."

"Mahdi?"

"Blow them now."

"Mahdi! We had only the three. Now two. There will be none left to force the girl to us in Beirut!"

"The infidel fools won't know that. Blow them now!"

"My brothers, Mahdi..."

"Allah will welcome them. Send the signal. Now."

A long pause, the silence of the encryption seeming to pulse within it.

"It is done, Mahdi. The arming sequence has started."

"Thirty minutes?"

"It is so."

"Are you within the blast radius of Sword Three?"

A choked chuckle. "It is in the trunk of my car, Mahdi. And I am approaching the city of sin now."

"You are a brave man. The Prophet himself will welcome you. Peace be upon him, and upon you, my son."

Zurvan cut the link. *You little bitch! May the next one you find blow you to atoms.*

O'Donnell Enclave, Waimanu, HI | Saturday 0641 HST

Joshua ran down the hall and stormed into the Council Chambers.

"Okay, TC's on the horn to Washington, he's..." he stopped short at the global consciousness display on the monitor in front of Eva.

"Jesus! It's really ramping up. We've never seen a chi-square go berserk like..."

Eva thrust out her hand.

"Come, Josh, we have to go. Quickly."

The chi-square stat... it must mean... Logic lattices flashed down through multivariate probabilities and converged in an instant. He looked at Eva. "The devices are armed, aren't they?" He put both hands behind his back. "No. You can't go."

I'm going," she snapped. "Stay if you want. Or give me your hand."

Her face was pale, but her eyes blazed with the strange light of full intention. *Shit! She will, too.* He reached out his hand.

She took it. "Another freighter, Josh. Two defenders, I think. I'll put us inside the room, I hope. Take the one closest to you. I'll get the other."

"Wait!" Joshua's fingers flew over the keyboard. "The third nuke, we'll have to pick that off right afterwards..." *Shit! The computers haven't locked in the coordinates yet.*

"Come on, Josh!"

"Looks like it's near Vegas, but..."

"Come on, dammit!" She seized his hand and they vanished.

He took two steps across the small stateroom and slammed the heel of his hand under the chin of an astonished young man in a steward's uniform. An energy plane blazed from his left hand as he spun around, but there was no need.

Eva stared wide-eyed at the blood-spurting mess she'd made of the other man's body as it slid down the opposite wall.

Joshua yanked the suitcase off the bed one-handed, dropped it between them and put Eva's left hand on the handle. He slapped her face lightly.

The girl shook herself and took his hand and they were gone.

The suitcase dropped into the swell of open ocean, and they were back in the Council Chambers before he could take a breath.

Joshua grabbed a wastebasket from alongside the wall and shoved it in Eva's hands, then ran to his console and fought to steady his hand within the control plane. His fingers twitched rapid-fire instructions.

"Come on, come on," he urged it, "plot the goddamn coordinates!"

The big wall screen displayed a satellite view of the city of Las Vegas, but with only probability circles, not the crosshairs of determined coordinates. He focused intently on it, willing his computer array to produce an answer.

Dimly, he heard Demuzzio's frantic feet pounding down the hallway outside the Chamber.

Dimly, he heard Eva vomiting into the wastebasket. She gasped in air, choked, vomited more. She screamed something unintelligible.

The global consciousness plot on her console monitor spiked upward, yanking his attention away.

The big wall screen flashed, a terrible white brilliance.

Eva screamed again and Joshua spun toward her.

She collapsed like an empty sack.

He dove across the polished stone floor to catch her.

O'Donnell Enclave, Waimanu, HI | Saturday 0644 HST

TC Demuzzio froze in shock as he skidded into the Council Chamber. Eva collapsed and Joshua caught her, both of them limned in the brilliant light playing across the floor. The light faded as he turned toward its source.

"No! God, no!"

The glare on the big wall screen faded as the filters kicked in on the camera in the orbiting satellite. The enclave computers began to compensate for saturation and hue in the satellite's signal, and the wall screen suddenly confirmed his fear: a mushroom cloud rose over Las Vegas.

Demuzzio's legs went weak, but he clamped down hard on his reactions. *Nothing I can do about that.* He spun toward Eva and Joshua and knelt beside them.

"What happened?"

Eva spasmed and regurgitated. Her brother rolled her on her side, swiped out her mouth with his fingers and bent down to listen to her breathing.

"I don't know, TC. She killed a man. But I don't think that's it. I think it was..." he nodded at the wall screen.

"Jesus! You were there? You got irradiated?"

"No. We were here when it went up."

Eva's eyes flicked madly between the two of them, then rolled up in her head.

Joshua grunted as if hit. "Get Sarah and Elia, now!"

Demuzzio started for the door, but there was no need; both women ran in.

Sarah crouched over Eva and touched her forehead for a brief moment. Then she snapped orders. "Thomas, move aside! Elia, across from me!" She pushed Joshua to her left. "Rest her head against your knees, Joshua. Her airway is clear?"

"Yes."

"Thomas! Get that highlighter from the table."

He did.

"Joshua, she may have a seizure. If she does, hold it in her mouth."

Joshua looked stricken. "Epilepsy? You never..."

"No. But her consciousness was ranging wide when..." Sarah nodded at the wall screen. "There probably was feedback to the physical brain."

Joshua groaned.

Demuzzio groaned with him. *Not my little Eva!* He paced nervously at her feet as Sarah and Elia took the girl's hands and clasped their other hands across her chest. The overhead lights seemed to flicker.

Eva's eyes opened but didn't see Demuzzio; they focused on the screen across the room. He followed her gaze. The satellite camera angle had shifted lower as it moved across the sky. The top of the blast cloud rose into a shear layer below the tropopause and was streaming eastward over the desert.

"Dark song in the wind," Eva whispered. Then she shuddered and passed out again.

O'Donnell Enclave, Waimanu, HI | Saturday 1159 HST

Sara and Elia held Eva's hands, their other hands clasped across the girl's belly. They chanted, rhythmically, musically, a harmony of soothing. Eva heard them, far down the canyon of her distant mind. Her phantom Sisters were closer, circling about, weaving a protective cocoon around the pain.

"I have to get out of bed," she whispered to them.

Not yet, Little Mother, not yet.

"I have things to do. My work..."

You have healing to do.

The pain roared in, as if to make the Sisters' point, but their cocoon tightened down around it. She exhaled and drifted away. Her mind ran down its distant canyon, recursive, chasing back along her genetic timeline, groping for an answer. She slowed and stopped at an ancient one. A white-robed Sister smiled at her.

Hello, Little Mother.

"I've never been this far back, Mary."

You had no need.

"You look like Mom."

The Sister nodded.

"Except your hair is dark, like mine."

Traits carry down.

"So he didn't die on the cross."

No. It was staged. A close thing, though.

"How?"

A drug in the watered rag. It fooled the Centurions.

"Ah."

And Joseph bribed Herod.

"Joseph? His father?"

No. Joseph of Arimathea.

"And Joseph revived him? In the tomb?"

No. Nicodemus and I did that. A very close thing.

"Nicodemus?"

The being you call... Eva felt delicate tendrils searching her mind... *Hamilton O'Donnell.*

"You had the power back then? I thought..."

The tendrils searched her mind again. *Some. Nothing like yours, Little Mother; but enough, barely.*

"I think I have a similar problem."

Indeed.

"I'm looking for a solution."

The Sister shrugged. *Events forced our solution. The Zealots saw him as a king, descended from David through his father's line... and as high priest, descended from Aaron through his mother's line.*

"Embodying earlier Christos myths, the Egyptians, Horus?"

Yes. The Messiah of many legends.

"What happened?"

We erred. The world wasn't ready. The Christ's message was love. The Zealots' was power.

Eva nodded. "Centuries of Roman domination. The Zealots wanted their country back. Their culture... their lives..."

Her Sister nodded back at her.

"And the Romans wiped them out in the wars that followed."

So I see in your mind.

Eva shuddered.

I cannot see your future, Little Mother. The woman's eyes brimmed with compassion.

"I know," Eva said sadly. "Neither can I."

Her mind slid off on a tangent. "Line of David, line of Aaron. So his genes... they had to be preserved down through generations. For me, or one like me. You saved him for that."

Nicodemus and the Sisterhood saved him for that, child. I saved him for love.

Eva smiled at the image. "And after three days in the tomb, he was well enough to make an appearance. To what end?"

To recast the old myth, to incarnate it, make it even more powerful.

"And then wait. That was your solution?"

That was the outcome. The history I see in your mind says it failed as a solution.

Eva shrugged. "Maybe. And then?"

I carried him back to Egypt, to the Therapeuti, the mystics with whom he trained.

"More healing?"

He was weak, infected. It took some time for full recovery.

"And then?"

The Zealots came after us, but we escaped to Galatia.

"Thank you, Sister Mary of Magdala," Eva said formally. "You have been most helpful."

Her mind pondered that historical outcome, parsing it for a solution that would better fit modern times. *So maybe,* she reflected, *just maybe... there is another possibility.* She pawed for that possibility until fatigue eventually drove her mind to flee into the comforting blankness of deep sleep.

Hours later Eva opened her eyes to a bedroom dim and cool. The clock read almost eight PM. Her stomach growled, but that was her only physical discomfort. Spiritual pain was there, but locked away by the Sisters' protective cocoon. She shrugged into a clean sweat suit and walked out barefoot into the enclave. The twins greeted her with silent hugs. She tousled their hair and went toward the voices coming down the long hallway from the Council Chamber.

Everyone was intent on the big wall screen, watching Muhammad Zurvan decry the attack on Las Vegas. Eva stopped in the doorway behind them, watching silently, parsing the emotions that whirled around them.

Demuzzio's held pure red rage. "Crocodile tears, the son of a bitch!"

Joshua's held despair. "He had that speech pre-canned, ready to go. He's even smarter than we thought. A lot."

Elia's emotions tasted of both rage and despair, but she was silent. Sarah also sat silent, but her emotions were more controlled, nuanced by thoughtfulness.

Eva looked at their backs and sighed; life would become immeasurably more difficult for them now. Her Sisters took up station around her mind.

You will do what you must, Little Mother.

"I know."

You are the One, now being born.

Eva winced as the impossible burden of that came crushing down.

Birthing is pain.

She felt their cocoon encapsulating her pain crack open. Her fingernails scraped the wood of the doorjamb. Dimly she saw those at the table turning in their chairs at the sound. A vision of future generations stretched out in front of her, their existence a matter of flickering probabilities.

You are the Earth Mother, little one.

The pain spilled over Eva, a flood of agony. She let it wash through her. "Earth Mother," she repeated, accepting the burden, the pain. Her Sisters nodded in approval as they spun slowly around her, helping, showing the way.

Earth Mother, they affirmed.

"Yes," she sobbed.

Give your sadness to the sea...

"I'll try," she sobbed.

...your sorrow to the sky.

Chapter 10

UMC Headquarters, Anaheim, CA | Saturday 2353 PDT

Robert Blake watched his big monitor screen as Eva walked slowly into the Nova Council Chamber at the Waimanu enclave. He worked his keyboard so that the high-definition vidcam there homed in on her face and dimmed down the surroundings. *She's older*, he thought, *and sadder. Poor child.* He let practiced sympathy flow across his face, knowing that his hologram in the Chamber would render it in faithful high-definition for those around the table.

Eva sat down carefully as her brother steadied her elbow. She patted his hand and nodded thanks to all the concerned faces, some physical, some holographic. "I'm okay. It... hurts, but I'm okay." Her eyes moved across the group, lingering a moment on each, then stopped on his hologram. She swallowed hard and looked down at the table to compose herself. The camera picked up a tear in her left eye. She blinked and smiled at him. "Pastor Bob. Please. Your take on Zurvan's speech? Was it really that good?"

"As a professional cleric?" Blake measured his words. "I'd say it was right up there, Eva. Compassion, but with a strong embedded message. He comes across as quite reasonable, even to non-Muslims. Sure, he's a fundamentalist, but no one would suspect he was a psychopath."

He watched the tear trickle down her cheek, and spoke gently. "Are you sure he is?"

"Oh, he is, all right" Joshua answered for her. "You're new to the Council, so you don't know the history."

"This asshole is the most dangerous man in the world," Demuzzio added, "seven years ago he kidnapped Eva and almost killed Josh. We'll fill you in on the history when we have more time."

Joshua nodded to confirm. "But for now, it's enough that you understand he did this thing. His denouncement of the 'Sword of Islam' is just a cover, so he can seem like a reasonable human being. But he did it. We have absolutely no doubt."

Eva sighed and brushed the tear away. "Next time you're here, Pastor Bob, I'll fill you in on my personal experiences with the man, years ago. Uncle Tee is right." She sighed again, let her gaze linger on his hologram a moment, then looked around at the other faces. Her voice broke when she asked the question. "Anybody know the casualty count?"

"You're not to blame, Eva," Blake almost whispered.

"We've told her that," Elia said.

"She knows that," Joshua added.

Blake studied the girl's worn face. *Yes she does. But the pain is no less for the knowing.* He wondered if that could be a point of leverage. *She needs to be comforted.*

"I want to know the casualty count," Eva demanded.

Joshua looked helplessly at the faces around the big table. "They're just estimates, Eva, based on population stats and property records."

"How many people?"

"It actually detonated south of the city, off Interstate 15. A lot of desert, not much development..."

"How many?"

"...and the winds were from the northwest, so the plume and fallout missed the big population centers..."

"How many?"

Joshua sighed. "Earl says probably thirteen thousand prompt fatalities, mostly from the pressure wave. The eventual total may be three times that, from radiation sickness."

Eva's face paled. She put her head down on the table. Blake watched sobs wrack the slim shoulders.

"It's late. We're going offline," Joshua announced abruptly. He reached his left hand out to his sister while his right went to the console. Blake's monitor went black. He shut down the holo camera and leaned back in his chair to consider the man who'd been sitting across the room from him, out of the camera's pickup.

"A wedge there, boy," the Senator said, "you see it?"

Blake raised an eyebrow. *Let him tell me; he likes to do that.*

"The little bitch needs some comfortin' boy. Some solace. I saw the way she looked at you."

"You think?"

"Get your ass back out to Hawaii, son. Seize the moment. Be her father figure. Or maybe somethin' else." He made a crude groping gesture.

"I was just out there on Thursday," Blake objected, "and I've got a big agenda this week, I don't know if I..."

"Bullshit, boy. After your service tomorrow, you got a week until your next. You got time."

"Senator, there are other UMC problems, I can't just..."

The fat man got up and waddled over to him. He looked down and smiled his crocodilian smile. "Do it. And get those DNA samples. Don't forget this time."

"I didn't forget last time, Senator. There just wasn't an opportunity. If they see me doing it, this whole thing is blown. I have to be very careful."

"They trust you, boy. You're a Council member now. The inner circle."

"I'm also the newest member, and trust is relative."

"Nah, you proved yourself with that nice little sermon at the National Cathedral last week. And you coaxed the President to say the same god-damn thing." The man leaned over and got right in his face. The alcohol and ketone-laden breath made Blake wince. "They owe you. They trust you. Use it!"

The fat man belched, hitched up his belt and walked to the office door.

"Smile as you walk me out of here, son. Put on a good show for your night staff. Image is everythin', ya know?"

O'Donnell Enclave, Waimanu, HI | Saturday 2037 HST

Eva sipped a protein drink as she studied Sarah and Elia across the kitchen table. *They're my Sisters, and I love them. But do I dare disclose?* The images of her older, ancestral Sisters circled around the two, debating. *No, not yet*, she finally agreed with them.

Sarah looked at her keenly. "Eva, if you feel better, if the nourishment picks you up, I'd like to get you into the scanner and see if the trauma made any changes in your cortex."

"Another MRI benchmark?"

"It could be important."

"I don't sense there's any physical damage to my brain, Sarah. It's all been to my soul."

"Yet there are feedback loops, you know that," Elia interjected.

Eva nodded. *Better than you do, Elia. Years ago I used them to damp down the trauma in your memories. Sarah's too.* "Okay, sure. I am feeling better. You put some of your herbs in this drink, didn't you, Elia?"

Elia and Sarah both nodded.

Eva smiled. "Thanks. I needed a boost; can't trigger serotonin if I don't have the raw materials."

Joshua entered the kitchen. "Pastor Bob just called. Wanted to be sure you're alright, kiddo. Said he's heading here as soon as his Sunday service is over and he clears his UMC schedule." He looked at Eva quizzically. She caught the developing blush and tamped it down.

"Tomorrow afternoon, then?"

"I imagine," Joshua answered.

Elia looked at her husband. Sarah coughed into her hand.

Eva couldn't help but smile. *Am I that obvious?* The interweaving emotional patterns dancing around the three of them mimicked her own conflicted state.

"It's just that we know you, dear," Sarah answered the silent question for all of them. "I doubt if anyone else would notice."

"Do you..." Eva paused to reassert blush control, "think Pastor Bob notices?"

Joshua shrugged off the question. The pattern around him turned darker. "You're only fifteen years old, Eva. And just barely into Nova puberty. He's not going to reciprocate your feelings; he can't. So what the man notices or not isn't relevant."

You can protect me against many things, brother, but not against love. "My body is fifteen, Josh. My mind is millennia."

Sarah and Elia exchanged a look that went past Joshua. The patterns around the two brightened with amusement. *Yes, they would know. Their ancestral Sisters were a lively bunch, too.*

Joshua tried another tack. "Relevance still is an issue, Eva. You haven't time to be distracted by an infatuation."

She felt a flash of irritation. "So why didn't you tell him not to come?"

"Because it's not properly my call, honey. It's yours. You know his number; you can tell him to cancel."

I'm sorry for causing you grief, brother, but... let's look at it a different way. "His wife died last fall, Josh."

Her brother nodded. "Car accident. How he dealt with it actually is what led us to consider him for the Council."

"Yes. I remember... the empathy, the forgiveness... you think maybe he's a pre-Nova? Like you?"

"Possibly. Manifests as a different skill set, though, is my guess. More outer-directed than inner-directed like mine. Why?"

"Because — infatuation or not — I have this feeling that he could be crucial to our success."

"Any specifics to this feeling? I mean, he's got enormous appeal and a huge following, but is there anything else I can factor into my probability projections?"

"Josh, I have no idea. Sorry. And hey, maybe it *is* just my changing hormones."

With a rueful smile, Joshua accepted her concession. "But you're not going to cancel? Because you need to actually see him to figure it out?"

"Yeah, to figure it out." *And because I can't keep pulling petals off daisies to ask if he loves me or loves me not. And because I really can't read him; he somehow screens his emotional patterns with so much complexity. And because that's so exciting...*

Sarah nodded. Elia nodded.

Joshua studied the three of them a long moment before he spoke. "Okay, then."

UMC Headquarters, Anaheim, CA | Sunday 1247 PDT

Robert Blake paused in gathering papers to look at his distorted reflection in the glass of a cluttered desk. The angle made his cheeks seem more drawn, the dark circles under his eyes deeper. *I'm a little gaunt. But that fit the sermon perfectly, didn't it?*

His other secure connection buzzed. He walked over to watch the encryption algorithms verify it then hit the connection link. The Senator's florid face filled the screen. It was a smaller monitor than the one provided by the Nova Council, but just as capable; it showed the tiny dark growth under the fat man's nose. *I hope that's cancerous.*

"Yes, Senator. I'm on my way. Jet's warming up at SNA."

"Good." The face grinned. "I watched your sermon, son. You got a real nice touch."

Nice touch? It was brilliant, Senator, and you know it. "Maybe I should go into politics."

"Haw! Mebbe so. Lemme know, son; I could do a fund-raiser. Not that you'd need it."

"So you think I got the right tone?"

"Tone? Boy, they was cryin' when they walked into your church. But they was goddamn dehydrated when they left." The man's jowls jiggled appreciatively. "And you cryin', there at the end, perfect! Ain't seen nobody pull that off as good since Clinton."

It was perfect. But I also truly felt it. "I had friends in Vegas, Senator, no word on them. And a UMC church there is gone."

The face on the screen got a blank look for a moment. Then the man shrugged. "Nothin' to be done about that, son; it'll take another week for FEMA and NRC to get their shit sorted out. So keep those thoughts pinned to your sleeve, where people can see 'em."

Am I that cynical? The Senator must have read his expression; the jowls jiggled with mirth.

"And cry whenever you in a photo op, Pastor Bob. Why, I'm bettin' you gonna get UMC back more membership next week than you lost last week. Fuckin' brilliant, whether you meant to pump those tears or not."

It was, and I did. But there's more to it than that, Senator; I actually do feel it. Blake changed the subject. "Any actual casualty count yet? That you can share with me, that is?"

"Yeah, my Committee gets hourly postings, here..." his face left the screen and the camera showed the Capitol dome behind. Some papers rustled. "A little shy of nine thousand dead, as of mid-mornin'."

"That will go up."

"Yeah, sure. We got mobile triage trailers around the whole fuckin' area now; they're startin' to front-end the hospitals."

"Nobody's gone in the hot zone yet?"

"Naw. Just recon drone flyovers. But that won't build the body count much, it was a low-population area."

It was also where my church was. But he probably knows that. Blake rubbed the back of his stiff neck. The Senator rustled more papers.

"Hang on, boy. I got a new translation here. Those 'Sword of Islam' assholes are sayin' Sin City got what it deserved. Home of the American Satan, all that bullshit."

"And Zurvan?"

More papers rustled. "Don't look like I got anythin' you ain't got, son. The fucker is smart, I'll give him that. Still comin' off as compassionate. Sayin' their Qur'an doesn't like innocents killed."

"The Council thinks he's behind it, even though he's disowning Sword of Islam."

"Yeah. So does NSA, but they're still tryin' to nail it down."

Blake scribbled a note to himself. "I've got a plane waiting on the tarmac, Senator. Anything else that might be useful to me in Hawaii?"

"Well, yeah! The little bitch got shell-shocked, right?"

"Something like that, I guess."

"So, she got hurt. Her people gotta be pissed."

"I'm sure."

"So jack 'em up a little more."

"Why?"

"Why? Because this is a great opportunity, son. We got us another 9-11 here. A better one — nothin' like gettin' nuked to jack up the public. God bless America, we're finally gonna kick some Islamic ass."

"The President's always been careful to identify which asses to kick, Senator. He won't do anything indiscriminately."

"Exactly, son. So get your buddies in Hawaii to target us some asses."

"Eva's calling the shots now, I think. And she may not want to do that."

"Why not?"

"Could lead to open war."

"Hell, son, war's comin' anyway. And war's good for the economy. You better put a buncha defense stocks in your portfolio."

"I'll leave them to your portfolio, Senator. I'd have a serious image problem if it came out. A man of God is supposed to have scruples."

"Scruples? Son, you leveraged the previous administration into a public-private deal that let UMC work around the separation of church and state. And I watched how you did it. Nice mix of blackmail and pressure and money."

How did he find that out? "For a good end, Senator. UMC charities have picked up what the government can't afford anymore."

"And the end justifies the means, don't it always? Scruples, my ass." The jowls quivered with more amusement. "Besides, in this here town we got a vaccination for scruples."

"Called politics?"

"Don't be stealin' my punch lines, son." The jowl-quivering escalated into laughter that cut off as abruptly as if a plug had been pulled. "And I sure as shit don't need no morality lecture from a preacher who whacked his wife."

Blake looked around his office for an answer. His twin daughters looked back at him from the only picture on his desk. *They're about the same age as the O'Donnell boys.* "No, Senator. I guess you don't."

"Go catch your plane, boy. And come back with those fuckin' DNA samples for me, you man of God, you." The jowls jiggled one last time as his monitor went dark.

A man of God. Is that what I am? Or am I the same as Pope Innocent, who wasn't?

O'Donnell Enclave, Waimanu, HI | Sunday 1601 HST

"Blake's plane will touch down in twenty minutes at the Waimea strip," Demuzzio announced.

Joshua watched what had been intense focus fade from his sister's face. "Eva," he barked, "we need to wrap up our thoughts here so Adrienne and Carol can pass them along to the President."

She grinned at him. "The President's picked the right tone, Josh; you know that. His speech will be fine. You and Uncle Tee can tidy up our input, undangle any participles. I have to go tidy up me."

"Tidy up you..." He let exasperation color the words. "Why? Isn't that your favorite sweat suit you're wearing?"

Mr. Bojangles stretched in Eva's lap and meowed languidly.

She grinned wider and dumped the cat on the floor. Then she patted Joshua's shoulder and walked out. The cat stalked after her down the hall, with a final meow back over his burly shoulder.

"Guess you been told," Demuzzio observed.

Joshua shook his head. *Right in the middle of the worst fucking crisis the world has ever seen.*

Demuzzio's computer beeped. He tapped a key and read the message. "Looks like the White House wants to talk to you, Josh. Carol."

"Violette? The NSC?" She wants me? Or the Council?"

Demuzzio glanced back at the monitor. "Just you. Privately. Soonest." He cocked an eyebrow.

Joshua shrugged. "Sure, why not."

"Okay then, I'll mosey on down to Waimea, pick up Eva's favorite preacher."

"The SIO roving patrol can collect him, TC."

"Ah, I need to get out, get some air. I'll do it." Demuzzio stretched and walked to the Chamber door. "The secure connection code Carol said to use is on my screen." He waved and walked out.

Joshua fingered the code on the monitor into his control plane and waited for the government's long encryption algorithm to complete the handshake. The green secure connection icon began blinking, then the face of the National Security Coordinator appeared.

I wonder if I look as tired, Joshua thought but didn't ask.

"Carol. Nice to see you. How come you and The Man aren't watching March Madness? Aren't both your alma maters squaring off in the Final Four about now? They decided to play it?"

"We're hoping to get to it maybe by halftime, Joshua."

"That bad, huh? Well... I know the feeling."

"I'm sure. But right now we've got our own madness to deal with... please forgive me, but I stumbled across something and I've got a personal question for you."

He opened his hands to invite it.

"First, I should tell you," she said, "in case you don't already know. I'm a Sister."

"I actually didn't know, Carol." *But it makes perfect sense; as a smart ghetto child the Sisterhood would have rescued you early.* "Uncle Ham compartmentalized SIO real tightly, and I never wanted to fool with that structure. I'm just a... a regent, I guess, until Eva assumes command."

"Does me being a Sister make you more comfortable, Joshua?"

"Absolutely."

Her image on the monitor went contemplative.

Joshua just watched her watch him. *She'll have to get to it in her own way.* The woman's image finally nodded.

"I, ah... rumor has it you put together a list."

"A list of...?"

She struggled with her words. "A list of men to be... removed. Or their influence somehow nullified. In a contingency. A sort of a doomsday list of those who would stop *Nova sapiens* evolution."

Not as well compartmentalized as I thought, evidently. Joshua gave a slight nod with his indirect answer. "Well... it would be logical to develop such a thing as an end-game strategy, *n'est-ce pas?*"

"You neither confirm nor deny?" She smiled at him. "That's such a Washington thing, Joshua."

The issue tumbled down through a logic lattice. *Oh, I see her problem.* "He's not on the list, Carol. If there is one."

She smiled more broadly, some of the tiredness leaving her face.

"And if he had been," Joshua added, "you would have been involved, and in full agreement with the contingency plan. If there is one. Those are the SIO rules."

"I know, Joshua. But you're not a Sister, and..."

"I abide by their rules, Carol." He stared directly into the camera for emphasis. "Always."

She stared back at him and the smile moved up to her eyes.

"Here," he said, working his fingers in the control plane, "I'm sending you our markup and some other thoughts for the speech. We left in the split infinitives, I know he's partial to them."

The computer beeped and the secure transmission icon beeped. The NSC looked off to her side.

"Got it, thanks, Joshua. Listen, I'm sorry if I..."

"Carol," he interrupted, "*de nada*. Finish the speech, then go have some beer and popcorn with the Prez and watch your Final Four game." He sat back in his chair and chuckled. "If your alma mater loses, you're probably gonna whack the guy anyway."

Carol Violette laughed, conceding the point. "A strong possibility!" The screen went dark.

O'Donnell Enclave, Waimanu, HI | Sunday 1657 HST

Joshua sat alone and quiet as questions about his contingency hit list ran down multiple paths through latticework logic. *Who leaked and why? Had to be somebody here. Elia or Sarah? They're Sisters, they may have discretion under the SIO rules that I don't. Or Eva? The locus will probably let her write her own rules at this point. One of the thirteen thousand Sisters designated as hitters? But they've all sworn. Or TC? He knows Carol from back when. But why leak? Any of them?* No answers came out of the lattice except *insufficient data* or *too many variables.*

He stood and stretched as voices sounded down the hall. *Do I need to know? It's still compartmentalized; Carol just had a rumor, not the list itself. Do I even want to know?* He set all the questions aside and arranged a friendly expression on his face as Demuzzio escorted Pastor Robert Blake into the Council Chamber.

Joshua shook the man's hand. "Thanks for coming, Bob. I think Eva's over the worst of it, but it's kind of you to spare the time..."

Demuzzio's mouth dropped open as Eva appeared in the Council Chamber, her eyes sparkling and fixed intently on Robert Blake's face. She wore a variant of the traditional Hawaiian muumuu, one with a wide neck showing modest cleavage that hinted successfully at developing breasts beneath. It hung on her like some sort of cohesive fluid, swaying seductively. Fragrant orchids were woven into her curly hair.

Joshua heard the air pop, turned and saw her. *Jesus... this is my baby sister? She's drop-dead gorgeous. And is that an underwire bra? I'm gonna kill Elia.*

"Pastor Bob," she said, "so nice to see you again." She brushed past Joshua, took one of the leis from around her neck and reached up to drape it over Blake's dumbstruck head. "I think we forgot to give you the customary Hawaiian greeting last time you were here." She stretched up and kissed the tall man on his cheek.

She caught her brother's expression and smiled serenely. Then she kissed Blake on his other cheek.

Chapter 11

O'Donnell Enclave, Waimanu, HI | Sunday 1831 HST

This is going reasonably well, Eva told herself. The vibrational patterns in the auras around the dinner table agreed with her. Even the dark overtones of Joshua's guardian context had been tempered by the easy manner in which Robert Blake slid into the conversation. *Way to go, Pastor Bob; you're a good Councilor. And counselor.*

"So we're all agreed in principle? I have to get out there more? Make myself more visible and accessible?" Eva asked.

Joshua looked troubled. "In principle, that makes sense, Sis. But in the details it gets very sticky."

"Your safety being the main sticky detail, Eva," Demuzzio added.

"So. Public appearances, but only safe ones? How do we arrange that, Uncle Tee? Deploy SIO Security like the Secret Service? Send inspection teams to a site, clear buildings, lock down perimeters? You know we haven't the resources. Besides, armed guards would detract from my message."

Joshua exchanged a glance with Demuzzio, but nodded agreement with his sister. "She's got a point, TC. We're preaching that *Novas* are no threat. If Eva's no threat to anyone, why would she need protection?"

"Because of all the nutcases out there. The public understands that."

Eva responded. "Probably they do, Uncle Tee, but it's still better to demonstrate in the strongest way possible that we're no threat."

Demuzzio rubbed his head in frustration, and ticked off his fingers. "Gandhi. Two Kennedys. King. The Pope before last..."

I love it that you protect me, Uncle Tee. I love that you're my godfather. She smiled at him. "My brother is my shield."

"Dammit, Eva! Yeah, close in; none better. But any half-competent big-bore sharpshooter, from a half-mile away..."

"You can't eliminate risk."

"But you can limit it. Don't pre-announce. Just show up, appear at something already being covered by the media. Like Wall Street."

"Screw up their event?"

"Nah. They'd bless you for the extra coverage."

"I have an idea along those lines, Eva," Blake interjected. "Stay with situations that are more intrinsically safe."

Eva leaned forward, intent. "Okay..."

Blake blinked. "And symbolism is the key, I think. You may think this is self-serving, but... I have to be in DC tomorrow. We're doing a big UMC baptism ceremony at the Reflecting Pool on Wednesday."

Baptize me? Cool! Eva watched the vibrations in the various auras around the table shift in tone and texture, and elected to stay silent.

"Pastor Bob," Elia said gently, "Eva is not exactly a Christian."

The minister shook his head. "On the contrary, she's as Christian a person as I've ever met."

"Philosophically. Spiritually. But not religiously," Joshua amended, his aura darkening. "And a baptism would offend other faiths."

"Not necessarily. The water symbolism is almost universal; it's been in human cultural heritage for millennia — Christian, Buddhist, Muslim, Jew, native traditions, some of the earliest pagan ones."

And I'm a Pisces. My dolphin friends baptized me a long time ago, Pastor Bob. Eva managed to keep the grin off her face.

Sarah spoke, her aura contemplative. "But the symbolism is manifested differently for different religions. And each claims a certain exclusivity."

"It plays right into the Messiah myth," Elia offered. Eva watched the younger woman's aura slide into the contemplative state.

"Myth?" Robert Blake managed to look offended.

"Oh, stop it, Pastor Bob," Sarah clucked at him. "You're not really a biblical literalist, even though that's the popular perception, and even though you slant your sermons that way."

He smiled comfortably at them. "I'm not?"

Ah, now there's something, finally. I think that *pattern shows a little deception.* Eva grinned at him; the prospect of penetrating the complex cloud of the man's emotions was becoming unbearably exciting. *I need a baseline, some benchmarks...*

"No, you're not," Elia confirmed before Eva could say it. "No; you fully understand the Christos allegory and metaphor. Its antecedents. The god within."

"In fact," Sarah added, "that's what gives your message its real power. You connect the gospel words with their true meaning. What Jesus and the other mystics really intended."

Blake laughed as he looked around the table. "Well... let's not say that too loudly, okay?"

Damn. I can't pull any baseline out of that pattern *at all.* Eva laughed with him, studying how his pattern's texture changed in response to her laughter. *What I need is Josh's latticework brain to analyze all these little telltales in a nice detached objective way. I'm just too involved.* Dim images of her ancestral sisters faded into the patterns around Blake and offered opinions. Some were thoughtful. Some were lewd. All were underpinned by compassion.

"Eva?" Sarah asked gently, returning her to the moment.

Behind Blake, the light on the deck outside changed into that peculiar and transient golden tinge caused by refraction of the setting sun's rays over the old Mauna Kea volcano to the south.

"Oh! Pastor Bob, quick! This is so beautiful! You gotta see it." She caught his hand and led him out onto the deck overlooking Waimanu Bay. Her other hand held behind her signaled for no one to follow.

Demuzzio raised an eyebrow to Joshua. Sarah and Elia smiled.

UMC Aircraft Hangar, John Wayne Airport, CA | Monday 1320 PDT

"Chewin' gum?" The Senator looked at the vials in the small chiller case, his fat belly shielding them from the view of the mechanics servicing the airplane. "That gonna work?"

"Best I could manage, Senator. I couldn't exactly do mouth swabs on those boys, could I?"

"Huh," the man grunted displeasure, "I'll see what the lab says."

"The one marked G is Gaelan; I is Ibrahim."

"Okay, son. I'm outta here." The fat man snapped the case shut, slid it in a jacket pocket. He scowled and turned toward the waiting limousine. "Bless you, Pastor Bob," he yelled back over his shoulder, smiling for the benefit of any watching technicians in the hangar.

Blake made a reflexive cross blessing toward the man's back. The pilot approached.

"Reverend? We're topped off. We can be airborne in fifteen minutes if you want to press on to Washington right now. We'd make Dulles around 10 PM local. Can't do DC National, it's still in lockdown."

"Crew time?"

"We're still good, sir. Within the window. Thanks for asking."

Blake looked at him, then up at the sleek aircraft, debating.

"You look tired, sir," the pilot added solicitously, "if you'd like to over-night here we could get a real early start tomorrow... you could say hi to your girls this afternoon."

"No. They're upstate with their grandma."

"Safer there," the pilot agreed. "Moved my family to the country too." He cocked an eyebrow at Blake. "The Senator say anything about more attacks?"

"No."

"Anything about when we might strike back?"

Blake frowned at him. "He wouldn't say, even if he knew. I really don't know any more than the general public, Tom. I believe the President when he said an appropriate time and an appropriate target."

"Problematic. I wouldn't want his job right now."

"I've prayed with the man, Tom. His faith is serving him well."

The pilot nodded. "Just wondering about the flight plan, sir. Any areas I should avoid?"

Bullshit, Tom. You're wondering along with the rest of the country why the President's behaving like he knows the terrorists don't have another shoe to drop. You're wondering about my connections to the man, and my sudden flights out to visit our new species in Hawaii, and how that all ties together. "Other than Washington, you mean?"

The pilot returned his crooked grin, still fishing. "Getting a little surreal, isn't it?"

Blake nodded, noncommittal. "That it is. File for the fastest route, Tom. We'll leave in fifteen minutes." He strode around the tail of the aircraft and climbed aboard.

Later, as the small jet climbed steeply to its cruising altitude, he told the crew not to disturb him. He sat back in the recliner to contemplate developments, his bible opened in his lap.

We're all gamblers in this game, he thought. The President was gambling on Eva and Joshua being right about the global consciousness not seeing any more nuke attacks on the near horizon. *He's being so measured that if he's wrong, if we get hit again, he loses big in the election this fall.*

Zurvan was gambling on staying hidden, and on not being exposed for what he really is. *If he's wrong, he's dead; that's a big downside risk.*

The Senator was gambling on his ability to keep managing and leveraging his power and image. *If he's wrong, so what? Disgrace. Impeachment. Jail time is pretty remote.*

Eva and her Council were gambling on their own ability to make people believe the Novas are no threat. *But is that even possible? A new species, edging out an old one? What bigger threat than evolution?*

And me? He was gambling on being smart enough to finesse all the players into the outcome he wanted. Power. *But am I that smart? Can I do it?*

Too many variables, he realized. Sooner or later such maneuvering had to stumble, even his. So...timing. Timing was the key. If he could keep his game together just long enough, play the forces off each other at just the right times, he could both destroy the Senator and get control over Eva and the Novas. *Good thing I'm smarter than all the rest of the players, Eva included. All... except maybe for Joshua O'Donnell, the certified genius. So he ought to be taken out of the game early. How do I do that?*

He closed the Bible in his lap and drummed his fingertips on its worn leather cover. The little jet arrowed east and the sun moved west and the shadows lengthened inside the cabin.

O'Donnell Enclave, Waimanu, HI | Tuesday 1754 HST

"She doesn't have to let the water touch her body, you know." Elia half-smiled at Joshua as she walked out of the waterfall. The cold fresh water had hardened her nipples under the Spandex swimsuit and she enjoyed how her husband's eyes roved over them admiringly. Then he looked up, troubled.

"You think?"

"Within her skill level, probably. Why, Joshua? You worried about the Reflecting Pool being contaminated?"

He shrugged and stepped under the waterfall to rinse off his own sweat and salt from their swim. "Not really; I doubt if there's any organism or toxin her immune system can't deal with."

"What, then?"

"A different kind of contamination. Baptism is powerful symbolism; Pastor Bob got that right. This thing could get spun any number of ways. Including out of control."

"Oh. Political contamination. Or religious." *And what sort of outcome does your beautiful latticework logic project there, my love?*

He answered the silent question in her face. "Too complex, Elia. Too many variables, too many possibilities."

"They'll narrow, surely, once the ball starts rolling," she observed.

"Yeah, sure. But by then we've rolled the ball onto a crazy slippery slope. Pastor Bob is okay, I think, even if he does have an agenda. But if he baptizes Eva, we're seen as aligned. Christian. This isn't a good thing. The Novas really need to transcend religion, so that they're no threat to anyone."

"Transcendence of any religion? That could be an even greater threat, Joshua."

"Yeah," he sighed, "I know that too."

"Well... Eva wants to do it, it seems."

"Yeah," he sighed again.

"And she has good instincts."

He gave her a crooked grin. "Usually."

She laughed. "But now that she's in love..."

"Love is a variable not easily worked into a logic lattice, Elia."

She nodded. "Love can cloud vision. Or make it clear."

Another crooked grin. "You're not a big help, El."

"Eva has good instincts," she affirmed, patting his cheek. "What other choice do you have anyway? Your baby sister is in charge now."

"She'd listen. Maybe not do it, if I was dead-set against it."

"But to be dead-set against it, your logic would have to compute all the most probable outcomes as bad."

He nodded. "And I can't compute anything. Bupkis."

"So, you go with Eva's instincts. You have before."

"I'm scared, Elia."

She put her arm around his muscled waist as they walked the path from the waterfall to the concealed door into the enclave.

"I know," she said.

O'Donnell Enclave, Waimanu, HI | Tuesday 1818 HST

Sarah watched TC Demuzzio swear at the monitor showing the couple approaching the enclave door.

"Dinnertime, Thomas. Can you pull yourself away?"

He jerked the chair around. "Josh is gonna cave."

Yes, he will, Thomas. He has no real choice. She just nodded at him.

"So, I'm the only one left thinks this is a shitty idea, Sarah?"

"It's actually not a bad idea. You just don't like exposing Eva. But that's easy to fix; she appears, gets baptized, disappears."

"Too much risk, Sarah."

She sat down in the console chair beside him and patted his forearm sympathetically.

"It's not just this one single exposure," Demuzzio continued, "if she does this, she's... aligned herself. And that's bad."

"Baptism in Pastor Bob's UMC makes her a target for other denominations, you think?"

"Paints a target right on her."

"For whom?"

"Any radical nutcases..."

"I think she's got a target on her now, Thomas. That she has yet to profess any particular faith... that she's ignoring all questions... the nutcase blogs are running wild with that."

"Yeah. I've been studying some of them just now," Demuzzio grunted, pointing at the computer monitor below the camera screen.

Sarah shrugged. "So maybe this will calm them down."

Demuzzio rubbed the top of his head, clockwise. She smiled at the consistency of his mannerisms. *I think he's enlarging his bald spot.* "Thomas, it's not all bad. The atheists like her; the secularists love her."

"Those groups are the more rational part of the population, Sarah. They don't generally shoot people. And they're in the minority."

"Oh, Thomas. Look. Eva has decided. I agree with her. Elia agrees with her. Joshua does too, even if he is late to the table. Will it work? I don't know, but I think..."

"What?"

"That it's better to take some action, get Eva out there, because that way people can see who she is, before they get caught up in someone else's concepts of who she is."

"And peoples' concepts are influenced by what they want to believe, yada yada; yeah, I've heard that song too, Sarah. Logically, it all makes sense for Eva to show her true self, which is beauty and truth and light and so many other things. But still..."

She put her hand back on his forearm. "You're scared."

"I'm terrified."

"As are we all," Sarah acknowledged. *Even though we researched it with her, scripted it out in accordance with all the power of many myths behind it, it's still a gamble. A roll of the dice in the middle of chaos.*

"We really have no choice, Thomas; we can't stay mute. There's too much craziness and speculation that Eva or the Novas are somehow at the bottom of the K'Shmar effects, and even the nuclear bomb at Las Vegas. Too many conspiracy theorists, getting too much traction on the internet."

He nodded. "All feeding into worries about the human race being phased out. I get it. But this place can take a nuke and not even feel it. She's safe here. Out there..."

They sat contemplative for a moment, looking at each other. His arm was warm under her hand. *You're a good man, Thomas Charles Demuzzio. You love your god-daughter like she was your own. But she's no longer yours. The child has grown up; she belongs to the world now. A new world. So that's where she has to be.*

Gaelan and Ibrahim ran into the room. "We're hungry," the twins announced in unison. "Aunt Eva says to come help her with dinner."

"Because Mom and Dad are in the shower," Ibrahim said helpfully.

"Together," Gaelan added, and giggled.

"You think they're making us another brother?" Ibrahim looked hopeful.

"Sister!" Gaelan was emphatic.

Sarah patted Demuzzio's arm and stood. "I'm sure your parents will tell you when the time comes."

"Maybe we can help," Ibrahim looked thoughtful.

"Good idea; let's all go help Eva with dinner."

Gaelan looked at his brother then at Sarah. "No, he means help them make a baby."

"Because Mom is blocking conception," Ibrahim said.

"She's sheathing the ova." Gaelan added.

Demuzzio cocked an eyebrow.

Sarah stood speechless.

You little devils! How could you know the Sisterhood's techniques for control of the bloodlines? She opened her mouth but no words would come. Both boys giggled.

"The locus told us," Ibrahim offered.

"Not in so many words," Gaelan amended.

The locus? Told them? How? What's going on here? This is totally outside anything we... Sarah recovered her composure. "Boys. There are some questions you don't ask. You just don't. Okay?"

"But how would we know which?" Ibrahim put on a face of false innocence. Gaelan adopted an earnest look, to bookend his brother's. Lights seemed to dance in their matching indigo eyes and flicker back and forth between them, a wilder echo of the crystalline pattern registered by their father's logic.

They're just too damn precocious. Sarah countered with sternness. "If you know enough to ask that question, you're smart enough to know the answer. Don't be messing with Doctor Sarah."

They looked chagrined.

And especially don't enquire into your own origins, boys. Please! Your father hasn't. And he's pretty smart. Wise, too. "Kitchen," she ordered, pointing. They scampered out the door and down the hall.

"What the hell was that about?" Demuzzio rubbed his head again.

"I'm not really sure," Sarah admitted. She touched his elbow and they followed the twins down the long hall to the kitchen.

O'Donnell Enclave, Waimanu, HI | Wednesday 0515 HST

They stood watching the televised ceremony on the big screen in the Council Chamber. Robert Blake, Pastor Bob to millions of faithful in the United Ministries of Christ, stood knee-deep in the water of the Reflecting Pool at the Lincoln Memorial in Washington, DC. Joshua had the sound muted as he studied Eva in her long white muumuu. Eva studied the scene on the screen, a procession of people moving slowly down the temporary steps into the shallow water. At intervals the camera zoomed in on Blake's face.

"He looks happy," she observed.

"They're likely big donors; he should look happy." Her brother gave her a wry smile that she ignored. "That water looks cold," he added. "And it's cloudy in DC. Mid-morning and not even sixty degrees yet. I don't know why he doesn't hold off until summer."

"The moment, Joshua. Just before Easter is the right time. He has such an innate sense for the symbolism."

"Milking the myth."

She just smiled at that. *As we will also, brother. Don't go sanctimonious on me.*

He shrugged. "SIO Security says it's clear, Eva. So... anytime you're ready."

"We'll wait just a bit. I need to be the last in line."

"Oh? And what would that be symbolizing?"

"The first one now will later be last," she sang.

"Um. Not sure I fully grasp the nuances here, kiddo."

Neither do I Josh, but they're important. I especially need to tease Pastor Bob a bit; see if I can pick up a little worry on his face. She answered obliquely. "Timing is critical."

"There are things you're not telling me, Eva."

Oh, you are so damn smart, brother. "When I was in the fog forest in Irian Jaya, Josh..."

"I remember."

"I was adopted by Klancko and his tribe."

"The little forest people. Who were there but weren't."

"Yeah. Now I need to be adopted by different... tribes."

"To stay non-denominational?"

"To stay... adoptable."

"That's a bit circular, Eva."

"I know."

"You want all tribes... faiths, cultures, whatever... to adopt you."

"Most of them, anyway."

"So the trick is to have all tribes see you as their own? Like animals can sniff out one of their own pack? Recognition at some very fundamental level?"

"Yes. Fundamental... thank you."

"And the baptism symbology is really that powerful?"

She shrugged. "It's a start."

Eva watched the crystalline patterns of her brother's logic lattices brighten and flex around him. *Your mind is such a beautiful thing, Joshua.*

"A neat trick, if it's possible," he conceded. But the brightness faded. "Which doesn't seem likely."

"Trust me, Joshua. It is."

He stared at her, his lattices brightening again. "You said 'a start'.... which means maybe you see a middle and an end. You want to share your strategy with your big brother? I'm feeling a little left out here."

She glanced at him. *Share? Share my ambivalence with you, brother? My uncertainty? Introduce more imponderables into the chaos your logic cannot process? Would that be helpful or hurtful?* The questions went unanswered as her attention went back to the screen.

"Oh. There's the last one coming up now, Josh!"

As she flicked the white shawl up around her shoulders, white forms flickered into being in her mind's other vision and circled around. One of the oldest acknowledged her problem: *Jesus was uncertain too, Little Mother. He almost did not step into the river to be baptized.*

So why did he?

The power of the ancient myth overtook him, I think.

As with me?

As with you. The Sister that had been Mary of Magdala smiled at her. *But your world is a different place. And you are better prepared.*

Still, I'm rolling the dice.

You are.

Eva nodded and took a calming breath. She tugged the white shawl tighter around her shoulders and briefly adjusted the flowers woven in her hair. She took her brother's hand and transposed them both to the rim of the pool. Then she stepped down into the water, alone, answering Pastor Bob's smile with her own.

When the baptism was done, Eva took the minister's hand and walked up the steps out of the pool. She formed just enough of an energy field around both of them to be visible against the cloudy day. People gasped and moved aside as they walked together to the podium. Joshua looked bemused.

Eva leaned her head against the tall man's arm and whispered. "I need to say a few words. Quickly. Then Josh and I have to go."

Blake made a sweeping gesture toward the microphone. She tapped it then pitched her voice into a pleasant mid-range. Her Sisters circled around in her other vision, coaching on tone and cadence. She gave herself over to be their instrument, letting them play her voice far better than she could herself, filling her message with eloquence and power and love.

"There are many traditions," she began. "and we respect them all. I speak to you for all the Novas, because I am the oldest. This morning we honor the Christian faith. Later today we will honor the Islamic. And the Buddhist. And the Judaic. And many others."

A part of Eva saw Joshua begin to smile, saw Robert Blake struggle to keep his pleased expression fixed on his face. Another part of her listened to the multitude of Sister voices, which somehow merged into the one single voice coming from her throat.

"Some call us a new species," she continued. "That is not especially accurate. We are an incremental change, a natural evolutionary step. We will be different in some ways, yes, but alike in many others. Your faiths are our faiths. Your children are us. We need you. We love you."

She found the other words, the powerful water allegories she and Sarah and Elia and her long-dead Sisters had crafted over the past two days, and cast them over the enthralled multitude. Ripples of emotion came back, then waves. They cohered around the cadence of her words, a resonance, and suddenly it was all working. A momentary break in the clouds swung a shaft of sunlight across the end of the Reflecting Pool and illuminated the statue of Lincoln inside his Memorial.

Eva Connard concluded her message, gazing for a moment out over the silent audience. Then she turned, kissed a dumbfounded Robert Blake chastely on the cheek and walked through dead silence to her brother.

"Come on, bro," she whispered. "I've got to take another plunge, before I dry off."

She took his hand and they were gone.

Chapter 12

Gonabadi Monastery, Boroujerd, Iran | Wednesday 1918 IRT

Joshua's ears popped as they materialized at a slightly higher elevation, in a walled courtyard. The building, he saw, was classic Islamic mosque architecture. Distant mountains dimmed in the fading twilight, but a rising moon bathed the dome and its minaret in pale silver.

"I don't think Muslims have a baptism ritual, Eva," he objected.

"Not in the literalist Christian sense, Josh, but in the broader sense of purification, preparation for prayer or spiritual contact or initiation... that's almost universal, and..."

A tall woman, unveiled, stepped from the wall's shadows, addressing Eva in unaccented English. "Sayyida. Welcome to our Nematollahi Gonabadi order. Spiritual initiation, I heard you say." She smiled. "Yes. The Semah awaits. Your timing is good, if we hasten."

"...it goes way back," Eva concluded to Josh, "to Leviticus, and Numbers. As you probably know."

And even before that, in oral traditions, Joshua's eidetic memory agreed. *Ritual washing was just good practical control over disease vectors. But the traditions were always couched in superstition, a path to power for the elders. How religions usually work.*

The woman turned and strode quickly toward a large wooden door. Eva followed her. Joshua followed them, his logic lattice questioning factors of ancient tradition versus those of current reality. *Worked, yeah. But now? Now it's a different ballgame, isn't it?* The lattice yielded no answer. He hurried to catch up with the two.

When the door opened, the sounds of reed and percussion instruments wove with chanting male and female voices to envelop them. Joshua felt his body begin to resonate and instinctively stepped in front of Eva to shield her.

"I'll be fine, Josh," Eva yelled in his ear as she nudged him aside. "Stand over there. Just watch."

Just watch? The resonance of the drums seemed decidedly martial, and flooded caution into the back of his brain. He fought it down. *Just watch. Just watch, she said.* Soon enough, the reeds and chanting shifted to a more pleasant vibration. He let out a long breath through pursed lips, a warrior's calming mantra, then stationed himself where Eva had pointed. He surveyed the room and its occupants. *Plenty of knives, but those are no problem. And no handguns, better yet.*

Several of the dancing celebrants had long thin needles or knives stuck through their faces or neck, but were not bleeding much. They bowed to Eva and backed out of the circle of drummers. She stepped out of her sandals and walked through flat pans of water. Women offered her bowls; she rinsed her hands in one and poured another over her bowed head. Silence cloaked the room; Joshua could hear only shallow fast breathing.

This is a special moment; something they've been anticipating. Why? Eva walked into the center of the circle and began to dance, a controlled slow spinning, an epicycle around the perimeter of the circle. A logic lattice formed in his mind as he studied her purposeful motions. *She's adding something to the traditional Semah dervish-dance. What?* The lattice gave no answer, but instead slid down a parallel analytical path. *This is very old*, his logic concluded at the end of it, *so the Sisterhood planted it genetically for this moment. A legend, and Eva's triggering it.*

Voices broke the silence, confirming his conclusion. "Sayyida," the chant started, a soft whisper. The candles ensconced around the room flickered.

Joshua watched his little sister move fluidly into her Semah dance, modifying the whirling patterns that were alleged to bring a dancer into communion with God. *I've seen Elia do that... I hope Eva's not going to...* But she did; after a few minutes her motions became subtly more erotic. A few more minutes, and not so subtly, but still blending seamlessly with the increasing tempo of the music. *Ah, Jesus! She'd better know how to control this once she starts...*

The planes of the girl's face seemed to change slightly in the shifting light and shadow, becoming leaner, more sharply defined. More adult. More a grown woman. *Dammit, Eva!*

"Fatima!" Wonder grew on the faces as the sacred name spilled out of multiple mouths and chased around the domed room in a syncopated rhythm.

More minutes passed and the drumbeat hardened. The pacing picked up again. Musicians and audience began to quiver in synchrony with Eva's motions.

The candles blew out. Electric lights on the circular walls faded to orange filament embers. The moon swelled in the single high window in the vaulted ceiling and shone down on the dancing girl, a bright spotlight. Eva's long white muumuu glittered and became almost translucent, the lithe body underneath a display of pure moving art. All eyes locked on her movements. *Induced hypnagogic state*, Joshua realized, *she's got total control.* He watched a mélange of pain and ecstasy play across the faces opposite him.

The chant changed and quickened and another name melded into it. "Kira!"

As Eva whirled, she scooped up water from the bowls and held globes of it in gravity fields in her hands. She loosed droplets of water from her grasp; they flew as shards of silver moonlight off her swinging hands, first into the circle of musicians, then into the audience beyond, splintering into all hues of the rainbow as they went. A woman screamed and fell writhing to the floor.

As the music crescendoed, a young male flute player stood and blew an ululating high note. His hips thrust fiercely and dampness spread into his thin robe at the crotch. All those in the room save Joshua had their heads back and eyes closed, even the musicians as they played on. Their palpable conjoined ecstasy ran over him like a freight train. His knees went wobbly.

A synchrous series of gasps matched the final notes of the music. *Jesus. I wouldn't have believed it. Simultaneous orgasms. Forty people here, male and female both.*

The music tailed off into a single composite moan, and the crowd collapsed to the floor as one organism. *Which they were*, the detached analytical part of Joshua's mind accepted, *in that final moment. Communion with God is erotic?* He shook his head to clear it. *No. They were so totally raptured, all of them, that it had to be an implanted suggestion. The Sisterhood cultured it, millennia, probably. What else don't I know, little sister?*

Eva, who had ended the dance in an implausibly graceful position on the floor, raised herself with equal grace. She turned full circle, arms out, smiling. The light on her faded and the muumuu became just fabric again. The overhead electric lights came back up. She walked to her brother, people bowing silently out of her path. She took his hand and pulled him toward the door. A low wail of loss broke the crowd's silence and followed them into the courtyard, but the door closed it off.

Joshua composed his mind, pushing aside the sight of her glowing skin and the smell of the sweat and sexual pheromones spilling off it. *I need to bring her down.* He forced his voice to casual inquiry: "You're a helluva dancer, kiddo. Where'd you pick up that dervish stuff?"

"Kira."

"One of your Sisters?"

"Kira Khatum. Rumi's second wife. Actually a Christian, captured in the Crusades."

"A dead Sister."

Eva smiled. "Physically, anyway."

He grimaced. "You let her dance in your body?"

"Vibrations, Josh. Her... resonances... were dancing my body. Bringing an old legend to life." She laughed. "But I'm still me, which is what you're asking."

Joshua's mind raced, but to no avail, so he changed topics again. "Okay... I guess this ceremony had a water element to it, so even if it wasn't a baptism I guess I see the point. But why do it in the first place? The Sufis are a relatively small part of the Islamic population. Nothing like the size of the UMC. And this was just a tiny gathering. Where's the leverage?"

"You saw the three veiled women against the back wall?"

"Yeah. Sisters. I could tell. Not SIO Security, though; they would have acknowledged my hand signal."

"You saw them spread out?"

"Yeah. Worried me for a moment. Seemed like they were getting different angles on you... oh... they were filming? Microcameras?"

"Yep. You'll see it when we get back to the enclave. See all of our..." she giggled, "...little ventures. Nicely edited for max impact. Sarah and Elia are doing that right now, then streaming them out on the internet."

Joshua sighed. "The internet, all of our ventures. Okay, I guess. What's next?"

"There's a Hindu ritual. On the Ganges."

"Good God, Eva! You have any energy left for this?"

"Oh, yes," she said softly, "plenty."

She took his hand and they were gone.

UMC Capitol Office, Washington, DC | Wednesday 2216 EDT

"What the fuck is that little bitch doin'?" the Senator demanded.

Consolidating power, you fat asshole. It's brilliant, Robert Blake thought, looking down on a deserted K Street from his Washington UMC office. But he gave a more oblique answer. "It makes sense, Senator. She can't align herself — or the Novas — with one religion, or culture, or country."

"She fucked you over, boy. You thought the little bitch was in love with your sorry ass."

In his mind Blake replayed Eva draping a lei around his neck the last time they'd met. She had arranged it carefully to fall an equal distance in front and back, touching him casually. But exquisitely. *Her dusky skin glowed. I smelled her desire, underlying the flower fragrance. The heat came off her, but with no sweat or flush.* A flash of heat hit his groin now as he looked out the window. He took a moment to straighten his suddenly wobbly knees as he turned away from the window and addressed the Senator.

"She is in love, I'm pretty sure. But she's also complicated. And she didn't fuck me over; not really. She made me the first stop; put the Christian faith first, specifically my UMC. That says something."

"Nah, it says shit; she fucked you over good."

Their conversation halted for a moment as they watched the monitor. Eva and her brother disappeared from the banks of the Ganges River in India. A horde of Hindus wailed in a language they didn't understand, but the loss and longing was apparent. That latest streamed video faded to black then restarted.

"A big operation," Blake noted. "At least three cameras. Professionally done. Not live, I think, because there's been some editing and interleaving. Some effects added too."

The fat man grunted. "What's your point, boy?"

"It's not trivial to do that sort of show, Senator. I know, I've done them. They had people in place. All prepared. Probably it was scripted tightly, camera angles and everything. A lot of planning went into each of these. Lots of resources. Lots of money."

The Senator slammed his hand on the console and the picture jittered. "Resources, money, professionally done. And you didn't know diddly-squat about it," the Senator sneered. "You! You part of the inner circle, boy, the fuckin' Nova Council itself. You even the one that suggested this goddamn baptism thing! And you didn't know shit!"

"I doubt if anyone did. Her brother looked surprised, too, when they left the Memorial."

"You tellin' me the little bitch just runs around and does whatever she wants?"

Blake shrugged. "She's a god, after all. In practical terms, anyway."

"God, huh? We oughta yank her fuckin' passport," the Senator muttered, "slow her down some."

"Technically, she's got dual citizenship, and the fix is in pretty solid with her Irish passport. Besides, passports are a State Department function, under the Executive. You think the President is going to stop her?"

"I realize that, son. I ain't some dumb hick."

"Besides, Senator, some of her outreach to different religions and cultures can be played into what you'd like to accomplish."

"Yeah? Talk to me, boy. What is it I want to accomplish?"

"Consolidation of your own power. You want a war to do that. You want to wipe out Islamic radicals. The President wants to educate them."

"So?"

"So Eva, by that dance with the Sufis, gave Muslim conservatives a direct slap in the face. Wahhabis, for example. Or any of the more dogmatic Sunni or Shiite sects."

"You tellin' me the towel-heads gonna get worked up over a fuckin' dance, son? Shee-it, the bitch wasn't even naked; just looked like it there for awhile. I seen more skin on belly-dancers."

I'll bet you have, Senator. Lap-dancers, too. "It's not just that, Senator. It's how the message resonated. The dervish-dance and Rumi's poetry trigger some deep reactions in what are essentially a pretty mystical people. Some of the channels Eva touched are next to the Qur'an in holiness. Broad appeal. Deep into fundamental roots of the psyches in those cultures."

"Yeah, so? Where you goin' with this, boy?"

"Power doesn't like her. But the people do."

The fat man's dark eyes went turgid with frustration. "So? Spell it out for me, goddammit."

"So far most blogs have been just knee-jerk responses, Senator, but you can bet your bottom dollar their ayatollahs are churning out fatwas now. There's no way they can ignore this; the psychology runs too deep. They'll have to counter it. Strongly. Pretty soon there'll be vitriolic stuff spewed all over the internet."

"And then they'll do somethin' stupid; that what you're sayin', boy? Overt action?"

"Almost inevitable. They'll give the President an identifiable target."

"And he'll have to bomb the camel-fuckers; that what you're sayin'?"

"He won't have much choice, politically."

"And then we got ourselves a nice little war." The Senator gave him a toothy grin.

"Better yet, most of the world sees it as a just war," Blake added.

The Senator's grin faded. "Yeah, maybe. But still, you gotta get control over that little bitch, Pastor Bob. She's movin' too fuckin' fast for us. That's dangerous. Nail her down. Get your sorry ass back to Hawaii. She's in love, boy; so go nail her down! With your goddamn dick!"

O'Donnell Enclave, Waimanu, HI | Thursday 0712 HST

In the enclave the next morning, Eva stirred in her bed as morning light brightened the opposite wall. She rubbed her eyes and giggled at the funny dreams she'd been having and almost rolled back into sleep. But then she sat straight up. *No! I actually did those things. Wow!* She giggled again as she swung her legs off the bed. *But did I do them properly?*

The Sisters who had been guarding her dreams took form and circled around in her other vision, wisps of greater light in the brightening room. The chatter among them condensed as they circled, and came out in a consensus: *You have done well, Young Mother.*

Eva smiled, pleased at the external confirmation but internally still disconcerted by the memories. *Enormous forces were untethered last night.* The visions simply nodded agreement and faded away. She dressed and scrubbed her face. The white muumuu lay in a pile on the floor by the shower, wilted flowers on top of it. She threw the flowers in the trash and tossed the dress into the hamper. Then she took a deep breath and walked out of her room. *All right, Josh, let's see how angry you are with me this morning.*

"Thanks for letting me sleep," she said as she entered the kitchen, "I needed it.

"You'll need this too." Elia handed her a tall cool glass. The smell of fresh guava and honey pulled the trigger on a suddenly ravenous appetite. She sucked it down gratefully and held it out for a refill.

"So?" she asked Joshua as he turned from the stove.

"Good job, kiddo."

"Tell me. Exactly."

"Sarah will, soon as she comes back with the latest poll data. Basically, approval ratings are up, anxiety levels are down. Significant changes." He smiled as he walked to the table, skillet in hand. "Here, have some pancakes."

Sarah came in as she was wolfing down breakfast. Eva listened carefully, not pausing in her steady food intake. The briefing moved succinctly from a general summary to specific targeted cultures and religions.

"Urgent problems?" Eva asked, "or anything we need to try to undo? Apologize for? Spin a different way?" She slurped more of the honeyed guava juice. "Like right away this morning?"

"Thomas is lining up the Council, Eva," Sarah replied, "we'll go live in the Chamber as soon as you've stuffed yourself sufficiently. They'll give us a good range of opinions."

"Okay. But tell me now, did I screw anything up badly?" She drained the pitcher into her glass and belched. "Scusi. Why aren't the Islamic numbers tracking the general trends?"

The three faces traded a glance; she read it easily. *They've been debating this.* "Is there coffee?"

Joshua reached for the stove and brought her the pot.

"Eva... I'm... ah... sure you know this, but your dance with the Sufis... that was blatantly sexual."

Eva felt her mind go dreamy. A distant chuckle sounded from one of her more libidinous dead Sisters.

"Yes. It was." Her focus tightened down on him. "That's how those things are. So?"

"I watched all the videos we streamed to the internet, Eva, before you got up."

"No wonder you look tired."

He shrugged off the sympathy. "Even edited — and believe me, Sarah and Elia scrubbed it pretty well — that one blew the beards right off the ayatollahs."

Eva giggled. "I actually tried hard not to offend, Josh."

"Eva! You cannot do these things and not offend."

"Which cultural segment? Break it down for me. Adverse stats are mostly from the hyper-conservatives, aren't they?"

Sarah flipped a few printout pages. "Yes. Wahhabis. Some other Sunni tribes. A number of the Shiite sects."

"You just fed Zurvan more ammunition." Joshua observed sourly. "He'll jump all over this. Western decadence coupled to Islamic deviants."

"The Sufis loved it, Josh."

"So they did. They've adopted you, sis, big-time." Her brother smiled at her. "But they're just a tiny minority. Relatively unimportant. And deviants, according to the conservative factions."

"Doesn't matter. Sufism is the mystical tradition within Islam, Josh."

"I know, but..."

"No, listen. Sufism has planted roots. The dancing, the ecstasy, the vibrations, the connectedness to the divine. The mystics' threads run through all the Islamic sects, Josh; Shiite, Sunni, even Wahhabi. All of them, irrespective of orthodoxy. And they run deep."

"As in embedded in the genome by the culture deep?" He got thoughtful. She watched the crystalline logic begin to shimmer in his aura.

"You're so smart, Josh."

"So... oh! Rumi's poetry... the Mathnawi..."

"Yeah. The allegory, the symbology. Deep threads, Josh."

The latticework structure brightened around him as he worked it through. "Jesus and the Therapeuti mystics practiced similar trance-states, driven by music and chant and dance. So did many cultures before them. And after, like Rumi. So Rumi just... structured it better?"

The three women watched him intently as his logic lattice concluded to answer his own question: "No. His wife Kira Khatum structured it. Then it was nurtured as a Sufi ritual. Over millennia. By the Sisterhood." He smiled and made a hat-tipping motion with his hand. "Ladies."

The three women burst out laughing.

Joshua shook his head ruefully. "It improves our chances of success, clearly, but..." Eva watched the lattice glow around him again, "it makes computing any sort of probabilities almost impossible. Too much of a wild card."

"I can learn to speak the high language of Rumi, too, Josh," Eva added softly. "And *my* poetry will cut Zurvan off at the knees." She giggled. "Or maybe a foot higher. Run *that* through a logic lattice."

O'Donnell Enclave, Waimanu, HI | Thursday 0736 HST

In the Nova Council Chamber, TC Demuzzio idly worked the console controls, lining up the eight off-site Council members for the holoconference and verifying their secure transmission channels. On the small monitor inset into the console, Adrienne O'Meara was relaying recent anomalies detected by NSA on their global consciousness network.

"I'm really worried about this, TC," she said.

He nodded at her image on the screen. Even the low-resolution transmitter on her car's dashboard couldn't hide the worry lines in her face as she continued. "Tell Eva and Josh, okay? Tell them to look hard at what my people will be sending them. Then use your own network to cross-check, okay?"

"I will. But we've seen this sort of squirrelly behavior in the GC before, Adrienne. Sometimes it doesn't mean any..."

"Or maybe it meant something and we didn't realize what, TC. Just tell them to look at it, please. The differential of the correlation fit. It somehow seems synched with Abe's biofield resonance."

"Along with two others in the DC area besides your son, right?" He thought it through. "And they've gotta be Novas, otherwise they wouldn't show up on the GC, right? Okay, I got that."

"Abe is sick, TC. Aaron says he goes in and out of phases where he's almost schizoid. It can't be just the fever, it can't."

"Maybe you should take him to the hospital, Adrienne."

"And ask them what? Is a psychic effect making him sick? Or is his sickness causing a psychic effect?"

He watched worry chew at her face and made the offer. "You and Aaron can bring your son here, Adrienne. Doctor Sarah knows more about Novas than anyone else on the planet." Her image gave him a wan smile and the worry softened a little.

"Kind of you. Thanks. Look, I'm just about home now. I've got a random event generator with me. I'll put it next to Abe and connect it to the network and maybe we'll be able to pick out a pattern."

"You and your NSA team must already have some ideas about the pattern, Adrienne; you said there's some synchrony. So what should I tell Eva and Josh?"

Demuzzio watched the image of her face turn aside as the woman rolled the steering wheel, and heard tires squeal as she braked.

"I'm home. The pattern... an alarm bell, TC. Tell them I think it's an alarm bell."

O'Donnell Enclave, Waimanu, HI | Thursday 0751 HST

He's rubbing his head again, Sarah noted as she entered the Council Chamber, *what's the crisis now?*

"Thomas," she said aloud, "you can queue up the holos. Eva's brushing her teeth and changing. Elia and Joshua are right behind me. We can do it right on the hour, I think."

Demuzzio's hand left his head and worked his keyboard, sending the standby message to Council members across the planet. The laser arrays that would create their holographic images hummed to life.

"We got another problem, Sarah. Maybe."

"So I saw."

"Huh?"

She smiled. "Just tell me."

He did, and the deep queasiness of the unknown seeped into her mind.

"Abraham? Adrienne and Aaron's boy? A Nova?"

"Yup. Plus two other Novas in the DC area."

"Novas don't generally get sick, Thomas." *At least not for long. And schizoid? Zurvan's K'Shmar shouldn't work on them. So what's going on?*

"Yeah, I know," Demuzzio responded.

"Adrienne's with him now?"

"Yeah, she just got home. It's two in the afternoon there. She'll miss our Council pow-wow."

Sarah heard Elia and Joshua coming down the long hall and made her decision. "We'll talk about it after the meeting, I think."

Demuzzio nodded agreement.

Joshua and Elia entered the room behind her.

Eva materialized next to Sarah with a pop of displaced air, bathing her in the fragrance of the crown of flowers on her head. Sarah inhaled appreciatively. *Fresh Frangipani, woven in a Maile vine. Nice symbolism... but for what?* Eva noted her sideways glance and giggled. *Peace with Council members that she didn't keep plugged into her plan? No, they wouldn't recognize it. A message to Pastor Bob, probably.* Eva giggled some more as she slid into the center seat. *And she's not really a child anymore, is she?*

The holograms of distant Council members flashed into existence in sequence, seven of them. Adrienne's spot stayed dark.

"Aloha and thank you for coming," Eva began as she usually did. "Adrienne is evidently...?" She looked at Demuzzio. He shook his head.

"Maybe later," he said, "we'll leave the channel open."

"Okay," Eva continued, "first, let me apologize for the consternation our little ventures out of the enclave have caused. I'm sorry, but I just felt we had to go proactive."

Earl Phillips spread his hands. "It evidently worked. More upside than downside, I think. At least that's how NSA figures it."

Carol Violette nodded agreement. "And the President was pleased when I briefed him at lunch. All of your videos have gone viral. Even crashed a few of the bigger website servers. It's huge."

"Taking some heat off his other problems," Joshua surmised.

"Yeah. He says thanks," Carol responded.

Sarah watched faces as she raised the main question. "Eva asked me earlier — and that's really the chief topic of our meeting this morning — if there are any urgent problems created. You've all seen all the videos at this point."

"Specifically, did we create any situation that we need to try to undo or explain or apologize for, like right away?" Eva added.

The holograms pondered that for a moment.

"Well, the Pope didn't seem happy when he baptized you, Eva," Robert Blake offered.

Sarah saw Eva brighten visibly and straighten a wayward blossom in the lei over her ear as she answered.

"But he did it, Pastor Bob. And his security detail gave our Sisters free rein in filming."

Blake shrugged. "He had to realize he'd better get the Church on the bandwagon whether he liked it or not."

Eva nodded. "So he wasn't happy. But he wasn't coerced either."

"All sorts of coercion, Eva," Blake offered, smiling. "He was the last one on your list... purposefully?"

That's one smart man, Sarah thought, *to intuit our design.*

Eva raised an eyebrow of invitation.

"The Pope knows power when he sees it," Blake expanded, "so you made sure he could see most of the other videos before you dropped in on him."

Eva concealed the smile behind her response. "He's a rational being, Pastor Bob."

"Rational, yes. But there's a deeper level. He's studied the mystics. He's one himself, I suspect."

Sarah stared at Blake's hologram. *Well, well, Pastor Bob, full marks. Another good intuition. The Gnostics were the mystics of the early Church, and those threads were planted deep too. For our Sisterhood to tug on when necessary.*

Eva shrugged. "Either way, the Pope sees what's coming. He knows he'll have to steer a careful course or his Church will collapse."

"Power adapts," Robert Blake acknowledged.

Sarah sighed. *Yes, Pastor Bob, when it sees it can't prevail.*

She sighed again, loudly enough that Eva cast a wondering glance at her. *And what poetry do you have for Christians, Eva, to help them adapt?*

Chapter 13

Hechal Shlomo, Jerusalem, Israel | Thursday 2259 IST

"What do I believe?" Eva repeated their question and let her eyes walk the bearded faces of seven members of the Chief Rabbinate Council as she considered how best to answer it. *Seven of seventeen. So ten are locked in their orthodoxy and won't meet with a woman directly. Will that be a problem?* She glanced at Joshua. He stood on her right, wearing a yarmulke, muscled arms folded across his chest. His lips quirked up slightly at her predicament, but the resonance of his logic lattice gave no hint of what he was evaluating. *Well*, she thought, *these seven agreed to see me; they deserve more than just diplomacy.*

So Eva answered honestly. "I believe the ancient allegories. I believe the story that starts with the human incarnation and resurrection of the sun-god in Egyptian myth. I believe in the rituals that became your Hebrew and Hellenic mysteries, then later Gnostic and Christian and Mithraic. The ancients saw this allegory as personal evolution: development of the god within. Given their times and knowledge, that's what their mystics taught. What some of your own mystical traditions teach today: that ultimately we all know God."

The resonances that flitted around the rabbis' biofields appeared, in her other vision, to be in roughly equal measure. *Curiosity. Uncertainty. Fear.* Several of the rabbis nodded. Others frowned.

"As a Nova-becoming," Eva continued, "I have the benefit of a... longer view. I believe that all humankind is a cradle for moral evolution."

"Some say you already are a god, Eva Connard," a rabbi whose beard had not quite gone all gray challenged. He frowned, testing her. "Do you say that?"

She shrugged and smiled at him. *Now some diplomacy.* "I can do things that seem god-like, that are beyond the capabilities of *Homo sapiens*. It seems so natural, I wouldn't call myself a god. But in this particular evolutionary context... oh... I guess 'god' is a relative term."

The rabbi's frown changed to a reluctant slow grin. "Ah yes. We're Jews, Eva Connard. 'Relative' we understand."

The mood lightened as smiles ran around the group.

Eva smiled along with them then got to the point. "You have a number of young Novas in your country, sirs. Over the next few years, at some point in their adolescence or early adulthood they will become like me. Please do not fear them; they are not gods, they are simply the next version of mankind. They must be loved and cherished, just like other children."

"That is your message to us tonight, Eva Connard?"

"And protected," she added, "from those who are fearful."

"You wish us to convey that message?"

"Yes. Please."

"We are scholars, young lady. We have no real power."

"You have the power of your influence. You are respected for your wisdom."

The seven rabbis considered that, and Eva watched their faces as they talked. A few phrases she understood as they traded citations from the Torah and Talmud, references to Ruth and Sarah and prophets. But she parsed more meaning from their resonances than their speech. *Curiosity, increased. Uncertainty, not much changed. Fear, down a bit.*

Finally, the grayest of the beards asked the question: "There is no reason to fear?" All seven faces stared at her intently.

"None," Eva answered firmly, "none at all." *They love to argue, and they'll do it all night. But we're out of time here. I'll be hopeful.*

She smiled at them, took Joshua's hand and transposed eastward to their next stop.

Al-Askariya Mosque, Kut, Iraq | Friday 0022 AST

"I have spoken of this briefly with several of you before..." Eva acknowledged to the eleven ayatollahs of the Supreme Council. She took a moment to inhale the cooler midnight air draining into the back room of their rebuilt Golden Mosque, calming herself and composing her thoughts. She studied the resonances around the bearded faces, calibrating her approach. *They deserve honesty as much as the Rabbinate, but how many have the same appreciation of relativism?* She looked at Joshua's guarded face and wary stance. He gave a tiny shrug. *Strictly my call, huh? Thanks, bro.* She watched the Council's faces carefully as she continued.

"...that many followers of the Christian New Testament, and also of your Qur'an and hadiths, have missed the allegorical nature of the mystics' teachings. They took the meaning of the writings to be literal, Tafsir. With all due respect to the Prophet, peace be upon him, this is not what he intended. Nor is it what Jesus intended."

"You lecture us, Eva Connard? Tell us how to interpret our own holy scriptures?" The old ayatollah's voice was mild but his eyes were challenging and dark. The resonances of his biofield signaled his emotional state clearly. *Some fear. A lot of confusion. But no antipathy, that's interesting.*

"I only observe that other traditions exist in Islam; for instance the allegorical interpretations of your mystics, Ta'wil."

"Those Sufis with whom you danced?" The cleric's tone seemed to turn derogatory. "Their myths?"

Eva felt Joshua tense beside her. *But his biofield didn't change, Josh; he's just testing me,* she thought. She touched her brother's arm lightly and opted for a soft answer. "Yes; my friends of the dance. Their myths. But all religions have their mystics, Sayyid. A necessary element, it seems."

"They suffer for it, too, it seems, Eva Connard."

All too often, in any faith, she agreed. "But not at *your* hands, Sayyid. You, and this Council in particular, have a history of reason and compassion in dealing with your Sufis. And in fact with other cultures and faiths in your communities. Turcomans, Assyrians, Christians. This is why we chose to come before your Council."

The cleric weighed her words for a long silent moment.

"And we thank you for making time for us at this odd hour," she added, keeping her eyes focused on his, letting her other vision evaluate the resonances building around the rest of the group. Against expectations, their biofields were becoming friendlier. Finally the man spoke, his tone neutral.

"So... the purpose of your visit tonight, Eva Connard?"

"Fear."

"Fear? Whose?"

"Yours, Sayyid. And that of many Muslims. And ours too."

He nodded. "The stories? The internet?"

She nodded, silent. *Our new cultural barometer.*

He looked at her keenly. "The Sword of Islam? Nuclear blackmail? We have no part of that."

"We know. But the fact is that many Muslims truly want to see me handed over in Mecca. To be tried as a witch."

"Backward Arab zealots," the cleric snorted. "The rest of Islam grieves for your loss of innocents in Nevada."

"There are others, Imam," she started, "Muhammad Zurvan..."

"Zurvan spouts nonsense."

Eva felt the start of relief. *Good! But go cautiously here; we cannot prove Zurvan is tied to the Sword of Islam.* "We agree. But some of your brethren are calling him the Mahdi already."

"True. But those too are the zealots, the fringe. Not all Muslims are the fundamentalists we often seem to those outside, Sayyida."

In her peripheral vision, Eva noted Joshua's left eyebrow tick up at the unexpected honorific. *Sayyida, huh? Either word travels fast from Qom, or does he see Fatima's image in me, too? Or... ah, thank you, Sisters; you've been here ahead of me.*

"True Muslims, most of us, ignore neither our modern world nor our ancient allegories," the cleric came back to her earlier point. His expression got rueful as he tapped the case on his belt. "All aspects of both being instantly available on our cell phones."

Fleeting smiles came and went beneath several of the beards. Eva and Joshua smiled with them.

"Fear," Eva repeated. "Fear is Zurvan's weapon. He will use it against us, and against your own voices of reason and compassion."

"Your purpose here is to warn us?"

"To warn about your children. You have a number of young Novas in your countries. They will become like me when they come of age. They will be different, they will have strange powers. But they should not be feared, they are just the next version of mankind. They must be loved and cherished, just like other children. Not attacked, nor tried as witches or warlocks."

"And you think it may come to that, Eva Connard?"

"We think Zurvan and those like him will try to bring it to that, yes. Not only in Islam, but in other faiths as well. Fear," she repeated, "will be their weapon."

Bearded faces showed understanding. Their resonances shifted subtly into a more compassionate pattern.

"Please protect your children," she added.

"Sayyida," the old cleric acknowledged, nodding respectfully.

She touched Joshua's arm, transposing them westward.

Vatican City, Rome, Italy | Thursday 2345 CET

"I can become the Christos myth in this millennium if I choose, *Sua Santità*. I can be the Second Coming of the Christ." Eva softened her words for the old man, but answered his question honestly.

The Pope got a bemused expression. "With the same outcome, my child?"

"Well... hopefully not the bad parts," she admitted.

They studied each other across the short distance in a corner of the deserted papal reception hall. The Cardinal Camerlengo and nine visiting cardinals looked on, transfixed. She read their biofields with her other vision, easily parsing emotional resonances. *Uncertainty. Ambivalence. Fear;*

a lot of it; more than at the other meetings. Interesting. She smiled at them all, her gaze flitting over faces, and saw the fear damp down a little.

"But that's our last resort," Eva clarified. "I'm not interested in starting another religion." She watched the fear resonance drop further as it cycled through the cardinals; it leveled off about where it had been at the Jewish and Muslim councils.

"We did wonder," the Camerlengo explained, "since there seems to be quite a popular groundswell along those lines on the internet."

"We are not encouraging it."

"You don't have to, Eva," the younger man added, "but you're not denying it. And your Sisterhood structured the psychodynamics so cleverly that once released the myth will feed on itself."

He knows of the Sisterhood? Wow! Josh must be having a fit. She glanced at her brother, and saw the resonance of a logic lattice flare into brightness as he considered the implications.

She turned back to the Pope and examined his biofield more closely; the resonances had shifted drastically upon hearing her words. *Weariness, or... Oh. Resignation. Suddenly he sees it. What started as the secularization of Europe is now the end game for his Church. Novas will have no need of religion. The poor man.*

"I'm sorry, *Santitá*," she said softly.

The old man stirred in his chair and spread his hands dismissively. "You requested a meeting to ask our help, child. What is it that you need?"

"There are a number of young Novas being born in the many countries with a Catholic population. As they grow into adolescence or early adulthood they will become like me. But they are not gods; they are just the next version of mankind."

"Yet for this they will be demonized," the Pope anticipated her, "by those of any faith who remain ignorant or fearful."

"They must be loved and cherished, just like other children. And protected..." Eva's voice broke, finally, from the weight of that plea. She swallowed. "...from those who fear them."

"And you wish us to convey this message to our faithful?"

"You will help?"

"I baptized you, Eva Connard. I will do what I can."

"Thank you, *Santitá*.

"We will pray for you, my child."

"Please," Eva agreed. "And for us all."

She composed her mind, leaned into her brother and whispered in his ear. "Slight elevation change coming up, Josh. Exhale, then swallow."

As soon as he did, she blinked the tears from her eyes, took her brother's hand and transposed them from the Vatican.

Vessagiri Hermitage, Anuradhapura, Sri Lanka | Friday 0347 AST

"Ayya Sangamitra," Eva greeted the slender woman with the shaved head of a Buddhist nun, "thank you for all your efforts, my Sister." The woman nodded a silent greeting, placing her palms together in front of her lips and bowing slightly. Eva turned to the rest of the Sanga Council and returned the bow. "Arya-Sanga," she said, "you have done all we could ask. Thank you."

"The warrior-sisters have been deployed, Young Mother. As you ordered," Sangamitra offered.

Eva stifled a smile. *Her tone is neutral, but it's really a question.* She read the woman's biofield resonance without difficulty. *Approval. But ambiguity. And distaste.* The same general pattern traced over the biofields of half the Buddhist council. Distaste flickered up when they switched their wide eyes to Joshua with his folded arms and panther-like relaxation. It flickered down again when they looked back at her. *Yeah, I have the same problem.* She stifled a sigh. *Your tradition is peace. I understand. But Joshua is needed, as are my warrior-sisters.* She gave the simplest answer she could to the woman's unspoken question.

"It *is* necessary. Your warrior-sisters will do whatever they must to defend and protect the young Novas." She paused to let her eyes roam the faces. "But nothing more."

The shared resonance of the assemblage shifted slightly, its light splintering into a pattern that included hopefulness and acceptance.

"Bless you," Eva said, "for keeping watch over the children. Thank you."

She took her brother's hand and transposed them home to Waimanu.

Jebel Uweinat, Libya | Friday 0303 CAT

Muhammad Zurvan cursed in three languages as he studied the panel of statistics on his monitor screen. The tide of Muslim commentary that had been running strongly in his favor was beginning to recede.

"Clever little bitch, aren't you," he said to the smaller inset image on the screen of Eva dancing wildly with the Sufis in their ritual, "embedding yourself in different religions, using their ceremonies, conditioning their myths for your own entry." He watched the girl spin and dip and turn, the flaring white dress a teasing minimal cover to her superbly conditioned young body, an elemental appeal. "Very clever. But I see what you are doing."

He fondled himself as her dance ended, then switched off the inset screen. "I will have you, Eva Connard. I will have you and your power," he whispered.

But the statistical trend lines plotted by his cultural psychometrics algorithms continued to decline. He snarled at them and turned off the monitor.

O'Donnell Enclave, Waimanu, HI | Friday 1549 HST

"Those meetings went pretty well," Eva said around the mouthful of lasagna she was wolfing down, "overall. Don't you think?"

Sarah nodded. "Except for that last one. And all the indicators have shifted another few points. So your instincts were right."

Mr. Bojangles meowed a second affirmative opinion and rubbed against Sarah's ankle. She absently kicked off a sandal and drew her foot along the big tomcat's back. Purring, he ambled off to a corner of the kitchen where he sat steadily contemplating the two of them.

Eva scrunched her nose at the cat over another mouthful. He responded with another meow.

Aren't they a pair, Sarah thought, for the umpteenth time. "Almost seems human, the way that cat acts sometimes, Eva."

"Almost," she agreed, swallowing and smiling.

Sarah saw the starcross light flicker in Eva's indigo eyes and snapped her vision back to the cat. *I could swear... no, that had to be an after-image.* The cat's gray eyes regarded her calmly. He yawned and stretched.

My interest in your connection with Eva is of so little consequence to you, Mr. Bo? The cat yawned again, confirming it. "Wish I could get you two in the MRI together somehow, Eva."

The girl grinned at her. "Mister Bo? Hah! You'd never catch him."

"A quantum cat?"

"Something like that." Another starcross flickered briefly in Eva's eyes as she glanced at the cat and back to Sarah. She looked down at the empty plate then picked it up and licked it.

"Why does transposing make me so damn hungry, Sarah? There's not much physical energy involved."

"You're burning calories somehow, Eva. Like a marathoner. Faster, actually." *How adroitly the child changes the subject!*

"Think you and Josh will figure out why?"

"Eventually. It's beyond my medical experience, but I think it's just a question of Josh getting his mind around enough dimensions to see how the mass-energy balance works with Novas." Sarah shrugged. "Ask him when he gets back. He took the twins and Elia swimming in the bay."

"Blowing off some steam?"

"Oh, I don't think he's that angry with you."

"Everything went pretty well, I thought, except that last attempt."

"Seventeen and one is a pretty good record," Sarah agreed.

"I had to try, Sarah. That last one, the fundamentalists; I had to try."

"I know you did, Eva. I would have done the same, probably. But Joshua doesn't like blood on his hands any more than you do."

Sarah put both hands on Eva's shoulders and continued. "He doesn't like you asking for trouble. At least not without warning him in advance."

"Yeah," Eva admitted, "that was a mistake." She slugged down the last of a pitcher of honeyed guava juice and belched. "I'll go apologize."

Sarah watched as the girl ran from the kitchen onto the deck and jumped the rail, whooping as she soared down toward the bay a thousand feet below.

Mr. Bojangles jumped up on the rail, watching her fall. Sarah came out on the deck to join him, in time to see a jet of water rise up from the surface to cradle the girl's impact. A shard of reflected light off the water below flickered around the cat's narrowed pupils in a star-cross pattern.

Ah! Caught you that time, Mister Bo, she thought.

The cat yawned at her again.

UMC Capitol Office, Washington, DC | Friday 2231 EDT

"It's a prion, son. Lovely little bugger," the Senator mused, holding the vial of amber liquid up to the light. "Resistant to heat, ultraviolet, most disinfectants. Tiny, goes airborne real easy, stays up a long time. Only affects Nova kids, because they're the only ones with the PrYx gene mutation. — dunno what the fuck that is, but that's what my lab boys say, anyway."

"So they inhale it?" The Reverend Robert Blake stared at the vial in fascination.

"Up the nose, into the blood, straight to the brain, son. Targets the new neuron connections as they're forming. Quick little bugger, too. Incubation is only a coupla days. Breeds like a motherfucker, faster than a cold virus."

"Is it fatal?"

"Probably. No way to tell yet, boy. Didn't have no animal trials. Had to do our own clinical trials right here, on that kid Abraham and them other two out in Germantown. Not FDA-approved." He guffawed at his own humor. "And a few others you don't need to know about."

A few others? Blake forced his expression to stay neutral. "Symptoms?" he asked.

"First the usual shit; fever, chills. Then they disconnect, go sorta like autistic. Then they hallucinate. And then," the Senator grinned wolfishly, "you gonna love this, boy... then they get mean."

"Mean?"

"Yeah. As in homicidal."

It clicked over suddenly in Blake's mind. *This wasn't an overnight project.* "So... you've had research going on for a while now, Senator?"

The fat man chuckled. "Bet your sweet bippie, son. Years."

"Why?"

"Why? Boy, you still wet in backa them ears? These Novas, we don't get control of 'em, they're gonna fuck up this great country of ours. Gonna give us all this peace and love shit."

The Senator wiped a little spittle from his lips. "Can't have that, boy. We didn't get to be the most powerful nation on earth that way. We got there because we got the biggest bombs and the best military. And that's the way it should be."

The man is certifiably insane, Blake thought, *I've got to find a way out from under his blackmail. Then I'll kill him.*

The Senator laughed and shook his head, as if he knew what Blake was thinking. "Okay, Pastor Bob, you gonna do two things for me." He handed Blake the vial. "You gonna dose that enclave in Hawaii. Spray this into their ventilation system."

Blake took the vial gingerly.

The Senator was amused. "The disease can't hurt you, son. Give you a cold, maybe; that's all."

"When am I supposed to do this? I'm going back to California tomorrow. And Sunday is my service."

"Yeah, yeah. Monday is fine, boy."

"They'll know it was me, Senator. Process of elimination. They're very smart."

"Nah. You could be just a carrier. An innocent bystander. Besides, you're gonna visit the O'Meara boy at Johns Hopkins tomorrow, son. Lay your hands on the poor lad, give him that good ol' blessin' of yours. Before they figger out he should be in isolation. So mebbe you pick it up there."

Blake nodded. *Crazy as a loon, but smart. And Eva and Joshua have been all over the globe, inhaling God knows what. It's decent cover.* He temporized anyway.

"Maybe. But I still don't like it. They're too smart. Especially Joshua. Look at how they pre-empted Zurvan's next move with those meetings over the past two days."

"Yeah, that was cute, son. Smart. But I don't give a shit if you like it or not. You just gotta do it."

Blake sighed. *Yes I do.*

O'Donnell Enclave, Waimanu, HI | Saturday 1022 HST

The morning meeting of the Council had been as upbeat as any since the crisis began. Taking the initiative instead of reacting had delivered a good outcome. The social psychometrics were now running in their favor, and even the stock markets were up worldwide. Eva had declared a day of relaxation and decompression. But for her it was also a day of reflection. She walked on the black volcanic sand with her brother, talking, working her way to the one bad outcome of their seventeen meetings across the planet.

Joshua put his arm around her shoulders when she finally brought it up. *Yes, it was messy*, he thought, *but they gave us no choice.* That was too blunt an answer so he softened it. "Every culture has its own paradigm, Eva," he offered, "its own lens for seeing reality."

"I know," she replied, her voice sad.

"And some of those lenses are defective."

"They distort the light," she agreed.

"Sometimes those lenses are even opaque," he continued. "In the middle ages, the Church hierarchy wouldn't even look through Galileo's telescope because they *knew* the moons of Jupiter couldn't possibly be there."

"And it's the same with the Novas for those fundamentalist Muslims, you think?"

"You're a fifteen-year-old heathen female. Not Allah. So you can't possibly be a god."

"Too big a shift of the paradigm?"

"Huge. It would upend everything they believe. They couldn't tolerate that. It would have destroyed their reality. So they had to destroy you."

"I had to try, Josh. I had to reach out."

"Yeah, kiddo, I guess, maybe so." *Love thine enemy.*

"They didn't have to attack us! Clerics, for God's sake!"

But I warned you they would; the logic was inescapable. He stifled that thought, and not wanting to add to her misery, just shrugged. "But they did, Eva. Guns. We had no choice."

"What was the body count?" She looked up at him sadly.

"I don't know. I did what I had to. You did what you had to. Then you took us out of there."

She squinted up at him through tears that sparkled in the morning light, and patted his hand as it squeezed her shoulder.

Chapter 14

Jebel Uweinat, Libya | Sunday 0103 CAT

Muhammad Zurvan studied the reports intently as they scrolled down his monitor. The opportunities they hinted at played at the edges of his mind, both irritating and enticing. He fed the new statistics into his game-theory algorithm, but got the same result. With the steady attrition of his K'Shmar relay stations, he was losing the ability to degrade minds. *Which means I'm losing the credibility battle.*

"How are you doing that, little Eva?" he spoke to the empty air. "The first one destroyed itself under the intruder protocol; but the others... frying the electronics with no trace? Clever girl, aren't you! Or is it your infernal brother?"

Cycling the stations on and off had worked to a degree; probably preventing their weapon — whatever it was — from getting a fix on the physical location. But only for awhile. He snarled at the monitor as another station went down, its icon turning black.

"Juarez, Mexico. I have operatives, I can place another one easily. But they could take it out just as easily." Rage fought with curiosity, but reason came down to arbitrate. He forced himself to sit back and look for a pattern among the sites that had been taken out, and got an idea.

"All in daylight." He punched the keyboard, his long fingers moving with speed and precision, calling up databases, picking off numbers, inserting them into correlation algorithms. Data began to scroll down the screen.

"Ah! All on clear sunny days. The sun high in the sky. What does that mean?"

The answer came easily enough. An energy weapon. A beam of some sort. Little moisture in the sky to absorb its energy. And daylight? So if it ionizes the air, it won't be visible? He began muttering aloud again, but softly, so that Muammar outside the cave door wouldn't hear him.

"Clever, little bitch! But the resources? Do you have them? And the platform, an aircraft?" Probably, he concluded. The organization Hamilton O'Donnell had put together was very wealthy, even though that wealth was managed in ways that made it impossible to assess.

He scrolled through the data again. *But no. Even with those resources... too many countries. Too far apart. Too much bureaucracy to go through to get overflights. Too many questions raised.*

"What then, my little Eva? Do you have one of those solar aircraft that lurks so high in the stratosphere no one can see it?

He looked at the data again, computing distances and vectors in his head. *No. And besides, they can carry no serious payload, just spy cameras and a transmitter. An energy converter and beam device would be too heavy.*

"So. Your government has a space-based weapon, does it? And they use it for you, my little bitch. How nice!" He laughed. "How many treaties does *that* violate, I wonder, hmm? Possibly my friends in Russia and China would be interested."

But the United States would bluster and deny, and buy time, and still keep picking off his K'Shmar sites. And there was little he could do to counter that, except for constantly replacing the electronics or possibly using mobile platforms. He punched numbers into a projection algorithm and felt his rage grow as the answer came clear: in this war of attrition he would lose all the sites in weeks, a few months at the most.

Will it matter? His plan depended on the K'Shmar effect to create chaos, fill the minds of the weak with fear, nudge them toward unthinking violence, herd them toward his ends. But many were following him without such prodding. He closed his eyes and let his mind play with probabilities.

An hour later, he opened them. The K'Shmar ultimately would fail to serve its planned purpose, he concluded, but until then was a useful diversionary tactic. They couldn't know where he was going with it, so their need to react had to be keeping them off balance. And their own secretiveness was a giveaway; they had used the beam even inside their own country rather than sending police or military. That he understood. Making public the existence of a weapon like the K'Shmar, which worked on minds below the level of rationality... that would cause widespread panic.

He smiled at the thought. "Fear and chaos. Maybe I'll disclose the K'Shmar, after all the sites are wiped out. Show it to be a device of the Novas and the US government, but beamed from space. Even in its death it can serve a useful propaganda purpose." He filed that thought away for future consideration and came back to the present, a very interesting present.

"So. That brings us to your offer, Senator. The virus. Yes, I do have the resources to distribute it. My faithful *Jaesh* is everywhere, especially in countries to which you have no access. And even in your own country."

He tapped a message into the encrypted system that would confirm his interest in a possible collaboration against the great danger that *Nova sapiens* represented to the established order, studied it, and hit the Send button. *You are a disgusting fat infidel, Senator. But the enemy of my enemies is my friend.*

Sarez Dam, Khorog, Tajikistan | Sunday 0815 TJT

The sun rising over the Pamir Range to the east bathed the construction works of the massive dam below in bright light. Eva inhaled the mountain air and took a moment to admire the scene. Mr. Bojangles, curled around the back of her neck, purred agreement with Eva. She put a hand on the big tomcat to steady him and stepped off the rampart, dropping smoothly to the secured area a hundred feet below. The woman guarding it spun and dropped into a crouch, the machine pistol whipping up in a blur.

"Sorry, Sister," Eva said in Farsi, her hands opening outward, "didn't mean to startle you."

The pistol lowered as the woman composed herself. "Sayyida," she acknowledged in clear English, "welcome to the Pamir."

"Thank you," Eva said, studying her. *Interesting how that matrilineal strain is so naturally persistent. Blond hair, green eyes. Twenty-three hundred years down from Alexander, and a disproportionate fraction of these Ismaili women are SIO warrior class. Exactly like Mom. After this crisis is over I'll ask Josh to help me trace the alleles.*

The woman studied Eva in return, grinning at the cat on her shoulder. She looked around. "Your brother, Sayyida? The Protector?"

Eva shrugged. "Other urgent matters. Only friends here, right?"

The woman smiled and nodded. "The Aga Khan is having breakfast. May I bring you some?" She motioned toward a yurt at the far side of the cleared area.

Eva shook her head. "Possibly some of your crazy coffee, that's all. I mean no disrespect to your custom or your spiritual leader, but I haven't much time. And, I'm sorry, you are...?"

"Ayesha."

"Ah. A fine name for a Sister."

As they walked toward the yurt the woman leaned in a little to examine the cat. "Your friend here? Is he hungry? A little mountain mouse, perhaps?"

Eva laughed. "Mr. Bo is a vegetarian today, I think."

Ayesha reached in and stroked the big tom behind the ears. His loud purring vibrated through Eva's neck. "You have a friend," Eva told her.

The woman stroked him again and nodded. "A good one to have, I think." She raised the entry flap of the yurt. "Uncle? You have a visitor. Visitors."

Eva bent down to enter, and the big tomcat jumped down and preceded her into the tent. The man inside stood up and offered her his hand.

"You didn't need to come personally, Eva. You know our organization will help, as your uncle has helped our Ismailis..."

Mr. Bojangles rubbed against the tall man's ankles and meowed. He stooped down and ran his hand along the cat's back.

"... over many years, going back to my great-grandfather." He looked closely at the cat and smiled. "Isn't that right, ancient one?"

The cat meowed again.

"I'm bringing you a gift, Sayyid." She reached into her jacket. "This is a copy, of course. The original was just couriered to your headquarters in Geneva."

He took it from her hand, a quizzical look on his face, and thumbed the book open. He frowned. "I'm afraid I can't interpret this. My father knew the ancient dialects, but..."

"We added an English translation, second half of the book. Look on page 179."

He did. His brow furrowed. His mouth twitched. "Well. Thank you... I think."

Eva laughed. "I know. A double-edged sword. Still, it belongs to you, more than anyone. And it may have a use."

"Legitimacy?"

Eva gestured toward the yurt entry, and the half-built hydroelectric dam on the Panj River. "Your good works speak for your legitimacy."

He laughed. "Eva Connard, the diplomat. My father's old friend — your Uncle Hamilton — he taught you well, I see. Sit down, please."

He waited until she sat in the canvas chair then sat in his. Mr. Bojangles jumped into his lap and settled, purring. The bodyguard entered with an ornate coffee server and small cups, and put them on the folding table.

"Thank you, Ayesha."

"It's strong," the woman warned Eva. She smiled at them and withdrew.

The Aga Khan poured them both the thick black coffee. "How did you come by this artifact?" He put the book on the table and tapped it.

"Accidentally. And recently."

He smiled at that. "Legally?"

Eva smiled innocently. "If you steal back from a thief, is it theft?"

He laughed. "Repercussions?"

"Not with respect to ownership." Eva felt the pain wash across her face but made no attempt to hide it. "The thief is no longer with us."

The man nodded sympathetically as Eva continued.

"But, if you use it, yes, of course... repercussions, denial. Your niece's namesake is known for her collection of the Prophet's hadiths. No one knew she kept a journal about her husband's family and offspring."

"So the heritage we claim for our Ismailis is true? The Aga Khan line is descended from the Prophet Muhammad through his daughter Fatima?" She watched his resonances build and shift. *Joy. Curiosity. Fear, a little.*

"Indisputably." Eva blew on the hot coffee and held the small cup under her nose. She put it down and added sugar.

"As you are also, Eva, if the stories I'm hearing are accurate," he offered.

She nodded and sipped the coffee. "Not quite. I look like Fatima, apparently, but we have... different mothers."

The man studied her and elected not to pursue that. "And what would you have me do with this information?" He tapped the book again, and then tapped the cat in his lap. "You and your old friend here."

Good question, she thought, *and one even Josh couldn't answer. Too many variables, too much chaos around it.* She sipped more of the coffee, enjoying the way it bit the back of her throat.

"I don't know," she confessed.

Mr. Bojangles meowed.

"But I think there may come a time..."

The man stroked the cat and waited patiently.

"...you'll just know that time, I think," she concluded lamely. *I'm as puzzled as you are, Imam. But unlike many Muslims your Ismailis see no conflict with other cultures or beliefs, and have consistently adapted easily to modern times and thinking. Your people treat women and even heathens as equals. So who better to receive this legacy?*

She shrugged, drained the coffee cup, and stood up. Mr. Bojangles leapt across the table into her arms. The Aga Khan stood. Eva stepped around the table and kissed the tall man on the cheek.

Then she stepped back, formed the intention, and was instantly in her bedroom halfway across the planet in Hawaii. An after-image of the man's thoughtful face painted itself on the cumulus clouds that sat on the horizon beyond her deck.

Good luck, she told it. *You'll know the time when it comes. I hope.*

"Another seed sowed, Bo," she said.

Mr. Bojangles stretched, stalked out on the deck and meowed.

O'Donnell Enclave, Waimanu, HI | Monday 1822 HST

With the sun sinking in the western Pacific and barely enough daylight remaining, the small UMC jet eased down onto the runway at Waimea's Barking Sands Airport. Robert Blake contemplated the deadly vial in his hand and half-listened to his secure cell phone.

"Yes, Senator, I understand," he said. *The death of a species? Or its control? Who knows? You're rolling the dice, Senator. And I'm one of them.* The man's encrypted voice was tinny in his ear, and the vowels sounded elongated.

"You'd better, son. The shit in that vial is worth nearly a hunnert million out-of-pocket."

"I appreciate that, Senator. There won't be any problem on my end. We've landed now, headed toward the hangar. I've got to go."

"Awright. Don't fail me boy. Squirt that shit all over their fuckin' enclave. We need a leg up on these people, capisce?"

The phone gave the three-tone signal of a dropped secure connection. Blake took a deep breath, let it out slowly, and turned the vial around one last time in his hand. Then he opened his overnight bag and slipped it into a canister of shaving cream modified to conceal it. The jet eased into the hangar and the engines spun down. The copilot opened the door and lowered the steps for him.

"Thanks, Tom," Blake said. "Get yourselves a good night's sleep in Waimea. I'll call you in the morning, let you know what the agenda is going to be for the flight back."

He walked out of the hangar to the nondescript SUV that had just driven up, and threw his bag in the back seat.

"TC, good evening. Nice to see you again."

"Pastor Bob," the man acknowledged, "nice to have you back. Eva's looking forward to talking with you."

And what do I say to that? He just nodded noncommittally and climbed in. The cat sitting on the dashboard meowed a greeting. "Mr. Bojangles riding shotgun?"

Demuzzio laughed. "He likes to get away from time to time. Eva says he's a vegetarian, but I think the cat goes out at night to collect a square meal. He'll stop me at the bridge, you watch."

"Really?"

"Oh, yeah. Slips down into that ravine, the Kaimu Gulch. Stream at the bottom, probably good hunting. Mice or something."

"You're not worried about something bigger getting him? This is a pretty wild part of the Big Island, I understand."

"Hasn't happened yet. I think he's too smart for that. Damn cat seems almost human some days. Anyway, he goes where he wants."

Mr. Bojangles yawned at them and flattened himself on the dashboard as Demuzzio put the car in gear.

"I saw Abraham on Saturday," Blake ventured.

"O'Meara? He's at Johns Hopkins, right? How's he doing?"

Blake paused. "Not well. They've got him sedated. He tried to attack the nursing staff."

"Shit. Tell Eva. Tell Sarah. It may be important. How are the parents handling it?"

"Not well either. Adrienne is totally wiped out, and Aaron, he's the father, right? Aaron is a little better, but he's still pretty frazzled."

"Anything we can do for them?" Demuzzio had to clear his throat to ask the question.

"I prayed over the lad, TC. Laid on my hands. I felt the Lord move in me. That gave the parents some comfort, I think." Blake studied the man's profile in the lights of the dashboard. "The medical staff is the best, and they know that Novas are different, so hopefully it's just a matter of time before they figure out what's wrong."

"Shit! Tell Eva and Sarah everything you know, and all you heard, every damn last little scrap," Demuzzio grunted, "they may want to bring him here." He turned right off the paved road and bumped down a narrow gravel road. There was silence as they proceeded through a rain forest, a twin cone of headlights bouncing off trees and vines and orchids.

Mr. Bojangles stretched and stood up on the dashboard, and Demuzzio pulled himself up in the driver's seat to see over him.

"Yeah, yeah. Your stop, I know."

They jounced over a narrow wood-planked bridge and Demuzzio stopped and opened the door. The cat meowed once and jumped out, vanishing instantly in the gloom.

"Happy hunting," Demuzzio called after him.

Ten minutes later they pulled up to a cabin and into the covered carport alongside it. Demuzzio rolled down the window and spoke the words that always sounded Gaelic to Blake. The pad on which they'd parked descended into the gloom of an underground garage hollowed out of the old volcanic basalt. They drove off the pad and parked alongside a dozen similarly non-descript 4-wheel drive trucks and SUVs. Demuzzio waved to the armed women across the big chamber, picked Blake's bag from the back seat and walked toward the elevator.

"It always amazes me, TC, the amount of money that went into this, and how little the outside world knows about it."

"Yeah. But old man O'Donnell built most of this thing right after Pearl, when the military was feeling the need for some super-security. Donated it, actually. Then he bought it from DOD in the sixties. Back then there was hardly anybody on this part of the island. Just pineapple plantations and cattle ranches southwest of here. Sleepy little place."

"Modern elevator, though," Blake noted as they got into it.

"Yeah. It's a little trickier these days, but money still talks. And big money yells."

"A quiet yell, evidently."

"That's what we pay a premium for, Pastor Bob."

"This is the only way in and out?"

"Naw. There are a bunch of trails carved out of the cliff. Walk down 'em some time. But this is the only vehicle access."

The elevator door opened to a smiling Eva, holding out a lei. The fragrance of the flowers wrapped itself around him.

O'Donnell Enclave, Waimanu, HI | Monday 2309 HST

"Eva needs to see this," Elia told Sarah, "preferably right now, if we can pull her away from Pastor Bob."

Dinner had followed the man's arrival. There'd been a comfortable sense of normality to it until, after dessert, he'd related his visit to the O'Meara's hospital watch over their son Abraham. That had dropped them all rudely back into harsh reality.

Sarah returned to her laboratory to plug Blake's observations into computer models that almost rivaled Joshua's capacity for analysis. Elia followed her to help, after putting the twins to bed. And now the two of them sat looking at the model results.

"Josh thought it was a possibility, Sarah."

"He never said anything to me."

"His logic lattice couldn't put any probability to it. I think it was more his gut than his head. So he never mentioned it."

"A designed infectious agent." The older woman tapped the screen and it seemed to Elia that the lines in her face grew deeper. "And the Johns Hopkins people never picked up anything in the blood work. Nothing. So it might not even be a virus; might be just some kind of genetic fragment or combination of fragments. That's one devilishly clever agent."

"You need to bring Abraham here, Sarah?"

"Hmm. No. I don't think so. I know more about Nova brain physiology than anyone, but we don't have the equipment, and I'm guessing my immunology background isn't up to their level either."

This thing wasn't developed overnight, Elia suddenly realized, and said so.

"Good point. Years of development, probably. So we haven't kept our Novas as far under the radar as we thought. Damn."

"The disease has got to be something specific to the Nova genetic makeup, right, Sarah? There's no record of any outbreak in the normal population."

"Right. And now I'm really worried. I need to ask Pastor Bob if Aaron or Adrienne were sick. I must be tired. I should have done that."

"We all could be carriers?"

"Exactly."

"If we could isolate the vector..." Elia began.

"Yes. Good idea." Sarah closed the analysis panel on the monitor, clicked on the communication icon and spoke into the pickup. "Eva? Where are you?"

No response came back. Elia toggled the security scanner. The system hunted for a few seconds then a popup screen showed an image of two figures on the beach below.

"Unless she's with Josh, she's not supposed to go without a communicator," Elia began. But then the image showed Eva raising the device to her ear. Her voice was clear enough over the rumble of surf for Elia to detect the irritation. "Yes, Sarah? I'm on the beach. Pastor Bob is admiring it in the moonlight."

"If you can break away, we have some new analyses we'd like to ask you about Abraham...

Eva interrupted. "Analyses? Can't you ask Josh?"

Elia spoke into the pickup. "Josh is still in Los Alamos, Eva." *As you know full well.* "Helping them reverse-engineer that K'Shmar installation the government managed to capture intact. He's flying back tomorrow... unless you want to go pick him up right now."

The girl thought about it. "No. If I bring him back here, he'll go to work. On the airplane maybe he'll sleep. He needs that."

Weak, Eva. You can rationalize much better than that, Elia thought as she let her eyebrow convey that to the older woman.

Sarah spoke more forcefully. "Okay, Eva. But we still need to talk with you about Abraham and the virus, or whatever it is. And some other Novas are showing symptoms. And the GCN is getting twitchy again. When are you coming up?"

"Oh... shortly, I guess." Eva's voice sounded half-dreamy, half-exasperated. Her communicator clicked off.

Sarah raised her own eyebrow.

Elia nodded. "Joshua may need some sleep," she offered, "but I just think she doesn't want him standing between her and Pastor Bob."

Sarah laughed. "No kidding, Sherlock. Actually, I think she finessed Joshua's absence."

"Really? The timing is... oh. She saw some convergence in the variables, and intended the outcome? Tricky to do, when it involves people rather than just natural phenomena."

"She's capable of it, I think, at this point."

"So what's she going to do with Pastor Bob on the black sand down there? *Intend* his clothes off and roll around with him in the moonlight?"

"She probably could do that, I think, at this point in her development. But that would be... coercive, so she wouldn't."

Yes, it would be. But who are we to judge? Elia smiled at the older woman. "Are you sure?"

O'Donnell Enclave, Waimanu, HI | Tuesday 0710 HST

"Nah. She's right here, Carol," TC Demuzzio answered the woman's query. "She's still sleeping. That midnight news about a designed virus, or whatever it is, hit her like a mule kick. Why?"

"Good. Don't let her flit off anywhere in the next ten minutes," the response came back from the National Security Coordinator. "The President's going to launch."

"Launch? What?"

"Missiles. From a Trident. Offshore of Somalia."

"Jesus. The Sword of Islam's in Somalia, huh?" *Eva probably knows that, from GCN anomalies. Why didn't she say anything?*

"Yes. And our intel says they're sitting on a couple more Russian suitcase nukes, maybe four or five, in a deep bunker near the coast."

"Shit! That's gonna hurt Eva. The mass casualties at Vegas nearly ripped her apart." *That's why she didn't. If the nukes aren't moving, they're not a threat. Why risk grabbing them?*

"No real choice, TC. Their stash is too deep for conventional bunker busters, and if we sent in troops to take it, they'd blow their nukes anyway. And our troops with them."

"The Prez isn't worried about the downside?"

"Sure he is. But he made the call anyway. And for the record, everybody here agrees with him. Sends a message."

"Yeah, I guess I agree too." Demuzzio rubbed the top of his head until Carol Violette broke the silence.

"And, TC? He understands Eva's sensitivity. There's not much of a population around that bunker. The Navy has chased all the fishermen out of the blast zone offshore. And we waited for the right weather. There's a strong west wind; it'll take the fallout over the Indian Ocean. A developing typhoon out there will scrub it pretty clean. India won't see any of it. Really, we waited for the optimum conditions. Best we could do. Tell her that, please."

TC Demuzzio thanked the President's NSC politely and set the phone gently in its cradle. Then he kicked the wastebasket the length of his Security Center. *Goddammit! Sure it's the right thing. But it'll give Zurvan another wedge to set back the progress she's made with Muslim moderates.*

He slammed his fist into the wall by the console. *And casualties? The last thing that poor girl needs is another fucking mule kick to her soul. I'd better go wake Sarah.*

Chapter 15

Jebel Uweinat, Libya | Tuesday 2121 CAT

He was growing unaccountably fond of the old Sanusi, Zurvan realized as they talked. The man's near-illiteracy did not occlude his native intelligence. *He asks thoughtful questions, and it is good to have someone to talk to.* He rewarded the most recent question with an answer, putting it in a non-technical context.

"A battle in end-times like these, Muammar, will have cycles, ups and downs, like waves upon the sea. Lately, the accursed Novas have been riding a crest, winning more converts to their falsehoods than we are winning to our truths."

Muammar squinted at the plots the computer had drawn on the monitor screen, and nodded. "But the trend will reverse, Mahdi, surely, in time. It is Allah's will for the end of days!"

Interesting. An uneducated Bedouin grasps the meaning of trend plots on a computer screen. "In time, yes, Muammar, of course. But unfortunately I misread the strength of little Eva's appeal to our more weak-minded Muslim brethren." *And I let them regain the initiative; that was stupid.*

"Shaitan is clever, Mahdi."

"Indeed, Muammar. So, right now, we must begin to reverse his gains. It is time to show the world what these devil-spawn will become."

"Allahu akbar!"

"Tell me what you think, Muammar, after you watch this." Zurvan told the man. "I especially want to know what you feel."

"The Nova boy murdering his family, Mahdi? You have decided to release that?"

"It is time, yes." Zurvan hit the icon on the screen to play his latest construct, watching the rapt attention on the old man's face, parsing his emotional overtones from the baseline of impressions he'd built up of the man over the last few days.

Images of carefully-selected Muslim artwork unfolded and blended into each other hypnotically in the introductory scene. Zurvan's sonorous voiceover began, pacing the images to quotes of the Prophet, a synchrony he'd adapted from the earliest K'Shmar experiments. Muammar began nodding his head with the cadence. Spiritual credentials established, the voiceover slid smoothly into introduction of the narrator.

"This is Muhammad Zurvan. I speak not only from within myself, but from, I believe, the spirit of the Mahdi."

Muammar jumped with joy. "Mahdi! You finally declare yourself! Allahu akbar!"

The man swings between sage and imbecile! Zurvan paused the video.

"Muammar, I did no such thing! Hear me! Such declarations have to be developed with excruciating care." He pushed the man back down into his chair. "Hear me on this! You address me as Mahdi, and yes, I accept that; you are a son of the desert, you may have the true sight. But to the rest of the world, to much of Islam, the Mahdi may be more a spirit than a person. I must be careful, and humble, and let the faithful declare me."

"You are the Mahdi," Muammar said, the light of certainty shining in his eyes.

But a totally faithful imbecile. Zurvan smiled at the thought. "Well. Muammar, please... I would like you to watch this video entirely through, without interrupting. I will ask your opinion after."

"I understand, Mahdi."

"Good." Zurvan clicked the play button again.

"My friends," his voiceover intoned, "I did not agree with the Sword of Islam, nor with their nuclear attack on the United States. But I have come to realize that those martyrs — though misguided — had a sense of the truth of the matter. The Novas, as they call themselves, are not the innocents they would have you believe."

Muammar's face remained open, expectant.

Good, Zurvan thought as his voiceover continued.

"What I am about to show you is terrible. You may not be able to watch. Children certainly should not watch."

Pain and worry chased each other across Muammar's face.

Better yet. When people are already scared of what the Novas may represent, it takes little to make them fear one more thing.

Police file photos of the murder scene came on, gruesome in their detail. Then a video of the boy was shown; he was being interviewed in a police station, matter-of-factly reciting why he killed his parents and siblings, decrying them as worthless "normal" humans. Just trash.

"My friends," Zurvan's voiceover continued with great sadness, "this is true; it was not staged. I have verified it. The authorities in Lebanon have verified it. And the boy has escaped their custody, no doubt using his Nova powers. They have no idea where he is."

Muammar inhaled sharply, even though he already knew the gist of the story, and fear took over his face.

Excellent. When the senses signal danger, the brain loses logical reasoning. You are almost there, my Muammar.

The camera zoomed on the boy's face as he ended his calm recitation. The odd lights that Zurvan remembered so well from his own unfortunate encounter with Eva and Joshua years ago flickered in the boy's eyes.

"Shaitan!" Muammar couldn't contain himself. The video faded slowly to black, the strange eyes fading last. Terror took over the man's face.

Thank you, Muammar; that tells me what I need to know. Zurvan flicked the stop button before the video could replay. *Of course, the boy was not a Nova, not quite, and we had to subject him to days of exposure to the K'Shmar to condition him to kill.*

Zurvan stifled his upwelling laughter and adopted a sad expression. *And afterward my Jaesh had to spirit him miraculously away from the police... but still, it all worked nicely, it seems.* He studied a trembling Muammar.

"Well?" he asked.

O'Donnell Enclave, Waimanu, HI | Tuesday 1017 HST

TC Demuzzio shuddered and clicked out of the internet site — one of many — that carried English translations of Zurvan's short video. *We were doing pretty well with our war of ideas, he thought, and then this. And the fucking thing's gone viral.*

"Gotta have another pow-wow," he muttered, "soon as Josh gets here."

"Absolutely," Sarah agreed, coming into the Security Center behind him. "This is a disaster."

"You think it was faked?"

"I don't know, Thomas. The empathy gene would seem to make Novas incapable of that kind of brutality, but maybe..."

"He wasn't really a Nova?"

"Well, he was starting to show a decent trace on the GCN just as he hit puberty, so he was in transition, maybe a year behind Eva. But... oh, it's so complex, the expression of that genetic sequence."

"You telling me there's gonna be some bad apples, Sarah?"

"We thought not, Thomas. We hoped not. The predictions seemed pretty solid. But Joshua will have to re-run them with some looser constraints on the variables."

"I already have," Joshua said as he walked in the door, "in my head, on the airplane back. And it doesn't change things much; it's still a convergent series. That gene expression should have withstood almost any kind of other influence. But I'll verify that; run the whole genome association on our mainframe."

Demuzzio rubbed his head. Sarah turned up her hands in inquiry.

"So they manipulated this kid somehow; turned him homicidal," Joshua clarified. "It didn't happen naturally, I'm convinced of that. Where's Eva? Does she know yet?"

Demuzzio swung the monitor around so Joshua could see it. "No. She's down on the beach... with her new best friend. Pastor Bob." He rubbed his head some more, looking at the distant figures on the black sand. "Again."

"Tell her..." Joshua paused, "no, ask her... if she would please come up for a Council meeting in thirty minutes."

Demuzzio did that. He watched Eva lift her communicator. She didn't argue. *Must have read my tone.*

"Okay, Uncle Tee. Coming," came out of the speaker.

"I've got the intact K'Shmar transponder that Los Alamos was reverse-engineering; I put it down in the lab."

"Surprised the government let you have it," Demuzzio grunted.

"Pandora's Box, TC. The President ordered them to stop."

"Took it away from his scientists and gave it to you?"

Joshua shrugged. "Lots of them, TC. Only one of me. He's a smart man. Controlling access."

"Trusts you, too."

"Yeah."

"Well, you destroyed it once, years ago."

"Or so I thought."

"This K'Shmar is different, though, isn't it?" Sarah asked.

Demuzzio watched the pain lines deepen around the young man's eyes. *Don't blame yourself for screwing up, bro. Even your mind can't see every possibility.* He put his hand on Joshua's shoulder and squeezed.

"Different, yes," Joshua answered. "Very. The old K'Shmar was a sledgehammer. This new one is a scalpel. Or a better analogy would be a thousand little scalpels."

"It takes longer to carve up the rational forebrain and let loose the hind brain, but it's much more subtle," Sarah guessed. "Harder for anyone to sense their reasoning is being degraded. Insidious."

Joshua stared at her. "Very good, Sarah. Where'd that come from?"

Sarah stared back at him then at Demuzzio. "I don't know," she said, puzzled.

Jebel Uweinat, Libya | Wednesday 0155 CAT

Muhammad Zurvan stood in front of the green screen, focusing his attention on the blinking light of the video camera. He'd positioned Muammar just behind the camera as a target for his monologue, as a barometer for his cadence. *A physical audience makes me even more eloquent,* he thought. He nodded to Muammar and the blinking light went solid. Zurvan lowered his head and studied the floor for a moment, arranging his expression: *great sadness, a tear or two.* When he felt the wetness trickle down his cheek, he raised his head ever so slowly to the camera, to Muammar's face behind it, and began to speak in the high language of the poet Rumi.

"My friends, my fellow Muslims, peoples of all faiths everywhere, I am Muhammad Zurvan. Many of you have heard me speak before." He paused a moment as a marker for the later insertion of an appropriate graphic during editing.

"I have fasted and I have prayed. I have investigated, using all the resources at my command." *Yes, first remind them of your credibility, your integrity, your purity of spirit.* He spoke additional words to that effect, in the proper soothing cadence. Then...

"I have reflected at great length on the crisis facing us in these perilous times." *Second, remind them of their free-floating anxiety, the disruptive threat that a new species represents.* He let his voice grow a bit more strained, and went on with words that would elevate their fear in any language. Then...

"I have concluded that *Nova sapiens* is a genetic experiment, a construct of the West. It is not Allah's will, nor his way." He paused for effect. "Of this I have conclusive proof." *Third, play on their fears. When already fearful about being displaced by a new form of humanity, make them see it as a plot. A frightened brain loses logical reasoning.* He spoke more words, conditioning their thoughts further. Then...

"And worse, I have gathered evidence that the government of the United States has attempted to influence your minds. From a satellite in space they send a beam to distort your perceptions of reality, to blind you to the meaning of what is happening. Some minds have broken under this assault. That is why you hear stories of violence increasing, in all societies." *Fourth, deepen the plot. Assign the blame. Give them a target.* He did that, playing on their predisposition to believe in conspiracies. Then...

Zurvan chose his closing words with care, commanding the look of great sadness to take over his face again, eliciting sympathy for him and his endeavors, another subtle bit of conditioning. "They will hunt me, my friends. They cannot stand the light of truth I shine on their foul enterprise. But the spirit of the Mahdi moves in me; it will keep me safe, Allah willing."

He looked at the camera steadily for a long moment, projecting his intensity into it. Then he concluded...

"These Nova children must be found. They must be isolated and controlled, before their powers develop. At this point, they are innocents; they did not ask to be made into the monsters they will become. I am a man of God. I have children of my own. I wish no harm to come to these Nova children, but if allowed to evolve they will hold you and me in no higher regard than an ant. So... find them, take them into your custody and care, and together we will pray to Allah to determine what should be done."

Behind the camera, Muammar was weeping openly, though he had understood only some of the high language.

Yes, thank you, Muammar, I agree; it was *brilliant!* Zurvan let his intensity bleed away then nodded to the old man to shut the camera off. *No need for another take. A day or two to edit and insert the background and its subliminals, and when* this *one is released we will have seized the initiative completely back from you, my little Eva.*

He turned away from Muammar, fighting to control the laughter so ready to spill out, knowing that the man would interpret his trembling as grief.

O'Donnell Enclave, Waimanu, HI | Tuesday 1409 HST

The Council meeting had been long and intense. Now opinions narrowed across and around the big table, questing for targets. Eva half-listened to them, and half-listened to the commentary of the spirit-Sisters who circled the table in her other vision.

"We gotta find that asshole and whack him," Demuzzio said.

Joshua shrugged. "He's in North Africa, probably, but it's too big a haystack. We need more convergence in the probability algorithms before we stand a reasonable chance of finding him."

"The desert," Sarah added. "Zurvan is... a serpent of the desert."

Which covers most of North Africa, Eva thought, *doesn't narrow it much.* Joshua echoed her aloud. *But the serpent? That's an interesting simile from you, Sarah.*

The Sisters stopped circling and exchanged glances. *Yes it is,* they agreed.

Robert Blake sat in the chair on Eva's right, his long legs stretched out comfortably. *He looks so at home.* He'd taken the seat, normally Joshua's, when her brother had gone to the kitchen to get them all juice drinks. And he hadn't gotten out of it. *Is that a message?*

The images of her Sisters began to dance around her. They shed spirit-petals from a spirit-daisy, chanting merrily. *He loves me. He loves me not.*

Eva glared at the images and forced her attention back to the discussion.

"Forget about finding Zurvan," Joshua advised. "We need to focus on undoing his latest message. Eva?"

"I tend to agree with you, Josh. I don't think the boy was a Nova, either."

"Not a defective gene?" Elia asked.

"It's always a possibility, I guess," Sarah answered. "But it comes down through the X-chromosome, matrilineal, RNA. Very stable."

"Eva? You've got the best inside track on this. Can you tell us how males might be different?"

"Um." Eva let her gaze drift unfocused to the darkness of the rock ceiling above the lights, considering the question. *My Pastor Bob is nearly a Nova, Josh, almost like you. Just a different skill set. Do you know that?*

Though he was two feet away, she felt the man's body heat radiate toward her through the cool dry air of the enclave. She remembered the feel of his hand on her arm when she cried at Zurvan's narration of the Nova boy's homicidal state, how he had occasionally touched her shoulder as they walked the beach. Her skin still tingled in both spots. *And yet he keeps his distance. Why is that?* Her other vision demanded help from the circling Sisters: *read his mind for me, dammit!*

They shrugged, collectively.

We are immanent only in your mind, Young Mother. We see only through your senses or your other perceptions. We have no existence apart from you and our collective memories encoded in your genetic structure. You know we cannot read his mind; why do you ask?

I'm just so frustrated. Eva sighed. *Robert is just too complex, like he's got too many layers or something. I need to peel them away.*

Why? one asked.

Enjoy a little mystery, another advised.

She gave Blake a sidelong glance and wondered if the hunger in the man's eyes was a reflection of hers, or something else. *He's been a widow for a long time. Does he still love his dead wife?* The man turned his head and sneezed into his hand. *Hope he's not allergic to me.* "Bless you," she said.

"Eva?" Sarah's voice brought her back to the question.

"I don't think he was a true Nova, Josh. I agree with your analysis. But... males are funny, you know. Your Y-chromosome has been shedding pieces like crazy, for a long time now."

"Millennia," Sarah agreed.

"Josh?" Eva prompted, as she watched the signature resonance of a logic lattice build around him.

"I gave myself over to the first K'Shmar field in Irian Jaya, Eva. I ceded control to my beast."

"I remember." She watched his resonance overlay with complex patterns. *Grief. Pride. Hurt. Satisfaction.* She felt him brush them aside, to let the lattice run to its conclusion. "And?" she prompted again.

"If a Nova, or a near-Nova, could be persuaded — or conditioned, or forced somehow — to submit to the K'Shmar..." Joshua began.

"How?" Elia asked. "And why would they submit?"

"... because they were deceived into believing the greater good required them to become weapons, is why. How... they believe, so they simply volunteer."

"I think built into the RNA is a shield ..." Sarah began to object. Eva held up her hand and nodded at her brother to finish.

"Yeah, Sarah. For females. And to an extent for males, I guess we've established that reasonably well; but..." Joshua shrugged, "we need to run a lot of permutations on the mainframe. See how big the problem could be."

Eva scanned the faces around her, one by one. *Worried. Josh most of all.*

"And I think there's another possibility that we haven't considered," her brother continued.

The faces waited for the other shoe to drop.

"Logic says Zurvan's next move is inciting a pogrom. Hunt Novas. Destroy them."

Demuzzio began rubbing his head. "Why, Josh? He wants control, power. If he destroys them, he's lost his resource."

"No, he'll try to accumulate a more controllable population. Younger ones. So he's got time to condition them. Make them into his kind of Novas."

"That's not possible." Elia voiced flat denial. "Conditioning can't overcome the strength and resilience of that genetic makeup."

Eva watched tears form in the woman's eyes. *Your twins won't become monsters, no, Elia. There is great strength and protection in culture and nurture. But not all Nova boys have the family or culture of Gaelan and Ibrahim. So there will be problems.* She felt her own eyes start to tear as she answered.

"I'm not totally sure, Elia, but I wouldn't think it could happen in any great numbers. Zurvan would have to pick the ones in stressed childhood circumstances, and condition them to believe all other Novas are a threat. Then they might act defensively." She felt a tear run down her cheek and her voice broke. "Like we do, Josh, when we need to."

Robert Blake reached out and put his hand on her forearm again. It tingled. He stood up.

"I'm sorry, folks," he said, "but I'm not capable of adding much to a scientific discussion. And I really do have to go. My UMC mission in the Philippines needs me there in person to counter some of Zurvan's craziness.

Big Muslim population in the south, Mindanao; they're right on the fence."

Demuzzio grunted and stood. "I'll drive you to Waimea."

Blake gave Eva's arm a gentle squeeze and kissed her cheek.

She managed to damp down a forlorn expression and smile him out the door.

His sneeze echoed back from the long hall outside. *Hope he's not getting sick.*

Hickam Air Force Base, Honolulu, HI | Tuesday 1623 HST

The small UMC jet slid smoothly into the approach to the outer runway that jointly served Honolulu International and Hickam Air Force Base. *I made a plausible exit,* Blake thought, *and it's true enough that we couldn't take off from Waimea's short runway with enough fuel loaded to make Mindanao non-stop.*

"My tracks are covered, I think, Senator," he spoke into the encrypted phone, "thanks for asking." The irony apparently went by unnoted. "What's so urgent?" he prompted. The Senator let the silence drag for a few moments. Blake could visualize the man grinning at him, eyes an empty darkness above his toothy smile.

"Urgent, yeah. Son, so long as you headed in the right direction, you gonna be doin' a little chore for me, awright?"

"What would that be, Senator?"

"You gonna hand off cartons of this virus shit to the Philippine representative of our new bestest buddy... Muhammad Zurvan."

Blake stared out the window as the aircraft banked and the island of Oahu came into view. *Cartons. So they can mass-produce it. Which means I'm just seeing the surface of something that's been a very long time in development.* He controlled his voice. *And he's going to hand it to a radical who could destroy everything?*

Blake fought to make his voice even. "So now we're involved with a power-mad zealot? How's that going to work, Senator?"

"Like a charm, boy. Zurvan is already the devil. So it takes their possible attention off us. Off you. It buys us time, lets us get some control. We're close to an antidote for this little bugger. Some kinda gene therapy. Once we have it, we can do some quid pro quo."

Blake nodded. *Crazy, but brilliant. And if they can mass-produce it, they've already got the antidote. So you're playing me on that one, Senator.*

"We trade lives for power, boy. Like always."

Blake nodded again. *Like always.*

The Senator continued. "And don't worry about Zurvan. He's a tool, that's all. We'll use him then make sure he takes the rap. Hell, he's already ripe for it."

Yes he is, Blake admitted. "So what's my story, Senator?"

"Our friends in the military just delivered the shit to Hickam," the voice explained, "on military transport. It's an emergency delivery of vaccine to those poor folks in the Philippines. Turns out there actually is a flu epidemic there. Bad one. And our military happened to have a lot of excess inventory." A belly laugh rumbled through the phone, oddly distorted by the encryption software. "Doncha love it when it all your shit comes together like this, son?"

Blake probed, looking for weaknesses. "So... since I'm headed that way anyway, I'm just saving the taxpayers a few bucks? That it? What's the story when the people expecting the vaccine don't get it? Hijacked on the highway?"

"Aw, son, you think I'm totally heartless?" Another belly laugh rumbled through. "Half the shit is flu vaccine, half is our virus. They'll get it sorted out when you land. Don't worry about it. It'll happen."

It'll happen, Blake agreed, *just like it always has in the past with your operations. So now you've told me more about how far your reach extends, Senator. Not only the defense and pharmaceutical industries, but into the military, and overseas too.*

"I'm impressed, Senator," he said, and meant it.

"Once you on the ground, boy, the air traffic controller's gonna tell your pilot to taxi to the military side. He'll ask you if that's okay. Tell him yeah, tell him about the mercy mission. Thirteen hunnert forty-two pounds extra weight."

"I'm not sure the plane has the capacity..."

"Sure it does, son. We checked. Think we want five hunnert million bucks of our good hard work fetchin' up in the Pacific?"

"I guess not."

"Just do it, son. Call me when you touch down at Bangoy."

The phone went dead abruptly, and the loss-of-encryption tone followed immediately.

Chapter 16

O'Donnell Enclave, Waimanu, HI | Wednesday 0909 HST

Yesterday afternoon's long Council meeting had never really stopped, Eva realized, it just morphed into an ongoing debate. Council members from different time zones had checked in and out during the night, leaving their ideas, updating them on the pulse of the cultures or communities they monitored. *Too much chaos, Josh says; too many variables, no convergence.* Her spirit-Sisters circled slowly about in her other vision, silent, watching.

She thought about how tired her brother looked, how tired they all looked, and felt an unaccustomed weariness in her body. *Not so much physical, just some kind of reflection of the uncertainty around us.* Her breakfast seemed bland and tasteless as she toyed with it.

"I didn't say it was a good solution, kiddo," Joshua repeated last night's opinion as he entered the kitchen, "I just said it was optimal."

"Optimal. But if we collect the Novas, bring them to safe havens, Josh — like the consensus that seemed to be emerging last night — what does that say?"

"Does it matter? When their lives might be at risk?"

"Sure it does, brother. You taught me that." She smiled wanly at him. "We go by probabilities. Where 'optimal' sometimes means the lesser of two evils."

"I can compute the probabilities, Eva. But these have so wide an error band around them they're practically useless. Too much chaos."

"So where does that leave us? The Council consensus?"

"And your... intuition, Sis." He turned away to open the refrigerator.

"Thanks, Josh." Eva grimaced. *So it all comes down to me.*

Several of her Sisters nodded agreement. *As always it must, Young Mother. You are the One. The Becoming.*

Lives are at stake. Innocents. The unfairness of being forced into such a position brought tears to Eva's eyes.

Her Sisters were saddened but stern. *Fate comes for you, as it will.*

She blinked away tears and her other vision and focused on her brother. "My intuition says leave them in place, Josh."

He turned back toward her, surprised. The pitcher shook momentarily as he poured himself a glassful. His eyebrow invited her to explain.

"I can't explain," she answered. "Other than... tapestries. Or the sensation of threads weaving into a tapestry."

He got a reflective look. "I've had sensations like that. When I was younger."

She nodded. "You told me."

He sat down across from her and sipped his juice, studying her face. "Yeah, so I did. Threads of light, running through my fingers. I was dreaming, or in some sort of altered consciousness state. Nine years old." He looked wistful. "Doesn't happen anymore. Hasn't for a while."

And it won't again. When you hit puberty, Josh, your lovely latticework logic fully displaced it. She smiled at him. *And that's nearly as good, except when it comes to handling chaos.* "I know," she said.

"These tapestries... you see the future in them?"

"No. I see — maybe — possibilities for futures."

He nodded. "I remember."

They looked at each other silently for a while. She watched the resonance of his logic lattice brighten.

"I'm okay with that, Eva. But humor me here... I mean, there are logistical problems with rounding up the Novas and getting them to safe enclaves, but it could be done, I think. Their families, too."

"And what does that say," Eva restated her earlier question, "that Novas are a commodity, to be hoarded? If we start that, governments will follow."

"Might not be a bad thing; it would keep them out of Zurvan's hands."

"A slippery slope, Josh."

"Yeah. Power. I know. But if we leave the Novas in place, the warrior Sisters are spread too thin to protect them all." He sighed. "I trust you, Eva; your intuitions, your tapestries, I trust you completely; I want you to know that."

"Thanks."

"But contingencies..."

"I know."

"Can we have a contingency plan to snatch some Nova kids that we think may be in imminent danger? You and I transpose and get them?"

"Bring them where? Back here?"

"Yeah. We have room in the lower levels. Probably for a couple hundred if it came to that."

"A big concentration of Novas might just make this a big target, Josh."

"So? A suitcase or tactical nuke wouldn't do much, Eva, the enclave is pretty hardened. This was one of the survivability centers during the Cold War. They'd need an H-Bomb."

"Our government has those. A missile. A direct hit."

"Can't do much about that. And it seems totally unlikely anyway." He shrugged. "And *our* hands aren't the wrong ones for Novas to fall into. The President trusted me enough to take the K'Shmar away from his scientists at Los Alamos."

The President, yes, Josh. But I'm not so sure about the rest of Washington. She returned his shrug.

"At this point, you're the only one I can take along for a ride. Because our resonances mesh, or something like that."

"But if a kid was a Nova, or close to it...?"

"Oh... possibly. You're close to being Nova, maybe that's part of it. But I think mostly the ability is just because we... mesh. We have since Irian Jaya. And we have the same mother, that's part of it somehow."

She watched the resonance of his logic lattice wax and wane as it sorted through possibilities but ultimately went down an alternate path. "Tell me about your tapestry, Eva," he demanded. "What is it telling you?"

"This is not a sharp message like you get from your logic, Josh."

"I know that, kiddo. I remember the sensation; just threads of possibilities."

"Okay. Basically, I guess, my instinct is that Novas aren't just some power resource to be hoarded and protected. One of the threads... I mean, what sort of feedback would that put in the genome? What would the second generation of Novas be like?"

"They'd be alive."

"Maybe. But scared? And defensive? That's totally dangerous."

Eva's mind played with threads she hadn't told him about, the dark ones that wove in the tapestry toward possible bad outcomes. *Yes, my Sisters... fate comes for me, as it will.*

Jebel Uweinat, Libya | Wednesday 2311 CAT

"Guard it well, Muammar. No one enters. None from the village. None of your friends. No one." Muhammad Zurvan studied the old zealot's face. *Good. He will do as I command.*

"With my life, Mahdi," Muammar confirmed. "When will you return?"

I'm actually going to miss the old fool. He clasped the man's shoulder. "When Allah wills it, Muammar. The end of days is coming. Who can say where that will take us?"

"It will take us to victory! You are the Mahdi! You will sit with the Prophet and the Christ and the angels, and condemn the infidels to the fire!"

Let us hope so, old man. But you will likely see the fire first. Unless my instincts fail me, Joshua O'Donnell and his friends at the NSA are tightening the probabilities around this place.

"Allah will protect you, Mahdi, wherever you go," Muammar continued. "Allahu akbar!"

It may be quick and clean, Muammar; an airstrike. But more likely a team of their Special Forces; they will want to know what's here. He looked the old man straight in the eyes.

"The enemy may come. You understand what is needed." *An unnecessary statement really; but confirm it for me, Muammar.*

"My village will defeat them, Mahdi. We will feed the infidels to our dogs."

Zurvan suppressed a smile. *More likely your villagers will not hear them or see them, Muammar. Even your wily sons of the desert cannot overcome their technology.* "And should they still come knocking at this cave door, Muammar..."

"I will go to my reward, Mahdi; and the infidel to his hell." He held up the box with the arming switch and red button.

Zurvan studied the lined face one last time. *Yes you will, old fool; as a martyr. And good luck with your seventy virgins.* He drew the man to him, kissed both cheeks and strode out to the idling jeep that would take him southeast to the helicopter waiting in the Nubian desert of northern Sudan. He nodded to the driver and pointed away from the village, silently thanking the Senator for providing the windows in the spy satellite coverage. In the calm night air, he knew, the dust of their passage would settle back to make their tracks indistinguishable from the many others that crisscrossed the desolation. He settled back for the long ride, mentally recounting his preparations.

Tonight, Muammar will release the video indicting the Novas as the cause of the world's problems.

By the time I get to Khartoum tomorrow morning the offensive will be mine again, little Eva.

By the time my swift jet gets to Mindanao tomorrow night, the Senator's shipment will have arrived. He made a mental note. *Have the authorities at Davao delay the American minister's departure from Bangoy Airport. I really must meet this man who conspires with me.*

The moon eased out from under a stream of heavy cirrus cloud, sharpening the rock and shadows of the desert. He laughed aloud. *Two men of God, conspiring to own the power, to own the world. Delicious!*

O'Donnell Enclave, Waimanu, HI | Wednesday 2358 HST

Eva had done what she could, crafting a message to counteract Zurvan's latest. It wouldn't change many of the minds that carried his vision of reality, Sarah realized, but it might change a few. *And a few might be enough,* she thought, *tipping points go one way or the other.*

Eva, exhausted, had gone to bed after taping the message, saying it was the best they could do. Joshua had followed right after, dead on his feet from working three days straight. That left the three of them in the Council Chamber, watching the final edit play through one more time.

"Elia? Thomas?" Sarah asked them, "final thoughts?"

They both shook their heads no.

"It's beautiful," Elia offered, "straight from her heart."

"So was Zurvan's," Demuzzio grunted, "or so it appeared. The lying sack of shit."

Life or death of the human race comes down to competing messages? Sarah shook her head wearily as she fingered her virtual control plane to broadcast Eva's rebuttal across the internet.

"You're right, Thomas. Somehow we need to expose the man for what he is. So that even his believers see his evil." *Saying that for the fortieth time, however, doesn't elicit how to accomplish it.*

"Eva said she had an idea," Elia said over a yawn, "maybe she'll wake up in the morning with a brilliant scheme."

"Let's hope," Demuzzio answered. "We're back to reacting. Puts us in a bad position. I don't like it."

Sarah stifled her own yawn. "Get some sleep, Elia. Go curl up with your husband. Comfort him in his dreams."

The young woman nodded agreement and exited the Council Chamber stretching and yawning. The two remaining watched her go.

Demuzzio tapped the keyboard and his monitor froze the closed-caption translation of Zurvan's speech. He rubbed his head in frustration as he spoke. "I mean, look at this shit, Sarah!" He swung the monitor toward her and tapped Zurvan's words with his finger. "How the hell can anybody believe that if you listen to Eva, 'you invite the devil to play in your heads...'? I mean, that's been a standard of religious fundamentalists for years! And it's so lame! Nobody believes that kind of shit anymore." His finger stabbed at the words decisively. "So that's the area we should attack next. Maybe that's what Eva's idea is."

"Maybe. But keep in mind that sort of exhortation is sound psychology for Zurvan's audience, Thomas. Not listening to the other side keeps their beliefs from getting derailed by any countervailing logic."

"Maybe the unthinking, the uneducated..."

"Much of their world, then." She smiled wanly. "I'm sorry to say."

"So Eva will leave it unrebutted?"

"Hmm? No, but I think she'll be very subtle with her response."

Demuzzio looked at her thoughtfully. "How does a neurosurgeon like you pick up all this psych stuff, Sarah?"

"I'm a Sister, too. Intuitiveness comes naturally to us." *Good question, though.* Sarah took a deep breath and changed the subject before he could pursue it further.

"Look, we've done what we can for now on the message front, Thomas, and twenty minutes ago Carol sent me an email." She pushed a paper copy across the table to him. "There's a bigger devil out there. NIH has got some initial typing results on the Nova virus."

"And it's man-made," Demuzzio guessed, "like we thought?"

"Yes." She felt bleakness twist her face.

"Something else?"

"Other Nova hits are coming up. Early symptoms like Abraham O'Meara. They may be testing it."

"Where?"

"Big cities. Just this country, apparently; not international."

"Jesus." The big man began rubbing his head again. "So it originated here, in this country? The kid in Beirut, the star of Zurvan's last show, the virus didn't get him?"

"Probably not. Looks like Josh was right, that boy probably was subjected to the K'Shmar or some other form of mind degradation. The police there took some swabs; they're headed to NIH now. But I don't think they'll find anything." Sarah watched the big man's mind process that.

"The normal population? Us poor regular humans?"

"Nothing. Maybe some light symptoms, like a cold."

"Shit! Pastor Bob was sneezing when he left here."

"I know. And he did visit Abraham and his parents at Johns Hopkins..."

"Shit! Does Elia know too?"

"No. I decided to let her sleep. Josh, too. They need it desperately. And we don't know yet how the virus is communicated, Thomas," Sara cautioned. "All we can really do is keep a close eye on the twins."

"Infects all humans, but only affects Novas? Isn't that crazy, Sarah?"

"Not really. There are precedents. HIV infections lead to AIDS in humans, for example, but not in other primates."

"And now we're the primates..." He gave her a rueful smile.

Becoming obsolete has never bothered him. She studied the lined face studying hers and the old longing slanted in from an unprotected angle. She returned his rueful smile. *Yes, I love you too, Thomas. I'd like to comfort you like Elia is comforting Joshua.* But longstanding doubts denied that possibility. *There are shadows in my Sister soul that I don't understand, Thomas. I just know I dare not let them touch you.*

Sarah shook off those thoughts and returned to the subject. "And apparently it's not exactly a virus; in some ways it acts like a prion. It was designed. It's clever, it's adaptive."

Demuzzio shook his head. "Designed. Jesus."

"Our knowledge gaps are really large when it comes to the ninety-eight percent of our genome that doesn't code for proteins, Thomas. But that percent doesn't contain just inactive junk genes either; there are plenty of functional sequences in there. We just don't know their function."

"So there's no defense? No vaccine?" His bleak face mirrored her own.

She sighed. "No question there will be. But it takes time"

She watched his face as he reasoned through the implications.

"Takes time to develop a designer virus — whatever it is — in the first place, right, Sarah? And money, too? Big money?"

She nodded.

"So there are major players out there that don't want the Nova evolution to happen. And they've been working on it awhile." His bleak look got bleaker.

"Or more likely they want to control it."

"Yeah. Yeah, I get that. Okay. Go to bed now, Sarah. I'm pissed enough I can't sleep, so I'll start running Josh's contingency plans, see what the Sisterhood can do to get some protection or isolation around as many Nova kids as we can."

She nodded, stood, kissed him lightly on the cheek, and left the Council Chamber, her bare feet silent on the polished stone floor.

Cargo Terminal Warehouse, Davao, Philippines | Thursday 2359 PHT

Restless, Robert Blake paced the floor of the largely empty warehouse. He glanced occasionally at the neatly divided sets of cartons, and occasionally at the close-mouthed policeman standing by the only unlocked exit. *Why would they want to keep me? And why here, with the shipments?* He worked at keeping his expression neutral and controlled the urge to wipe his sweaty palms.

The shipment of mixed flu vaccine and Nova virus had blown right through customs: smiling agents accompanied by smiling doctors just looked at the label on the top of each box and spoke their effusive thanks to the United States and the United Ministries of Christ. Then he'd gone his way, south to the UMC mission, and the cartons had gone onto a truck. He hadn't expected to see them again. He paced another lap around them. Then his cell phone rang, blinking into encrypted mode.

"Don't be gettin' nervous, son," the Senator rasped, "just a little adjustment to our plan."

"Dammit, Senator. I'm in an overheated humid warehouse and I should have been airborne a half-hour ago."

"Now, boy, you a man of the cloth. Don't be swearin' like that." A laugh erupted. "When you doin' the Lord's work." The laugh just as abruptly cut off.

"What adjustments? Something go wrong?"

"Nah. They got the shit sorted. You see them two piles?"

"Of cartons? Yes."

"The original boxes with the blue stickers have the flu vaccine. They're goin' out in the mornin'. The other boxes got our little Nova surprise." Another laugh erupted. "They're gonna be picked up in about ten minutes. By someone you just *gotta* meet, son." More laughter, then the connection dropped off.

Someone I have to meet? Blake flipped the phone closed and resumed his pacing. *My Maker? Has the Senator decided I'm expendable? No, that doesn't make sense; he needs me too much.* He calmed himself by resuming his pacing.

Exactly ten minutes later, a tall bearded man strode through the door. He waved the guard out, smiling a mouthful of white teeth.

"Doctor Blake," Muhammad Zurvan said as he stuck out his hand, "a pleasure to meet you. I'm sorry to be late."

Blake clamped down hard on his shock, and took the hand. *Long delicate fingers, but the grip is strong,* he thought inanely. "Mullah Zurvan. Nice to meet you, too."

Zurvan laughed, showing lots of white teeth. "Questionable, from your expression."

Blake rearranged it to polite neutrality as the man continued.

"How does my person compare to the pictures in my dossier, and to the internet videos, do you think?"

Do I think? Well, the man is a megalomaniac, so stroke him. "You have certain... presence... I think, that can't be captured by media."

"Ah! As do you, my dear doctor... of divinity, isn't it?" Zurvan laughed. "Of course we have a certain presence, you and I; we need it in our business."

"I didn't expect you to pick up the shipment personally," Blake changed the subject.

"Nor did I. But I have a proposition for you. Of which your Senator approves, by the way."

Blake straightened up and forced a polite expression as he studied Zurvan. *He's almost exactly my height.* "And that is...?"

The man's smile widened to show more white teeth, but the dark eyes lost their humor. "I want the girl. I want you to deliver her."

"Eva? Impossible."

"For you? A member of their inner council? One of twelve people she entrusts with her secrets, her life?"

Blake shook his head, but Zurvan persisted. "And she loves you."

Blake nodded. "So she's vulnerable. But there's Joshua, and Demuzzio... and a Sisterhood security detail around the enclave... it's impossible."

Zurvan laughed. "You say it's impossible, but you didn't object."

Blake studied the man, collecting his thoughts. *This is crazy. I told the Senator way too much. And now he's got some wild scheme going with Zurvan.* He shrugged. "I'm not in a position to object to anything the Senator approves of, let's just leave it at that."

"Ah! How refreshingly Western! A politician with leverage on a cleric. In our culture it's usually the opposite."

"I've noticed."

Zurvan laughed again. "My dear Doctor Blake. I don't know what that leverage is, but I can probably neutralize it. And of course I can reward you with money. Enormous sums of money, in fact, outside of any inconvenient oversight of your church or your government."

A shroud of inevitability descended on Blake. *At some point I'll be found out, regardless of what happens with the Senator's or this man's scheme to control the Novas. I'll need to protect myself from that.* It took only a moment to decide to listen. "An interesting offer, and I'd be inclined to discuss it... but Eva probably can escape from any kind of entrapment, I think. So it's still impossible."

"Not so," Zurvan said, dark eyes studying him. "Not so at all. Let me tell you how it can be done..."

O'Donnell Enclave, Waimanu, HI | Friday 1859 HST

The Council meeting ended on an upbeat note, Eva thought with some satisfaction, *even though we're still behind where we'd like to be with the Islamics.* Now she smiled across the dinner table at Robert Blake. He'd appeared unexpectedly in mid-afternoon, en route from the Philippines back to California. He'd come in time to catch most of the Council meeting, and stayed for dinner.

He smiled back at her and shook his head. "No, Eva. I'm sorry. As much as I'd like to, as beautiful as the Bay is in the moonlight, as interesting as our conversations always are... I can't walk with you this evening. I really have to get back to California."

She let him see her face fall. It didn't work. He looked at his watch.

"In the next few minutes, actually. The plane should be refueled and pre-flighted by now. TC, can you get me to Waimea?"

"Aww, I wanted to hear about your trip to the Philippines, Pastor Bob," Eva interjected. "Was it a success?"

Demuzzio glanced at her but answered Blake. "Sure, no problem."

"Thanks," Blake said, standing. "Eva, yes, I'd say it was a success. Some of the mission's congregation was wavering, but my personal appearance backed them away from the edge. And that I brought a big load of flu vaccine from our government probably helped too. They're in the hardest-hit area."

Eva smiled, trying to decode the resonance of the man's biofield, and why it seemed to conflict with his behavior. *He's been a good guest. Attentive. Thoughtful. Helpful in his contributions to the Council. Like always. But...*

"I'm glad it worked out well," she said, standing and walking to him, kissing him on the cheek. The man's resonance didn't change. She stepped back and let him leave, controlling an errant tear. *So unresponsive. Totally frustrating. Darkness around him now. What happened? Doesn't he love me? Did he ever? Or has the evil in the world just caught up and overwhelmed him with grief?*

As she watched him follow Demuzzio out, Eva reflected on her constantly evolving perceptions of reality, and whether those were a help or a hindrance in decoding the complex resonances of life and love. She sent her spirit-Sisters chasing after Robert Blake down the stone corridor, but they returned with no added perspective, just a collective shrug. *We see only with your eyes, we perceive only what you do, Young Mother.*

Eva sighed. None of her genetic predecessors had been a Becoming, a Nova evolving through puberty; only Mary of Magdala had come close. So as much as she asked, and as much as they wanted to, her spirit-Sisters could not predict when or how she would develop. *As a Nova, will I have a universal perspective? Or, like Zen practitioners claim, no need for a perspective at all?*

She sighed again, thinking of the darkness building around the man she loved, seeing its threads reaching out from him, weaving into the tapestry, but unable to see the possibilities they created.

Fate comes for me, as it will.

Chapter 17

O'Donnell Enclave, Waimanu, HI | Friday 2307 HST

The vials of serum sat placidly on the laboratory bench in front of Elia, secured in a holder. *They might represent the end of a species, yet they get just a small standard biohazard label? That doesn't seem right,* she thought inanely.

She'd ridden with Demuzzio to drop Pastor Bob off at the Waimea airstrip, then they'd driven to Kona to meet the government's fast jet and pick up the serum shipment from the National Institutes of Health in Bethesda. She switched her gaze to Sarah, who was thumbing through printouts and diagrams of genetic structures that had accompanied the shipment. For almost five years she'd been Sarah's assistant and student; coupled with her intensive Sisterhood training that gave her more knowledge about molecular biology than most doctoral candidates. She absorbed each page as Sarah handed them to her, flicking her gaze to the vials in between pages. Finally the older woman handed her the last page and rubbed her eyes as she spoke.

"What do you think, Elia?"

"The vials make me nervous, just having them here."

"Live cultures. I know; me too."

"Why did Eva want them?"

"I think she has more faith in us than the government." Sarah patted the pile of printouts. "What NIH does — and they're very good at it — is methodical science. But that takes time."

"We don't have time," Elia admitted. *That scares the hell out of me.*

Mr. Bojangles stalked into the laboratory and meowed loudly.

"Mister Bo agrees, apparently." Sarah dropped a sandal off her foot so the big tomcat could massage himself on it. "And we're probably better at outside-the-box thinking."

"Should I go wake up Josh? Eva?"

"No, Elia. We're much fresher. Let's see what we can come up with first." Sarah spread out the color-coded diagrams on the lab bench and the two women studied them.

Later, Elia broke a long silence, tracing the letters in a diagram. "Sarah, look, that makes sense. It looks like the HAR-1."

"The first human accelerated region?" Sarah flipped through the printouts. "But it isn't, not exactly. Here they're calling it HAR-X."

"That makes sense; it's still in that region of the genome... the part that evolved us from chimps."

"And what is evolving *Nova sapiens* from us." Sarah stepped down from the high lab chair and stretched her back. "But HAR-1 doesn't encode proteins, it encodes... oh."

They looked at each other with widened eyes. "Matrilineal, it comes down through the female?" Elia offered.

Sarah nodded. "Um. And to this the Sisterhood owes its existence, I suppose. Although behavioral and cultural changes probably encouraged the Nova gene along the way."

"Sisters just three generations ago knew nothing about a double helix or the nature of the genome, Sarah. Six generations ago... they barely knew any biochemistry."

"But they knew their ultimate objective. Pretty good for seat-of-the-pants bloodline breeding, isn't it?"

It is, Elia agreed, fingering a vial nervously. *Now tell me what this breeding says about the present.*

Sarah handed her the printout. "It seems like HAR-X encodes an entirely new type of RNA structure. It's still the same 118-letter snippet of genomic code as HAR-1, but twenty-three of the letters are shifted."

"As opposed to eighteen in the chimp-to-human shift, if I remember correctly, Sarah?"

"Which makes it an even more remarkable shift. And it's stable; evolution has made it a positive selection, not just a random mutation."

"In one generation?"

"I know, I know. But... no, it's been around for ages; has to have been, to be that stable. So our ancestors had it, going way, way back. It just got triggered with Eva's generation. Then, boom!"

"Ancestral fragments can be dangerous, Sarah."

"Such as?"

"Evolution taking one step forward and two steps back. Maybe more."

"Specifically?"

"HIV evolved from a relic retrovirus. Chimps still have protection, they don't get very sick, but humans get AIDS."

Sarah patted her hand. "Always the good student, Elia. More specifically? Related to this case?"

Elia thought for a moment. "The HAR-1 is active in neurons that — if they malfunction — are linked to the onset of schizophrenia."

"An inability to distinguish reality, symptoms of ...?"

"Abraham O'Meara. The others too, I guess, from what I hear. So that's it?"

"Maybe. But ancestral fragments also can be beneficial with no downside. HAR-2 gave early humans wrist and thumb development that allowed use of complex tools."

"But still, it's a good place to start, this HAR-X?"

"I agree." Sarah waved the printouts. "This NIH work is very solid, so far as I can tell. I think we just need to accept it and move on."

"To a cure."

"Hopefully. At least to a preventive vaccine or something similar."

Elia held up the first page summary of the printouts. "They don't know the exact form of the virus..."

"...or retrovirus, or whatever..." Sarah equivocated.

"...but they do know the area of the Nova gene." Elia felt a flash of hope.

It was mirrored in Sarah's eyes. "And they think they may have isolated the active site."

"Have they started shot-gunning it with likely protective candidates? Did you ask?"

"Yesterday. And all the big labs are involved, Elia, a massive effort."

"Think they'll turn up something?"

"Inevitably. Method always does."

"But in time?"

Elia watched the older woman's incipient yawn slide into a long sigh.

"I agree with Eva," Sarah said. "We're probably faster at outside-the-box stuff. So... make some coffee and let's get to it."

O'Donnell Enclave, Waimanu, HI | Saturday 0606 HST

TC Demuzzio dealt with the last of the overnight messages on the monitor in his Security Center and nodded with satisfaction. The warrior Sisters of the SIO were doing everything humanly possible to protect the Nova children. According to the polls, Eva's message had been well received and was drawing support away from Zurvan. *A good night,* he thought, *maybe a very good one. So why did I wake up so goddamn edgy?*

He watched his left hand tremble as it reached toward the coffee cup. He raised the cup, inhaled the biting aroma, then put it down without drinking. *Too much coffee?*

Mr. Bojangles leapt from the floor in a fluid motion, walked across the desk and perched in front of the monitor. After one low negative-sounding meow, the cat just sat there regarding him gravely.

"Naw, that's not it, Mister Bo. I drink coffee like water," he agreed, "I always have." He reached out his big fist and let the cat rub his whiskers against it. The contact gave him a sudden insight. *The locus is ramping up, even I can sense it.* The sensation approximated what he'd felt in upcountry Vietnam and Laos many years ago. Not something imminent, like the cessation of jungle birdsong that preceded an ambush, but definitely anticipatory. *The locus. The power. Like at the pool in Irian Jaya. That's what it is.*

"Dammit. You feel that, Bo?"

The cat lay down facing him, Sphinx-like.

"It gives me a bad feeling. Like the shit's gonna hit the fan soon," Demuzzio said as he steadied his hand and sipped the coffee.

The cat nodded. *'Tis probable*, an Irish lilt responded in Demuzzio's head.

His hand shook, sloshing coffee on the tabletop. *I didn't hear that*, he thought.

Ah, but ye did, lad. Mr. Bojangles sniffed at the puddled coffee, licked it, wrinkled his nose and returned to his Sphinx position. *Ye know ye did.*

Demuzzio set the cup down gingerly and stared at the cat. He let his mind replay indirect memories of Hamilton O'Donnell, the reclusive mysterious billionaire uncle of Joshua and Eva who for some reason he'd never actually met face-to-face. *But I've heard the family's stories, I've seen tapes of the man doing his good works in the world. That gravelly voice with the Irish brogue is unmistakable. And Sarah has told me the Sisterhood legends.*

Demuzzio swallowed his disbelief along with the coffee and spoke.

"All right, let's say I did hear that, Alexander Hamilton Shaughnessy O'Donnell. Why now? You've been dead for, what... seven years?"

Death is overrated.

"Your body disappeared from the LA morgue."

So it did. The Sisterhood made it so, bless their good works. My apologies to the coroner, but 'twould have confused the poor man.

Demuzzio struggled with the preposterous. "And now you're a cat...."

A tenant, merely.

The man rubbed his head. "Do I need to speak out loud?"

Mr. Bojangles seemed to shrug. *It better focuses your thoughts.*

Intuition struck. "You've been a tenant in other bodies, haven't you? A bigger cat — Eva's tiger companion in Irian Jaya?"

The cat yawned dismissively.

"Human bodies, too?"

Gracious hosts, all.

"For how long?"

The cat seemed almost sad. *Millennia.*

"We could use some help here, Mr. Supernatural Bojangles O'Donnell."

I cannot.

"Why?" Other memories surfaced, indistinct at first, then crystallized around remnants of conversations he'd overheard Eva have with Sarah and Elia. "Some SIO thing? Called the Covenants?"

Aye, always those. But the convergence of probabilities constrains me now, more than the Covenants.

"I don't understand."

As Eva and the Novas mature, I decay. The new fruit no longer requires the husk.

That concept buzzed around indeterminately in Demuzzio's mind, a waspish irritant.

"Dammit! You love that girl. You've got to help."

'Tis what Jesus said. But I could not then, lad; nor can I now. These threads of probabilities run forward in time and only the child may weave them.

On that thought, Mr. Bojangles stretched and jumped to the floor.

"Where are you going?" Demuzzio shouted.

To the ravine.

"What? What the fuck for?"

To do what cats do for stress.

"Hunt?"

A sense of wry humor accompanied the returning answer. *My host's taste in birds is atrocious.*

"Yeah? What's down in the ravine besides birds?"

Memories.

O'Donnell Enclave, Waimanu, HI | Saturday 0624 HST

Joshua O'Donnell's body thrashed as his mind swam upward toward consciousness. He awoke sweating, dream fragments following him: Mom and John in the ravine, the streamflow pushing the SUV with their unconscious bodies toward the deeper pools and certain drowning. In his dream he couldn't pull them out. *But that never happened, did it? Calm down.*

He steadied his breathing and put a hand out toward his wife. Elia's side of the bed was empty but still warm. He rolled into it, inhaling her fragrance on the pillow. He chased the fading dream fragments a little further. *Something. Oh. Threads, possibilities. They could have died. Another few minutes, probably would have.*

Joshua rolled on his back and stared at the morning light creeping across the ceiling, ordering his thoughts. *But they didn't. Mom and John are safe, down in the vault. Locked in some kind of stasis even Eva doesn't understand. But the locus has them, it's protecting them, nurturing them somehow.*

His mind sent the question into a logic lattice: *how can that be? No breathing, no heartbeat, brains unharmed but in deep comas, bodies that are healthy but need no liquids, no food... how can that be?* The lattice spun its Boolean way downward through years of accumulated observations and hypotheses but came out to the same indeterminate place it always had: *insufficient data.* The only thing that was clear was that the power locus at Waimanu could, when it chose, suspend time. *And what does that say about the nature of our reality?* No logic lattice arose to even nibble at that one.

He threw off the covers and sat on the side of the bed. *Dreams. Did I rest at all?* His body still had the leaden weariness it had carried to bed hours ago. *And my pulse rate is up. Why am I so twitchy?* He suddenly recalled another dream fragment, the tapestry again, its threads weaving toward an outcome. *Mine, Eva's. Elia's, the twins, the Novas, humanity.* Bands of uncertainty jiggled the threads with their harsh resonances. *I haven't had the tapestry vision, this mind-metaphor, in years. Why now?* The uncertainty within those threads rolled across him as the cause of his mental state became clear: *it's not just me; the locus is twitchy, that's what I'm feeling.*

"Elia?"

No answer came.

He stood. Dizziness seized him on the way to the bathroom, then nausea. In the mirror, his face was flushed. He splashed cold water on it. *What the hell? I'm never sick!* He leaned heavily on the sink, trying to control his breathing.

"Joshua?" Elia's voice came down the hall, urgent, the sound of running feet with it.

"Joshua, come quick! Sarah says the twins are infected. And the locus..." her voice broke, "can't you feel it?"

Rage flooded him and twisted the face in the mirror, his face.

"Joshua?" Elia asked uncertainly.

He spun to face her, blades of pure energy rippling from his fingers like fiery claws. She stumbled backward and screamed.

O'Donnell Enclave, Waimanu, HI | Saturday 1448 HST

In her laboratory, Sarah watched Joshua fidget while he watched the gene sequence analyzer working on his blood sample. She put a hand on his shoulder and formed an intention to quiet his mind. It had little effect: *there isn't sufficient channeling,* she thought. *The locus is too... what? Preoccupied? Distraught?* She squeezed his shoulder anyway, for the human comfort of it. Hard muscles tensed and rippled under her fingers.

"We don't really need this, Sarah," he said, "it's obvious I've got the virus."

"But we don't know what it may do to you, Joshua. Or how it works on almost-Novas."

"We know what it did to that kid in Beirut."

"*May* have done," she corrected. "But we all agree it's more likely he got driven into psychosis by the K'Shmar."

"The virus is a plausible alternate hypothesis. Logic says so."

Maybe it does and maybe it doesn't, Joshua. I wonder if your cognitive functions are being affected. She tested that: "Similar behaviors can come from different causes. And so far as we can tell the virus is only loose in the DC area, not overseas. Certainly not Beirut."

Joshua shrugged. "Airplanes, travelers, there's a lot of traffic between Washington and the Mideast. Flu in the past has spread like wildfire."

Sarah shrugged back at him. "You don't have that wide-open receptor on the Nova gene, because you don't have the Nova gene."

"No, but I've got some kind of vulnerability. I can feel it. Sarah, I went through a lot of changes when I gave myself over to the Irian Jaya locus years ago. And I was eighteen, still maturing... so who's to say that didn't create some genetic anomalies? I *was* a Nova, actually, for the time that the locus owned me."

"But you recovered, got control of your mind back. Drove out the demons Eva calls your wolves. Your prefrontal cortex tamed your runaway amygdala."

"Yeah, but Eva did most of that, not me. I was totally lost in the blood-lust. Just like that poor kid in Beirut."

"Still... Ockham's Razor says that boy was a K'Shmar effect." *And you know it does, Joshua. So what is it?*

Unexpectedly, he answered. "What if I turn homicidal?" He swallowed hard. "What then? I need to be gone. Away from here."

"I've got fMRI scans of your brain, don't forget, Joshua. They show hyper thickening in your prefrontal cortex. You'll be able to control yourself."

He looked speculative. "You say that too easily."

"I'm a neuroscientist and a physician," she dismissed his uncertainty. *And a Sister, and Sisters have their instincts.* "Eva helped you before, so did Elia." *And we can't afford to lose you now.*

"A razor's edge, before." His lip trembled.

"What?"

"Never mind, Sarah." He gathered himself. "Let's hope you're right. While Eva and Elia are working on the twins, what can we do?"

Good. Focus on the immediate. Action is a tonic for worry. "Well, Thomas is prodding the government's investigation of who created this virus."

"Tested in the DC area. Where NIH facilities are clustered. They're chasing that connection, right?"

"Right. But that's probably long-term. These people are clever."

She watched him process that for a moment. *Yes, Joshua, a black operation within the government. It will be buried deep; too deep for us to uncover in the limited time we have now.*

He nodded. "Okay. Since the twins have it, and I'm sick, Eva's been exposed. All of us have."

"But there's the good news. Her blood shows some natural immunity; the viruses are getting scrubbed as soon as they attach to the site. Their replication rate has a cap."

"You can tell? For sure?"

"There are some pretty good markers; we've got a quick test. I'm comfortable with that. For now."

"But if it replicates faster in Gaelan and Ibrahim? And I'm a carrier, so what if I start generating like mad? Then Eva's subjected to a heavier exposure. I need to be gone."

Eva walked in.

"Like hell you do," she said.

O'Donnell Enclave, Waimanu, HI | Saturday 2120 HST

Eva watched the three across the table from her. They picked at a thrown-together dinner, desultory. She felt oddly distanced from them, in spite of the deep and abiding love they all shared. *Why is that? Do I look at them from a different reality? Is the locus hyperactivity affecting my perception? Or am I trying to balance it off by being calm and detached? Or am I getting sick too?*

In spite of the urgent, and now personal, threat posed by an infection loose in their enclave, she felt reasonably calm. *Why is that?* Her spirit-Sisters circled around in her other vision, but had no answers either. Except that from the Sisterhood mythos: *You are the One.*

"I don't know what that means," she said aloud.

Nor do we, they replied.

"Eva?" Sarah's worried voice brought her back.

"Sorry, Sarah, my thoughts were elsewhere. Continue your summary, please."

The woman studied her, then nodded. "The good news is — I think

— that the Nova genetic structure is adaptive. It responds to information from outside the organism."

"This isn't anything new, Sarah."

"No, I mean in the short term. The structure learns. It probably can be taught, once the organism develops to a certain point."

"What point? Puberty?"

"My guess is that it's not purely biological; it's some other kind of maturation."

"Emotional? Intellectual? Spiritual?"

"It has to do with the global consciousness, I think."

"A feedback loop from the outside," Joshua expanded.

"I think you guys are right," Eva answered. "That feels right. Only it's more of a pipeline. Or maybe a... tide; it has that kind of cyclical sense to it."

"Like the effects culture or environment has always had on the evolution of all species," Sarah expanded, "subtle influences feeding back into the genetic makeup of individuals, favoring those mutations that move the species forward. But with the Novas it's not millennia; it happens on an individual basis, in their lifetime."

"Then that's also the bad news." Joshua winced as he said it. "Some mutations move the species back."

"Well. Yes, theoretically that could happen with the Novas, I suppose," Sarah acknowledged. "But the main point here is that maybe there's a way to get a message to the right Nova gene, teach it to protect itself."

Eva watched a logic lattice form around Joshua. *Your sickness has dimmed you down, brother, but I'm glad to see your mind is still functional.* "So if it can be taught... how do we get the message to it? Sarah? Josh?"

Her brother shook his head as the lattice glow faded. Sara answered for them both. "We don't know enough molecular biochemistry. It'll have to be the folks at NIH."

"You're better at outside-the-box, both of you." Eva countered, "Elia too."

"Yes, but you have to have a certain threshold of knowledge about what's inside the box," Joshua answered, "and I'm not there. Not at that level of specialized science. Neither is Sarah. Certainly not Elia."

No, you're not, Eva thought. But maybe, just maybe, there are other pathways besides science. Sisters materialized in her other vision, weaving their circle around her. *Yes, Young Mother, other ways of knowing.*

And they would be? Eva demanded.

Uncertainty flickered around the circle. *For you to discover. Only you. None of us has gone so far.*

She nodded, dismissing her spirits, filing their thoughts away for another time. Then she changed the subject.

"Josh, I'm infected, but I'm not getting sick. So my immune system, or *some* system, is keeping up with it but the twins aren't."

Sarah nodded. "They're generally following Abraham's pattern, but I think their connection with the locus is slowing things."

Her brother looked scared. "Let's hope. That's why the locus has gone so antsy, I think. It mirrors some of what's going on in their brains."

"Yet it's not mirroring mine. I know this," Eva said.

"Because there's nothing happening with you, with your brain; the virus is hitting the receptor but it's sliding off or something, sis."

"Is it an age thing or a sex thing?"

"Not sure. And those are only two of the obvious variables."

"How many variables total?"

"Hundreds, probably, within the body and genetic structures. NIH is puzzling some of them out."

"But that takes time," Eva said, looking at Joshua's ragged face. *His Nova sons, my nephews. And they probably don't have a lot of time; Abraham O'Meara is only hanging on by a whisker.* "Elia is calming the locus, Josh, holding their hands; that seems to be slowing the virus down." He looked back at her, lost.

Sarah cleared her throat and spoke. "And NIH says there are exposure factors, same as with any contagion. If you're hit with an initial high exposure — a higher concentration of the organisms — that gives them a head start."

TC Demuzzio, the third member of their desultory dinner group, finally spoke up. "Pastor Bob brought it in, from contact with Abraham. We should have known. *I* should have known."

"Pastor Bob didn't know," Eva said defensively. "And we didn't even know what it was at that point; and certainly not that it was contagious."

"Of course not. But we shouldn't allow him back. We don't know how long carriers will be contagious. He was sneezing and coughing pretty good when I dropped him at the airport."

Sarah shrugged. "Too late for quarantine, Thomas. We've all been exposed. If you're not feeling like a cold or flu is coming on, you will shortly. I know I do." She sneezed into a napkin. "Excuse me."

That seemed to be a signal. Eva stood. "Look, let's get some rest. Josh, I know you're going to sit with Elia and the boys, but if you can sleep while you're holding their hands, do it."

He stared at her a long moment, eyes flickering with the energy of his struggle for control. *Help them*, those eyes demanded.

"I will, Josh," she answered aloud. *I don't know how yet, but I will.* "Sarah, get some rest too. Then if you can relieve Elia in a few hours? Wake me a few hours after that."

"Rotate watches, keep the locus slowed down so that the infection slows down?"

"Exactly."

"Good plan."

Eva nodded acknowledgment, and even as she turned down the hallway to her bedroom began the Sisterhood mantra that would bring relaxation and sleep, even in the midst of chaos. *God, I need to rest. We all do.*

But a puzzle followed her into bed and down into the first level of sleep: *I was with Pastor Bob more than anybody for the time he was here. Close to him. In his space.* That memory lightened her face as she rolled on her side. *The twins hardly put in an appearance at all. So I had all the exposure, they had hardly any.* Her smile faded as she turned her face into the pillow. Something niggled at the back of her mind, but the mantra did its work and she dropped into oblivion.

Hours later, drifting upward into REM sleep, her mind's hands played with the threads of a tapestry that wove toward an uncertain future. The threads sang as she wove options downstream, sometimes a bright major chord, sometimes a dissonant minor key. Her spirit-Sisters wove around her in contrapuntal harmonics. She laughed and cried and debated with them all in turn, ending with the most ancient Sister she'd been able to resurrect from her elegantly coded genetic memory: Mary of Magdala.

A different culture in a different place, Eva admitted; *still... a religion is an option.* Though asleep she whispered to start the discussion: "In your time the earth-mother myth had been taken over by monotheistic traditions with a male-centric god figure."

Mr. Bojangles leapt from the floor onto the bed and watched her attentively, ears cocked forward.

So I see in your view of history, the thought floated back to her from her oldest spirit-Sister, carrying a nuance of uncertainty.

"My view is not accurate?" Eva whispered.

Mary shrugged. *It's not everything.*

"So the Sisterhood has always said," Eva agreed. But then she pressed her: "This is a different time, and the world is a smaller place. More educated. More rational. What's the real danger in this option?"

A cult would form around you. More educated and more rational just means a more dangerous religion. It would grow. She picked the modern word for the concept out of Eva's mind and added it. *Exponentially.*

"Is that a bad thing?"

You know it is. Empires come and empires go.

"Yeah, guess I do." Eva smiled wearily, defeated by her own intuitions: the threads wove that option to an outcome that just pushed the darkness further into the future, and not by much. She let go of them.

"I didn't like the idea of becoming a Messiah anyway."

Mary nodded. *I see that. Jesus felt the same way.*

"A reluctant Messiah?"

Very. But like his namesake your brother Joshua, he was — again came a modern word — *an optimizer.*

"The lesser evil?"

So he thought.

"And was it?"

At the time? It seemed so. The Zealots would have brought Roman destruction down on the entire Jewish population. A firestorm of ethnic cleansing. Loss of essential bloodlines for the Sisterhood.

"And now? With the history you see in my mind?"

Who can say, Young Mother? But the history in your mind says certain cycles are inevitable.

The strands of the tapestry wove on relentlessly in Eva's mind, their threads a complex chorus of many possibilities good and bad. "I'm running out of options," she whispered.

Mary of Magdala's green eyes darkened with sadness. *It is the goodness and love in you that will hurt you the most.*

The mental alarm clock she'd set went off, and Eva stirred and woke up. Mr. Bojangles meowed a greeting.

Chapter 18

O'Donnell Enclave, Waimanu, HI | Sunday 0555 HST

Joshua O'Donnell sat motionless on the lanai suspended from the cliff face. A false dawn brightened the sky in the east, dimming the brilliance of the stars in the clear morning air. His ears pricked back at a soft sound inside the kitchen behind. He smiled grimly. *An animal reflex. My ears haven't done that since Irian Jaya. Right before I killed a whole lot of people.*

"Put on some coffee?" Eva's voice carried out through the French doors.

He stretched out of the lotus position and stood up. With the lapse in focus, his fingers twitched and thrummed with planes of angry energy wanting release.

"Sure," he agreed quietly. The resonance left his fingers.

"How you doing?" Eva stepped out onto the deck. "Your control?"

"I have to watch it every second."

"And otherwise? Your body?"

"I ache. I'm sick. I feel... less capable, diminished." His fingers glowed with anger. "Right when I'm needed the most. I hate that."

"Part of that diminished feeling may be us, Josh."

"Huh?"

"We wrapped an intention around you. A little psychic cocoon, to keep you safe."

"Oh. You mean to keep everybody here safe from me?"

"Oh, you're a spinning buzz-saw, brother, no doubt about that. But no, the intention is to keep you safe from yourself."

A growl came from his mouth, unbidden. "I want to go hunting."

"I know, Josh," Eva replied sadly, "but until the virus runs its course in you, or until we find some way to manage its effects, we can't turn you loose, even on our enemies. Trust me on this."

"So the locus has me in a straitjacket?" Joshua felt the planes of energy rippling through that other dimension, reaching for him, enticing. Little flares crackled around his fingertips.

"The locus is very busy, yes. You, and the twins. We're trying to direct its energy. Which is really our energy, I guess; it's so hard to separate cause and effect."

Joshua felt his ears twitch forward as the coffee machine beeped.

The twitch wasn't lost on Eva. She held out her hand. "Come on, let's get some breakfast. I think I heard TC coming down the hall. Then I need to spell Elia. And you need to go back to bed."

The three of them made breakfast together, then ate food they didn't want but knew they had to eat. The act induced some semblance of normality. Joshua tried to answer Demuzzio's string of questions about the power locus and its protective functions.

"The universe is conscious, TC, and consciousness is self-organizing," he began. "That's the first thing."

"And the locus here, and others around the world, they're focal points?"

"Yeah, a close enough analogy. They're intersections of meridians of quantum coherence around the planet, places where standing waves form. The intersections are locations with extreme coherence in the global consciousness."

"Huh. Okay, what's the second thing?"

"Reality is multidimensional, and subject to intentionality."

"Here? At this locus?"

"Everywhere, actually. But much more... apparent... at a locus. And of course Eva and other Novas carry multidimensionality with them."

The older man rubbed his head while he considered that.

"So why are you asking, TC? You've heard all this before."

Demuzzio nodded agreement, but rubbed his head some more as he swallowed a well-chewed mouthful of breakfast. Finally he spoke.

"I talked to your Uncle Hamilton yesterday."

Eva glanced at him. "Oh?"

"Yeah. Alexander Hamilton Shaughnessy O'Donnell. In his alter ego."

"Mr. Bojangles?" Eva eked out a smile. "The locus is doing strange things, isn't it?"

Joshua looked at her. "I always wondered. But you never said anything, Eva."

"I couldn't, really. You loved your Uncle Ham so much. But at some level Josh, you knew. I've heard you having conversations with Mister Bo yourself."

"One-way."

Eva shrugged. "Oh?" She gave him another wan smile. "Really?"

Demuzzio looked back and forth between them. "Jesus," he said, rubbing his head. "What's next? This locus... does it have a mind of its own? Is it... intelligent?"

"Intelligent? Depends on what that means, I guess, TC," Joshua answered. "Probably not, in the classical sense of reasoning. But it is... aware, would be the best way to describe it."

"It takes on the characteristics of the consciousnesses in its area," Eva added, "it's really a reflection of all of us in the enclave."

"Including your deceased uncle, now a tomcat? Not sure I understand this," Demuzzio said.

"Join the crowd, TC," Joshua answered, "I don't either. Too many dimensions."

Eva saw her security chief wince as he made the connection. "A reflection of all of us. So that means Gaelan and Ibrahim, and you too, Josh. Am I right?"

She nodded.

"And the twins, being infected, are headed toward psychosis. You, Josh... you're worried about control of your own state of mind. And the three of you are "reflections" in the locus?"

Joshua looked at his sister. "Yeah."

"Shit." Demuzzio looked glum.

"It's not that bad, Uncle Tee," Eva counseled. "Sara and Elia and I have formed intentions. Josh is being... helped. The progression of the twins' disease is being slowed."

"Something," Demuzzio grunted. He grabbed a napkin and sneezed into it.

Eva continued. "But that's why the locus has gotten so antsy; why my uncle's consciousness could have a conversation with you."

"Antsy," Demuzzio muttered, "me having a conversation with a cat. Yeah, I'd say that's antsy."

Joshua smiled through his pain. "Uncle Ham was always full of surprises."

O'Donnell Enclave, Waimanu, HI | Sunday 0637 HST

Eva wasn't surprised to see Elia on the bed with the twins, centered between them, holding their hands as they slept. Elia's eyes were closed too, but in the trance that was the Sisterhood's variation of *samadhi*, not sleep.

Sarah shrugged at Eva's raised eyebrow. "A mother. She wouldn't leave them. I couldn't make her go to her own bed."

Eva nodded. "Our intention is holding?"

Sarah looked at the laptop on the bedside table and turned it toward Eva. "I guess. Their immune systems certainly are working overtime. But look, we're just suppressing the symptoms, not attacking the disease."

Without some sort of physical change agent — some kind of antidote or vaccine — the psychic linkages of our intention are only a delaying tactic, Eva acknowledged. *Better than nothing, but a long way from where we need to be.*

Sarah traced the twins' parallel brain resonance patterns on the screen with her forefinger. "And Ibrahim is more affected than Gaelan."

Eva studied the laptop display. "Sarah, am I reading this right? Gaelan is getting entrained in Ibrahim's pattern?"

The older woman nodded. "It seems so. Slowly dragging him down."

"So their mind connection is problematic?"

She sighed. "We could we try to separate their minds more."

Eva winced. "Triage?"

Sarah put on her physician face and stayed carefully clinical. "What the effects of separation would be I don't know."

"They've always been so close," Eva whispered.

"They're fraternal, of course, not identical. I still don't know why you wouldn't let me run their gene sequence until now, Eva."

Because you would have picked up on the anomalies, immediately. But Eva didn't give voice to that thought; she covered it by pretending to study the laptop screen. Sarah conceded her the contemplative time, a little, before she spoke.

"Now I know, Eva," she said softly. "I know. And it explains why Ibrahim is more susceptible."

Eva winced again. "No such thing as a bad seed, Sarah. Not here, in this locus with all of us. This environment is too nurturing."

"Even at eighteen, Elia had enough Sisterhood training to terminate the pregnancy, Eva. Bloodline control is taught even before puberty."

"Punish an innocent for the sins of the father?" Eva shook her head. *Besides, the Sisterhood termination intention would have aborted Gaelan, too. And Gaelan is Josh's. I see why she couldn't do it.*

Sarah sighed, a long deep human sound, her clinician's distance evaporating. "You do keep a lot of secrets, Eva. From all of us."

A flat statement, that; but with no complaint, no lack of trust. Eva raised her eyes from the laptop and addressed Sarah squarely: "I thought it best."

"Elia has suffered a long time."

"*That* secret is hers to keep, Sarah."

"At some subliminal level, Joshua probably knows. Unless..."

"Yes. She did."

"A violation of Sisterhood principles, an intention that keeps a beloved partner from the truth. A serious sin."

"I know. And Joshua being Joshua, her intention would have been overcome by his intellect at some point. So I sinned too, Sarah."

"You reinforced Elia's intention?"

"I did. And the locus has kept it stable all these years. My brother does *not* know that Ibrahim was fathered by Muhammad Zurvan."

The older woman went silent, glancing at the trio on the bed, then the laptop, then Eva. "If we need to triage, knowing that may help Joshua with acceptance."

"We're not going to triage, Sarah. We're going to save both twins."

"How?"

"I don't know. Yet."

"In the meantime, reinforce the intention? Be nice to have a circle of six."

"Josh has to stay away; especially physical contact. The twins would pick up his resonances, worsen their condition. We need a male surrogate. Uncle Tee?"

"Not psychically strong enough, Eva. A fine mind. A fine man. But not ready. I should have spent more time working with him."

"I wish Pastor Bob were here. He could stand in, I think."

"Maybe. My guess is he's strong enough, close enough to Nova status." The woman reached out to touch Eva's arm. "But right now he's back on the West Coast for his Palm Sunday services. This is a big Judeo-Christian week; Palm Sunday today, then Passover, Good Friday, Easter. The projections show his messages will do enormous good for bringing sanity to the Nova debate."

It was Eva's turn to sigh. "Yeah, you're right. But I'm going to call him anyway. Maybe there's some way he can squeeze in a visit. For this morning we'll do a circle of five, like before. I'll be the focal point, taking Elia's place between the twins. This time, Sarah, I want you to take Ibrahim's hand, not Gaelan's."

"I think I have a better connection with Gaelan."

"No you don't," Eva snapped. Sarah's eyebrows shot up. *Shit! That was too emphatic. Sarah picked right up on it. Now she'll think about it, and about my secrets; then maybe she'll get serious about dredging up those memories the locus and I blocked away from her fragile mind. Shit!*

UMC Headquarters, Anaheim, CA | Sunday 1357 PDT

Pastor Robert Blake sat in the solitude of his inner sanctum in southern California, thinking hard, sketching strategies and timelines on a big pad. He tore off the latest and set it beside the others on the conference table, then walked around studying the sketches in turn. *Convergence. Fast, too fast. Pretty soon I'll have no way out. I have to act.*

He gathered up the papers and began feeding them to a shredder, trying to find something more positive to reflect on. The morning service had gone well, he thought, and his Palm Sunday simile was brilliant. *I gave myself the latitude to reverse position on the Nova issue if I need to, and no one even realizes that; they just think I'm being even-handed. Ecumenical.* He laughed harshly as the last paper went into the shredder. *Maybe the Senator was right; I should have been a politician.*

His cell phone beeped the pattern for an incoming encrypted call. He looked at the security code and exhaled. "In the morning, God; in the afternoon, the devil." He thumbed the accept button.

"Nice homily this mornin', Pastor Bob. Good bookend to the meetin' you had with our new mutual friend last Thursday," the Senator's voice said. "Heard all about it."

"Zurvan's plan is crazy."

"Crazy enough to work?"

"I'm thinking about it."

"Well you best git to thinkin' harder. Time's a-runnin' on us, boy; I can feel it."

Blake said nothing.

"T'were done, t'were best done quickly," the Senator quoted.

"Shakespeare, Senator?"

The man guffawed. "I ain't no backwoods hick, son."

"No, you're not, Senator. Far from it." *And even though you misquote Shakespeare, you certainly are a verbal chameleon, with a dialect of the moment. Any one of a dozen, in fact. Why you always choose your screwball hillbilly persona with me is a total mystery.*

The Senator chuckled, tinny and hollow in the encrypted transmission; then he spoke almost kindly. "Son, they ain't no backwoods hicks over in Hawaii, either. My read is you better get your ass over there and carry out Zurvan's plan before they start to figger things out."

"Right now they're preoccupied with the infection. It probably is a good time," Blake agreed. "But I've got a Church to run, and this is a big week coming up."

"Yeah, yeah, I see your problem. Listen, I ain't a member of that Nova Council, Pastor Bob. You got a better sense than I got about timin'. So you gonna have to make that call. But make sure you get it right, because it's your ass in the sling." The Senator guffawed again. "Keep me posted, boy." He clicked off abruptly.

Blake put the phone down and walked over to the window. The bright afternoon sun through the clear air painted a sharp shadow of the temple's cross on the grounds of his church. A dim reflection of his face looked back at him from the glass, gaunt from the dehydrating effects of the virus.

I never told you about the Sisterhood's warrior cadre, did I, Senator? A word to Eva or her brother and you're history. They'd go through your security people like shit through a goose. So unfortunate Joshua is so smart that I can't make that happen without implicating myself.

He walked back to his desk and studied the statistics downloading to his computer from the enclave's global consciousness monitoring network. Joshua had tagged the latest plot with a brief message: *A lot of convergence. Things are coming to a head. Global consciousness is anticipatory. Some key event is imminent.*

"That it is," he agreed, "my very problem." Easter Sunday was a week away. He clicked the download to run in the background and brought up his schedule for the week. *Doable*, he decided. And Eva had asked him to come, practically begged. So he wouldn't be overtly insinuating himself; he'd just be doing his Christian duty to comfort the afflicted. No suspicions raised there.

His words echoed back at him: *In the morning, God; in the afternoon, the devil.* "And then, Eva," he said softly, "there's you." He picked up the phone to call the enclave.

O'Donnell Enclave, Waimanu, HI | *Sunday 1110 HST*

"Sure, no problem," Demuzzio told the image of Pastor Bob on his monitor, "just let me know your ETA once you get organized."

"I'm sorry, TC," Blake offered, "I couldn't be sorrier." The image's expression was truly woeful.

"Look, don't worry about it. You didn't know it was contagious; we didn't know. And we probably should have. Water under the bridge. We just go on from here," Demuzzio told him brusquely.

"If I show up there now I'm not a hazard?"

The man looks like my sister's beagle the time she threw him out in the rain, Demuzzio thought, and softened his voice. "Sarah says no. And Eva wants to see you. That's good enough for me."

"I won't make anyone worse?"

"Nah. We all feel like shit, but the twins are the only ones in imminent danger."

"Eva? Joshua?"

"Eva's actually got the fewest symptoms. Josh is screwed up, but the ladies and the locus are shielding him somehow."

"Shielding him?"

"No idea how, Bob; it's way beyond me. But it's slowing the twins' slide, too." *And there's some other crazy shit going on here,* Demuzzio thought, but didn't offer it to the man's confused expression. *Be nice to have a visit by a normal human being from outside, actually.*

"Okay, TC. Thanks for your kindness. Please tell Eva I'll be there as soon as I can re-arrange my schedule." The minister nodded and his image blinked out.

Demuzzio turned to the big tomcat sprawled on the Security Center console observing the exchange.

"And speaking of other crazy shit... we on speaking terms again, old man?"

Mr. Bojangles stretched and sat up and meowed.

"That's affirmative?"

Gray eyes flickered erratically with a shimmering pattern of light. Demuzzio pushed his chair back from the console and studied the cat.

"I know I'm repeating myself, but we really could use your help here, Mr. Bojangles O'Donnell."

If a cat could appear thoughtful and sad, the big tom achieved it. "And fuck your Sisterhood Covenants," he added. "You've broken them before. Josh told me."

The response seemed to come from some great mental distance, as if sadness degraded its strength. *I had more latitude then.*

"Why not now?"

Convergence. Constrained probabilities. And my presence in this reality is wanin'. As I explained.

Demuzzio rubbed his head then slammed his hand on the console. "You're fucking useless."

Aye, lad. How I feel, too. The cat rose onto all fours.

"So why are telling me this shit?"

I owe it to ye, lad. Mr. Bojangles jumped down off the console. His parting thought slid into oblivion in Demuzzio's mind as the cat padded out the door.

Demuzzio slammed his hand down again. Then he forced calm on himself as he answered the next call. The image of Carol Violette came up on his monitor screen.

"How's my favorite National Security Coordinator today, Carol?"

"Shitty, TC."

He felt his forced grin evaporate, and groaned. "Tell me."

"The tide has shifted, I think. Parts of the third-world, particularly Islamic parts, are going to hell in a hand basket. Zurvan is making real inroads with us nuking Somalia. He twisted it brilliantly."

"Does that matter?"

"By itself, maybe not. But there are more reported atrocities by young Novas, and all their spin-doctors and conspiracists... and Jesus, we really need Eva to put out a brilliant counter."

"Eva's running on empty, Carol. The twins, Josh... that's where her focus is. Where it has to be."

"I know, TC. I know." The classic planes of the woman's face showed the hollowness of fatigue as she looked down at some papers. "Look, we know you guys are preoccupied, so we've put together a script. If she could tape it and get it on the news channels and the internet, we think that would help. Or something like it; we're not trying to be directive here."

"Sure, Carol; download it. I'll see what we can do."

The woman's hand moved off-screen and the incoming secure transmission icon blinked on Demuzzio's monitor. "Got it," he said. "Anything else?"

"I know how busy Sarah and Elia must be with the twins, TC. But can you pass some stuff along to Sarah when she has a breather?"

"Sure. Shoot it to me."

The NSC's hand went off-screen again, and the transmission icon on Demuzzio's monitor lit up again as she explained. "The feedback we're getting from NIH is that there's a window of maximum susceptibility to the virus, because of how the gene gets expressed."

"That's new. An age window?"

"Yes. Between six and maturity for boys. Narrower for girls, maybe nine to puberty. And the gene structure itself in girls seems to provide them a bit more protection."

"So that's why we're only picking up male cases?"

"No longer true, TC. As of last night. Check your global consciousness network. There are some female cases now. Not many, but enough to indicate an infection trend."

"Eva's well into puberty. That's why she hasn't caught it?"

"It's probably not that she's immune... she actually must have the virus in her system. She's just less susceptible to its attack."

"Heavy exposure could override that?"

The woman sighed. "We don't know."

"Thanks, Carol," he said dryly. "Anything else?"

Her hazel eyes studied him. Her face seemed to become more wearied. "Ah, TC. That's enough, don't you think?"

He nodded.

She nodded in return and clicked off.

Demuzzio scanned the downloaded infectious disease data from NIH and shook his head. *The world outside is going to hell. We're not doing much better in here. Gaelan and Ibrahim may be dying. Josh is sick and may be dangerous. The locus is going nuts. Eva may be at risk. And the architect of this whole bloody mess is now a fucking cat who can't help. Jesus!*

O'Donnell Enclave, Waimanu, HI | Sunday 1616 HST

"Elia," Eva probed gently, "your opinion, please." Her sister-in-law's haggard face looked back at her, helpless.

"You could die," she whispered.

So I could. The thought hung starkly in Eva's mind. She glanced at Sarah's troubled face, then re-focused on Elia.

"I cannot ask you to do this thing," the woman sobbed. "The Novas, their future..."

Eva made her voice calm and soothing, giving them both some space. "But we agree that the intention cannot hold. In spite of our reinforcing it this morning, the virus is winning. Sarah, do you concur with that?"

"Yes," the older woman croaked, clearing her throat, "I do. But we could wait for Pastor Bob; try the reinforcement again, with him as a sixth."

"I cannot fetch him by transposition. And nothing else is fast enough; the twins will be irretrievable if we delay any longer. We've been over this."

Two agonized faces silently acknowledged that truth.

Eva went on, bending them to her relentless logic. *I learned at my brother's knee.*

"And we will not sacrifice Ibrahim to save Gaelan. We are agreed? Then this is the only way?"

"You could die!" Elia wailed.

"I *could*. Your twins *will*."

"Joshua..." Elia began.

"We'll leave him a note," Eva said firmly.

"The craziness in the world outside..." Sarah began.

"I've taped the message. Uncle Tee can send it to Washington. They can get it out just as well as we can. It's a powerful message. It will buy us some time, I think, while this happens."

"It's never been done. It may only be a legend," Sarah objected.

"Not true. Mary of Magdala did it."

"Two thousand years," Elia whispered.

"Yes," Eva agreed calmly. She penciled a note for Joshua and taped it to show through the glass door of the infirmary as she instructed the two women. "We'll do it right here, so we can stay with the twins. Elia, get the mattress off that other bed. Put it in the corner, so they can see from the door that we're okay."

Eva's spirit-Sisters spun around her, the dissonance of their own sharply divided opinions and loyalties washing over her. She ignored it.

"Sarah. Get the syringe. Please."

Eva thanked her spirit-Sisters for their disparate views and pushed them off to a distant part of her mind. She sat on the mattress in a lotus, her back braced in the corner, composing her thoughts, her arm bared for injection of the virus.

As Sarah slid the plunger down, Eva fixed her gaze on her twin nephews in the bed across the room. *I intend to fix you guys pretty soon. I just have to get my body and the locus to manufacture the right antibodies. Hang in there.*

Elia and Sarah sat on the mattress beside her and joined hands. They picked up Eva's ancient Sisterhood chant, the one that would lead Eva to the no-place and no-time of the null state. *I will become one with the locus. There, neither time nor space will matter.*

In her expanding consciousness, Eva heard the dolphins offshore of Waimanu Bay. They sang to her.

Chapter 19

O'Donnell Enclave, Waimanu, HI | Sunday 2211 HST

These women make me nervous, Robert Blake thought as the SUV jounced down the old logging trail in the dark, *and I pray to God the Senator has some high level talent to neutralize them.*

"So, Marta, how is it that there's such a small security force here? I would've thought... given Eva's growing public visibility..." he let his question trail off, open-ended.

His driver glanced at him and shrugged. "That's how Eva wants it, Dr. Blake."

"And you haven't had a problem with visitors? Autograph hunters? Nut cases?"

"No, not really. The general public really has no idea where the enclave is. 'Somewhere on the Big Island... maybe' — that's the typical guess."

"But a few people must have figured it out."

"Sure. But there's a checkpoint at the highway turnoff; the Army stops most of them."

"I never saw the checkpoint."

"You wouldn't." She gave him another quick glance and a half-smile.

"Ah. They recognize your vehicles, stop all the rest?"

She nodded. "Your tax dollars at work."

He laughed. "Worth every penny. So, no vehicles, but still a few visitors? On what, foot, helicopter...?"

Marta slowed the car as they passed over the bridge and studied him for a long moment.

"Oops, I'm sorry..." Blake offered, "...if I'm prying into security areas. I'm just curious. And concerned, of course."

She eased the SUV off the bridge as she answered. "No problem. Eva's standing instructions are to answer any question of any Council member."

"That's interesting."

"Drives TC a little batty. He worries about a Councilor getting abducted and squeezed for the information." She gave him a wry smile. "But to answer your question, yes, we get an occasional hiker. If they get as far as the enclave upper entrance we just escort them out; no harm, no foul. The Army talks to them; cites the Patriot Act. We haven't seen any come back."

"Don't you worry about — how do I say this — more troublesome visitors? I mean, for instance if one has grabbed me and pulled out my fingernails to make me cooperate?"

"I do. TC does. But it would take a very good sapper team to take out the Army patrols and get to us. And even if we're all taken out, no one can get into the enclave itself, either from our surface entrance up here or the trails from the beach or around the cliff."

"No one? Really? How?"

"The locus stops them."

"I'm confused, Marta. I come and go at will. No ID, no keypad, no retinal scan, no nothing."

"Eva has keyed your consciousness to the locus. You have access."

"Oh. The ultimate security check? So if I'm being pushed along, a gun at my head, missing all my fingernails, the locus will let me in but hold my captors back?"

"Exactly."

"Wow. How does it do that?"

"I'm not sure. The force is not so much physical as it is psychic, I think. But the effect is physical; it stops people cold. We tested it out on a few of the Army guys."

"Stopped them cold?" He let the wonder run through his voice, and wasn't faking it.

Marta nodded. "So it's the ultimate escape hatch, too. Keep that in mind if you're ever in a hostage position. Of course, when your captors discovered they couldn't come along, they might still shoot you from a distance. The locus can't work on a bullet."

She gave him another half-smile. "So if it should ever come to that, Dr. Blake, get through the portal fast; then go around the corner to put a solid wall between you and whoever wants to shoot you. Joshua actually re-engineered both entrances with that in mind. I'll show you on the way in."

Minutes later, the hydraulic carport pad lowered down and they drove into the garage bay. Across it next to the guard room was the portal leading down to the enclave. He replayed his prior entry over in his mind and nodded. *Concrete walls, thick, a left and a right and a left before the elevator. More recent than the rest of the government's Cold War construction project.*

He smiled at the woman as they walked unhindered through the portal and his recollection was verified.

"Good information, Marta. Thank you."

She smiled back as she set his bag on the elevator floor and pushed the button for him.

"Enjoy your stay, Dr. Blake."

Abu Sayyaf SH, General Santos City, Philippines | Tuesday 0416 PHT

Muhammad Zurvan stood beside the rear window of the Abu Sayyaf safehouse. From the darkened room he contemplated the tall spire of the new mosque in the distance. A clearing in the clouds let the light of a waxing moon set the spire's brightness off against the rusted steel roofs in the middle distance. He contemplated it as he considered the questions posed by the three young men, citizens of the United States, poised to do his bidding.

One of them coughed politely into the long silence.

"Mahdi?" Another one finally queried.

Zurvan held up an index finger, his back still toward them, his gaze still out the window. *Let them steep a little longer in the nimbus the moonlight casts around me. Their malleable minds will make it a sacred thing in the reporting, later.* He smiled at the moon but suppressed a chuckle. *Of such small things is godhood born.*

"Patience, my young zealots," he instructed softly without turning, "these are complex questions; I commune with the Prophet for his counsel."

Their audible intakes of breath made him shudder with the strain of repressed laughter. *And they will report that as my body trembling to the touch of Allah, no doubt.* He breathed slowly, controlling his mirth and returning to the questions at hand. They were indeed complex. *I must come out at the end as a savior, not a destroyer. So the K'Shmar devices cannot be my doing. Care is required.*

"Yes," he finally answered," we will deploy all the remaining devices. Do it quickly. Place them in populated areas where the enemy cannot target them from space without collateral damage."

"They will come with police and soldiers, on the ground, Mahdi," the most analytical of the three observed, "and destroy them anyway."

"Of course. But that is the point. It will take them time; it will cause chaos. Chaos is our friend in this struggle, my *Jaesh*. We cannot do outright battle with the enemy. Not yet. Ours must be the most subtle of guerilla warfare."

"Then are we to release the rumor-enhancers embedded in the K'Shmar signal, Mahdi?"

"Yes, absolutely, enable that software as you turn them on. The people in your adopted country do not trust their government. And many are receptive to conspiracy theories. Start the rumors on your internet blogs simultaneously."

"It seems so quick, Mahdi," the youngest of the three asked, "are the end times upon us so soon?"

The man met his gaze for a moment then looked at the floor. Zurvan studied him, then the other two in turn. *They are not stupid, just blind.*

He ignored that question and continued. "Blame for the technology must rest with the West, my *Jaesh*," he continued. "So we must make the K'Shmar their own weapon. You know the story. Invented at MIT. Used secretly by the government for years to control its citizens, manipulate markets. Tell that story in the blogs."

"After they have destroyed all the devices, Mahdi, we will have only the virus as a weapon against the cursed Novas. It seems like we are using our ammunition too fast."

"A fair objection. But no; we are not. To answer your earlier question, the end times are indeed upon us. A matter of months, maybe only weeks." *And maybe even sooner. I feel the convergence, I can smell the blood coming, almost taste it.* "You have given the virus to your brethren? They are releasing it in the designated areas?"

"Yes, Mahdi."

"Good. Then all is well, my *Jaesh*. On this K'Shmar activation, do as I say, and do not concern yourself with timing. Trust in me, in the Prophet, in Allah. All will be well."

"Allahu akbar," the three shouted in unison. They raised their eyes to his, and Zurvan saw the glitter of the fanatic. "Allahu akbar," he echoed softly.

O'Donnell Enclave, Waimanu, HI | Monday 1512 HST

Almost a full day had passed since the three Sisters chanted themselves downward into the null. Now, Eva floated outside the box of her physical brain, her mind entangled with aspects of Sarah's and Elia's in a triune identity. *But not a complete triune,* she had advised them as the chant worked its magic, *you are unique individuals and must not be subsumed in me.* She had formed the intention, precise in its scope and clarity, to prevent that very thing. *Besides,* she'd said as they watched their protection take form, *we all have our secrets.* Under better circumstances that might have been funny.

The part of Eva's mind that was an aspect of Elia chased backward in time, seeking the memes that had converged to affect the *Nova sapiens* genetic code. They jointly sought clues in the interaction between mind and body.

"The virus is a biological problem in a physical body, Eva," Elia had objected before they started, "and memes are genes of the culture, not the body. Why seek answers there?"

"There are feedback loops."

"Yes, agreed, but they operate over generations."

"They used to. Now they're faster. The internet."

"Still... I think you would be better served if I helped Sarah on the biological side..."

"No, Elia. Trust me on this. You have an awareness of these feedback loops that transcends the limitations of perspective. A feeling for it, intuitive and deeply instinctual. Sarah doesn't have that; she's much more scientific, rational."

Elia had struggled, then agreed, dubiously. Together they now chased down the labyrinth of cultural ideas that mold the present realities.

Simultaneously the second part of Eva's mind, the part that was an aspect of Sarah's, studied the changes the virus was wreaking in her own body. Eva felt that damage in a distant way, and with Sarah's help tried to parse the meaning of what she felt into a biochemical context. Useful hints were developing.

"The *Nova* gene has a designed weakness, doesn't it, Sarah?"

"I think so."

"Why? And by whom?"

"A failsafe, probably. Ask your Uncle Hamilton."

"A failsafe for what?"

"If the Novas turn to the darkness, a way to reset evolution without destroying civilization. I presume, anyway."

"A safety valve in case the *Novas* are a destructive aberration... okay, but we know that's not going to be the case, don't we?"

"Now we do, Eva. But the Nova mutation is old, millennia. Who could know, then, how it would evolve?"

"And the memes, the culture, could have fed into its development, in ways both good and bad?"

"Exactly."

"That's what Josh said to me one time."

"He was guessing, but then he's good at that."

"He gave it a high probability, Sarah."

"Then he experienced it personally, no doubt," the woman's consciousness responded.

No doubt at all, Sarah. You saw Joshua's primal darkness first hand, though you don't remember. Eva suppressed the thought before it could escape, and pursued her inquiry. "A created vulnerability I understand, I guess. But who recognized it? Who was even looking?"

"You know the answer, Eva. It's always the same."

"Power. If you can destroy a thing, you have control."

The older woman's long sigh pervaded their shared consciousness. "It doesn't matter, really. What we have to do is find an antidote or a vaccination. Or both, preferably."

"Change the lock, our *Nova* gene, so their key no longer fits?"

"Or ambush the key before it enters the lock."

"So how can we ambush it with cellular effects?"

"I don't know. But we need a genetic solution."

Eva Connard drifted in the null, aware of many realities but owned by none. The third part of her mind, the part solely hers within the triune, queried her spirit-Sisters as they spiraled around her.

"What stopped the *Nova* development in the past? The golden age of Greece, there was a moment... And before that, in Egypt with Nefertiti, another... What happened?"

"Too many gods," one Sister opined.

"What you now call the memes... they were confused," added another.

"Insufficiently focused," amended a third, "to create the feedback loop that would generate a clean Nova strain."

"You knew that then?" Eva was surprised.

"No, Young Mother; in the past we were stumbling along, following only general principles of breeding and knowledge of bloodlines."

"But you know it now."

"We see it in your mind, how it has come together in your present."

"It happened before. Or it came close. Jesus of Nazareth."

"Jesus was a surrogate. Mary of Magdala had the power."

Eva focused on one of the spiraling white forms, calling her to the fore. "Mary?"

"The meme was not right for a woman," Mary of Magdala answered. "The Jewish culture of the times, its predecessor Egyptian Christos myths, all demanded a man as savior."

"So you gave him your power?"

"I acted through him."

"Did he know that?"

"Eventually." The woman seemed sad. Eva shifted gears.

"You weren't ready yourself?"

"I did not have your power, Young Mother. Nor did the Magdala locus have the power of this one. Nor did I have your confidence."

"But my Uncle Ham took your hand."

"The priest I knew as Melchizedek, yes."

"And you and he worked out the plan with Jesus?"

The woman almost smiled. "It seemed like a good idea at the time."

"It violated the Covenants."

"So I see now, from the hindsight of your mind in your time. The present always is more clear once it becomes the past."

"You could have been the One of the Sisterhood myths. But you failed, and the Covenants suppressed the Nova gene for two thousand years." Eva laid it out as a blunt truth. *And one that I'm stuck with.*

Mary nodded agreement. "Many generations, I see. Until your mother and father passed the Covenants' monkey trap test, and conceived you."

Eva toyed with an intuition, a distant mental itch. *That past plays into this present somehow,* Eva thought to herself, *and Mary's history has a lesson for me. If Elia and I can figure out what it is. Reconfiguring memes, somehow.*

"Did I fail?" Mary continued, picking through the history in Eva's mind. "No... you are my daughter, many times removed. And what is time to the dead? The potential was preserved, the Nova bloodlines."

Eva felt Sarah's consciousness summoning her back to their triune state. She thanked the circling forms.

"Making progress here, my Sisters."

The cold reality of the virus ravaging her body displaced the warmth of her matrilineal line as she dismissed them. Their composite concern chased after her.

"We hope you make enough of it before you die, Young Mother."

O'Donnell Enclave, Waimanu, HI | Monday 1810 PDT

"Are you sure they're okay?" Robert Blake switched his gaze back and forth between the two men. "Over a day now? Why aren't their muscles cramping? Why isn't their blood circulation screwed up? Why... I'm not a doctor, but why..."

Demuzzio shrugged, with the wry look of a man who has seen many mysteries and understood none. Joshua answered.

"They've put themselves in the null state. Time has no meaning for them."

"For their minds, okay, I can see that. But for their physical bodies?"

"Autopilot, I guess. Something like that. Their autonomic systems are slowed, but the locus is managing muscle tone and peripheral blood flow. Or I assume so, anyway; you can see contraction ripples periodically." Joshua gave the same shrug as Demuzzio. "Look, I've got to get back to the twins,

Bob. Head to the kitchen; TC will get you something to eat. I'll join you later."

"Can I do anything for them? I feel useless."

"Pray, Pastor Bob."

Blake let himself smile. "I thought you were agnostic, Joshua."

"Only with respect to your version of God." The young man smiled wanly back at him, squeezing his shoulder as he left the room. "Pray, Bob. It can't hurt."

Later, chewing a sandwich provided by Demuzzio, he contemplated the uncertainties. *So, do I act tonight? What would happen if I did? What would the locus do? What could it do? Is my free pass enough to get me out of here carrying Eva?*

Demuzzio came back into the kitchen, sighed tiredly and pulled up a chair. Blake picked up the thread of their earlier conversation.

"So Eva is safe, TC? And Sarah and Elia? There's no danger in this null state?"

"Not from the null state itself. I've seen Eva go there before. From the virus, yeah; that could kill her, I guess"

"We can't bring her out of it? This null state? Maybe I could talk her into going to a medical facility."

"I don't know. Maybe. But we're not going to try. She left very precise instructions."

"She's fifteen! Does she know what she's doing?"

That got a tired guffaw. "If she doesn't, Pastor Bob, then sure as shit none of the rest of us do."

"Still, I'm worried, TC."

"Yeah. Me too, a little. But Eva knows what she's doing."

Demuzzio contemplated the last of the sandwich and turned toward the refrigerator. Blake's soft reply stopped him.

"My wife was in a coma for two weeks before she died, TC. She looked okay, propped up in that hospital bed. Like Eva looks now. But then she slipped away." He let the practiced sadness slip over his face, and felt an eye moisten. He dabbed at it with the napkin.

"I know." Demuzzio's expression softened.

"You know?"

"We checked you out, Pastor Bob. When Eva wanted you on the Council. Sorry."

"Oh. It never occurred to me, but of course... you would have to do that." Blake paused to adopt his own wry expression at the natural question. *What the hell, just ask him.* "Find out anything interesting?"

"Naw. For a preacher, you're clean as a whistle."

"I had a somewhat misspent youth, TC."

"Yeah, I saw that. But didn't we all. And your calling cured you."

"I found Jesus."

"Uh huh." Demuzzio was non-committal. He opened the refrigerator and pulled out sandwich makings.

Blake studied the man's profile. *He wants to tell me something. Give it time.* He watched in silence as the man fussed with sandwich makings on the sideboard.

"But some of your friends aren't," Demuzzio said after a long pause.

"Huh? Aren't what?"

"As clean as you. So you should be careful."

"Careful. Okay. Anyone in particular?"

Another pause.

"Calhoun Smith."

"The Senator?"

Demuzzio grunted. "Be careful of him, Pastor Bob. I think he's dirty."

"He's a friend to the *Novas*, TC. Or at least he's neutral."

"He's a politician. He's a friend to himself."

Blake pondered that. *I wonder if they've got any leverage I could use.* "Well... they all serve their own interests, TC. And I wouldn't call him a friend, actually. He's a member of our UMC congregation, been very helpful to the church. Never asked for anything in return." He made his tone non-committal, inviting more disclosure.

Demuzzio just grunted, taking a bite of his sandwich.

Blake put a little measured distaste in his tone. "So how is he... dirty?"

"Oh, nothing actionable, Bob. But there are enough hints. The man's a player. His ends justify his means. Be careful of him."

"Okay. Thanks for letting me know. Why'd it come up, anyway? There's not much of a connection." *Although there's more than I thought, and TC isn't telling me everything here.*

"Intersecting spheres."

"What?"

"Josh ginned up some software. We run it on anybody we want to check out."

"All the Council members?"

Demuzzio nodded. "You're in good company."

"So I am." He raised his glass and clinked Demuzzio's, still thinking through the decision. *Intersecting spheres. Software. Running on the supercomputers they've got downstairs, making little connections, tying them together. So they must have picked up some of my early meetings with the Senator, before we got more careful. Means a clock is ticking. If Joshua wasn't so sick... if TC wasn't so distracted... if they start picking at my accidental carrier story... So... do I act tonight, or not?*

O'Donnell Enclave, Waimanu, HI | Monday 2323 HST

Demuzzio studied the man for a long moment. *I like this preacher. He's honest. Eva says he's okay. He's a Council member, for God's sake. So why do I have this itch?* He answered the man's question so he didn't have to answer his own.

"Sure, Bob. It's a clear night, good moon out there. You've been to the beach before, with Eva. You know the way. Walk and pray all you want. Go for it. The locus will let you back in, no problem."

Later, as the clock ticked past midnight, Demuzzio watched from the lanai off the kitchen. Hundreds of feet below and a quarter mile away a solitary figure paced the black sand at the edge of Waimanu Bay.

"Pastor Bob praying out there?" Joshua asked as he walked out from the kitchen.

"Yeah."

"Good place for it. Hope it does some good."

"Me too. How are the twins?"

"Resting okay. But the locus is sitting on them pretty hard, I think; especially Ibrahim. There has to be a cost for that deep a suppression, eventually."

"And the ladies are still in never-never land."

Joshua sighed.

Demuzzio rubbed his head. "Little Eva. My god-daughter rolled the damn dice, didn't she?"

"We all have to roll the dice at some point, TC. And Eva has a more direct path to knowledge. She had no choice but to try it."

"Sure she had a choice. Wait for NIH to figure it out."

"Yeah, the scientific path is tried and true. The scientists at NIH will develop the knowledge eventually, but not soon enough. Ibrahim will die, then probably Gaelan. And a lot more Novas will be infected and die. My logic lattice puts the probability over ninety percent."

"Eva doesn't compute like you do."

"In this case she did, with Sarah. I can read the underpinnings in her note; she thought it through quite carefully. I even agree with her logic." A half-smile flickered and was gone. "But logic didn't drive her choice, TC. Love did."

Demuzzio groaned. *No answer for that.* He walked to the rail and looked out over the moonlit bay. The lone figure in the distance caught his eye.

"What's he doing, making a phone call? Josh, can you see that far?"

"Pastor Bob?" Joshua squinted. "Looks like it. Maybe he's calling his flock, getting them to pray with him. That actually might help; the power of a combined intention."

Demuzzio's mind rebelled at the helplessness and ambivalence he felt. *Reduced to prayer and hope and Eva's fucking long-shot roll of the dice.* He rubbed his head and sat down hard on a chair.

"A child's love is a powerful thing, TC," Joshua said softly, almost as if he'd read his mind.

Chapter 20

O'Donnell Enclave, Waimanu, HI | Tuesday 0909 HST

Elia sat silent, watching her image of Sarah apportion itself into the triune composite, watching her own image do the same. *Like intersecting circles,* she thought; *like one of my husband's Venn diagrams. But animate: fluid and shifting.* Their overlapping consciousnesses sat within some indeterminate region of space-time. She was simultaneously within the circle of herself and the smaller triangle of their intersecting triune. *It seeks to be,* she accepted, feeling the triune's powerful pull. *But it is dangerous for me to let go.*

That thought trickled over into their commonality but was rejected.

"No, Elia," Eva soothed her, "my intention is holding. Your individuality is protected."

"I have secrets, Eva," she admitted from that protected place, "terrible ones."

A wave of compassion swept outward from their triune entity, a composite waveform of her own self with Sarah and Eva. It quieted her mind and took the edge off her pain. *As do we all. A time for that later,* was the combined sense, *we have urgent work now.*

Elia reached out a tendril of her mind to touch the twins, and sensed Joshua was with them. The locus had all three cocooned in a protective psychic embrace, she saw. *That's enough. It has to be. My best purpose is here. Their safety is here.* She forced herself away and dropped more deeply into the triune. She found the balance point that Eva's intention had set: a psychic col area, a saddleback where energy in balanced energy out, where she could be both a triune identity and herself. She chanted the Sisterhood intention rhythms to keep floating at that balance point. *I have two minds now.*

The triune mind focused down on its chase of the virus and possible means to block its attack. Elia shifted attention to the herself portion of her mind. She directed it backward in time along the line of her hereditary spirit-Sisters, seeking in their RNA-preserved memories instances of cultural memes favoring Nova evolution. In an era centuries before Christ's, she stopped to commune with Sanghamitra.

"You brought Buddhism and tolerance and peace to Ceylon," Elia said. The dim shape brightened in response.

"Non-violence, at least," the shape answered.

"In an era that was quite violent."

"As I see in your mind; your view of our history from twenty-three centuries later. Is your era any less?"

"I hope so."

The vision took on better-defined facial features and smiled at Elia enigmatically. "I do too," she said.

She looks like me, the cast of her eyes. "Ashoka, your father," Elia continued, "went from a murdering conqueror to a peacemaking emperor. And he changed the culture. How?"

"My mother."

"Devi?"

"Yes. Also there was what you call a power locus in Ujjain."

"Ah." *Does a locus develop on its own or does it come to a place where there is to be power? A new question. An interesting puzzle for my husband. If we survive.*

"How?" Elia repeated.

"She made him look at what he had done, the aftermath of the battle at Kalinga. The burning, the corpses, the wailing children..." Visions of those cascaded across Elia's vision. She felt the sorrow like a hammer blow: *Devi was a nurse.*

"And his personal redemption changed the culture?"

"He re-set what you call the memes, yes."

"He had such power? To change a culture that quickly?"

"He was emperor," Sanghamitra said simply. "And then he had Devi and the power locus." She thought for a moment more and smiled at some glad memory of her father, the man who had been both an emperor and spiritual leader of India. "And he strode the path of the Buddha. He was right. People knew that, in their hearts. They became... healthier."

In their hearts. Yes, there's that. "I need your help, Sanghamitra. Violence, atrocities... are they necessary?"

"Can people see good if there is no evil?"

An old question. "Is that your answer?"

"I don't know," the image of her ancient ancestor said sadly. As Elia emerged from her racial memory, the woman added "I hope so."

Evil. Was that why Eva wouldn't let Joshua destroy the mad mullah seven years ago? Is he the evil that the world must see to understand the good of the Novas? Did she foresee that? And what of the memes? How would Zurvan fit into reconfiguring them? The thoughts swirled around in Elia's mind as she shifted attention back to her triune mind.

"Any luck?" Sarah asked.

"I don't know. Maybe. You?"

"No. The past has its brilliance, but no more knowledge of biochemistry than I have. A wasted effort." Sarah's thought carried the charred overtone of time fleeting away from hope.

"I wish we could commune with each other's spirit-Sisters."

"Step outside our own RNA? Not possible. And why would that help, anyway?

"I don't know, Sarah. But I think in looking at your heritage you have too much of yourself, you lose... not objectivity, maybe... but perspective?"

"Some of my memories are false, Elia. But I don't know why."

Eva's attention slid fully back into their triune at that point.

"Give me some good news," she said.

"Nothing," Sarah replied. "Odd slants on ideas. Knowledge that the mind can cause or enhance immune system responses, but not the biochemical level of detail we need to defeat this virus."

"Elia?" Eva asked wearily. "A counterattack through the culture? The power of combined intention?"

"Sanghamitra thinks the memes can be reconfigured. Love and tolerance from *Homo sapiens* will feed into the *Nova* neural networks, maybe protect the gene from future assault. But the price is knowledge of the horror and evil."

"An ancient concept. Biblical. Buddhist. Sumerian, long before them." Their triune mind examined the concept, using their separate perspectives, turning it over and inside out. "An enduring myth... that's... helpful," Eva concluded. "Thank you, Elia. No use now, maybe, but in the future... an epigenetic factor, operating downstream..."

"Is there a future?" Elia loosed her doubt into the triune.

Eva nodded acknowledgment of the question's validity but not agreement with the doubt. "Support me, Sisters, while I search it out."

O'Donnell Enclave, Waimanu, HI | Tuesday 1012 HST

The three women sat unmoving on the mattress laid on the floor, Eva braced in the corner, Sarah on her left, Elia on her right. The energy field flickering around them was apparent to Demuzzio only in his peripheral vision; it went away if he looked at the women directly. He glanced at Joshua's twin sons in the bed across the clinic room and saw the same energy signature.

"The field is intensifying, I think," he told Joshua. *And is that a good sign or a bad one?*

"A sort of waviness out of the corner of my eye? That's all I see," Robert Blake asked.

"I see, or maybe sense, more of the spectrum than you," Joshua answered. "It's really quite beautiful — splintered light, coming back together."

"You ever see that before? With Eva?" Blake was curious.

"No. Never."

Blake looked at his watch. "It's been... what... forty hours since they went into this trance? Joshua, we need to pull them out of it."

"Jesus spent forty days and nights in the desert," Joshua whispered.

"Huh?" Blake looked confused to Demuzzio.

"Never mind. The normal rules of physiology don't apply where they're at, Bob. And Eva's note specifically says don't try to break the trance."

Demuzzio looked up at Joshua's flat tone, and then across at Blake. He watched anger flash across the man's face. *Careful, Pastor Bob, we're all friends here.*

But the man was stubborn. "Even if their metabolisms are slowed way down, Joshua, they'll dehydrate."

"No. The locus is involved with both them and the twins. Eva's got a protocol of some sort running. An intention." Joshua's tone was even flatter. He knelt beside Elia.

Demuzzio put his hand on the minister's shoulder. "Let it go, Bob. Josh is right. Eva's word is law here, now."

The man opened his mouth anyway. "I'm worried, dammit!"

"We all are, Bob." The irritation left Joshua's voice. "But look." He gently pinched a fold of skin on Elia's inside forearm. It melded back smoothly when released. "No dehydration."

"Yeah," Demuzzio agreed. *I wonder how the locus is doing that?* He watched Joshua do similar pinches of Eva and Sarah with the same effect. *Absorption from the air?* He dismissed the question immediately. *What the fuck do I know? They're okay; that's all we need. Be happy, Pastor Bob.*

But the man still looked angry as he spoke. "Well, at least let's shift their positions, Joshua. That lotus has to be restricting circulation by now."

Demuzzio shook his head slightly, warning him off. *You're a Councilor and Eva's friend, but don't press it. Josh is edgy. He could boot your ass out of here.* He watched the man's expression smooth out as he got his feelings under control. His shoulders slumped in acknowledgment.

"All right. Then I'll pray over them, Joshua."

"Pray all you want. But do *not* touch them, Bob." Joshua looked hard at him. "Please," he added, and dropped his head in his hands.

O'Donnell Enclave, Waimanu, HI | Tuesday 1617HST

Eva sensed Sarah and Elia supporting her, their two consciousnesses overlapping hers, forming the tri-part base upon which the Waimanu power locus fixed. She let that power roll through her and felt the corresponding mind-shivers of her Sisters. Their triune dropped deeper into Eva's cellular makeup, seeking to understand it, looking for the key that would defeat the virus. *I know it's there*, she arrowed encouragement after the departing triune.

The herself portion of her mind that remained in her awareness vaguely sensed her physical body, seeing it as an indistinct ghost. Now through that ghost came another, a cadence walking toward her: Pastor Bob, praying.

She greeted it with vibrations of warmth and love.

They slid uneasily around his cadence, and wouldn't mesh.

"Robert," she crooned, "it's me. Eva."

Nothing. His cadence was a veil.

"Don't you know me?"

Nothing.

"I know you, though. I'm glad you came."

Nothing.

"I could force your mind to open to mine, I think."

A vague stirring, a dip in the cadence of his prayer.

"But I won't do that," she responded. "I've already sinned enough with Sarah and Elia." *For their own good, of course; their traumas were unbearable.*

"Have I done the right thing, Robert? Playing God with them, even with the best of intentions... is that right? I've never been sure." *Elia knows her secrets, down deep, and Sarah is beginning to understand that her memories are not all hers. If I've made a mistake we may all pay the price.*

Eva sighed. "I wish we could talk, Pastor Bob. I really need a confessor."

Another stirring in the cadence. *Uncertainty, ambivalence. Yes, Robert, I know those all too well.*

"But I'll never play God with you, my love. Even though now... I can read some of your thoughts. Superficial ones, I think. Forty hours... has it been that long? And forty days and forty nights. Yes, I know that allegory." *But I'm my own devil, n'est-ce pas? As are we all? You certainly cannot be.*

Eva slipped the lightest of mind touches through the veil around his presence in her mind. The reaction was sharp, defensive, an immediate distancing. The cadence of his prayer stuttered, then stopped altogether.

"Oh! I'm sorry. I didn't mean to..." She eased vibrations of warmth and love toward him. But his fear had turned his veil into a wall; she tasted it solidifying. *Damn! It has to be scary. I can't blame him.*

But how she'd felt walking with him on the beach flooded out the logic of that thought. Her mind wailed. *I need you, Robert!*

O'Donnell Enclave, Waimanu, HI | Tuesday 2121 HST

"Two days now! Eva, where are you?" Joshua whispered to her closed eyes. *Maybe Bob is right. Maybe it's time to intervene.* He picked up Eva's note and re-read it. Mr. Bojangles padded into the clinic and meowed.

"Do you know, Uncle Ham?" The cat jumped onto the mattress among the three women and stared at him unblinkingly. "Know where they are? How they're doing? What I should do?"

No response. The cat remained a Sphinx.

"Everything's turning to shit outside, Ham. Again. Eva's message helped, but now the tide has turned back."

The cat blinked slowly.

"We need her showing herself to the world, active. The rumors are esca-lating. Carol and the President and our Councilors and friends are doing all they can, but they're not Eva."

The cat blinked again. Twice.

"Pastor Bob will have to get back soon, with Good Friday and Easter coming up. And he could do us much more good if he were actively herding his flock our way. But he needs to talk to Eva for some reason."

Joshua groaned as he stood up from his kneeling position. *My knees feel like they're ninety years old.* He walked across the room to the twins' bed and sat on it, propped up between them. He took their small hands in his big hard ones. *I have to be strong and stay sane.* Vibrations formed around their threesome and reached out across the room to the women in the opposite corner. They meshed and moved in hypnotic synchrony, reflected in the glittering gray eyes of Mr. Bojangles. Joshua let the weariness take his body, and his eyes closed. As sleep took him down, he drove his conscious-ness toward a mind-dance with his dead uncle.

"We really need your help, Uncle Ham."

The after-image of the cat looked at him sadly.

"I am weak, Joshua; 'tis all I can do to hang onto this earthly hook Mr. Bojangles so graciously provides."

"The locus, can't it help you?"

"It helps Eva now. My stewardship has passed. I have not much longer in this plane."

"I said goodbye to you twice seven years ago; must I do it again now?"

"Aye, lad. Shortly."

Joshua let out a long sigh, a half-sob.

Mr. Bojangles blinked. "Your space-time is not all there is, laddie."

"So I've noticed. But it's all *I* have. I'm no *Nova*."

The cat studied him thoughtfully. "Nor was, for example, Aristarchus. Yet he stepped outside the perspectives of his time."

"And got a truer vision of reality, yeah. Over twenty-three centuries ago. Determined the earth orbited the sun, not vice-versa. What's your point, Uncle Ham?"

"Knowledge has grown since; exponentially. And into more subtle regions."

"Nuclear physics, quantum mechanics, lately the Higgs boson? Our tools are better; more inferential."

"I speak less of knowledge about the physical world than the mental."

"Oh. We know now that consciousness is not just an epiphenomenon of the physical brain..."

"Aye, lad; 'tis fundamental; causal to how the world manifests."

"And Novas know this from an early age, Uncle Ham, sure... and after puberty some of them may be able to manipulate the physical world like Eva. Still, I'm missing your point."

"For everythin' its season, Joshua."

"Still."

"The light of Aristarchus had to await Copernicus before it flowered. Darkness intervened."

In his dream state, Joshua trembled. "We have days, not centuries, and those who would bring back the dark ages are in full cry out there."

The cat seemed sad. "I know," it said. Then Mr. Bojangles faded into the vibrations flowing across some indeterminate space between the two corners of the room.

Joshua watched those vibrations form patterns of splintered light around the three women. At times they melded into coherence, as if a reverse prism had melded them into a gentle comforting golden glow. At other times they became dissonant, incoherent, and darkness crept in.

A last thought seemed to come from a great distance, weary of its travel. "Trust in your little sister, lad."

O'Donnell Enclave, Waimanu, HI | Tuesday 2345 HST

Awareness beyond the limitation of perspective, their triune realized as it dove down into the cellular level in Eva's physical brain, *that's what we need here.*

Their composite consciousness had chased down a multitude of neural pathways, trying to comprehend the view from inside. It was vastly different from the outside view each of them was used to: the detailed fMRI scans, the electron-microscopy of cell structure.

"I think this is how the tire sees the road, as opposed to the driver," Elia lamented.

"I can't change my perspective that easily, Eva," Sarah complained. The science is too ingrained in my mind. I can't get away from all that training, looking at the world a certain way... I..."

Eva cut her off. "It doesn't matter, Sarah. In fact it's been useful that we see it different ways, I think. Look now."

Their sense of headlong motion slowed to a crawl as the triune hung in a stream of blood flow feeding neural circuits.

"This is it," Eva continued, "We've found it. I'm sure."

"How do you know?" Elia asked.

"Shh. Just watch."

On a neuron below them, an attack played out.

"Ah. Okay, I see it now," Sarah said. "Just what NIH thought. A pretty simple agent. Its protein wrapper only made it behave like a prion."

"It's got genetic material, RNA, or fragments. I see them!" Elia became excited.

"And look at it dock. It's gone asymmetrical, like HIV." Eva was analytical.

"It's not an enveloping mechanism, Eva. See, the wrapper is staying outside the cell; just RNA is slipping in."

"That's fast, Sarah; it means this virus has a unique enzyme, doesn't it?"

"Wow, look at it go. Copying itself. No latency at all!" Elia let her excitement run.

Eva watched the process play out. "It's not destroying the cell."

A thought came to Elia. "Sarah, a unique enzyme means NIH can probably synthesize an antiviral to block reproduction, right?"

"I can do that myself," Eva grunted, "now that we've seen it. Hang on."

The triune drove deeper, into the sub-structures of the infected cell.

"Look, Sarah, Elia. Tell me what you see."

"Three genes in this region — they encode the growth progression for the Nova gene. The virus RNA material inserts itself... here. Yes!"

"Can you block the insertion?"

"Watch me."

"Eva!"

"What?"

"Be careful! The Nova gene probably performs more than one function; most genes do. And functions are encoded by more than one gene. Pleiotropy. You know this."

"I do."

"We should study it more."

"There's no time."

"Time means nothing to the locus."

"But it does to the outside world."

The debate raged for only a brief moment; a composite entity can't argue with itself for very long.

"There, it's done," Eva whispered. "We're propagating the change through my bloodstream."

The triune watched that happen.

"Your system will have to scavenge out the damaged cells," Sarah noted. "You'll be sick for a while yet, I think. Several days is my guess."

"Incapacitated for a while, too, Sarah. I feel that. Hope I don't have to transpose or fight. I probably can't."

The triune withdrew its composite consciousness from the cellular level of Eva's brain and paused to watch macro elements of her biochemistry manifest. At some far remove, she felt her body start to repair itself.

Its duty done, the triune dissolved back into the three separate entities, to their herself minds.

"We played God." Elia said in wonderment.

"So we did," Sarah confirmed, her voice edgy with concern. "How do you feel about that, Eva?"

"Nervous. Exhausted. And hot. Very hot. Come on, Sisters, let's go home."

Chapter 21

Tonight, Blake thought, *it will have to be tonight.* From his stool beside the door, he studied the three women. *Regardless of whether she comes out of this trance or not.* He looked across the room at Joshua's sallow face, a mask of fatigue and pain even in sleep. The twins beside him twitched restlessly. *They're all beaten down. I'll chance it. Tonight.*

Sarah opened her eyes and looked around quizzically. Elia followed suit. They stared at Joshua and the twins, then at Blake. Then they rose together, standing up and stretching as if they had been sitting in a lotus for only minutes. *That's amazing.*

"Welcome back," he said.

Sarah nodded. "Success, I think." She knelt and put her hand on Eva's forehead and opened one eye. The dilated pupil flashed an amethyst star-shape directly at Blake. He froze. *Almost as if my mind is pinned down.* Transfixed, he could only stare back. Sarah let Eva's eyelid drop. His sense of mobility returned, a slow-motion recapture of control over his legs and arms. *What the hell was that? Does she know?*

"She's burning up," Elia said.

"We've got to get her in a shower, quick," Sarah responded.

Eva mumbled something as the two women lifted her. They paused. Elia's knee buckled. "I'm too weak," she moaned.

"Let me help," Blake said, taking three quick steps across the room. "I'll get her into a shower."

He caught up Eva in his arms, lifting her away from the two women. Her left arm clung weakly around his neck, her right hung flaccid. *Jesus! Burning up is an understatement.* Energies tingled his skin, and waves of heat throbbed where their bodies made contact. Her face seemed to flicker in and out, a hologram losing coherence.

"Waterfall," Eva mumbled into Blake's neck.

"Waterfall, she says," he repeated to the women.

Sarah nodded. "Good idea." She pulled them through the clinic door. "Elia, stay here. Wake Joshua. Tell him there's hope. Hope at last."

Blake trotted down the long hall behind the older woman, Eva light in his arms. *Hope at last.* "What hope exactly, Sarah?"

"An antidote for the infected Novas. Protection for the uninfected."

"Wow! Both? Great! But it will take time to ramp up. Won't it?"

Sarah stumbled, almost pulling them all down in a heap. As she recovered, Blake saw her face aging, its fatigue lines deepening almost as he watched. *After they left the trance, they started to fade. I wonder how far down they'll drop.* He slowed. "You okay, Sarah?"

"Keep going. The waterfall," she said through gritted teeth.

And how long they'll need to recover. Blake's mind began playing with options. The enclave portal slid open and they swung right, onto the path cut in the side of the cliff. Directly ahead and down a bit lay the wider ledge and its pool. The waterfall into it was a torrent. *Big rain overnight.*

Eva mewed like a starving kitten, her breath hot and rancid against his face. She turned her head and strained weakly toward the water.

Sarah sank to her knees then dropped to all fours as they reached the pool. "Go!" she gasped, "under the waterfall."

Blake paused, tempted. "What will it do?" *Push Sarah off this cliff and take Eva down to the beach. Call the Senator's extraction team.*

"It must be an energy sink for the locus. Bleed Eva's level down. Equilibrate her. Go!"

No. No time to ad-lib. Stay with the plan; it's still a good one. "Equilibrate her to what?" he asked as he stepped carefully into the pool.

"This reality!"

"She's been elsewhere?"

"Yes! "

Blake waded carefully across the slickened pool bottom, his feet feeling for unevenness. *Elsewhere. What does that mean?* The spray from the falling water enveloped them. Eva mewed again and twisted in his grasp, both her arms reaching out to the falling water. He held her firmly. A breast rolled under his hand, its heat emphasized against the cold water up to his waist. He stepped forward gingerly into the waterfall. It almost knocked Eva out of his arms, but she turned and grabbed him around his neck.

Sarah called something unintelligible above the roar of the falls.

"What?" he yelled.

The woman's voice got louder. Blake saw her shape approach, vague through the spilling water. "Keep her there until she's ready. She'll tell you, I think."

You think? How recovered will she be? And what does she know? He shrugged, holding the girl tightly. *Guess I'm committed.* The wry observation from a Chinese fortune cookie flashed through his mind. *A thief wastes time wondering what others steal from him.*

Sarah came a little closer, struggling to see into the water. "She needs to burn off all the energy, so she can re-cohere," she yelled.

Re-cohere? The sun took that moment to lift above the tree canopy shading the waterfall. The colors of the rainbow played through the water and across them both.

O'Donnell Enclave, Waimanu, HI | Wednesday 1111 HST

Re-cohere. Thank you, Sarah. Thus keyed, Eva reached her mind out through the falling water to the locus. She found the harmonic she needed and meshed with it to help the cool water rein in her runaway metabolism. It worked, after a fashion. *A cure that also kills the test organism isn't the best success.*

She kept it up, and the water glittered in response. Its droplets became heat sinks for the residual energy she needed to dissipate so her vibrations could match the different energy plane in this reality. *How can you pick up energy leaving a null state?* She dismissed the question immediately. *A curiosity for Josh, later.* But a caution, nonetheless. She would have to be careful. *I'm a totally new thing. Anything I haven't done before might be dangerous.*

As the threat to her body diminished, Eva's awareness spiraled outward. Sensations spiraled inward. Blake's hand on her breast as he carried her into the waterfall. The way his body felt now, strong and steady. The mystery of his mind, his conflicted thoughts and how he sheltered them.

She squeezed her arms around his neck and kissed his cheek. "Robert. Okay now. Put me down please."

He did, gently, keeping an arm around her waist until she found her footing. Her knees barely supported her. *I'm weaker than I thought.* Her bare feet sought to pull the strength of the locus through the rock floor of the pool, but only a little trickled into her body. *I'm not back in phase yet.* Intuition said it would take a while. She needed to rest, desperately, but there were urgent matters first. She put her left arm around Blake's waist for support and stepped out of the waterfall.

"You look like hell, Sarah," she told the bedraggled figure standing in the pool in front of her.

The woman hugged her. "You should see yourself, dear."

"But we did it, Sarah!" Eva turned to Blake. "Robert. Find Elia, please. Ask her to bring all the sterile sample jars she can find in the lab. Quickly."

He looked at her, hesitating. "You can barely stand up."

"I'll be okay. Quickly now!"

The man turned and vaulted out of the pool and trotted up the cliff-side path. Eva and Sarah limped to the side of the pool and helped each other climb out. They sat on the side, tired beyond belief. The tropical sun climbed higher above the tree.

"Oh, that feels good. I was starting to get cold."

"You've equilibrated then, Eva? You still look a little... fuzzy. You sure you're back with us?"

"Yeah. It's just that all sorts of energies were flying around me. I wasn't sure what to do. But the water worked."

"What happened?"

"I truly don't know. The three of us were fine in the triune. But when we split back to ourselves, and I went to follow you out of the null... I don't know."

"Something happened. What did it feel like?"

"Like the null wanted to hold me. I had to really burn some energy... like I was an electron climbing to a higher state."

"The null hasn't done that before?"

"No. Maybe it's just that I'm closer to my future evolutionary state? I don't know, Sarah. It took me all that energy to get back here, and I wasn't able to bleed it off fast enough. It had no place to go. Without the waterfall, it might have fried me."

"Why the waterfall? Why not just a cold shower?"

"Your guess was right, Sarah. It wasn't just my body needing cooling. My being needed... re-alignment with this place. Coherence."

The two pondered that mystery for a moment.

Sarah shook her head tiredly. "What now?"

"Now I spit in the specimen jars, and you send them out to each lab that's working on this, but save one so you can sequence the genome."

"And the twins?"

"Rub my spit in their eye. Should work. The optic nerve is a direct path. That's fastest."

"Okay. Let's go then." Sarah struggled upright.

Blake came trotting with boxes of sample jars, Elia limping behind.

"Not yet. I need the waterfall's water, I think."

Sarah cocked an eyebrow. "Surface runoff. Biological contaminants. We've got distilled water in the lab."

"This water is a better matrix, Sarah. Nourished by the locus."

The older woman shook her head wonderingly. "Are you sure? How is it...," she began, but then cut off the question. "If you say so." She took the first box from Blake and walked with Eva through the pool.

Eva filled a jar half full with the falling water, then spat in it.

The four of them formed a little production line, passing the filled jars back to Elia on the rim of the pool. Eva watched her stack them carefully back into the boxes, smiling through tears and exhaustion.

O'Donnell Enclave, Waimanu, HI | Wednesday 1331 HST

Blake had acted the dutiful gofer for the past two hours, helping in the lab with the sample shipments. He'd watched Eva take a mouthful of the collected water and dribble it carefully in the corners of the twins' eyes. She'd rubbed it in gently, like a salve. His confused mind had flashed with disconnected, inane thoughts. *The gospels say Jesus mixed his spit with dirt to cure the blind.*

Now, the most urgent actions accomplished, Eva lay on her bed under a light blanket. Blake held her right hand in both of his. Her left sought the shelf cut into the volcanic rock at the head of the bed. She brushed a small lamp and a few seashells aside and let her hand rest on the rock. It seemed to shimmer at the contact. He blinked and the effect was gone.

"You should sleep," he said, "everyone agrees."

Eva's drooping eyes widened, amethyst pupils flickering with the light of that strange energy as she stared at him. She smiled a little.

"I know."

"Then do it. I'll go back and help with the samples."

"You've done plenty. You've been a big help, Robert. You're an integral part of how this is all going to work out."

"Just my Christian duty. And speaking of which, I have to fly back to my church tonight. I may be gone before you wake up."

"Just hold my hand, Robert. Please."

She closed her eyes and he felt a faint trickle of energy run up his arms and down through his feet. A flicker chased around Eva's hand on the rock headboard. *Or did it?*

"I baptized you, Robert." An enigmatic half-smile.

He smiled back. "In the waterfall just now? Paying me back for baptizing you in Washington?" *Your body in my arms, your young breast under my hand. Your energy burning through us both. Yes, that was a baptism of sorts.*

"Your sins are forgiven, Robert," she said dreamily. A long sigh and she was asleep.

As her breathing slowed and deepened, Eva's hand went limp. Blake disengaged it gently and laid her arm across her chest. He sat still, thinking.

My sins forgiven? She grants me absolution? The implications bounced around his mind like spit on a hot griddle. *Does she know? Has she read my mind somehow?*

Blake walked around the bed and out onto the lanai where the satellite would pick up his cell phone. He punched in the number for his UMC Washington office, then keyed through to the answering machine that would keep the Senator apprised. He spoke unencrypted, an innocent-sounding message in case Demuzzio or anyone in the enclave were to pick it up.

"Bring the plane into Waimea, pre-flight it for turnaround tonight." *If she suspects, would she say anything? Why did she smile at me that way?* He continued with instructions, his phrasing embedding the codes that would alert the Senator's sapper team to stand by for action. He reviewed what he'd said and clicked off. He walked back into the room and studied the sleeping girl.

Eva called it her sacred pool. Her mother had one too, he remembered Eva telling him. *In the hills of New Hampshire.* He let little questions nibble at him, wondering if they might have relevance for his planning. *Does a locus follow these women around? Is flowing water some sort of carrier or context for this power?* Elia and Sarah had certainly seemed to get some energy back after working with Eva in the pool.

Much of Eva's conversation was laced with water metaphors, now that he thought about it. *But so what? Water is the biological basis for life, and the mythological basis for many paradigms.* That was nothing new. But Eva also had spoken of talking to the spirits of her maternal ancestors; she'd told him they cascaded like water down through the ages, to swirl around her. *Bringing accumulated wisdom. A heightened intuition.*

That metaphor bothered him. *Could she actually know I'm betraying her?*

He reviewed their interactions over the last several hours. *Probably not; no hints in her behavior.*

He reflected on his brief interactions with the others in the enclave. *No nuances, not a hint from anyone. I was just a part of the team, all of us working together. Demuzzio has a good poker face, but not that good. If he knew, I'd see it.*

Her intuition, Blake concluded with relief, may be telling her something, but she either doesn't know what it is, or she's rejected it. And she hasn't told anyone. So she may suspect but she can't really believe it. He sat down in the chair and spoke softly. "Isn't that right, Eva?"

Other factors tumbled through his mind. As the stressors drove Eva's development, the locus clearly was developing also. *They say the locus is not sentient, in any sense they understand; that it's just raw potential needing direction.* But how much longer would that be true? And therein lay a key question: *Will it protect her?*

O'Donnell Enclave, Waimanu, HI | Wednesday 1406 HST

Eva fell like a rock down the dark abyss of sleep, but part of her mind went sideways to a place where alpha brainwaves rode with thetas and some awareness persisted.

Isn't that right, Eva? Blake's dimly sensed question hung in her mind. There was an origin behind that question, but she couldn't summon it up. *Isn't what right?* She summoned her spirit-Sisters instead, and posed the question.

As they circled around her mind, several of the shapes coalesced into one. "A joint opinion? This is new."

"Rather a change in your perspective, brought about by your recent experience."

How will I describe this to Josh? The elegance of their composite vibrations... a standing wave? Harmonic coherence? Eva smiled as she spoke to the coalescence. "Our triune? So having had that joint experience with Sarah and Elia lets me perceive you... jointly? But you're all individual memories... encoded in my RNA."

The coalesced Sisters shrugged it off. "Perspective."

Eva shrugged too. "Okay. Your answer?"

"We see it in your mind. The man is conflicted."

"Why?"

Another shrug. "He hides his inner self well, for a man."

"Does he love me?"

"Possibly. Difficult to love a goddess, we suspect."

"He's very bright."

"A mind like quicksilver, Young Mother. Very much like your brother's."

Eva pondered that for a moment. *True enough, but I haven't time to pursue it. I have more immediate issues.* The coalescence slid apart into individual spirits, as if its transient existence had been solely to collaborate on the question of Robert Blake.

She posed a different question. "My genetic antidote, is it dangerous?"

Spirit-Sisters whirled around her in looping interactions, but no standing waves of coalescence formed.

"We have not your modern knowledge of the genetic and biological mechanisms involved," a singular one of them said.

Another one offered a caution. "You are the One, the First. You may attempt things that not one of us has done before. Some are bound to be dangerous."

A semi-coalescence formed, a sort of consensus, more hopeful. "You formed the intentions by combining those of ours that have proven effective over thousands of years. You observed all the Sisterhood protocols. There is nothing more you could have done."

"Thank you," Eva told them. *They're right, but we'll need to watch the outcomes carefully.*

Eva loosed the strictures on her brainwaves and let herself sink into sleep. As they left her mind, her spirit-Sisters nodded in harmony, all save one.

"There are those who will betray your trust, child," the cautionary voice warned, fading from her awareness. "We've seen it before."

O'Donnell Enclave, Waimanu, HI | Wednesday 1654 HST

In the small laboratory adjacent to the clinic, Joshua turned the vial slowly in his hand. The last open slot in the last shipping coolpack awaited it.

Beside him, Sarah prepared the genomic information that would accompany each shipment, along with the biohazard label that would go on each coolpack. She sensed his stillness and looked up.

"Don't even think it," she told him.

"I'm not a Nova, Sarah."

"You're close enough genetically for the virus to affect you."

"So Eva's cure should affect me, then."

She sighed. "It could also kill you. We've been over this."

"First of all do no harm? Hippocrates didn't have our problems, *Doctor Kruse.*"

Sarah smiled slightly at that. "You've seen the uncertainties yourself, Joshua. You've worked them all through your latticework logic. You can't get an answer. Or even a decent error band around the outcome probabilities."

"Yeah. I guess so." *But there's one wild card pathway I didn't mention. If Eva's cure didn't kill me, maybe it could turn me into a Nova. Maybe I could courier these samples to the labs by instant transposition, not wait for airplanes.*

"And the Waimanu locus is slowly bringing you back to health anyway, I think. A week is my guess. Just be patient, Joshua."

I was a Nova before, for three days in Irian Jaya...

"Joshua?" Sarah swung her stool to face him as he continued turning the vial.

...but I was also crazy. I tapped into my reptile brain. It took over. I killed a lot of people. And the locus in Irian Jaya helped me do it...

"Besides, you're Eva's protector," Sarah added. "You're too valuable to be a lab rat."

...not that they didn't deserve it. But do I want to walk that razor's edge again?

"Valuable. Yeah. I guess so," he acknowledged. His fingers itched for the power they once held, but there was no responding tingle. He let out a long breath and slid the last vial into its slot in the coolpack and closed the lid. "Take Pastor Bob up on his offer to courier these back to the coast?"

Sarah applied the label over the seal. "I think not. Marta's got the SIO jet warming up at Waimea. Bob's plane is still inbound. Hours count. We can get the samples to Vandenberg in five."

Joshua nodded. "Let the Air Force get them to the national labs? Good plan. I'll take them upstairs." He stacked the coolpacks and lifted, but then groaned and swore and lowered them to the lab bench.

"Use the cart, Joshua." Sarah took the top two and wrestled them onto the cart.

"I need to be healed," he said.

"You'll start getting better in a few days, I think."

I'd better.

Chapter 22

O'Donnell Enclave, Waimanu, HI | Wednesday 1819 HST

Four hours after falling asleep, Eva's brainwave pattern edged slowly up toward consciousness. She instinctively tightened the strictures around the pattern, shifting it into that waking dream state where she communed with her spirit-Sisters. They swirled around her, their patterns sometimes singular and sometimes coalescing.

"I want my parents back," she told them, almost wailing.

"You committed them to the care of this locus, this power you call Waimanu."

"I miss them terribly."

All the spirits coalesced into a wave of compassion. It rolled over her, comforting, but their response in her consciousness was dispassionate: "Your own mind says their time is not yet."

Eva reached out with her mind down to the deep room at the base of the enclave, where her parents lay locked in the stasis of no-time. Not dead, not alive; just locked, bodies and minds, in a place where time had no meaning. Her consciousness probed around the edges of that stasis field. As always in the past, she found no entry.

I need you, Mommy. Daddy too.

"Their time is not yet, Young Mother."

Eva sighed. "I put them there. I didn't know what else to do."

"You saved their lives."

"But for what?"

Uncertainty was their response. "Only you can answer that."

"You gave me the proper intentions. You told me what to do."

"You were eight years old. And desperate. Waimanu heard you."

"Why can't I get them back? Give me the right intentions, help me. Please."

"We are your past, Eva. We can only give you those intentions proven for us over millennia. We gave you those, to keep your parents safe. You wove them with Waimanu in a new way, unfamiliar to us. You wove them into the future. Only you can retrieve them."

"When?"

More uncertainty. "You are a Becoming. You will be The One of our legends. There will come a time, surely."

Some comfort leavened that uncertainty, and Eva let it wash over her. *Water bird. That's what Waimanu means in Hawaiian. Do you fly out there on the wings of the gulls, Mommy? Do you see me on the lanai, Daddy? I sat in your lap while we watched the whales birthing in the bay. Do you remember?*

"A time," she sighed and let it go. They were right. She had formed a triune with Sarah and Elia and driven their consciousnesses into the null. She'd used its absence of context to explore at the cellular level. They'd found a cure for the virus. She'd brought them back. Things no Sister had done before, not even Mary of Magdala. All the stuff of legends, foretold in allegory in the Sisterhood myths. A matter of time, and then she'd be able to retrieve her parents. Surely.

"My Becoming," she asked the swirling spirits, "and the legends. My parents are part of them."

"They fell to earth, and you are their union."

"An ancient myth."

"And a powerful one, yes."

"But it's your myth. Must I live it?"

"Have you an alternative?"

"I'd rather create my own myth."

The Sisters rippled in disharmony for a moment. "You are The One. You may do as you wish."

Eva nodded. "I might... but millennia of the Sisterhood's careful construction, its subtle conditioning of cultures, the resonance in DNA... my path has been mapped out by your myths, mostly."

"So it has."

"My problem right now is that path is sown with dissension and destruction. I think I represent too much of a change. I don't want my myth to become a religion, even if the Sisterhood has sown the seeds."

"Religion is a sure path to power."

"I don't want power. The Nova children are not paths to power, and must not be seen that way."

The sense that came back from several coalescing Sisters was practicality: no means to this evolutionary end would come easily.

"On the Sisterhood's path there is fear, violence, intolerance," Eva continued.

The coalesced Sisters countered: "Intolerance is intrinsic to most belief systems. So fear and violence always result from changing beliefs."

That's interesting, a part of Eva's mind observed, *this is a grouping of cautionary souls; they want to play devil's advocate. So my Sisters coalesce when their opinions or perspectives converge. They take sides and debate. Very democratic, just like our Nova Council.* "In the past, yes," Eva responded, "but today tolerance prevails."

"The present ecumenism is a pretense of respect for other creeds, not respect itself. Nor acceptance."

"But a pretense may become real, over time."

"When recognized as truth by a culture, over enough time, then embedded in DNA, yes. But there is little time left for that."

"So I need to play out the role the Sisterhood's created for me? A new Messiah? The Second Coming? Displace or overturn male-centric monotheistic belief systems?"

"Ours are older belief systems. Better ones, kinder and gentler, more holistic. More human. Better serving both old and new species. You know this, Young Mother."

"Agreed. But they should not be forced."

"No birth is without pain."

"You advise me to betray the trust of the people I've won over? Pastor Bob, the Pope, some of the Rabbinate Council, the Aga Khan, many other Muslim leaders... betray them all? Become an all-powerful Earth Mother, live out your Sisterhood myths, destroy other beliefs?"

"Destruction sometimes is needed for creation to proceed. Your survival may depend on it. And the Novas' survival."

Eva nodded. *As my brother has pointed out, many times.* "Well, you make a point," she conceded.

O'Donnell Enclave, Waimanu, HI | Wednesday 2002 EDT

The brain scan sections on the fMRI screen really were indeterminate, Elia thought. *Hope is just overriding his logic.* She studied her husband's worn face as he studied his son's images. *He needs to sleep, more than any of us.*

"Eva thinks the damage will be repaired, Joshua." Her voice sounded hoarse to her, even though she tried to soften it.

He grunted and keyed in an enlarged image and tapped the screen with a pencil. "You think those spongiform structures have gotten smaller?"

Humor him. "Maybe," she answered. "Yes, I think maybe so. But we don't know how a Nova might go about re-building. There is no baseline."

"Baseline. Yeah." He turned to look at her, eyes glittering for a moment. "Okay. Pull Ibrahim out. Let's look at Gaelan."

"Two eggs, love. They're fraternal, not identical," she reminded him. "A comparison may not mean much."

"Baseline," Joshua repeated.

A hard tone. Peremptory. Elia pushed the button and the imaging field collapsed. *He's tired; let's just get this over with and get him to bed.* The imaging

annulus slid backward and she lifted Ibrahim off the table and carried him
back to bed in the adjacent room. Joshua lifted Gaelan's limp form onto the
table and re-set the machine. Elia joined him in the shielded control booth.

"My father went crazy, you know," Joshua said as he worked the scanner's
controls. The annulus moved over Gaelan's head and upper body.

"Yes, Joshua. You've told me. Your biological father. Malcolm."

"Ibrahim has his coloring, other characteristics. Black Irish."

"That worries you?"

"I went crazy once."

"Yes, I know. Irian Jaya. Seven years ago. But the cause was outside your
head, not inside."

"This virus, or whatever it truly is, came from the outside, too."

"Eva thinks the damage will be repaired," Elia repeated.

"Still." He turned to look at her again. "A crazy Nova. A dark god. What
kind of a problem would that be for the world?"

"Inheritance of acquired traits," Elia countered, "requires their acquisition."

"Lamarckism? The modern variety, epigenetics?" Joshua twisted to look
at her.

"The crazed primal state you experienced in Irian Jaya came *after* the
twins were conceived, Joshua. So whatever was coded into your DNA from
that experience could not have been passed to them."

"But my father's could have."

"Your uncle Hamilton said it wasn't. Eva has said the same. Sarah has
mapped your genome, and she agrees." Elia paused, belatedly realizing her
error: *I should not have brought up epigenetics; his logic will chase that.*

It did. "Ibrahim went down so much faster than Gaelan. He has to be
more susceptible. Why?" he asked.

Dear Mother, he can't be going there! Not now of all times. "Both are distinct individuals, Joshua. Natural variability." She managed to suppress the
sudden quiver in her voice. *Two souls in my womb at the time of my terror, so
newly conceived. Who can say what markers were imprinted atop their genes?
Or what the downstream consequences would be as they evolve? Not even our
supercomputers can map that out.*

"And look here," Joshua pointed at the brain image just plotted on the
screen, "in this region of the cortex; Gaelan was much less affected than
Ibrahim."

Elia watched her husband's eyes change to the inward look that signaled
a logic lattice forming.

Not now. Distract him! She infused her tone with practicality, leavening it
with a hint of exasperation. "Heredity is only one factor, dear. Both our sons

have had the best of environments. Nurturance, love, support... we gave them *those* epigenetic markers. Their natures reflect it."

He lost the inward look and focused back on her, as she'd intended.

"Yeah, I suppose."

"You need to rest. Now!"

He yawned.

"Our boys will get better, Joshua. Gaelan quicker than Ibrahim, maybe, but they'll both be well."

He yawned again. "Eva says so," he acknowledged sleepily.

Relieved, Elia reached past him and shut down the fMRI. "Yes. She does." The machine's annulus withdrew from around Gaelan. She picked the child up and carried him to the bed beside his brother. She kissed one forehead, then the other. "Their fevers are down."

Joshua contemplated the twins from the foot of the bed, changing expressions fleeting across his face faster than she could decode. Finally he nodded.

"Good. I can sleep now?" His legs trembled and he fought to stay upright.

"I'll help you back to our bedroom, love."

"No. Here. I sleep with our boys."

"The locus sleeps with them, Joshua. You're better off in your own bed."

"No. Here." He crawled up onto the bed and wedged in between the twins, his big hands taking their little ones. "The locus can sleep with me too. Wake me if you need any..."

He closed his eyes and was gone from her.

"Joshua?"

An exhalation, a half-snore, was the only response Elia got.

"Sleep well, Joshua. Love them both."

She turned to the door. *I'll push in an extra bed and stay with them. Just as soon as I see if Sarah or TC or Pastor Bob need anything else.*

At the door she paused and looked back. *Love Gaelan, Joshua. He's our flesh and blood. And please love Ibrahim too. Even if you're not his biological father... he is your son in every other way. In all the ways that count. Epigenetics be damned.*

The agony of her long deception gnawed at her as she walked away down the hall, an ache, an emptiness where truth could have been, and arguably should have been. "When all this is over," she muttered, "if we're still alive... I will tell you, Joshua, I promise. But not yet." *A time for every purpose under heaven.*

O'Donnell Enclave, Waimanu, HI | Wednesday 2121 HST

Eva Connard pushed her arguing swirl of spirit-Sisters away to a distant part of her mind, but one thought lingered on: *no birth is without pain.*

Joshua the Practical would agree with that, she thought, but not without understanding the nature of her pain. Her Uncle Tee would gladly trade off her pain for that of a billion others. Sarah and Elia, on the other hand, would understand her dilemma at its root level. And Pastor Bob? Where would he come out? Would he marry an Earth Mother? Father her children? Would he forsake his UMC flock and the decades of work it took him to build it? *How could I even think to betray him like that?*

Thus summoned, the image of the Reverend Robert Blake approached in her dream state. He walked in the desert amid an expanse of sand and sun and sky; the desolate and unforgiving landscape seemed to wrap itself around him. *Looks familiar.* Eva let her mind swing around to different perspectives. In the distance, his small UMC jet sat on a runway, the air behind its engines distorted by heat waves. *Ah. The Waimea landing strip, the desert to the west.* Marta, their SIO security team leader, carried a bag up into the plane. *Marta?* Eva reminded herself this was a dream. *And Marta is gay; not interested in Robert.* Still, the scene conveyed uncertainty, with some unhappy feeling she couldn't quite identify. *The environment represents the truth of our circumstances?*

Thus stimulated, Eva's brainwaves shifted briefly toward an awake state. She felt her hand in his, and knew he was there with her. *Thank you for staying with me, Robert.* She squeezed his hand slightly and began to slide comfortably back down into her dream. *So I'm not the sole creator here; this dream has combined influences, yin and yang, its reality comes from both of us.*

But on that thought the hand holding hers turned cold, and uncertainty and unhappiness chased her back down into the dream. Her spirit-Sisters gathered around her, a protective cocoon as she contemplated her intended lover.

"He may not know you because he doesn't know himself," one of them offered.

"So sad for you," another one said.

"I am here to support you, Eva; you and your Novas..." Blake's image replied.

What's going on here? My ancestors communing with Robert?

Her Sisters began to swirl around them both on the desert plain, chanting and muttering. A coalescence formed. She recognized the distinct vibrational signature of the grouped cautionary souls as they spoke. "No, pastor, you are not. We've found you out."

Blake looked as forsaken as the sandy ground. "Please believe me Eva, I never wanted to hurt you."

Found out what? And are you responding to them, or to something you see in me? "Of course you wouldn't," Eva interjected, "that's just so obvious." *This is one crazy dream!*

"Don't bother with that wretched mask anymore," her cautionary Sisters screamed at Blake, "we don't believe you!"

Eva jerked back at the vehemence. "That's enough!" She glared at them, and the coalescence dissolved back into its component spirits, sulkily.

Blake turned away, his hand shading against the blazing sun, masking his eyes in shadow. "Anger is the devil's tool," he admonished.

"Words," one of her Sisters sneered, "rote words."

Eva bent to scoop up some of the gritty desert soil into her palm. *I keep feeling as if I should know something before I know it.* The hot sand slipped through her fingers, falling back to earth. Her hand grew cold. *My Sisters have never lied to me.*

"I would never betray you, Robert," she said.

O'Donnell Enclave, Waimanu, HI | Wednesday 2244 HST

Fractured images ran through Robert Blake's mind. Eva's hand had suddenly gone cold in his. *What was that about?* He disengaged, tucking her hand under the blanket. He reached up to take her other hand off the rock shelf above her head and tuck it in, too. But that hand was warm, in spite of having rested on cold rock. It tingled in his grasp; in the dim light it seemed to glow. He took it gingerly by the wrist and tucked that hand under the blanket also. *Spooky.*

Eva muttered something, soft and indistinguishable. Blake shivered and left the room. *Something changed just now.* He walked down the long stone corridor from the sleeping quarters. *What?*

Voices from the kitchen led him in. Sarah, Elia and Demuzzio sat around the table. The smell of rich native coffee wafted over him.

"You all look like hell," he said, letting his own face sag in weariness.

"That from a minister?" Demuzzio replied with a crooked grin. "You look like hell yourself, Pastor Bob. You want coffee? How's Eva?"

"Sleeping soundly. No fever, I think. How are the twins?"

"Asleep, too," Elia answered. "We ran fMRI scans on them. There's some early indication they're pulling out of it. Maybe."

"And Joshua?"

"Sleeping with them."

"His condition? Did he take Eva's cure?"

Sarah shook her head. "Too dangerous. He's a hybrid, a half-Nova. We don't know enough about how he would react. And he seems to be coming out of it naturally."

"But it's taking time... is he still weak? I can help get the vials to the airstrip."

"Oh. Forgot to tell you, Pastor Bob," Demuzzio interjected, "your jet was diverted to Kona. Waimea is socked in. Your HQ wants instructions, at your convenience."

"No problem. I can drive the antidote to Kona if Marta's crew can't be spared."

"Not necessary. The vials are already on their way. Our SIO-1 got in and out before the fog. They're en route to Vandenberg."

"Ah. Okay." *This is news. I've got to let the Senator know. And are they getting suspicious?* "I need to coordinate with my flight crew, then. Check in with my headquarters. Think I'll take a walk on the beach, clear my head while I'm talking to them." *So allay their suspicions, if they have any.* "Anyone want to walk with me?"

Three heads shook no.

"Anything else I can do for you? Help out with anything?"

"Nope," Demuzzio said, looking at the two women, "thanks for asking. I think we're all just gonna crash. Watch your step on the path, there's not as much fog here as at the airstrip, but not much light either."

"Ah. I'll just go sit by the waterfall, then. Get some fresh air." Blake gave them a weary smile matching their own and turned to the doorway.

"Pastor Bob," Demuzzio called out, "want coffee? A beer? Juice?"

"I'm fine, thanks, TC." He walked away down the corridor leading to the portal to the waterfall and its pool. *Is something not quite right to them?* He let their facial expressions and body language play back in his mind as he walked. *No. I'm just spooked.*

Robert Blake sat by the pool, confident that the noise of the falls would obscure any conversation that the security cameras might pick up, and punched the Senator's code into his cellphone.

O'Donnell Enclave, Waimanu, HI | Thursday 0817 HST

In her dreamscape desert west of Waimea, the quick tropical evening descended and the last of the volcanic sand trickled through Eva's fingers. *An hourglass out of time.*

"I have to let you go," she concluded.

"I love you, Eva." He spoke it forcefully.

She searched his face. "In our orchard, Robert, on the ridge, we have macadamia nut trees."

"Marta showed me, on the way in." He was puzzled.

"When they're pruned, or cut…"

"Yes, Eva?"

"Their sap runs red… like blood." A sword of pain sliced through her chest. Blake's face became pale and murky as twilight fading into darkness.

"Eva, listen, I don't know who I am," Blake started, "but you can help me…"

"No!" Eva screamed to the night sky. "I can't. I won't. You are not who you say you are. False kindness, false hope, false prophets…" She sneered. "I could squash your silly little religion, Reverend." A distant part of her mind screamed at her. *No, this isn't me!*

"Eva, the virus has weakened your mind and now your spirit. You imagine wrongs that don't exist."

His words diminished her to a sitting position. The lotus reminded her of moonlit evening meditation sessions with Joshua as they sat on the lanai and she practiced communing with the dolphins as they surfaced and plunged back under the waves off Waimanu Bay.

"I'm going to sit here in the darkness with you for a little bit now, Robert," she said. *I am so sad for you. For us.* She felt the remnants of the virus coursing through neural tissues. *What is the truth? Does the virus distort it?* Her eyes drooped as she transited no-time. When the dream resumed, it came on differently. "It doesn't matter so much," she told the spot on the sand where Robert Blake no longer waited with her. "I don't want you to worry. Or Joshua, or Elia, or anybody. I'm going to do what's best."

A rare rain came over the desert then, fog with it, and her spirit-Sisters formed from the mist. Her intention pulled one from the circle and moved it forward in her mind. "Tell me," she ordered Mary of Magdala, "about the betrayal."

"Judas had his own agenda," the woman replied sadly. "He was a Zadokite from the line of Aaron. They were traditionalists, exclusionary. He was caught up for a while in the love that we all had for my wandering Gnostic philosopher, my Jesus. But his love of power was greater."

"Like my Pastor Bob?"

"The parallels are close. The story would be the same."

"An old story."

Mary sighed. "An always story, Young Mother."

"So you made a mistake."

"The Sisterhood formed the legend, gave the myth its power, but the outcome we intended was love, not power."

"How close did you come?"

"Not very close, I see from the history in your mind... if it is accurate. But we were optimists. We thought the right time was upon us, that it would be an easy step to expand the golden age of Greece and Alexandria. We miscalculated."

Eva stared at the woman's flickering sad face. *Miscalculated? Some of the worst atrocities in human history followed for several centuries, in the name of Christian religion.* "And to rectify your miscalculation, your Sisters and my uncle — the being you called Joseph of Arimathea — recovered Jesus from the cross. You returned him to the Therapeuti, his mentors in Egypt. Your Sisterhood sanctuary."

"A minor locus at the time."

"And then?"

"We foresaw the damage the myth might do. We tried to unmake it..."

So that's why the first hundred years after Jesus contain no actual historical record of him, isn't it? Why his contemporary Philo in Egypt makes no mention of him? Philo's wife was a Sister.

"...but we couldn't."

"The legend you set up, the Christos myth, going back thousands of years before Jesus to the Egyptians, the Sumerians... it was too powerful, wasn't it?"

Mary nodded as she pulled the proper concept out of Eva's mind. "Once the genie was out of the bottle, it wouldn't go back in."

"So you created a derivative myth. Mine."

"Yes. But it is buried in racial memory, in what you call DNA, not articulated in literature."

"To what end?" Eva challenged. "Power changed the Jesus myth, in just a few short centuries, to suit its convenience." She let scenes from some of Mary's descendants play out in her mind, some of those who had first-hand knowledge of the violence done in God's name, some who had died from it. "Power corrupts," she said.

"The Novas will not be corruptible," Mary countered.

"Another Sisterhood gamble?"

"Our Covenants were observed. Your parents passed their monkey trap test and conceived you, Young Mother. A greater power thinks it is right. You are The One."

Eva sighed. "A time bomb in our DNA, and me the trigger? I don't have your confidence."

Eva dismissed her circle of spirit-Sisters and sought the blankness of the null. An indeterminate time later, morning sun streaming in from the lanai pulled her slowly up through levels of consciousness. She woke to find Mr. Bojangles curled against her, purring. She studied him carefully then nuzzled his head.

"I've made my decision, Uncle Ham."

Chapter 23

O'Donnell Enclave, Waimanu, HI | Thursday 1010 HST

Little Ibrahim O'Donnell twitched in the throes of the battle that his body fought with the virus. His brother Gaelan lay beside him, but more quietly and with more color in his cheeks. Joshua moved aside when Elia entered the room. As she knelt beside the twins, he stood behind her, resting his hands gently on her shoulders.

"How long?" Elia asked him.

"About twenty minutes, I think. I didn't wake up right away." *Or maybe it was longer... or maybe I was dreaming...*

Elia reached for his hands; he felt them tremble, clenching and unclenching in time to Ibrahim's motions.

"We should fetch Eva," he told her.

"She didn't say anything about this."

"No."

"I think the locus is losing its ability to manage so many issues, Joshua. Or losing its strength, or something. Something's happening. Don't you feel it?"

"I know I don't feel any better." *That's an understatement, but she has enough to worry about.* "The twins seemed improved when I woke up just before dawn," he added. "Both of them took some water by straw; they had a good sucking reflex even though they never came fully conscious."

"And now this?" She turned her head and gave him an agonized searching look. "With Ibrahim? Why?"

"No idea."

Ibrahim jerked then and his face turned paler, its handsome features contorted in a silent snarl. Gaelan moaned in his sleep and reached his hand toward his brother's. Elia leaned over the bed and soothed Ibrahim's sweating brow with her mother's touch. He twisted his head away, but one eye opened and blinked at her, its pupil dilated, crazed, flickering at her nervously.

"I'll get Eva," Joshua said, leaving the room. *And yes, I do feel like something is happening, Elia. Thank you for surfacing it. I think I've felt it before. Zurvan's cooked up some kind of surprise for us, somehow.*

O'Donnell Enclave, Waimanu, HI | Thursday 1011 HST

Eva struggled to stay upright as she walked down the hall from the Council Chamber. Uncertainty followed in her mind's wake: *is the locus weakening because I am, or conversely?* Did it matter? *When your resources become limited, you have to allocate. Triage.*

She could not be all things to all people, members of the Council had just advised her. And, after all, she had done what was most important, finding a cure for the Nova virus, they told her. *But three days without the world hearing from me, and it goes to hell in a hand basket? That's not fair!*

And just when she thought the corner had been turned and she could take a rest, there was this... thing... some psychic dark shadow burrowing into their enclave. *I should have seen it coming.* Her sandal caught an unevenness in the rock floor and she stumbled. Demuzzio, following, took quick steps and caught her.

"I think you should be back in bed, Eva."

"Can't."

"You gave the world a great little speech, honey. Let's get you something to eat and then back into bed."

"No. I need to see Ib again."

"He's doing okay last I heard. Both twins."

"When?"

"Around sunrise. Josh said they took some water, by mouth."

"No. Gaelan's okay, but Ib needs help."

He looked at her quizzically. "You haven't seen them. You came to me as soon as you woke up."

"Ib needs help," she repeated.

"Okay then, Eva. Lean on me."

They walked down the long hall, Demuzzio taking a lot of her weight. *Which isn't what it should be,* she realized. *Am I that dehydrated? Why?*

Joshua's footsteps sounded from around the corner. She read the urgency in their haste.

"TC, shut down the links to outside," he said. "The phone, the satellite dishes, everything."

"Huh?"

"There's a K'Shmar Field generator trained on us."

"What? How? And we're shielded!"

A hundred tiny connections clicked over in Eva's brain and added up. *He's right. And I sensed it but I'm so damn drained I never put it together.* She took her arm off Demuzzio's broad shoulder. "He's right, Uncle Tee. Do it."

"And then find the goddamn thing," Joshua added. "It can't be far away."

Demuzzio rubbed his head and objected. "The Army patrols just swept the property; there's nothing out there..."

"Tell them to sweep it again."

"... and we're not detecting any anomalies on the GCN, Josh."

"Wouldn't, this close to the locus."

Demuzzio looked doubtful. *He doesn't want to believe he could have failed us,* Eva thought. She squeezed his arm. "He's right, Uncle Tee."

"And look offshore," her brother instructed.

"Nothin' out there but the whale research vessel, Josh. And I checked that out yester... oh, sweet Jesus." Demuzzio's face went pale. "Zurvan used that cover before, didn't he? In Ireland."

"Probably."

"You think he's out there? Himself?"

"Not a chance. It's the usual research boat. Probably the usual crew; all good people. We know them. But I bet they've got a new crew member."

"Who's pretending to track the whales with some new kind of technology," Demuzzio added grimly, "I get it."

"Coast Guard," Joshua said, moving in to support Eva.

Demuzzio gently handed Eva off to her brother. "Roger that."

"But carefully," Eva whispered. "Those people are our friends. The whales' friends."

"Good point," her brother agreed. "Could get dicey, TC. Hostages or something. Before you shut everything down here, call Carol. Let her run the op."

Demuzzio turned and trotted down the hall. Eva took comfort in her brother's arm around her, but sensed its weakness. They both turned carefully back toward the infirmary.

"You'll feel better when we get the K'Shmar Field shut off," Joshua told her, "and the locus reasserts itself."

"Maybe. But the locus won't reassert."

"No?" His arm twitched at that news.

"No. Waimanu is weakening." *Its power is declining, or shifting elsewhere. Is it prescient? Or have my thoughts started it on its way?*

"I thought it was an ordering function. Too much chaos?"

"I don't know," she sighed.

"I was coming to get you, Eva. Ibrahim needs your help."

"I know." *As do you, brother. As do we all. The question is... with Waimanu fading will there be enough left of me to help all those who need it?*

Abu Sayyaf SH, General Santos City, Philippines | Thursday 0511 PHT

In the dark predawn hours, Muhammad Zurvan turned restlessly in the narrow bed of his safe house in the Philippine Islands. Sweat beaded his forehead, and in his dream he twisted away from a bony reaching hand. The hand stretched out, elongated, and stroked his sweat away.

The face of his Crone appeared above the hand, speaking soothing words in some language he only half-understood. He kept his head turned but his one open eye watched her hand nervously.

"I don't want love," he told her. "I want power."

"I know," she said, and the left half of her face morphed into that of a much younger woman.

Her dark eyes froze him, terrified him, but he was young and weak and couldn't move.

"Mama," he uttered, but no sound came out of his mouth. Kaleidoscopic images whipped across his vision, animating the face looming above him.

"Muhammad," that face whispered, fading in and out of focus.

"Ibrahim," an answering echo came from some uncertain middle distance.

Huge lips descended toward him, landing like a cloud on his forehead. He twisted his head to the other side, but the lips kissed him softly anyway.

"Muhammad," the face whispered again as it pulled back. Its lips became gnarled and split, and fangs grew from the blackness of its opening mouth. He tried to scream, but no sound would come.

"Ibrahim," the echo resonated, "look at your mother. Please."

The only mother Zurvan remembered, and only vaguely, was the one his father the Ayatollah had whipped to death when he was three years old. This face leaning over him had the same dark eyes.

"Muhammad," the whisper was harsher, and now he recognized it. His Crone. *You're dead, Hessa. You must be. The O'Donnell boy killed you. Go away, leave me.*

The face morphed again, more slowly, into the much younger prettier one. "Ibrahim," it called to him. A room swam into focus behind her face, a hospital look to it. His one open eye blinked. *No, not my mama.* Disbelief crumbled slowly, until... *You, child? You, Elia Gibran Baradei O'Donnell? The girl I tortured and raped in Irian Jaya years ago? Who the Crone said was my very own daughter?*

A hundred mental connections parsed the chaos of his dream and suddenly Zurvan knew it was more than a dream. *I am linked to a child's mind, but not my own from my childhood.*

Other connections followed, imposing order on the chaos, and the answer came with a flash of certainty: *the mind of Ibrahim O'Donnell. A Nova sapiens. And I am the boy's biological father. By union with my own daughter.* Astonishment was shoved aside by crazed mirth. It built and built into a crescendo that finally his mind could no longer contain, and it drove his body fully awake and off the narrow bed.

Muhammad Zurvan ran to the safe house window and howled his mad glee out into the humid tropical air, toward the mosque and its minaret, toward the moon beyond as it set in the western sky.

O'Donnell Enclave, Waimanu, HI | Thursday 1212 HST

"It should be okay, Joshua. This tranquilizer isn't a central nervous system depressant," Sarah said as she pressed the plunger. "It won't interfere with Eva's antidote." Ibrahim twitched as the needle pulled out. Joshua released his iron grip on his son's arm and watched his body relax. Elia had taken Eva to the kitchen for food, where Pastor Bob was preparing lunch.

"I'll stay with them, Joshua. Get something to eat. Please."

"I will. But a few questions..."

"Hmm?"

His mind flickered through chaotic combinations, unable in its weariness to form proper logic. *Ask anyway,* he thought, *maybe something will come together.*

"Epigenetics, Sarah. Imprinted markers on kids from their environment, their culture, their physical and mental and spiritual nourishment..."

"Yes, Joshua?" Sarah looked at him expectantly. "What?"

"They're just the software; they don't change the machine."

"Good analogy. The markers control the expression of the gene, but don't physically modify the underlying DNA. So yes, the software makes the computer run a different program, but it doesn't change any of the chips inside. What's the nature of your question?"

Joshua lowered his aching head into his hands. Even though he'd felt better after the electronic links to the outside world were cut, the depth of his son's misery dragged down his mind. *I'm too fuzzy, I can't even frame the right damn root question.*

Sarah tried to help. "Is that what you're asking, Joshua? About Eva's antidote?" She didn't wait for his answer. "Epigenetics isn't evolution; it doesn't change DNA. But the markers can control how a gene is expressed."

"For how long?" he mumbled. *Is that the right question?*

"The science is too new. Nobody really knows. Before Eva, epigenetic changes were mostly a biological response to an environmental stressor."

He raised his head to look at her. "The stress goes away, the gene goes back to its programmed expression."

"Exactly. But the residual effect can last through many generations before it fades."

"Eva's antidote, vaccine, whatever it is..."

"An incremental victory, Joshua," Sarah conceded, "and maybe temporary. But for now it's a good thing. A very good thing. The survival of an evolving species. Be happy. And go get some food. Guava juice, drink a quart; you need the fruit sugar and the vitamins."

He saw the compassion and wisdom in her eyes and nodded. *But I'll only be happy when Ibrahim turns back into his old self. And maybe not even then.*

"Fucker blew himself up," Demuzzio reported as he ran into the infirmary. "I watched from the lanai, saw it happen. He was right there, on the starboard side when the Coast Guard chopper lowered their team."

Well, that's unambiguous, at least. Joshua stood up, pushing on the bed for support. "Casualties?" he asked.

"Probably. But nobody was really close to him. And the explosion looked small, probably just a self-destruct for the machine, not a mass bomb."

"Okay, TC. Put all the links back up. I think we'll be okay."

"Navy's on the way to survey for subs. I asked Carol for that favor before we shut down comm. Just in case."

"Good idea." *And one I should have thought of too. What's the matter with me?* "Listen, TC. When you get the casualty report, just tell me, okay? Not Eva. Not yet. Those whale researchers were her friends."

Demuzzio nodded and left the infirmary.

Joshua straightened himself up wearily and spoke to Sarah with a half-smile. "Guava juice. Be happy. Incremental victory. Got it, Doctor Kruse."

He left Sarah with the twins and walked his worries down the hall to the stairs for the kitchen. *Incremental victory. But what if the damage to Ib is too great, what if his condition can't be reversed? Will he become some kind of chimera? Some uncertain state between Nova and Homo? Or something worse?*

And at the root of those questions, he realized, was a deeper one that his mind had never wanted to ask. It slid uneasily around the periphery of his consciousness, fuzzy and unformed, evading his attempts to bring it into focus.

O'Donnell Enclave, Waimanu, HI | *Thursday 1414 HST*

A distant pull, strange yet familiar. *The reason the locus is fading here is because it's building in Irian Jaya,* Eva Connard suddenly realized. *There's only so much order in chaos. And that order lives at the edges...*

Questions flowed from that. *Is the locus prescient? Anticipatory? Am I intended to return to Irian Jaya? Does the locus need to build there to receive me? Has it read my plan? Or am I somehow following its plan? Or are our plans converging? Karma?*

And what of free will: *does it exist or not for me?*

Eva took a deep breath, gathered her wandering thoughts and focused back on the twins. Eventually she lifted her hands off their foreheads.

"Sarah's right, Josh. They're pulling out of it. Both of them. Slowly. Gaelan first."

Her brother let out his breath, almost a whimper. He hugged her, hard. "Thank you, Sis."

She put her hand on his forehead. "You're healing, too... but... somehow I feel you have farther to go." *The edges of chaos are strange places, brother... intersections of quantum effects... multidimensional Mandelbrot sets, you yourself once called them. And those edges are constantly shifting. I will return to Irian Jaya, I think.*

O'Donnell Enclave, Waimanu, HI | Thursday 1657 HST

TC Demuzzio studied the image of Pastor Robert Blake on his monitor. The camera had a pretty good angle on the waterfall and pool, but wasn't close enough to pick up the sound of the phone conversation over the white noise of the running water. *If I could find a lip-reader...*

Certainly the operations of the preacher's ministry were none of anyone's business in the O'Donnell enclave. Certainly he had no business snooping. Certainly the man was a Nova Council member and had been vetted by Eva personally. *But still... those tiny tells: an eyebrow here, a bit of forced laughter there...* Competing parcels of logic and intuition tried to organize the suspicions in his mind. Then Joshua walked into the Security Center and his focus shifted.

"You're looking better, Josh." *Fatigue lines are still there, but his face isn't a death-skull. That's good.* "Much better, actually."

"Guava juice, TC. Doctor's orders. Been sucking it down all afternoon. I got pretty dehydrated, apparently. Eva more so."

"Sarah? Elia?"

"No. Or at least not much. The twins, some, but they're better too. Sarah took them off the IV's."

"You think it was the K'Shmar? The ship arrived offshore just after dawn."

"A factor, probably. The timing fits. But other things are happening; the situation is too damn complex, TC. Too many variables, and how they relate... synergistic, antagonistic... it's all gone chaotic."

"Yeah, the outside world too."

"Shit. Tell me."

"Sure you want to know?"

"I need to."

Demuzzio turned toward the console and keyed video clips onto the big screen. Thumbnails ran down its left side and a click brought one to enlarge and play, then another. Bangalore. Paris. Jakarta. London.

"Riots everywhere, Josh. Especially third world countries, especially Muslim. Zurvan's got 'em stoked. The cocksucker."

"Hunting Novas?"

"Yeah. Sisterhood's covering all they can."

"How many Nova kids have we lost?"

"That's not so bad, actually; just a handful. So far."

"So Zurvan got them stoked, but not organized."

"Yeah, some of that I think. But we've got Nova supporters in the general population. Some pitched battles to defend Novas. Shitload of collateral damage."

"The Sisterhood's myth? Eva said she wouldn't trigger it, except as a last resort."

"She didn't, Josh. I think it just came out of the conflict spontaneously."

"Another random factor."

"Fucking chaos," Demuzzio agreed. He keyed out of the video clips and threw some charts up. "The world markets tanked, all of them. The Nikkei looks like it'll open lower tomorrow. Everything else will probably slide along with it."

Joshua sighed, and Demuzzio thought the fatigue lines in his face deepened again.

"You send Eva's message out, TC?"

"I sent it to Carol, let her guzzy it up. We're all too frazzled here."

"Oh... good idea. She put it out?"

"Will shortly. The Prez will add his message, appeal for sanity, she said."

Joshua sighed again. "Let's hope it works." He nodded toward the small monitor with the security camera images. "What's Pastor Bob doing by the waterfall? Praying?"

"Coordinating with his UMC folks in California, I think."

"He needs to get back there. It's Easter week. Good Friday tomorrow."

"He said he can stay until after supper."

"Eva?"

"She wants him here, I think. As long as he can stay."

"You okay with that, TC? The relationship, I mean."

"No. But..." he shrugged, "love is love."

"And Eva is Eva."

"Yeah. About how I feel, too, Josh. Like one of those big rogue waves caught me offshore and now all I can do is go along for the ride."

They looked at each other for a while.

"Josh, about Pastor Bob..."

"Yeah?"

Eva walked into the Security Center.

"Aw, never mind," Demuzzio said.

Chapter 24

O'Donnell Enclave, Waimanu, HI | Thursday 1717 HST

The two of them sat, as Demuzzio had insisted, on the comfortable semicircular bench behind the kitchen table. They watched him work at preparing food for dinner. Eva nestled herself against her big brother's arm and rested her head on his shoulder. Mr. Bojangles leaped into her lap and settled into a steady purr. *Comforting*, she thought, *this eye of the storm.*

"Easy on those Habeneros, TC," Josh offered, "not everyone has your chrome-plated innards."

"Buncha wimps." The big man grinned at them and popped a piece of one in his mouth. "Besides, hot peppers are good for the immune system. The hell with all these genetic cures."

Eva laughed through her bone-chilling weariness. *Maybe he's right. They'd heat me up, anyway.*

"Please," Joshua added.

"Okay, okay. Don't worry about it; they temper down when they cook."

"I love you, Uncle Tee," Eva whispered.

A tear ran down the man's craggy cheek. "Maybe you're right, Josh." He rubbed his cheek on his shirt shoulder. "These local-grown are smokin' hot. I'll do half."

He scraped some of the pepper cuttings into a plastic bag. "I love you, too, honey." He wiped his other cheek then looked up at her. "And that was a great speech. We're getting the momentum back, I think. Josh?"

"The global consciousness ticked up strongly, TC. I'd say Eva generated a lot of empathy out there. It was a strong message. And Carol packaged it nicely."

"Think it'll stop the insanity out there?"

Good question. Eva's Sisters spiraled in and took station in their customary orbits. They offered varied opinions on the question, drawn from their own life experiences plus what they saw in her mind.

"Nothing is more difficult than establishing a new order of things," the Sister named Marietta said, "as I often told my Nicolo."

Heads nodded around the circle. "But love helps," another added.

The circle entities shifted and swayed and entered into different alignments, compositing their opinions for Eva.

"Power concedes nothing," one grouping said.

"Yet love is powerful," a second responded, "at evoking concessions."

Both things are true, Eva thought, *but not helpful. I need specifics.*

The first grouping hardened into a clear position. "Unleash the Sisterhood assassins, Young Mother. They are prepared. Your brother has worked out the plan with them, in all its intricate detail. Do it now, before the timing is lost."

"Not all of his targets have actually become enemies," Eva countered.

"Selectively, then. And become the god that evolution has made you."

Eva shook her head and asked for other perspectives: "Devi?"

A Sister separated from the second grouping, circling Eva at a slow thoughtful pace, giving Eva her thoughts. "Ashoka was a killer, a violent man in a violent time. But then he found his way."

"You showed him the way, Devi."

"A way can be shown, but it still must be found. My husband found it in the ruins of the torched buildings, in the cries of the dying, in the wails of their children. In the sorrow that he created."

"I would save my Robert, Devi. Make him my Ashoka for these modern times."

"Bah, wishful thinking," the first grouping countered. "The man loves power more than you, Young Mother. He will fail the monkey trap test."

"If he loves, he can be saved," Devi protested sadly. "There is always a chance."

The spirit-Sister thoughts rattled around in her mind as she listened concurrently to her brother's opinion in the physical world.

"Eva's message won't stop the insanity, TC. But my guess is it'll slow it down, give people a chance to think. That's what usually happens when the GCN shows an anticipatory response."

"Fired off ahead of the webcast, did it?"

"Yeah. Just after she taped it. Even before you sent it to Carol."

"Gives me the shivers when that happens."

"Me, too."

Even with her eyes shut, Eva saw Demuzzio studying her. *A scary thing, what you can't understand*, she agreed.

The distinctive sounds of Robert Blake's footsteps approached down the hall. She wormed closer against her brother for comfort and suspended the communion with her spirit-Sisters.

"Hey, Thomas," the man said as he entered, "security is your job. Food is mine."

"You seemed busy out there on the phone, Bob. And the pressure is off a little bit. We thought to leave you to take care of your church matters."

"Ah. Thanks. I think everything is back on track now. Where's Eva?"

Demuzzio nodded toward the corner and Blake turned around. Eva caught a scowl fleeting across his face, quickly smoothed over.

Oh, Robert! He's my brother. We've been through more trials together that you can imagine. She smiled at him until he smiled back. Only then did she raise her head off Joshua's shoulder and straighten up. *What was that look? Jealous or fearful?*

The big tomcat in her lap stopped purring. She stroked him absently.

O'Donnell Enclave, Waimanu, HI | *Thursday 1719 HST*

Robert Blake felt his face start to grimace again, but smoothed it over quickly. *That should be my shoulder she's leaning on.* He forced a smile. *I need her depending on me, just a little longer.*

"The pressure is off?" Blake sought the meaning in Demuzzio's statement. "You're recovering, Eva? Feeling better? And you, Joshua?"

"I wish," Joshua said.

Eva just groaned.

"No. It's the outside world that's feeling better, Bob," Demuzzio said to his back, "Eva's message gave us the momentum again."

"Maybe," Joshua cautioned.

"For a while," Eva added.

"Well, Sarah showed me the message you taped, Eva." Blake widened his smile. "It was masterful. Heartfelt. You made some converts."

"I'm not in the religion business, Robert."

"Maybe you should be." He kept his expression lightly amused. *And you will be, Eva, in a way. My way.*

"I'm an evolutionary development, not a messiah. Nor is any Nova."

"So you've said. And I believe you. Not messiahs, not devils. So when the crisis is over, maybe we could do a joint sermon?"

"Stop teasing me, Robert. I'm too tired."

Blake laughed. "Okay. But the world's response — that we're seeing on the GCN — that has to have knocked Zurvan and the other idiots off their pace."

"Some of those idiots are your televangelist colleagues, Bob," Demuzzio noted.

"Don't put me in the same clown car with them, now, TC. I'm a reasonable man."

"We know. Or you wouldn't be here."

Was there some kind of edge to that? Blake turned back to study Demuzzio.

Did that long encrypted phone call bother him? "Can I help you with dinner, TC? Anything?"

Demuzzio grunted. "Sure, Bob. Slice up these avocados and make a salad or a dessert or something."

His vibes are changing. The clock's running out on me. The Senator was right: it's got to be tonight. "Be happy to," he said, picking up one of the fruits and a paring knife. *Nothing like elbow-to-elbow shared labor to keep the trust alive.*

He changed the subject as he peeled. "Eva. The antidote? It's gone out? Anything I need to take back to the coast with me later?"

"We got the packages to Vandenberg. The Air Force flew them from there to the various labs; they're already synthesizing it."

Blake nodded. *Find out what you can now. You won't have a chance later. And you don't know what might be valuable.* "So tell me, how does it work? Sarah said it's a two-function solution, one change inside the DNA and one outside? Something about methylation?"

"I can't express it in biochemical terms, Robert, I haven't got the language."

"Yet you did it. Created a cure."

"Not by knowledge. By... feel, by intuition, by some kind of sensing of the way things should be."

"Well, okay. Tell me about that; I wouldn't understand the biochemistry anyway. Sarah said the antidote part is genetic, a repair to a vulnerability in the Nova gene that lets it fight the virus. I get that. But the epigenetic shield? I don't get that."

Eva looked at him, struggling for words. Joshua answered for her. "If the infection has set in, Bob, the antidote cures it. But if it hasn't set in, the vaccine is a shield that will keep it from attacking the genetic structure. It sits above the gene: ergo, epigenetic."

"Why two parts?"

"That's where Eva's intuition was so brilliant: because we don't know everything. The antidote is pretty serious cellular manipulation of a new human gene; it's risky and we can't predict all the outcomes."

"Probably some Novas will die from it," Eva said. Her lip quivered.

"So, Eva, you created a shield that sits on top of the gene?"

"I guess that's close enough in concept."

"And how does it work?"

"It closes off the pathway the virus takes into the cellular structure."

"I've read some about epigenetics... you have to read this stuff in my business, because evolution is such a tricky area for religion. I've read some of the work on the effects of the environment on fruit flies, worms, lab rats. But in humans?"

Joshua spread his hands. "Too complex. No scientist really knows."

"Yet the Sisterhood of the Implicate Order..." Blake started.

Eva raised an eyebrow. "Yes?"

"... has practiced epigenetics down through millennia..."

"Essentially, yes."

"... conditioning genetic development from the outside, through the culture, the environment..."

"You pried that out of Sarah? Clever!"

"... ultimately leading to actual changes in DNA, yes?"

"The mechanisms are still not fully understood, Robert. Even with modern mapping of the human genetic code."

"You understand this sort of thing raises issues with the more... traditional... of my religious brethren."

"Another knife for them to cut us with, yes." Eva's eyes flickered with light as she stared at him. "Is that a problem for you?"

"Not at all," he lied through his smile.

O'Donnell Enclave, Waimanu, HI | Thursday 1742 HST

The two of them sat alone in the Council Chamber, Eva having felt the need for a quieter place. Her brother waited patiently, respecting her need for reflection, for communion with her ancestral spirit-Sisters. She looked around the room, at its walls carved out of volcanic rock. *This is a good place, our enclave.*

"We'll eat supper here, Josh," she said, "and ask our virtual members to break bread with us."

"Convene the entire Council? Across time zones? Not that they'll mind, I guess..." Joshua got up without further question and removed from the big table the holographic projector keyed to Pastor Robert Blake. He pushed a spare chair against the table in its place. Seven projectors remained on the table, their dark lenses staring up into the space where the holograms of the Council members would shortly be projected.

"And we'll put a glass of wine in front of each projector," Eva added.

"You're too beat to be whimsical, Eva. Symbolic?"

"So we can toast each other."

"You have a feeling about this? That we've turned the corner?" Joshua shook his head. "All my logic says the battle isn't over yet."

"No," she agreed, her voice distant in her own ears, "it's not." *But it will be. Come to me, Sisters.* They did, spiraling into a tight protective circle around her mind. She asked her questions, seeking precedents, seeking their relevance to a more modern age.

"Many of us in your line of descent have been close to becoming a Nova, Eva," the spirit of Bathsheba told her. "But our old world was not ready for a female savior."

That made Eva grimace. "I'm not sure this modern one is either."

"So we chose to work through men," her Sister continued. "Gave them what power we had."

"You gave them magic and miracles."

"Yes. We guided, helped. It was a different time. The Sisterhood's gentle female gods of the forest and water and sky had been displaced by the angry conquering male gods. Patiently we fostered the proper environment for their minds; patiently we installed the proper influences — what you now call epigenetics — into the marrow of men. As I did in my lover, David, and our son Solomon after him. For centuries. Millennia, I see in your mind."

"And into the female line, too."

"Yes, certainly. We are glad to see our work come to fruit."

Eva thought about the concept. *Come to fruit. No birth without pain. Does the avocado Robert was peeling feel pain in nature when it ripens and splits asunder to spread its seed? I wonder.* Her query went off on a tangent as more of the ancient's memories presented themselves. A certain resonance hinted they could be relevant to her developing plan.

"Eva?" Joshua's voice came from some uncertain middle distance.

She held up a finger. "The more strands of great myths that are incorporated into a story, the more resonance it will have." She saw her brother nod and go silent, respecting her communion state. She went back to it, to Bathsheba: "The Pentateuch, ancient Sister, the first books of the Jewish Torah, and subsequently the Christian Bible, the Muslim Qur'an..."

"Yes, I edited those works, Young Mother. I did what I could to soften them. The Sisterhood has always taken targets of opportunity. Words are important. Their proper choice in documents that persist down through time can lead to subtle conditioning of the mind."

"For better or worse."

"Yes, of course."

"My modern world has images. Instantaneous."

"So I see in your mind. Your modern world moves much faster than my old world. And images can be even more powerful than words, more directly put into the soul."

Eva nodded. *Our conditioning is faster. The question is... can I make it fast enough?*

Bathsheba faded into a composite of spirits, some more ancient, some more modern, and their thoughts were as diverse as their experiences and personalities. Eva parsed them and pulled out commonalities as she exited the communion and set both feet back in reality. *The Christos myth, and its predecessors like Osiris in Egypt... yes, use them. But not, maybe, as the Sisterhood has intended.*

Joshua was watching her.

"Okay, Sis?"

She nodded. "Could you call down to the kitchen and ask them to put supper on the cart and bring it up here? I'm too tired to even move."

O'Donnell Enclave, Waimanu, HI | Thursday 1836 HST

Twelve expectant faces looked at him from around the big table, five physical and seven holographic.

"Of course, Eva, I'd be happy to do a blessing." He smiled at the assemblage. "I'm feeling a bit awkward since there are so many faiths represented here..."

That drew some return smiles. *These of all people appreciate the irony of the disruptive threat Novas represent to established religious traditions.*

"... so I'll just keep it generic." Blake paused and looked up at the sculpted rock ceiling of the Council Chamber while his practiced mind slid into something appropriate. He spread his arms wide to embrace them all then brought his hands together in prayer.

"Dear God, we ask that you bless this food and drink, and cause it to replenish and nurture not only the bodies, but also the minds and souls of all here who have labored so long and so hard to do Thy will. We ask that you bring our new species of human gently into this new day, and that the Nova children be greeted with love and understanding. We ask that you help all of humanity to resolve our differences and bring peace to these troubled times."

He lowered his eyes to Eva. *And would you be that God, Eva Connard? Or is there another, higher order of being behind you?*

She looked back at him evenly, a slight smile playing around her mouth. All faces turned toward her, both physical and holographic.

"Amen," Eva said.

Blake blinked. *You must realize that a God incarnate is fundamentally less manageable for us in the religion business. We much prefer our present inchoate deity; it can be molded to our needs and purposes. And you can't, child. Obviously.*

"I love you, Robert," Eva said aloud.

On his immediate left came a sharp inhalation of breath from Demuzzio. Blake watched other faces around the circle display a variety of emotions ranging from bemusement to consternation. *That's the first time she's said it publicly.*

"And I you too, Eva," he settled on an innocuous tone. *The way she smiled at me, like she's unreachable, behind bulletproof glass or something.* He shook his head, confused. *Does she know I'm betraying her?*

The dinner that followed was given over mostly to growing optimism as reports of favorable developments trickled in from various Councilor networks around the world. Blake listened without much comment; the uncertainty persisted unabated in his mind: *Has she read it in me somehow? Does she suspect?*

That uncertainty tempered a bit when she complimented his innovative avocado dessert, her speech natural and unweighted by any accompanying ambiguity. *So, no suspicion. Then tonight will work. They're all exhausted anyway, and the food will make them sleepier.*

On cue, Eva yawned and thanked all her Councilors in turn for joining in the supper. She stood up, a little bent at first, but then straightened and squared her shoulders.

"A toast to you all," Eva said, raising her glass.

Twelve glasses, physical and holographic, raised in reply as she spoke.

"Be the light where shadows still remain,

and if and when you ever need me...

be calling out my name:

Love, as always was and ever will be."

Silence deadened the Chamber. Twelve faces above raised glasses stared at Eva, frozen.

"Amen," Pastor Robert Blake finally said, and drank the wine.

"Amen," everyone echoed.

O'Donnell Enclave, Waimanu, HI | Thursday 2012 HST

The lights in the Council Chamber dimmed down behind them as they left. *The Council session was automatically taped and archived, as usual, so Josh will have it when he needs it,* Eva thought. Blake walked well ahead of her, pushing the cart with the dirty dishes and remnants of their meal. She leaned on her brother and spoke softly in his ear. "Robert has been a big help."

"Yeah. Really pitched in when we needed it. Not too proud to do anything. I like that." He put his right arm around her shoulders and squeezed. "It's okay if you love him, I guess."

Her left arm squeezed him back, reflexively. *It's easy to love someone for who they are, Josh. It's not so easy to love someone for who they should have been or could be.*

"Look, everybody," Blake offered as they trooped into the kitchen, "Why don't you all go off to bed? Or do whatever you need to. I'll clean up here."

"You're flying out tonight, right?" Demuzzio asked. "Back to the coast?"

"Soon as I'm done here, yes."

"I'll tell Marta to take you to Waimea. Call upstairs when you're ready, Bob."

"Okay, thanks. An hour, maybe."

"One last thing," Eva injected, "while we're all still here... if you wouldn't mind..."

They all turned to look at her.

"... a little prayer. A blessing."

They nodded.

"Over here." She went to the circular kitchen table, sat down and lit the single candle. "Alternating men and women."

They each sat where she gestured them into place.

"Robert, Josh, Uncle Tee. Join hands, please. On the table."

They did.

Without being asked, Sarah and Elia joined hands with Eva, and together they laid their forearms over the men's. In the middle of the human six-pointed star thus formed the candle flickered then burned more brightly. Eva began the chant, Elia followed, and then Sarah. Their chant became a song, complex and contrapuntal, in an old lost language, an ancient Sisterhood paean of life and death and sorrow and hope. The candle flared and cast splintered light on each of them.

As their song ended, the candle smoldered out.

"The locus is fading," Joshua whispered.

Eva opened eyes flickering with light and looked directly across the human star at Blake's pale face. *Without the Novas, we could slide back, Robert. Humanity could destroy itself.*

"Thank you all for humoring me," she said softly. "And now I'm going to bed." She kissed them on the cheek, one by one, Blake last.

As Eva walked alone down the long hall to her sleeping quarters, her spirit-Sisters took up station around her mind and she framed a question for Mary of Magdala: *When Judas kissed Jesus, did Jesus kiss him back?*

Chapter 25

O'Donnell Enclave, Waimanu, HI | Thursday 2311 HST

"Yes, tell Marta I'm packing and I'll be up in a moment," Blake told Demuzzio. "And then for God's sake get some sleep yourself, TC. The outside world doesn't look like it's going to implode overnight without your attention."

Demuzzio yawned hugely. "Yeah. Probably. The GCN's gone pretty flat. You're right, Bob." He lumbered out of the guest quarters. "Catch some z's yourself on your trip back. And good luck with your UMC Easter ceremony. Do us some good, okay? One of your great sermons?"

"Working on it," Blake spoke to the man's back. Demuzzio's hand waggled a V signal back over his shoulder as he turned down the corridor. *Excellent,* Blake thought, *he went left to the sleeping quarters. They'll all be clustered for exposure at the same time.*

He flipped open his suitcase and pulled out the dog-eared leather-covered bible, undid the gold clasp and removed one of the two small gas cylinders from its hollowed-out pages. He studied it for a moment. *Two rotations clockwise and a two-minute delay. The Senator had better be right.*

Blake pocketed the other cylinder, tossed the empty bible in his suitcase and zipped it up. Then he held a tissue to the vent in the lower wall beside the bed. It pulled against the grate and held there. He nodded. *I wonder where the Senator dug up those old construction drawings? You'd think that Hamilton O'Donnell would have found a way to purge them from DOD archives.* He shrugged and undid the loosened screws and set the grate aside. *Your intel has been perfect so far, Senator. I'm hoping it is this time too.* He looked at his watch, twisted the top of the cylinder twice, set it in the duct as far as he could reach, and screwed the grate back on, loosely.

The newest and greatest sleeping gas, the Senator had told him, always disabling but rarely fatal. Mathematical models gave it an hour to permeate the entire facility at a sufficient exposure level, he'd said.

"Hope you're right, Senator," Blake whispered to the grate as he picked up his suitcase and exited.

Trepidation and elation accompanied him up the hall in equal measure. *The die has been cast. No place to go but on.* That was a relief, in a strange way, from the ambivalence he'd felt when Eva had chanted her strange blessing over twelve clasped hands in the kitchen. The elevator to the surface stood open awaiting him. He punched the button, then spent the ride up arranging his face into its best pastoral expression.

"Good evening, Marta," he told the SIO guard waiting at the enclave's surface entry, "I'm all set to go."

"Evening, Doctor Blake."

"Running a tad late, actually. Can we hustle to the airport?"

"Not a problem." The woman nodded as she took his bag and held the SUV door open. "The only traffic this time of night is the occasional wild pig. Half an hour, tops."

He nodded. *Right on the mark with the Senator's schedule, good.*

"I've admired your sermons, sir," Marta said as the SUV dropped down the ramp to the gravel road. "Especially how you meshed them with some of Eva's addresses."

Blake relaxed. *If Eva has any suspicions, she didn't convey them to Demuzzio or this woman.* "Thank you, Marta. I try." He gave her his humble smile. *Get her take on current events, how they assess the risk to the enclave.* He chose to ease into it indirectly.

"How do you think the battle is going?"

"Battle, sir?"

"Struggle, whatever. The Novas and our voices of reason against the insanity out there?"

"A Council member would seem to have a better handle on that than a simple soldier, Dr. Blake."

He laughed at that. "Simple soldier, huh? Baloney, Marta; no one in the SIO is that. How do you think it's going?"

In the dim light from the dashboard Marta's expression went contemplative, and she concentrated on driving for a long moment before she spoke. "Seems to be playing out pretty much like the Sisterhood myth."

Blake nodded. "And what do you think of that myth?"

"No official opinion, sir."

"A personal one then. Unless you'd rather not say."

She gave him a quick sideways glance after they jounced over the bridge. "I wouldn't want to offend you."

"No, please. I'd like to hear your view. Straight and unvarnished."

"I don't like it. It's too bloody. Maybe a bit better than the Christian and Islamic end-times myth, but not by much."

"And yet you're ready for it."

"Prepare for the worst while you hope for the best."

"And is the enclave ready for the worst?" Blake slipped in the question casually. He was entitled to it, he figured, as a concerned Council member.

Marta sighed. "Honestly? If there's an attack I'd be worried. My team is down to three of us. Eva sent the others out to protect Nova kids across the world."

"But your Special Forces friends are still patrolling the forest?"

"Yeah. They're good. But they're pretty thin, too."

That's all I need to know, Marta. The Senator will fill me in on the rest, I'm sure. To deflect her from thinking about his questions too much he went back to natural curiosity. "The Sisterhood myth... is that a sort of mandatory belief?"

"Oh no, not at all. The SIO is a big tent, Dr. Blake. It accommodates a number of different personality types and belief systems. We all have our own opinions."

The SUV jounced across a wooden plank bridge.

"Thank you, Marta. That's been most informative."

O'Donnell Enclave, Waimanu, HI | Thursday 2327 HST

"Morning, TC," Carol Violette answered his call in a sprightly tone. "We're doing better on this end, I think. You guys?"

"You sound too damn good to be a NSC in a crisis like this," he snapped, "at what, 0530 in DC?"

The National Security Coordinator laughed. "I actually got three hours solid sleep on my West Wing office couch. You jealous?"

"I went to bed, but I got this niggling little thing running around in the back of my head, Carol. Wonder if you could give me a hand with it."

"Is it legal?"

"Maybe."

"Ah. Well, we're doing a brisk business in ambiguity over here these days." She laughed again. "Hey, I'm getting ready to give the Prez his morning brief at 0600. Can you tell me quick or should I call you back after?"

"NSA's monitoring cell phones around here, right?"

"Waimanu area? Absolutely. NSA has the area totally blanketed. Why?"

Demuzzio paused. *I must be crazy.* "Because Pastor Bob..."

"Yeah?"

He paused again. *Maybe paranoid.* "...spent a lot of the afternoon and evening outside on his cell phone."

"So? It's Easter, and he's got a huge congregation needing his attention. Especially now. It must be a nightmare for him, trying to manage that from a distance."

"Yeah, that's what he said. Except for the nightmare."

"He's a Council member, TC. Like you and me. He's fully engaged on the Nova side. What's your issue?"

"The call was encrypted."

"Most corporate stuff is these days; the technology cost is dropping like crazy. Again, so...?"

"He sat by the waterfall, so the security cam couldn't pick up any sound."

"Mmm."

"You think I'm paranoid, don't you?"

"Lack of sleep will do that sometimes, TC," she said gently.

"But still... you think NSA has it on tape? The conversation?"

"Oh sure."

"Could you have them decrypt it?"

"It would take a while. And some legal dancing... there are privacy issues."

"Will you?"

"Pastor Bob plays golf with the Prez. A bunch of Congressmen too."

"Will you?"

"If it was anyone but you, TC, I'd think they were nuts."

"Will you?"

The NSC sighed. "Okay. After I brief the Prez, I'll see what I can do."

"You gotta go, Carol. Sorry I'm cranky. Sorry I have to ask this." But Demuzzio felt the relief sweep over him now that the itch was scratched. *And suddenly I'm so tired I'm about to fall over sideways.*

Her voice came back from a greater distance. "You sound really beat, TC; more than just your cranky old self. But you're entitled. I'll get NSA to chase down Pastor Bob's conversation for you. Get some sleep."

"Thanks, Carol," he replied and clicked off. He blinked at the monitor screens but they wouldn't come into focus. Then he did fall off his chair, sideways.

Kamuela Airstrip, Waimea, HI | Thursday 2348HST

The UMC executive jet sat on a distant part of the taxiway, engines idling as they drove up to it. Marta carried Blake's bag up the stairs. As she swung it into the passenger compartment the Taser dart caught her in the thigh. A woman crouched over Marta's twitching body and jammed a device against her neck. Marta stopped twitching. The woman started undoing Marta's blouse and looked up at Blake.

"Why don't you just call me Marta, Dr. Blake? It'll save on the introductions."

He stared at the woman. *Quite an organization the Senator has.*

"Yes, that's right; I could be her twin," the woman read his mind.

"Your voice is slightly different... Marta."

She frowned. "Are there any voice-recognition security systems at the enclave?"

"Not that I know of."

The woman stared at him a long moment as she slipped into Marta's blouse. "Good," she said. She held up Marta's limp arm and wiggled it. "Any handprint scanners?"

"No."

"Good." She giggled and let the arm drop. "Saves a mess."

She pointed down the aircraft steps. "Get back in the car, rear seat, lie on the floor."

He did, watching her turn and wave at the cockpit. The hatch pulled in and the engines whined up. The woman slammed the back door.

"Stay down, doc."

"Nobody around this time of night... Marta."

"You never know. All it takes is one curious insomniac with a long lens and our plan is shit. Stay down."

"If I can't see, I can't guide you in."

Her hard laugh greeted that. "I know the way. Stay the hell down. Just tell me, how many other Sisters guarding the enclave?"

"Two."

"And they are where?"

"Across from the garage lift."

"All right. Now don't say a word until I tell you."

"Okay," he acknowledged, "but how are you going to..."

"Doc! Shut the fuck up. The plan is solid, it's playing out perfectly, that's all you need to know. You're just a chess piece now. You move when I tell you, talk when I tell you."

He grunted and lapsed into silence. Fifteen minutes later he felt the turn off the highway onto the graveled road to the enclave. Five minutes after that, through the gap between the front seats, he saw the woman waggle her fingers at the unseen soldiers at the checkpoint. Nothing happened, and the SUV jounced across the plank bridge over the ravine. Finally they pulled up at the enclave's surface entrance.

"Don't move," the woman cautioned. The pad holding the SUV began its slow descent.

Blake heard the back hatch open, then a zipper, then a metallic ratcheting sound.

"Stay here," she whispered over the rear seat, "I'll be back." The descent stopped.

He did, trying to use logic to keep uncertainty at arm's length. *She is competent. We got past the checkpoint.*

After brief moments filled with dull thuds and clattering echoes, the woman returned.

"Okay, Doc, all clear. Come on, you're gonna get the kid." She handed him a gas mask as he clambered out of the SUV. "You remember how to put this on?"

Blake nodded, and followed her into the subsurface garage.

"The Senator didn't share much of the plan with me past this point. He said you would be directing."

"Yeah, I'm field tactical. Well, here's the plan. First item: put Marta's troops down."

They rounded the corner and two women lay sprawled against the pocked concrete wall, in piles of bullet-ripped flesh and blood. One wide dead eye stared at him. Blake swallowed hard on the rising gorge. *What did I expect?*

"Don't be looking at us, bitch-Sister," the woman snarled and triggered a burst that vaporized the head. Then she smiled happily at Blake. "I'm just not happy with the Sisterhood, you understand."

He swallowed hard again. *This woman has issues.* "Evidently," he offered.

That brought the woman back to business. "Second item: after I nailed the bitches I cut the power to the security systems." She gestured to the ceiling. "But not until after that camera picked me up coming in and blowing them away." She giggled like a schoolgirl. "When the dust settles they'll see how Marta betrayed them. Their most trusted Sister guardian. Cool, huh?"

Blake forced his eyes away from the bloody mess as they walked toward the elevator. "So all the cameras in the enclave are off now?"

"Yup. You can go get the kid, unobserved. Far as they'll ever know, you were en route to the coast. Make sure you collect the gas cylinder."

"Joshua O'Donnell will figure it out, eventually."

"Maybe. But all the plan needs is a few more days, and he's toast. Why? You wanna off him while you're down there?"

The woman stopped as if she'd stepped in glue. "Really interesting shit. I wouldn't have believed it if I hadn't experienced it."

"The locus stop you?"

"Yeah. I can't go any further. Let me see you put your mask on, then come back here so I can check the seal."

He did, and she did.

"Okay, Pastor Bob. Third item: you go get the kid. You do not, repeat, do not do anything else. Just get the girl and the gas cylinder. If you're thinking about whacking Joshua O'Donnell, don't. The Senator's plan specifically says not to."

"Why?"

"Don't know. Not my brief. Not yours either."

He studied her through the lens of the mask, breath rasping in his ears. *It would be safer to kill him. All of them.*

The woman smiled and shook her head. "Don't."

He nodded acceptance. *So the plan uses them somehow. Probably sets Joshua on a vengeance rampage that they can spin to their advantage. Or something devious like that.*

"Good. Fourth item: you're not bringing the kid out this way. Carry her down the trail to the beach. There's gonna be a Zodiac and crew waiting to pick you up." She looked at her watch. "You got exactly eighteen minutes. Go!"

Hilo Harbor, Hilo, HI | Friday 0141 HST

Too late now, Eva admonished herself, *to reconsider.* The decisiveness of that thought might actually have been comforting had it not been punctuated by the ominous sound of a clanging bell.

A buoy? Where am I? What water? Her mind struggled toward a more conscious state but fell back into the waves of darkness lapping around her. *Surrender,* the waves whispered, *it's what you planned.*

Eva let go, and in the dream she drifted over dark water and onto a cold shore in dense fog. The mist seemed to swallow up the waxy brush beneath her hands as she clawed through it toward the sound's origin. Waves of numb paralysis disconnected her legs from her mind's control and she crawled, pulling herself by her arms across a muddy jungle floor into a clearing.

Dark windows glared at her as she pulled her way up rotted wooden steps. The bell was close now. *A missionary outpost? Here? Am I in old Hawaii?* The misty shape of a cross rose from the structure above her to confirm it. *But the land surrounding our enclave has no churches. Irian Jaya, then?*

Her mind fought back momentarily against the confusion and disorientation. *No, it can't be.* A veil of fog settled over her, obscuring all sense of place and time. *The null, then? But I didn't seek it.*

Triggered by that thought, she summoned her spirit-Sisters. A long line of white-robed figures spiraled in toward her mind, mingling with the clouded air. *Just smoky wraiths against the veil. Barely present.*

"We are here for you, Young Mother," they said, but their voices were dim and fractured.

"Where am I? Why can't I remember coming to this place? Have I joined the locus? Waimanu? Irian Jaya?"

The figures jittered with uncertainty. "This place is your mind's creation. Whether or not it exists independent of you we cannot say. We have no frame of reference save your mind."

Eva's eyes searched. In the fog were no anchor points to establish a reference, excepting the church.

"Well, if I made this place, I made whatever is inside the church." She sighed and moved wearily toward the entrance. *It's like swimming in molasses.* She forced herself to turn and look back, and beckoned her sisters to follow.

Inside, a dull green light illuminated withered pews and a degraded altar. There, a lonely figure kneeled in observance of a rusted, house-shaped box. *God's house, or a withered vestige?* Bracing herself against the sides of the pews, Eva pulled her body painfully forward along the aisle. When she finally reached the figure at the far end, she stretched a weary arm and clasped his shoulder.

In the deathly light, her father's countenance turned to look down on her.

"Daddy?" Tears welled and trailed down her cheeks. Collapsing forward, she wrapped her arms around him, dimly aware as she did so that the procession of her spirit-Sisters had formed a circle around them. "I've missed you!"

But as she wiped her eyes, the features before her shifted and changed. Her father's deep blue eyes lightened to gray and his jaw stretched, widening into the more rounded chin of Hamilton O'Donnell. Her joy came punctuated with puzzlement. *Maya. The world is not as it seems.*

On that thought, her uncle's face metamorphosed, the wrinkles of age receding, hair sprouting from the bald scalp. *Robert?* The rich color of the minister's eyes flickered, brightened, and made light shine through the stained glass windows.

"Walk with me, Eva." He held her up as they made their way back to the door. Outside, a searing sun had evaporated the fog. The tropical foliage sparkled with dew. Tombstones stood in the adjacent yard. Blake led her to a tree there and rested her against its trunk; then he approached one of the graves. A pot there held a single flower, stained with vibrant colors. Blake gripped the stem and tried to pull the flower from the pot. It didn't give way. He adjusted his grip, trying again. After a moment of puzzlement he lifted the pot instead and carried it to her.

The flower pulsed brightly and opened, displaying multiple layers of petals. But the petals all shaded toward red, and Eva felt unsettled: the flower had a predatory sense to it. *He should have left it alone and now it's angry.*

"Put it back," she told him.

As Blake obliged, a train of questions spilled from Eva's mind about the hidden message, but the cloud veil descended and her dream faded into it. *Maybe there are no answers.*

Charter MZ987, East of Johnson Atoll | *Friday 0319 HST*

She truly is a beautiful young woman, Robert Blake thought as he contemplated an inert Eva Connard strapped down on the seat across the airplane aisle. *Such a shame.* But he kept that perception out of his voice as he talked on his encrypted cell phone link.

"She's secured, Senator. Still out cold."

"You sure, boy?"

"Yes. She revived a bit when the oxygen feed cleared the nerve gas from her system, but that injection put her back down. What was it?"

The Senator ignored the question. "Well, Goddamn, son! This about as purty an operation as I've ever run." He laughed in a rumble of true mirth. "You check her breathin', her pulse?"

"Both slow and regular."

"Good. We don't wanna be deliverin' a dead body to our good buddy Muhammad, do we?"

"Somehow I don't recall that I was supposed to be the deliveryman, Senator."

"Aw, now, don't get your shorts all twisted, Reverend, little minor tactical change like that. Look, Zurvan sees you with the girl and not just a buncha my troops he don't know, it'll all go much smoother."

"The gun behind my ear didn't feel real smooth, Senator, pushing me onboard this aircraft." *And neither does the clear logic that says you've got about three devious subplots under your move.*

The man chuckled. "Well now, I'm truly sorry for that, son. I'll have a word with my lads afterwards."

Blake put some heat in his voice. "And I'm supposed to be halfway in the other direction, coming back to my California HQ for Good Friday. Getting ready for Easter Sunday. There are too many loose ends here, Senator."

"Aw, son, you gotta trust me more. No loose ends. You never actually got onboard your UMC jet in Waimea, did you?"

"Huh? No. Marta's double took me right back to the enclave. Why?"

"Marta's double... she a good look-alike, son?"

"Yes. Crazy as a loon, but a good physical match." *Where's this going?*

"Good as that match was," the Senator said with a higher pitched laugh, "we done you one better, boy."

Shit! "You're not serious!"

"Yup. The Right Reverend Doctor Robert Blake is gonna climb outta his UMC jet at John Wayne Airport in California a couple hours from now."

This is surreal. How long has he been planning it? "What, arm-in-arm with Marta, I suppose?"

"Aw, no. Poor Marta slipped and fell out the back hatch on climb-out. Lost at sea. Far enough out she won't wash up for a while, though." The Senator's laugh pitched yet higher, almost a giggle. "You puttin' this together yet, son?"

Blake heard only raspy breathing as the Senator lapsed into an expectant silence. *He's owned my flight crew for a while; that's nothing I hadn't suspected. But a double? Am I a dead man walking?* "We can still do business, Senator," he said shakily.

"I got three or four options here, son. Right now your twin is just gonna announce he's goin' into the desert to meditate. We'll have some pictures, maybe a little video with time-stamps. Keep your skirts clean of the shit that's gonna go down with our buddy Zurvan."

Bullshit, Senator. You've got something trickier up your sleeve. But he just grunted noncommittally.

"You deliver the girl, Reverend, we got you on a quick turnaround from Indonesia back to California. Private jet, with a bed and a shower. Home Saturday, well rested, plenty of time for your big Jesus show on Sunday."

Clever. My double wanders in the desert, not saying a thing, obviously troubled, meditating, praying. The Senator's given himself a lot of latitude. "I get back and my twin disappears?" Blake asked.

"Uh huh. We can still do business, you and me, son."

We can do your business, you mean, Senator. But you've got me neatly boxed. "Okay. I can live with that."

"To get back to your earlier question, boy... that injection is a nice little cocktail. Anesthetic, but when that wears off there's a residual motor muscle paralytic. Really advanced stuff, my people say."

"How long?"

"About… oh, maybe in an hour or two from now she'll wake up. But she won't be able to move for another six."

Blake stayed silent.

The Senator started to giggle. "Go ahead, boy. Do it. Fuck her brains out. You know you want to, that's your history. You got plenty of air miles to cover before you deliver the bitch. Your pilot and copilot won't be a problem." The giggle deepened into a coarse laugh. "And this would be a new first for you. Neanderthal fuckin' a Cro-Magnon. Life is good, huh?"

Blake stared across the aisle. "She loves me, Senator," he said softly.

The man exploded in mirth, forcing Blake to hold the phone away from his ear.

"Goodbye, Senator." He clicked off. *Sensory nerves but no motor nerves.* Blake stared at Eva's still form and licked his dry lips.

Chapter 26

Charter MZ987, South of Johnson Atoll | Friday 0420 HST

Am I the angry flower? Or is it the locus? Or is it our diune persona? Eva's thoughts scattered like dust on the Big Island's dry side in a downslope wind. *Waimanu? You're weak and fading, growing more distant.* An attempt to focus the analytical side of her brain fell short, but she sensed an answer to the circumstances around her. So she pursued it doggedly, resisting the cloud veil that wanted to descend over her mind.

Eventually, patches of memory surfaced. *A constant hum: an airplane or boat.* Her Robert's voice, speaking to someone not there. *Who's the Senator?* Eva tried to turn her head, without success. Neither would her eyes open. *I'm drugged. Oh, Robert!*

Eva chased down other patches of memory, fragments of a one-sided conversation. *On his cell phone.* And that unexpected tone in his voice had been subservience, she suspected. *Why? There are a hundred Senators, Robert. But only one of you. And you're a deliveryman?*

Another memory bit surfaced: Robert had spoken of a gun behind his ear, forcing him on an airplane. *This airplane!* Her heart leapt. *You were forced, Robert! I knew it! This Senator — whoever he is — is making you betray me. You probably had no choice. Or thought you had none. Oh, you should have told me! We could have dealt with it!*

Other fragments of conversation played across her improving awareness and became questions: *Marta? Doubles? Twins?* They confused her, but were overridden by the joy caused by his last statement: *She loves me, Senator.* And she still did, Eva admitted. *Even now, after betrayal, I love you, Robert.*

The effort of retrieving those recent memories sharpened her mind and pushed the cloud veil back a bit. She took inventory of her body. *I can feel. I can hear. But those are passive things. I can't activate anything. Some sort of block of the motor nerves but not the sensory?* She verified that, feeling the imprint of the airplane couch fabric under her back. *Can I bring back my motor nerves? I could probably see if I could open my eyes.* She tried, but without result. *Weird!*

Then she sensed him over her, his warm breath on her neck. Goosebumps ran up and down her skin but her eyes still wouldn't open. Fingers fumbled at her pajama shift and she felt it slide up to her hips and pull against her buttocks. *Robert? What are...*

A hand under the small of her back, another tug, and the shift bunched up under her shoulder blades. Cool air from the airplane ventilators blew on her exposed belly, then on her breasts as he lifted the front of the shift to her chin. She heard his breathing get deeper. *No, Robert! Not like this*, her mind wailed.

She felt her nipples contract and harden in the cool air. His tongue caressed the left one, then the right. His breathing deepened more, becoming almost a groaning as he kissed slowly down her rib cage to her bellybutton. She felt the moistness growing between her legs. *Autonomic response. That's all it is.* But her pheromones would tip him over the edge, surely. *Sisters, help me!* her mind screamed.

They spiraled in, their speed reflecting her urgency. Real-time slowed as her consciousness engaged with theirs. Robert Blake's breathing slowed to a ponderous pounding, deepening into a bass drum sound that finally elongated into a drawn-out resonance. The hands pulling at her panties moved downward only micrometrically.

"Your body wants him, Young Mother, there is no way to deny that," one spirit-Sister said, not unkindly.

"My mind does not. Nor my heart. Nor my soul. Not this way," Eva objected.

"Oh? We see ambivalence in your mind," another added, "your love is such a powerful thing."

"But if he takes me like this there is no hope for him!" Eva wailed.

A composite of several Sisters formed to contemplate that. "He has already betrayed you," the composite finally answered, "so there is no hope anyway."

"That was a forced betrayal! The Senator. It was not Robert's choosing; it couldn't have been!"

"No? Your love says that, Young Mother. We see no objective proof in your mind."

"He's a good man."

"Power has seduced many good men."

"Robert's not like that."

The composite was dismissive. "Bah. Your father passed his monkey trap test. As have many before and since. This man has not."

"And the choice is his," Eva conceded sadly.

"And the consequences. As always."

Her spirit-Sisters circled protectively around her mind, awaiting the outcome as Eva returned to real-time. *But your plan is my plan, Robert. Don't you know that? My fate is your fate.*

The fingers inside her panties ceased moving for a moment.

Charter MZ987, International Date Line | Saturday 0351 MHT

Blake paused, kneeling beside Eva as he had with all his previous victims, savoring the moment. He enjoyed the exquisite ambivalence he felt: the driving heat of his need versus the cold truth of violating a trust. *I wonder if a theologian would call that contrition.*

He sighed, laying his head on Eva's belly. "It's because I know the Devil so well that I'm such an effective man of God, darling." He ran his hands up her rib cage and pinched her nipples between his thumb and forefinger. He squeezed, hard, but got no reaction. "This new drug of the Senator's, Eva? I think I like his Rohypnol derivative better. At least with that one there's some response. But you? You're just a lump... unless..." He sniffed at her.

He slipped his thumbs back under the waistband and drew her panties down slowly. He fingered the wetness in them then rubbed his nose against her pubic thatch.

"My goodness, Eva. So damp! Is that an invitation?"

He drew a finger around her triangle. *Interesting,* the detached part of his mind offered, *no muscle control, but that part of her obviously works. Autonomic. But then I've always excelled at exciting it.*

He breathed in her aroma, and his erection responded with a pounding urgency that was almost painful. He made his mind clamp down on it. *Don't rush! Like the Senator says, we have lots of time.*

"Let me tell you, Eva darling, about the things like this I've done before." He ran his tongue delicately around her vulva.

"Ah, nothing quite so delicious as violating a trust. The ultimate betrayal. Yes, Eva, I'm guilty. I confess. I've done it many times. An urge I've had ever since puberty. Maybe before." He eased the panties down off her limp legs.

"And of course it got much easier after I started my ministry. Those young women who would come to me for counseling." *My need is a beast that has to be fed periodically. But my atonement is bringing massive numbers of people to God every day. I wonder if a moralist would consider that a tradeoff?*

"My wife, the poor dear, the mother of my twin girls — who as you know are the same age as Gaelan and Ibrahim — unraveled the truth. A sad day." He smiled down on Eva as he undid his belt.

"Then along comes the Senator. With some of my escapades on film. That's one of the problems with power, Eva. It makes you careless." Blake reached under the small of her back with his left hand and turned her on her side. His right hand swung the belt hard against her bare buttocks, a sharp crack that left a blazing red mark. Her face remained impassive, but beads of sweat popped out all over her body. *The autonomic system's response to pain. So the Senator is right, the sensory nerves are active. Excellent!*

"Anyway," Blake continued his soliloquy, "the Senator helped me resolve my little marital discord. Did I love my wife? Yes, of course. How can you not love the mother of your children? But she had to go. An extraordinarily well-contrived accident. Never any question. The Senator hires only the best." He kneeled beside Eva and began kissing the red welt.

"And there were several others after that, whose memories weren't totally emptied by the drugs; they had to go too. And naturally the Senator has my culpability in their murders neatly captured. So you see, Eva, I really had no choice here. Until I find a way to rid myself of the Senator, I have to dance to his tune."

He stood and whipped the belt across her again. "Not that I don't enjoy it." He knelt and began licking the welt, which had begun to bleed.

"Power, Eva, power. I do love it," he explained, glancing up at Eva's immobile face. Tears ran from the corners of her eyes. *Ah, another autonomic response.*

Charter MZ987, South of Marshall Islands | Saturday 0428 MHT

The circle of Eva's spirit-Sisters drew inward and tightened down protectively around her mind. *My fate is your fate, Robert! Can't you see that?* With her Sisters forming a shield, Eva retreated from the terrible reality of her physical sensations and drove her consciousness toward the unfeeling blankness of the null.

Images formed against the darkness, whispery traces of a past time; her Sisters parted to let them pass. Eva slid into the past, into her eight-year old mind, each detail recorded with exquisite sharpness:

Josh-wa and I sit at the sacred pool, dangling our legs in the water.

His are bigger, hairier.

At the bottom level of the enclave, Mom and Dad sleep cradled in the arms of Waimanu.

Their bodies are alive but frozen in time. A deed just done the day before, she recalled.

She spoke the same words, made the same promise, to the image of her brother now as she had then. "When I grow up to be a Nova, Josh-wa, I'm going to heal them."

His look was burdened with sadness and uncertainty. "Traumatic brain injuries, Eva, you heard what the neurosurgeons said. Just because they're breathing and their hearts are beating doesn't mean they're alive in any human sense."

"What's human, Josh-wa?" *A good question then and a good one now.*

"Their minds are damaged, honey. A full blast of the K'Shmar field at close quarters; their brains are atrophying."

Which is why they're here, Josh-wa.

Despite her brother's rational reluctance at an eight-year-old girl's insistence, he hadn't hesitated to do her will. Lara Picard and John Connard had been expeditiously transferred from the Honolulu hospital to Waimanu. *Night-time, military medevac, no questions asked, courtesy of a thankful government.* He'd stood apart as she and Elia had arranged the inert bodies side-by-side on the stone table and intertwined their fingers. He'd stood with his arm around Eva as she whispered the ancient words. He'd watched the dim glow form around them, mixed blue and green, the colors of their eyes, the colors of the waters in Waimanu Bay. He'd looked at her with lessening uncertainty and growing hope, a wondering in his own eyes.

"Sleep with Waimanu, I told them, Josh-wa," she said now to his image at the pool. *I couldn't answer you then, I didn't know I was speaking Galatian, the lost root language of the Celts. The Sisters helped me frame the intention and speak it properly.*

A sense of time slippage, a warp, and it seemed as if her memory of that time long ago had become a parallel present. She wiggled her toes in the pool, and watched little whorls of order rise from the water's randomness and float to the surface.

"Eva?" He stared at her. "What happened just now? You sort of... blinked."

"Don't know, Josh-wa," she replied from both inside and outside of her memories, "but the null has no time."

"Ah. So you put them there. On hold? Something like that?"

"Waimanu holds them. They are water-birds, Josh-wa."

He looked at her speculatively, the lights of a logic lattice flickering in his turquoise eyes. "Like water, consciousness is fluid," he agreed, "sort of."

"Their patterns dwell in the water, with Waimanu. When my time comes I can bring them back into their bodies. I will."

"Yes, there's that theory: consciousness has a map for the body, it knows what it should be, it can put it back together." Joshua nodded thoughtfully as a logic lattice completed its analysis. "And for the mind, too, I guess would be a logical extension..."

Her brother's voice trailed off as Eva's mind looked down on her parents, still side-by-side, still holding hands, lying at the base level of the enclave.

You see, my parents were friends, Robert, and true lovers. They were all that we could be and should be. Should have been. Eva let her sorrow dissolve along with the images and focused on one measure of hope: *Waimanu is fading, but it will hold my parents tight, even if it can do nothing else. My intention has always been its imperative.* Consoled a little, Eva Connard let her mind slide away into the nothingness of the null.

O'Donnell Enclave, Waimanu, HI | *Friday 0630 HST*

The sounds came to Joshua from a distance, echoing down some indeterminate cavernous space. *A dragging sound, rasping breath.* He realized he was on the stone floor of his sleeping quarters. *What happened? Is something coming for me?* Adrenaline shot through the fog in his head, driving him up on all fours. The room spun out of control. He fell sideways and vomited.

"Josh?" Demuzzio's slurred voice croaked from the hallway outside. "I'm coming. Hang on. Don't try to stand up."

"TC? What the hell?"

"Drugged. Gas, I think."

"Eva!"

"Gone." Demuzzio's single word carried an infinity of loss. He dragged himself to Joshua. "Stay horizontal."

Gone? No! More adrenaline speared through Joshua. He jacked himself up on all fours again and pushed off the floor with his hands to stand up. His feet had no feeling; they skidded in his vomit and he felt himself falling.

"Goddammit, Josh, I said stay hori..."

Demuzzio's voice was lost in a wave of vertigo that faded to blackness as Joshua hit the stone floor.

Eva. Where are you? Talk to me, kiddo. Tell me you're alive! Tell me you're okay! Fragmented images flashed across his mind. *The waterfall. The pool. We sat there, side by side. And then what?* The question forced coherence back. His mind instinctively focused on details, seeking that one invariant among all the competing probabilities, the one that would give him a solid place from which to cast his net of logic. *Love.*

"Josh," Demuzzio's voice finally penetrated, punctuated by slaps on the face, "I stuck out my arm, broke your fall, but you still whacked your head."

Joshua grunted, torn between real-time and that other state, from which Eva might or might not just have spoken to him. *Waimanu. The locus is love. But it's de-cohering. Eva? Talk to me!*

"You might have a concussion. Don't move."

"I'm okay, TC."

"Bullshit. Just stay there for a minute, okay?"

Joshua forced his mind to calm. "Elia, the twins. Sarah. What?"

"They're okay, Josh, far as I can tell. Breathing, pulses."

Thoughts clicked across, the beginnings of a logic lattice, and Joshua took steadying breaths. *In through the nose, out through pursed lips, ventilate.* The lattice began to run, and he fed his symptoms into it. It churned slowly, molasses instead of its normal lightning-quick fluidity. The confirmation when it came seemed to need verification. "Gas," he croaked to Demuzzio, "like the Russians used on the Chechnens?"

"Something like it, probably. More advanced."

"Where? Who?" He sat up slowly, Demuzzio's arm at his back.

"Military's got shit like that, I think. From DARPA. Hostage rescue situations."

"Pastor Bob?"

"He was gone. Probably en route to California when the gas hit us."

"Inside job." Joshua retched at the thought; a dry heave. "Had to be." *Is Waimanu so weak our defenses are lost?*

"Ventilation system, yeah. There are blueprints around somewhere. Air intake on the surface is hidden, though. I remember that much."

"Marta? Jamie? Susan?"

"Not answering, Josh. As soon as I can stand up I'll go topside and look."

"Makes no sense, TC. We should all be dead. Why just disable us?"

"Dunno. Can you stay sitting up?"

Joshua nodded.

"Okay. I'm going to open all the doors to the lanai. Get more air exchange." Demuzzio turned on his hands and knees and crawled away. Joshua hear the click of a latch and smelled the hibiscus shrubs clinging to the cliff wall outside. He breathed it in. *Eva smells like that, flowers in her hair.* His mind wailed. He suppressed it and began to crawl toward the door, to see to his wife and children.

Charter MZ987, East of Marshall Islands | Saturday 0433 MHT

Some fleeting sense of Joshua in the present relieved part of Eva's worry. *He's okay, and so are the rest of my family. Hurt, drugged, but safe.* At least that was the message she thought Waimanu was trying to convey. She formed a return message. *I'm glad you're okay, Josh. I'm sorry I had to leave you, but it's better this way. Or at least I hope it will be.* She wrapped her intention around the message and let it go. *I made my plan, Joshua. I rolled the dice. Now you must leave me to my fate.*

Eva withdrew from the null to check on her plan's progress. Spirit-Sisters cocooned more tightly around her mind, a shield against pain and betrayal as she moved back into reality. The aircraft hummed. Her body ached. A blanket had been thrown over her and tucked in; she could feel the fibers against abraded skin. Cautiously she tried to crack open an eye, wiggle a finger. *Nothing.* It didn't really matter, she decided; helplessness was part of her plan. That thought caused her Sisters to re-engage their debate; a lively exchange despite their growing weakness in her mind. Most of them now saw it her way, but not all.

"Your plan is too risky," that group of Sisters said, "better to go back to the Sisterhood's."

"I don't want to be a god," she dismissed their arguments gently, as she had before.

"You are the first, the One. You must not risk what the Sisterhood has planned for thousands of years."

"I have no issue with your objective. I seek better means."

"You are naïve. Seize the power. Be the Second Coming. It is the only certain way to protect the new species."

"Power. It brings war. Destruction. Death. Cruelty."

"True. But brief and clean, with a better tomorrow."

"My plan protects both Novas and humans."

"But at what cost, Young Mother? You will die."

"Death is overrated; my cat told me that."

"The Custodye can consider death irrelevant; you cannot."

Eva nodded. "I respect your opinion."

The composite shook their heads in an admixture of love and respect and frustration. "You will regret it."

Eva nodded as she dismissed them. *I may.*

She sensed Blake's breath over her face again and her mind went back to the drug-induced dream. *He put the flower back, but then he picked it up again. I wanted to, but couldn't stop his free choice.*

She drove her mind back to the scene, to examine its symbolism. The flower was Hibiscus kokio, an endangered species; Eva had restored it, with the help of Waimanu, extending its range further south on the Big Island. *My favorite red flowers, so pretty. But now its red means anger?*

With that question her mind continued along in metaphor and simile. *No, it's not the hibiscus, she realized. It's not a physical thing at all. Irian Jaya is my red flower. Beautiful, but angry. All the threads of my fate converge there, a nexus of power.* That made sense; that locus was primitive, unformed, and had remained dormant since she'd left it years ago. Its possibilities were not yet turning into probabilities nor hardening into inevitabilities. *But that's where this airplane is going, isn't it? The energy is fading in Hawaii, moving westward. Waiting for me.*

Her mind took a long fond look back. *Goodbye, Waimanu.* Eva formed a last intention carefully as she dropped back into the null. *Care for my family.*

Chapter 27

O'Donnell Enclave, Waimanu, HI | Friday 0651 HST

The long crawl down the hall and then the stairs, punctuated by waves of vertigo and dry heaving, left Joshua exhausted as he crawled toward the infirmary.

"They're okay," Elia announced as he entered, "they're not awake yet." She stood at the foot of the bed, bent halfway over it; she swayed, but her hands were locked solidly around the bed's rail.

She's recovering faster than me, Joshua thought as he crawled toward her, *or maybe the gas diffusion was less down here?*

"Eva's gone," he croaked at her.

"I know."

"How…?" He reached the bed and managed to pull himself up beside her on the rail. The room rolled, but he kept his grip on the rail and ignored it. "…do you know?"

Elia turned her head slowly and cautiously to look at him. Her eyes were wet, her breath foul with vomit. "She's no longer one with Waimanu. There's a… gap."

"Is she alive?"

"I think so."

I think so too. So there's hope. "Thank you."

"Your dizziness will pass, Joshua. Mine is fading. Stay here with the twins, I'll check Sarah and Thomas."

"TC's okay. He came to me. You stay. I'll revive Sarah if he hasn't."

She looked at him and lifted a hand to his face. "Better if you stay. I turned the twins on their sides in case they vomit."

He shook his head, and the room rolled again. *A clock is running.*

"I'll get Sarah," Elia said. "The two of us need to work with Waimanu quickly, before it de-coheres more."

"No," he croaked, "I'll send her down. TC and I need to see what Washington knows, get a hunt started." Joshua staggered away, bouncing off the doorframe but keeping himself upright by pure force of will.

"First chance," Elia yelled after him, "drink lots of water; it will flush out the residuals."

Joshua walked down the hall but crawled up the stairs, unwilling to risk falling backwards. Sarah met him at the top and helped him stand. She seemed more stable than he, but her face was ashen and lined.

"Elia's in the infirmary," he told her. "Twins are okay. She needs you to work with the locus."

Sarah nodded then sat and started bumping down the stairs. "We'll try, Joshua. Thomas is in the Security Center."

No hope in her voice. That's not good. Joshua staggered away, detouring by the kitchen. He drank directly from the sink faucet then filled two water bottles and stuck them in his pocket. The effort drained him and the kitchen spun. He stuck his head under the cold running water and held it there until the vertigo faded. Then he made his way cautiously down the hall.

Demuzzio had the National Security Coordinator on a video uplink. "No, TC," Carol Violette was saying, "we had no reports of anything from our roving patrols. They say Marta went out of the checkpoint with Pastor Bob, came back through without him. Then she went back out a bit later, and hasn't returned."

Demuzzio raised an eyebrow. Joshua shook his head as he dropped into the adjacent chair. *A warrior Sister? Impossible. All that conditioning, from the cradle almost.*

"I'm sorry, TC, Joshua. I tried to raise you a few times, earlier; but figured you all were just having a well-deserved rest."

"Had to be an inside job, Carol. The locus would have warded off any other penetrations."

"Unless Eva walked out on her own, before the gas hit. Have you looked at the security camera records? And are you even sure Eva's gone?"

Demuzzio glanced at Joshua for confirmation.

"She's not here." Joshua's voice broke before he could control it. *They have her. Who they are is a question, but not as important. We need to get her back.* He opened his mouth to speak but shut it to control a wave of nausea.

"Power to the camera circuits was cut, it looks like," Demuzzio added. "I'll check topside soon as I can walk better. But they're not answering. Not Marta or Susan or Jamie. We were penetrated, Eva was grabbed. Pretty obvious."

On the monitor, the NSC's eyes flicked back and forth between the two men. "The possibilities are limited. Waimanu only lets Nova Council members or your SIO guardians enter your enclave."

The statement hung in the air over the table, an ugly thing.

"NSA manage to decrypt Pastor Bob's phone call yet?"

"No, not yet, TC. But the man got off his airplane this morning in California, around 0700 local. I saw him on a video clip. He's evidently in the desert east of LA, some sort of Good Friday meditation. By himself, I think."

What's that about, TC? Joshua opened his mouth but shut it again. *Other matters are more urgent.* "Carol," he told her image, "TC and I will chase down everything we can here. If you can get the Agency working on air and boat traffic, satellite communications… and please, please, please, priority over everything else."

The NSC studied him for a moment. "Be good to narrow the search as much as we can. You sure Eva's off the island?"

A gamble, but there's Elia's instinct, and a gap in Waimanu where Eva used to be. "I'm sure," he said.

O'Donnell Enclave, Waimanu, HI | Friday 0712 HST

Demuzzio smelled it as the elevator door opened at the garage level, the coppery odor of blood and the sourness of cadavers. He clicked the safety off his Glock, stuck his head around the concrete abutment and quickly pulled it back. *Two down. Better be safe.*

"Alpha Two," he whispered into his handset.

"Here, Tango Charlie."

"Where are you?"

"Right outside."

"You been in?"

"Negative. Command post ordered no entry. We're on the hydraulic pad, three feet down."

"Can you see inside the bay?"

"Roger, most of it except below us. Two down. No activity. Infrared shows nothing."

And I can see the areas they can't. "Uh huh. Okay, Alpha Two. I'm coming out. Don't shoot me."

"Roger that."

Demuzzio slipped the handset inside his shirt pocket. Pistol at the ready, he walked across the garage bay to the two riddled bodies and crouched down to inspect them. *I'm sorry, Susan. Jamie.* Their weapons were still holstered. *You never had a chance, did you?*

"And where are you, Marta?" he whispered aloud.

The handset crackled in his pocket. "Say again, Tango Charlie?"

He stood up and took deep breaths through his mouth before he spoke. "Give me a minute, Alpha Two."

"Roger that, sir." Empathy permeated the three words.

Demuzzio turned and walked to the power panel. *The circuit breakers weren't marked, but they knew which ones to hit for the cameras. So the ones downstairs probably will be off, too.*

He flicked the breakers back on with his pistol muzzle, in case there were fingerprints. *But there won't be any; they're that good. And they had the wiring diagrams.* His sense of desperation ratcheted up. *Somebody got into DOD archives. This goes really, really deep. Smarts. Planning. Money, a lot of it. Over many years, probably.*

Demuzzio spoke into his handset. "Alpha Two, I'm belaying that order. I want a forensics team in here from the Bureau."

"Yes, sir. The entire enclave or just this surface entry?"

"Just up here." *They can't get to the elevator or downstairs anyway, unless…* his mind ran on, chasing possibilities… *a gap in Waimanu, Elia told Josh. And if the locus is weakening…*

The handset interrupted his thoughts; the voice soft. "I'm sorry, Tango Charlie." The voice went apologetic. "We saw nothing out of the ordinary. Not at the checkpoint, not any of the rovers. Just Marta, in and out."

"Not your fault, Alpha Two." *It's my goddamn fault,* his mind raged.

O'Donnell Enclave, Waimanu, HI | Friday 0715 HST

Joshua looked at Demuzzio, and saw the look reflected back at him. *Fear and frustration.* "You feel the same familiar tug at your mind before it let you back through?" he asked the man.

"Yeah, Josh. So if the locus is still active enough to check me, I'm thinking it's active enough to block off any intruders." Demuzzio rubbed his head.

"Presumably," Joshua agreed. *Security is survival; it's at the base level of Waimanu's function pyramid, like keeping Mom and Dad alive. It would be the last function to go.*

"But when I go back up I'll see if any of the troops can follow me to the elevator, break through Waimanu's ward."

Joshua nodded at him. "Good idea."

"And if the warding function is still active…" Demuzzio rubbed his head harder, as the ugly question came back to hang there between them.

Joshua nodded again. "Yeah." *Even a Trojan horse of some kind wouldn't get past Waimanu's gate; its security function is keyed to individual mind-patterns.* "And all the other possible entrants, Councilors, SIO troops, were elsewhere. Carol just called and confirmed that."

Demuzzio sighed. "Leaves Pastor Bob and Marta. But Pastor Bob was on his jet, maybe an hour out, headed toward California. And we know he arrived there. No time gaps. He doesn't fit the timeline. So that leaves Marta. And she's gone. No trace."

"Break all that training?" Joshua raised an eyebrow. *Not possible. She loves Eva. Loves us all, actually.* "She's been with us seven years."

Demuzzio spread his hands. "The K'Shmar, maybe? Some other kind of operant conditioning? Enough to turn her?"

"We probably can track her past movements, develop a history, but I really don't think she's been off-site enough for that kind of thing, TC. It takes time."

"Somebody has put a lot of time into this, Josh. A lot of money. Knows our systems."

Joshua sighed. A logic lattice ground away, laboriously, and spit out another possibility. "A different motivation, then? Not a bad one?"

"Like what?"

"Maybe she took Eva off to protect her?"

Demuzzio rubbed his head then nodded. "Protection of Eva would be about the only thing strong enough to overcome the training."

Joshua objected to his own idea. "The trouble with that, TC, is that I'm Eva's best protector, better than ten Martas, no matter how good she is."

"But not now, Josh. Not in your present state."

"True enough. Maybe she knows something we don't? Maybe she felt she had to act?"

Demuzzio shrugged. "Or she's under some kind of duress? Misdirection?"

"That's about the only thing that makes any sense at all, TC."

"So that's maybe why we're alive and not dead right now? Marta wanted to protect Eva but not hurt anyone else?"

"Or maybe Marta suspected the virus and the K'Shmar was getting the better of me, that I would lose it, become a hazard to everyone, maybe harm Eva." He grimaced. *I've been close to the edge.*

"No. That's logical, Josh, but it just doesn't feel right. And if she's got Eva stashed somewhere, it can't possibly be as safe as here." He rubbed his head some more. "Ah, fuck it; it's all speculation at this point, Josh. Listen, I think a couple of the real remote cameras outside have backup power and local memory, nanochips. I'll go check."

TC nailed it; Marta doesn't feel right for this. That means she's probably dead like Jamie and Susan. He looked up at Demuzzio's weary face. "Good luck. Hope you find something."

O'Donnell Enclave, Waimanu, HI | Friday 0722 HST

The two women stood on the lanai off the kitchen, taking deep breaths of the sea air to clear the drug residuals out of their bodies. Sarah spoke first. "Thomas might find something; those are the older cameras. But I don't think he'll see Marta on them."

Elia exhaled and nodded at Sarah. *I agree; Marta is not a candidate for this betrayal.* "You think she's dead?"

"Almost certainly."

"So… Pastor Bob, then. Even though there's no way he could possibly fit the timeline?"

Sarah shrugged. "Or a third party, unknown, with concurrent failure of Waimanu's warding."

The implausibility of both those things hung in the air between them, uncaring.

"Pastor Bob… could Eva be so blinded by her love?" Elia asked.

Sarah shrugged again. "An embryonic Nova? You wouldn't think so. But still, she's a fifteen-year old girl."

Elia pondered that. "Past a superficial level I cannot read that man well. He controls his emotions tightly. Almost secretive."

"But Eva could."

"She wouldn't intrude that deeply."

"You think not?"

"Her first love? She'd be circumspect. She as much as told us so."

Sarah sighed. "I remember now."

The silence built for a moment, punctuated only by the distant surf and the rustle of breeze through the hibiscus leaves on the cliff. Elia watched the older woman. *She's thinking the same thing.* She saw Sarah gather herself to voice it.

"There's a bigger question." Pain laced Sarah's statement.

Elia shivered. "I know. The Sisterhood's lonely quest prayer last night." *To seek that which is terrible to find but must be found.*

"An allegory. The truth is always painful."

"Last night? It was much more than the allegory we Sisters all learned. The way Eva sang her part… she improvised the chanting, made the meaning deeper, more complex. An intention."

"I know. I wish I'd understood more of it."

"Maybe it's meant to be understood later."

"Later? After what? It's a prayer of loss and mourning. A goodbye. Off on a journey, alone. But the way Eva sang it was not with closure, it was with hope of meeting again."

"Waimanu was fading, that was evident last night, even to my husband. He felt it."

"And what if it wasn't a goodbye to Waimanu, but to all of us?"

Elia chased memories back in time. "When Eva was small, when we first got here, she was an open book to read."

"And in our years in Waimanu she's grown subtle. A crafter of perceptions even at fifteen. If she didn't want to be read, she wouldn't be."

"And with what she's learned from Joshua's mind… you think we've been… crafted?"

The rising sun cast some heat on the volcanic cliffs and the breeze picked up in response. Elia ran through more recent memories. *Last night.*

"She opened her eyes and looked right at Pastor Bob when we concluded the prayer. Did you see? She impaled him with her truth."

"I saw his reaction."

"So Pastor Bob betrayed her. Betrayed all of us. That's what you're saying, Sarah? Your intuition, regardless of his timeline making it impossible?"

The older woman considered that for a long moment. "Yes. That's what I'm saying."

"But that's not the real question, is it?"

Sarah groaned. "No. It's… would Eva go willingly?"

"If she chose her path rather than having it forced on her…"

"The Sisterhood Covenants. If she has chosen, we must not intervene."

That fundamental prohibition now hung in the air between them, indifferent to their answer.

"Does she have foreknowledge?" Elia felt the edge of desperation in her question.

"Prescience? Maybe, of a kind. We just don't know what her capabilities might be."

Elia shook her head. "No. Eva would include us if in her plan if she could. Not to would be a betrayal of those she loves. She wouldn't do that."

Sarah groaned again, increasing her breathing as if to force clarity through her being. "But what if we would be obstacles? What if we would stand in the way of what she knows is right? Would she not step around us?"

Elia considered that for an even longer moment. "I'm not sure. So whether she left willing or forced, we simply do not know."

"This is a Nova female, coming of age. She plumbed the most intricate basis of her physical being. She changed her genetic structure to produce an antidote for the virus. Surely she could defeat any immobilizing agent."

"We shouldn't assume. She was almost totally drained by the effort to solve the virus, remember. And the sleeping gas is chemical, not biological."

"If willing, she would have left us a message, somehow."

"So we assume she was forced, and proceed?"

Sarah nodded. "Let us do what we can with Waimanu. There is some energy left. It may be enough."

O'Donnell Enclave, Waimanu, HI | Friday 0731 HST

The old tomcat stalked into the Security Center, wet and bedraggled and limping. He screeched as Joshua picked him up.

"Sorry, Bo." He put the cat on the table and carefully felt the left rear leg. "Doesn't feel like it's broken. Unfortunately, Eva's not here to fix you up. But then you know that, don't you?"

Aye, laddie, the words entered Joshua's mind fuzzily and he had to struggle to impose coherence on them. *Nor can I reach her consciousness. The die has been cast.*

"I got that. But while it's still rolling, could we nudge it in her favor?"

I don't think so, lad. The Covenants.

"Fuck the Covenants!"

Aye. I know how ye feel.

"I'm not a Sister! I didn't sign on."

Yer sister invoked them.

"When? And meaning what?"

Last night.

"The prayer? Or song, whatever it was?

Aye. The Sisterhood lonely quest song. With Eva's intention woven in. Very subtle, very thoughtful. Powerful.

"Intending what?"

The cat's gray eyes shimmered at him. *That the work be hers, and hers alone.*

"What work?"

Redemption.

"What?"

Beyond that I cannot say. If a cat's face could ever look miserable, Mister Bo had achieved it. *The Covenants have always been a two-edged sword, laddie.*

"Goddamn the Covenants! We have to get Eva back! Or at least help her somehow!"

The cat looked even more miserable. *Eva has withdrawn from Waimanu. She left no trace of her consciousness. I even stood in the pool, Waimanu's heart, trying to touch her mind. To no avail; she seeks her fate by herself.*

Great sadness permeated that thought. It sat as stark and dark in Joshua's mind as the memories that immediately followed it: *As did my old friend Jesus. But this time... with this redeemer... I cannot help. I'm de-cohering.*

The cat let out a piteous meowing wail.

Footsteps pounded down the hall. Demuzzio rounded the corner into the Security Center, excitedly waving a memory nanochip in his fingers. "I think we might have some footage here, Josh."

Mister Bo let out another wail.

"Bo? Hamilton?" He stared at the wet cat then looked at Joshua. "What the hell does that mean?"

Joshua buried his head in his hands. "It means Eva has a plan. And she didn't tell us. Doesn't want us."

Chapter 28

Joshua entered the infirmary, standing more or less upright. *His color is better,* Elia thought. *Or is that just wishful thinking?*

"Gaelan woke up," she told him. "He was conscious. He took a drink."

"I'll help Ib," the child had said, rolling on his side and throwing his arm across his brother's chest. Then he went back to sleep. *Or to whatever state he needed to be in. Young Novas… I wish I understood my own children.*

Joshua actually half-smiled at the scene. He walked gingerly around the bed. "Some good news at last? And Ibrahim?"

"Not yet. But I believe they both rest with Waimanu, together."

He reached out and took her shoulders. *I think his hands are trembling less.* He stared in her eyes. "This is a good thing, right?"

She watched tiny lights flicker around his turquoise irises. "I believe so," she answered carefully. "At least it feels like their minds are going back to their usual state of reciprocal entrainment."

"Not one consciousness dominating the other? You can tell this?"

"The fMRI is needed to confirm, but yes, it feels that way to me."

"Good news. I'll take it," Joshua repeated. He drew her in, hugged her tightly.

Elia's arms circled his waist and her hands ran up the small of his back, giving comfort. Her fingers sensed the separate but cumulative effects of the virus and the K'Shmar exposure and the sleeping gas residuals. *I'm happy you're alive, my husband. A lesser man would be dead.* Her fingers also felt underneath the tension in his muscles, finding their drivers: *frustration, confusion, loss, anger, hate.* She formed an intention. *Joshua, you will be strong, for all of us.* The knotted tissue relaxed a tiny bit and he released her to ask his hopeful question.

"The twins entraining again… does this mean the locus is re-cohering, filling in the gap Eva left, adjusting to rebalance its energy or something like that?"

"I think it is as Eva always told us, Joshua. Waimanu takes on the characteristics of all the consciousnesses in its area."

"So it's a composite reflection of us all…"

"In proportion, roughly, to the strengths of those consciousnesses."

"So Eva's the biggest piece."

"And you next, Joshua. *Be strong for us all,* her mind tried to weave the intention more tightly around him.

"But a step down. A big step." He looked at her curiously. "And then you?"

"Maybe. But I suspect the twins are increasingly immanent in Waimanu. Or were, before they were infected."

"Aren't they too young?"

"It would seem so, but who knows? They're twins; that might be a factor."

"With Eva gone, with that gap, can the rest of us flow in to fill it, somehow?"

She studied his face. *A general, marshaling his possible forces; he needs some hope.* "I don't know. The locus is an ordering function, Joshua; very close to your mathematical model of it, actually."

He nodded. "A reverse entropy system."

Elia watched the characteristic pattern of a logic lattice start to form. *So slow. Oh, Joshua!* "Like all of life, yes," she acknowledged. "But the feedback is from all creatures, all consciousnesses, great and small, within its reach: Sarah, Thomas, your Uncle Hamilton the cat. The mongoose and pigs and birds of the forest, the dolphins and whales of the water… we all are part of Waimanu."

Joshua nodded again, the dim glow of the logic lattice brightening his expression momentarily.

"And it was beginning to entrain Pastor Bob, I think," she added.

"Then when the K'Shmar wave hit us, when the twins regressed… especially Ibrahim…"

Don't go there, Joshua, please. Her mind screamed the command but she kept her face unchanged and turned to look at the boys.

"Elia, there's something nibbling at the back of my mind, that doesn't want to come out. A root question, something important."

"For now, or for the future?"

He grimaced. "If it's not coming to me, I guess it's for the future."

"You have much to do, Joshua, now. When this is over we will explore your question. Together, we will find an answer."

She gave his chest a little affirmative pat.

"Um. Yeah, good. Thanks. I'll get back with TC and call Carol. See what NSA came up with. When the boys wake up again, kiss them for me. Both of them."

Joshua turned carefully and walked out the door. "And call me," he said over his shoulder.

Elia exhaled a long breath and put her hands back on the twins.

O'Donnell Enclave, Waimanu, HI | Friday 0752 HST

The image on the remote camera's video showed Eva being carried out to the beach: Demuzzio recognized her pajama bottoms on a loose hanging leg. He froze the image and zoomed in on the back of the figure carrying her. *Too tall to be Marta,* Demuzzio decided, *that lets her off the hook.* He strained at the low-resolution image, shook his head and advanced through the subsequent frames one by one. Finally the figure turned its head just enough for certainty.

Demuzzio slammed his fist on the table. "Pastor Bob, you miserable son of a bitch!"

"It's him?" Joshua entered the Security Center and slumped into the chair beside Demuzzio. "You sure?"

"See for yourself." Demuzzio fingered the zoom controls.

Joshua closed his eyes, opened them, stared at the monitor.

"Oh, Eva," he finally said.

"Eva? Eva? Josh, this miserable bastard betrayed her!"

"She could have figured him out, TC. She chose not to."

"Why?"

"Love. How can you not trust someone you love?"

They stared at each other. Demuzzio put his head in his hands. "Two dead. Marta probably three. The rest of us fucked over by a virus and K'Shmar and sleeping gas. Eva kidnapped. What the hell kind of a security chief am I?"

"What kind of a guardian am I? What kind of a big brother?" Joshua spoke softly, no recrimination in his voice. "TC, it doesn't matter. It's done. Focus on what we do now."

Focus, yeah. With my god-daughter lost to a son of a bitch whose motivation we don't even know, can't even guess at. "I'm gonna kill that fucker with my bare hands," he growled, "slowly."

"I'll say it one more time, TC. You thought something was off, and you were the only one to suspect. You asked Carol to decrypt the phone conversation. You were ahead of all of us. No blame. Okay?"

"My god-daughter," he replied helplessly.

"TC, the locus entrains our consciousnesses. Eva's influence overshadows everyone else. And there's feedback. So if she trusted Blake we all probably were disposed to do the same. Nobody's fault. Now focus!"

"I'm gonna kill the fucker," Demuzzio repeated.

Joshua squeezed his shoulder, hard. "Stand in line." He flicked the video frames forward one at a time. "Now focus. What's that?"

"Looks like a Zodiac." More flick forwards. Even at the poor resolution it was clear Blake got into the arriving boat with her, Demuzzio saw. "Means Pastor Bob has a double in the California desert. From this point, he doesn't fit the timeline for the flight back. Not even if he had an F-16."

"Or the actual Blake is in the desert, and his double carried Eva out... if Waimanu's warding got breached somehow."

"I think that's unlikely, Josh."

"Yeah. Me too."

"Means Marta had a double too, but she couldn't get in to get downstairs. That's why Blake had to carry Eva out. Means Marta's dead."

"Sure looks like her in the checkpoint video."

"At night. Inside the car. Doesn't mean much."

"It means a pretty good stand-in."

"Wouldn't have to be that good; the troops were expecting to see something and they saw it. You know how that works, Josh."

"Yeah. Guess I do." Now it was Joshua's turn to bury his head in his hands; and when he spoke his voice was muffled. "Carol got any satellite images on boat and plane traffic yet?"

"Too early, I think. But the time hack on this clip will help narrow it." Demuzzio hit the speed dial on the fast video link to the White House, and the NSC answered immediately.

They ran the video clip for her. Then they watched her compose her face, but the strain came through in her voice.

"I agree. Marta's not involved, TC. I trained with her when we were kids, then all the way through college. I know her like the back of my hand. She's dead, I'm afraid."

More discussion ensued, strategies and tactics, roles, divisions of labor. Demuzzio listened to the NSC's summarization in admiration. *Damn, she's good. Maybe as smart as Josh. Decisive too.*

"We'll sit on the Blake angle for now," Carol Violette said. "Blake doesn't know we know. But we'll keep a drone on his double. Track him everywhere we can. His actions may tell us something useful."

"Okay, thank you, Carol. Let us know when you get the satellite imagery for the area. Or anything else useful," Demuzzio added.

The woman looked off-screen momentarily, then back at them. "There is something else, actually. Be good if you could think about what it means. Pull up your GCN plots; the energy level at Waimanu is ramping down, and Irian Jaya is ramping up."

O'Donnell Enclave, Waimanu, HI | Friday 0803 HST

In the infirmary, Sarah heard Demuzzio's boot-heels hitch-clicking down the polished rock floor outside. *Did he hurt himself retrieving that camera chip?* He limped in, followed by Joshua, silent in bare feet.

"Ankle, TC?"

"It's nothing, Sarah."

She patted the examining table beside the twins' bed. "Let me take a quick..."

"No time," Joshua interrupted brusquely. "Where's Elia?"

"The kitchen, getting some juice for the boys when they wake."

"Sarah. I need you and Elia to paste me together as well as you can. I need to go to Irian Jaya."

She felt the blood leave her face. "That place?" *How can I be so terrified of a place I've only heard about but never seen?* "Why? The locus there is unformed, primitive..." She stopped at the look on Joshua's face, and felt her own features turn almost as strange. *Or have I seen it?*

"Eva's headed there."

"How do you..."

"Our global consciousness net. Shows it's building; the energy patterns there are getting more coherent."

"While Waimanu here is decaying?"

"Exactly."

"That doesn't necessarily mean..."

"It does, dammit, Sarah. TC, get Elia please. Now."

Demuzzio limped off. Sarah patted the examining table and Joshua levered himself up on it.

"I think you should confirm, Joshua. Surely our friends in the government..." Sarah began.

"They're working on it," he snapped. "What should I do, lie back?"

"Please."

"I've been slowly starting to feel better."

She put three fingers against his right temple. *That's a bald-faced lie, Joshua.* "Feeling better relative to what? Your body is ridding itself of the gas residuals, that's all. The effects of the virus, and the K'Shmar exposure on top of that... all of this has to run its course before you can even begin getting back to normal."

As Sarah lowered his head to the pillow she had a sense of things unraveling, threads carefully crafted coming undone when the coherence imposed by a masterful intention began to decay. *Without Eva's immanence,*

Waimanu cannot maintain the tapestry. The truth will come out. Many truths.

"Give me the antidote, then," he said.

Sarah shook her head. "Eva's antidote could kill you."

"The probability is what?"

"Too high."

"Numerically."

"You're a chimera, Joshua. Half human, half Nova. It's either twenty-five or fifty percent, depending on the genes contributed by your parents and grandparents."

"Can you tailor it? Fit me better?"

"Eva might. Or some other Nova. Not me, not Elia. And Eva specifically didn't do that because she thought you would heal over time. With Waimanu's help."

Desperation ran across Joshua's face, unfettered. "Some of the gene-splicers at the national labs?"

"Maybe. In time. Years, I would guess."

"Irian Jaya! Dammit, I need to be strong!"

Demuzzio's limp and Elia's sandals sounded in the hallway outside. Sarah softened her voice into the soothing tone that would pervade the healing intention. "I've heard the stories, Joshua. I know it was a terrible place for you. Elia too."

"All right. Just fix me up as best you can, Sarah. You and Elia. I accept there aren't going to be any miracles. Whatever you can do will have to be enough."

Elia entered, resting on Demuzzio's arm, her face pale. "Joshua, love, I…" she swallowed a sob.

"Just help me, Elia. I've got to go to Irian Jaya. There's nothing else we can do."

Elia walked slowly to the other side of the table. She clasped his right hand in hers and put her left hand on his temple. Struggling, she matched Sarah's tone.

"Joshua, the locus there has a name in the language of the little forest folk. But we never knew what it was called. Eva never told us; wouldn't tell us. Only that it would sleep again…" her voice broke, "until its time."

"Its time is now," Joshua answered. "And so is mine. Begin, please."

On the other side of the table, Sarah clasped his left hand in hers and put her right on his temple. *We can work on the symptoms, Joshua, alleviate them to a degree, mask some of your pain. But whatever the virus and the K'Shmar and Eva's loss have done… that will require a deeper healing.* Her thoughts carried little hope, so she didn't bother saying them.

The two women began the chant.

O'Donnell Enclave, Waimanu, HI | Friday 0849 HST

"I do feel better," Joshua told them as he came out of the induced trance. "Vertigo's gone." His soldier mentality automatically catalogued body sensations. *Not as weak. Pain's there but not as bad. Not nearly normal, but a lot more functional. That'll do.* He sat up and swung his legs off the table. "And Waimanu has some juice left. I could feel it as you worked on me."

Sarah agreed. "I suspect Eva gave it instructions. Programmed a sequence."

"A shutdown sequence?"

Elia answered. "Possibly. But more likely a transition sequence."

"Imprinting Waimanu on Irian Jaya?"

Elia and Sarah exchanged a look. "That's an odd thought, Joshua," Elia said, turning his head to study his eyes. "It came out of a logic lattice just now, that possibility; didn't it?"

"My analytical capacity is coming back. Speeding up, anyway. Thank you, ladies."

Elia studied his face more intently. "Seems so. Just now your biofield has more of that typical crystalline shimmer it gets when your brain is running a lattice."

Joshua slid off the table and stood up. His balance was fine. *And so is my brain. Elia's right. Maybe not lightning-quick, but it's not mired in molasses anymore.* The lattice kept working away, chasing down the tangential probabilities of a reconfigured or reconfiguring locus. An odder thought popped out of it.

"Can you transpose me to Irian Jaya? If I could get there ahead of Eva..."

"I doubt it, Joshua," Sarah answered. "Elia?"

His wife paused, her eyes closed, and took a long moment before she shook her head. "No. I'm sorry, Joshua. We are not Novas. Without Eva as part of Waimanu, we are limited. The locus wants to help, I think, but now it lacks the coherence Eva's immanence gave it."

"It wants to help," Joshua watched their expressions closely, "so could you substitute?"

"For what? And why do you ask?"

"Yourselves for Eva. Because the three of you were in a trance for a long, long time, looking for a solution to the virus. I don't know how a Sisterhood triune trance works, but I think it's possible Eva's consciousness may have imprinted on yours."

"And thus the two of us together could substitute for her missing presence in Waimanu? Fill in the gap, bring back the coherence?" Elia watched his expression as closely as he was watching hers. She and Sarah exchanged a longer look before Sarah answered.

"Some kind of mutual imprinting is likely," Sarah conceded, "but that's probably the least of it. We have no idea how Eva manipulates space and time and energy."

The way they look at each other... it's not just uncertainty about the imprinting possibility; there's some ambivalence in how they feel about it. Joshua gave a mental shrug to push that anomaly into the background, and his logic lattice moved on to the next question.

"Okay. Now, if Eva imprints Waimanu on Irian Jaya... could she transpose me there?" He watched another shared look.

"You think that's her plan, Joshua?"

He sighed. "I don't know. Eva can't do formal structured logic trees and probabilities in her head like I can, but she's still very, very good at analysis. And her intuition might even give her an edge over me in evaluating pathways and probable outcomes. So yeah, I'd say she has a plan."

"You believe she allowed herself to be taken, don't you?"

"Not believe, not at this point. But I think it's a possibility."

Joshua watched both heads nod agreement with him. His logic lattice dropped out an incidental result: *they're ambivalent because if Eva had a plan, and if she actually intended to leave us out of it, the Sisterhood Covenants might say they shouldn't interfere.*

He straightened up and lightly touched the twins' tousled heads. As he walked to the door the lattice spat out another possibility: *equifinality, the concept from systems analysis that there's usually more than one way to a particular end. A Buddhist might call that an eight-fold path.*

"I'm not a Sister, ladies. I'm no longer constrained. Because what kind of rules stop you from helping someone you love?" He snapped the question at them as he walked out the door.

O'Donnell Enclave, Waimanu, HI | Friday 0927 *HST*

"NSA decrypted the phone call." The NSC's flat voice told Demuzzio the news wasn't good. *How much worse can it get?*

"Talk to me, Carol."

"This thing goes deep, TC. Blake was talking to the Senator..."

"Carol," he interrupted, "hang on a minute, I hear Josh coming. I want him to hear you directly, so I don't lose anything in the translation." *And let's hope the ladies succeeded in getting his eidetic memory resurrected.*

Joshua saw the NSC's image on Demuzzio's monitor and quickly slid into the chair beside him.

"Carol. What've you got?"

"Bad news. It's not just Blake, there's a huge conspiracy." The woman's hands moved over her keyboard. "Here, I'll play the decryption for you."

They listened in silence. Demuzzio felt the anger build. *I'm gonna kill both those fuckers. And everybody else that was part of this.* He watched his growing rage mirrored in Joshua's face, the deepening lines, the lips drawn back, the turquoise eyes flickering with light.

"Questions?" Carol Violette asked.

Demuzzio shook his head. *As crystal-clear an indictment as I've ever heard.*

Joshua had one. "The Senator is an educated man. Why's he talking to Blake like he's some hick?"

Carol nodded. "Yeah, I wonder, too. Some kind of crazy psych dynamic going on here, I don't know what. But the Senator is clearly directing a man who's one of the most powerful religious leaders in the world. Maybe it gives him a kick. I've always thought that man was bent."

"Bent doesn't begin to describe it," Demuzzio replied.

"And he keeps getting re-elected. This is his fifth term, TC."

"The most powerful player in Congress," Joshua noted.

Demuzzio watched the younger man take a deep breath and calm his emotions. *He's going analytical. I should too.* It was a struggle.

"There must be other conversations in NSA's databank, Carol."

"There are. Lots."

"So what do they say?"

"We don't know. Their encryption security is a floating algorithm, it changes each time."

Joshua nodded but Demuzzio needed clarification. "Meaning what? You gotta decrypt each one by itself?"

"Yes, TC. Days. Maybe only hours if our geeks can write some sort of optimization scheme. But still, it takes time."

Demuzzio slammed his palm on the table in frustration. The NSC's image on the monitor jittered.

"All stops are pulled out, TC. We'll be as quick as humanly possible," she added.

Joshua put a restraining hand on Demuzzio's forearm and changed the subject.

"Okay. Anything turn up on satellite?"

The woman grimaced. "More bad news. A departure from Hilo, 0219 this morning. Listed as a medical courier into Hickam.

"Hickam? Not Honolulu International?"

"Yeah. The military side."

"Did it land?"

"Uh huh. Touch-and-go, almost. Re-fueled and filed a minimal flight plan for Davao, in the Philippines."

"Our military pumped aviation fuel to kidnap my sister?"

"Looks that way. They didn't know, of course."

"And fewer questions on the military side…"

Demuzzio watched Joshua's eyes go distant.

"Carol," he said after a moment, "that's even worse news. It implies the Senator has an organization."

The woman agreed, glumly. "There was a black ops security blanket thrown over the flight; the duty officer didn't ask any questions."

"Jesus!"

"He was about the only one not involved. I've briefed the President. We'll take this apart, Joshua. I promise you."

"You'd better do it carefully, Carol. And watch your back every second. The President's too. You understand?"

"Had occurred to me, yes. Thanks."

"That Davao flight? You're watching it?"

"Absolutely."

"It's going to divert, Carol. Biak, or more likely, Jayapura."

The woman nodded. "Going to Irian Jaya. That's what I think too."

"Let it happen. We don't want to tip our hand."

"Also my reasoning, Joshua."

Joshua turned to Demuzzio. "Where's my SIO jet?"

"Inbound to Waimea. Fifteen minutes, maybe. Another twenty to refuel."

Joshua stood up. "Carol, I'm heading out. Whatever assets you have in the western Pacific…"

"Already in play," she replied, "Presidential tactical orders. We tried to avoid any command channels we thought might be bent."

"Good thinking! Thank you. I'll be in touch when I'm airborne."

Joshua pointed a finger at Demuzzio as he backed out of the Security Center, but said nothing.

"Got it," Demuzzio yelled after him. *Yeah, I'll take good care of the twins and the ladies for you Josh. You just get Eva back. And rip that fucker Blake apart for me. Or bring him back and I will.*

Chapter 29

Charter MZ987, North of Jayapura, Irian Jaya | Saturday 0656 JYT

After sessions of sating his urges, with catnaps in between, the Reverend Robert Blake buckled his victim into her seat with something like tenderness. The rising sun lit up the green island off the left side of the aircraft as it settled into the landing pattern for Jayapura.

"You know, Eva, I'm not exactly sure what our friend Zurvan has in mind for you. But if you should somehow survive it, I certainly hope that you were in the fertile part of your cycle." *I'd like a son or two to balance off my daughters. All Novas, of course.*

His cell phone vibrated and he patted her thigh. "Excuse me, Eva. I may need to take this." The screen icon showed the secure incoming call was from Zurvan.

"We're on final approach," he answered it.

"I know. A helicopter is waiting. Two men will transfer the girl, on a stretcher. Walk beside them. They will give you a white coat and hat."

"Preserving appearances?"

"We do not know who may be watching."

"Okay. Cover her face?"

"My men will do that."

"Do you have the balance of my funds?"

"Of course. When you deliver the girl to me, in the uplands."

"Why not here? I could turn around faster, be gone with the plane refueled."

"Ah, Doctor Blake. I regret that I must see the girl for myself, so that I can verify what I've paid for. Your friend the Senator is quite skilled at producing substitutes. As you no doubt know." A chuckle followed the sonorous words.

"Oh, it's Eva. I can guarantee that."

"Bring her to me." The connection cut off abruptly.

Blake looked at the cell phone screen. *Not dropped reception, the man hung up.* He started to call Zurvan back, but the plane's landing gear came down and he decided against it.

Blake drummed his fingers lightly on Eva's thigh. "Well, darling, if I do that, I'm out of my own hands and into his." His mind ratcheted up a notch, evaluating possibilities. "You think he has other plans for me? You think he might kill me? Hmm?"

Eva remained unresponsive.

"No, I don't think so," Blake continued his monologue, "smart as he is, he must know I've protected myself with records of our meeting. Mutually assured destruction."

He poked Eva in the side. "Besides, he could just as easily have me killed at this airport, I suppose. Those men who are going to trundle you off won't be physicians."

Blake shrugged. "You know, Eva, this isn't the way I envisioned things working out. Control is not in my own hands anymore; it's in the Senator's. Has been for years. This is his airplane, flown by his organization. And if I go upcountry to deliver you, then I'll be in Zurvan's hands.

"A problem for me, of course, both the Senator and Zurvan. You see, I suspect the Senator in his righteous anger has planned to unleash the dogs of war on Muslims. He probably has all the dots set up, ready to be connected; obviously he's a splendid long-range strategist. The President is a smart man, but he'll really have no choice. So the Senator will have his way. The evangelicals will push everyone over the edge. A new Crusade.

"And then Zurvan will do the same from his side, a jihad, and the mythologized final days will be upon us."

A single tear leaked out of Eva's right eye. He brushed it gently away with his thumb.

"I truly would have preferred to sit this out, Eva. To stay with you in your enclave or someplace else safe and watch the destruction go on.

"Ah, well, wishful thinking doesn't change my status much, Eva. Or yours either, for that matter. Much as I'd prefer it to be you and me against the world, I'm just a pawn in this game. For now, anyway, I just have to play it out."

The wheels of the small jet kissed the tarmac, and they were on the ground in Indonesia. He patted her thigh a last time.

"Of course you're the queen in this game, being the first Nova. Or you were, before I snatched you off the board. Now you're just a ticket, a means to an end for the three of us."

Jayapura Airport, Irian Jaya | Saturday 0700 JYT

Growing proximity to the locus in Irian Jaya nudged Eva's consciousness out of the null state. She heard the tail end of Blake's soliloquy as the plane's reverse thrusters cut back and it taxied more quietly.

"Oh, my, Eva. How right our Founding Fathers were. Jefferson calling Christianity a fable, Madison saying it created superstition, bigotry and persecution. And of course, Islam is the same, a Judeo-Christian derivative." The man chuckled. "I can say that, you know, as an insider."

Sisters! Eva's mind called out in dismay, and they spiraled inward toward her.

"Ah. There's the helicopter," he said. She sensed Blake's form leaning across her, looking out the window. One of her eyelids lifted; slowly, like it had a great weight on it. As the plane turned eastward a shaft of morning sun blinded her.

Her spirit-Sisters clustered in groups. The critical cluster accused her. *You leapt without looking, Young Mother.*

Eva struggled to close her eye against the blinding light, and the circling forms took on a more internal brightness as she answered them. *No. I saw possible futures. The nexus was clear. I leaped toward it.*

Blake's voice sounded in her ear, warm breath close. "Eva. George Washington got it right when he quoted Micah 4:4, 'everyone shall sit under his own vine and fig tree, and there shall be none to make him afraid'."

Her Sisters recoiled with an intensity almost physical. *This man is the serpent of his own myths.*

"It is truly is amazing that after more than two hundred years we've regressed from that sentiment sufficiently to be on the verge of war."

I loved this man, Eva answered her Sisters sorrowfully, *and I still love him.*

"I know you want peace, Eva," Blake continued. "Admirable. And I expect that the Novas, with their empathy gene, very likely could bring peace. But, you see, that wouldn't suit the Senator, or Zurvan. Or, come to think of it, even the established order, churches like mine."

A snake, her Sisters repeated.

"But of course there is no path to peace that doesn't run through war," he added.

"You're wrong," she croaked out of a dry throat. "Water. Please."

"My goodness. Coming out of it, are we? Well, of course. The least I can do." Blake reached into the seat pocket for a bottle, pulled up the valve and dribbled water into her mouth. "Hmm. You even have a swallow reflex. Excellent!" He dribbled more, patiently, as the airplane taxied.

"Thank you," she whispered.

"You're quite welcome, Eva," Blake answered. He pushed up the leg of her pajamas and she felt the pinch of a needle, almost an afterthought to the rest of the pain. "More of the paralytic, dear. Can't have you getting too frisky on us. By all accounts you were pretty dangerous last time you were in this country, what was it, seven years ago?"

Snake, her Sisters screamed in her mind.

But he's wrong again. The last time I was here was three years ago, when Joshua and I set up the nanocamera network. Our little research project to monitor activity at the pool as its locus slumbered.

Her spirit-Sisters de-clustered and spiraled around that thought. Their forms sometimes showed discrete identities, and sometimes merged, becoming shifting, weaving patterns of emotion and logic and history and prediction. At the end, the cluster she perceived as fully supportive of her plan had been reduced to a single Sister: Mary of Magdala. But the cluster that she perceived as critical of her plan had lost a few Sisters to the rationalist cluster.

After some internal debate, the rationalists offered their collective opinion: *It's a slim hope.*

Still the best hope, Eva countered.

The Sisterhood's plan is better, objected the critical cluster, *a surer outcome. And safer for you.*

No, and safer doesn't make it better. There would still be war. Societies would fall apart. Innocents would suffer and die. Eva was adamant.

The critics tried a new tack: *You cling to that belief because you're depressed.*

Eva rejected that out of hand. *Depressed? My plan is working!*

That it has to work at all is depressing, the rationalists noted.

Eva gave a mental shrug. *Conceded. But now I'm in the right place at the right time.*

You tell yourself that because it is your only solace, the critical cluster offered.

Possibly, Eva admitted.

The critics had found her weakness and struck. *Your plan betrays your family and friends, Young Mother. They love you. They would help you.*

That hurt, Eva whimpered.

The aircraft stopped next to the idling helicopter. The copilot nodded to Blake and opened the hatch. The two men in white coats pushed the gurney toward the aircraft as its stairs came down. Blake unfastened Eva's seatbelt.

She struggled to speak as his arms went under her, but the paralytic had begun its work. *You're wrong, Pastor Bob. There is a path to peace that doesn't run through war. One.*

Her spirit-Sisters faded into the background, arguing among themselves, their voices indecisive with worry. *You go to the place of your Becoming, Young Mother. We will see what paths await there.*

East Baliem Valley, Irian Jaya | Saturday 0712 JYT

It had been two days since that strange mind-contact with the boy Ibrahim O'Donnell, and Muhammad Zurvan still relished it. *Flesh of my flesh. I wonder if they know. I'll have to ask you, Eva Connard, when you arrive.*

He smiled at the prospect. *Soon now. Very soon.* "Cover that crucifix," he shouted to the two soldiers of his Philippine jaesh.

The two scurried to collect the branches trimmed off the crudely-fashioned cross laying on the ground, and began to pile them over it.

Zurvan did a slow rotation, scanning the waterfall and the pool and the mountains beyond and the valley below, remembering. *You and your tiger chased me into the river, Eva Connard, which delivered me to the forest folk. Who held me captive for seven long years.*

His ears twitched as they picked up what sounded like helicopter rotors in the distance. Other vibrations passed through him as well, more felt than identified. Except that they clearly were anticipatory: *years of payback, with interest.* The thought made him laugh.

He scanned the sky to the northeast, just above the treeline, but saw nothing. His own helicopter sat idle, on the wide volcanic rock shelf in front of the pool. He looked at his watch. *Another forty minutes yet. My mind is playing tricks on me.*

Zurvan felt that odd sort of connection with the place that he'd developed during his years of captivity. He did another rotation, looking around for the source of any vibrations. Except for a few birds circling overhead, there was nothing. He shook himself and dismissed the feelings. *This is a place of power; I'm feeling what I felt before, that's all.*

The dismissal gave him confidence. *My last visit was problematic, but this time I'm in control.* He smiled. *Full control!* Still, little uncertainties nibbled away at his mind, decisions to be made where the variables weren't clear, or were too fluid.

What will I do with Blake?

The temptation was to kill the man. Blake had his own agenda. *At some point his interests will diverge from mine. And his Senator's too, probably. We will compete for power.* He let his mind chase down possible divergent pathways for a while, then gave it up. *The Pastor may yet have more uses. And he can be manipulated by both money and power. Let him live, for the present.*

He shifted consideration to Eva Connard; she also now represented a nibbling uncertainty. His original plan had been to control her with the K'Shmar, strip the power of a Nova from her and keep her enslaved, mothering his children. In the seven years she owed him, she might make him that many Nova brats. *But the question now is, Eva, since I already have a Nova son and can probably steal him... is keeping you as a brood mare worth the danger you would bring?*

Zurvan shrugged, letting the confidence flood back in. *We'll see.*

West of Jayapura, Irian Jaya | Saturday 0749 JYT

The power built around Eva's mind as the helicopter drew closer to the locus in Irian Jaya. Along with that power came an element of recognition, like a wolf sniffing around a former pup who had gone off and grown up. She let herself sniff back. *Yes, we know each other. My name is Eva. You helped me out, years ago. My brother Joshua, too. We've visited a few times since, but didn't disturb you.*

It was not exactly a cosmic click, Eva thought, but it clearly was an acceptance, a meshing of her rhythms with something greater. It started in her mind and moved out into the reality of her body, along nerve and into muscle and bone, hinting at a more fundamental and complete connection than even the merging of Sisterhood minds. *We never named you. Joshua thought we should, but I wouldn't. It wasn't your time of becoming. But now it is.* A moment of whimsy seized her. *I'm going to call you Gabbatha.*

"Eva?" Blake leaned over and spoke loudly above the thwack-thwack of the helicopter rotors. "Did you just twitch? Should I give you another shot?"

She heard him, and didn't doubt that she'd twitched, but it had nothing to do with her immobilized muscles. She felt him watching her, even though her eyes were closed.

"I guess not. Probably just aircraft vibration." He pulled away.

Yes, Robert, a vibration. But not a physical one, not from the helicopter. I'm not surprised you felt it; you do have that near-Nova sensitivity. She dismissed him from her attention and focused back on the connection that was rapidly forming. Gabbatha, she saw, was tied to Waimanu by the threads of a probabilistic tapestry. *A conduit?* The energy flowing between them was fluid and laminar, but now and again roiling into turbulence where uncertainty obstructed it. *All life is probability.*

Blake's voice intruded again. "Irian Jaya is a place I've been only briefly in and out of, to thank our UMC missionaries. But you've had quite the experiences here, haven't you, Eva? Do you remember?"

Again she dismissed him; he sounded nervous, merely testing her, trying to get a reaction, seeing if she would remain paralyzed. But the closeness of his presence, his voice in her ear, brought the realization abruptly to the surface: yin and yang. *Waimanu is the male aspect; Gabbatha the female. Or what passes for the essence of those concepts.* She felt the energy flow between the two loci react to that recognition and confirm it, and the threads of probability wove the conduit more tightly. *Now I understand a little better. Maybe.* Eva's spirit-Sisters wove into the pattern, spiraling alongside the probabilities in the energy conduit.

Eva posed the question to their rationalist cluster. *Jesus was male. So he couldn't imprint Gabbatha when this locus existed in Palestine, could he?*

The rationalists agreed that must have been the case.

But unlike Jesus, I can imprint Gabbatha to suit my plan. Eva reached out to touch the probability threads, showing them how it could work.

The critical cluster spoke up. *You can still implement the Sisterhood's plan. The locus will give you the power to do this, we think. A catalyst.* A certain desperation sounded in their tone.

Eva shook her head. *Power brings war. Love brings peace.* She called her spirit-Sister Mary of Magdala forth from the complex spiraling patterns of energy and probability. *Isn't that so, Mary?*

That form nodded agreement. Another form left the rationalist cluster and spiraled to stand beside Mary. Eva smiled at her. *Devi? You agree with me now?*

Power has its place, as Ashoka showed me. But he came to love, and love is better.

Eva thanked her and addressed the critical cluster: *You see, Jesus and Mary, and Ashoka and Devi before them, could only reconfigure memes over time. It took generations of Sisterhood breeding and epigenetic reinforcement. But my present day is different; we have instant mass communication through the internet, and a parallel capacity for imprinting global consciousness. Almost instantaneously. My plan will work.*

A few Sisters shifted from the critical cluster to the rationalist cluster, but none joined Devi and Mary of Magdala. The pockets of Sisterly uncertainty in the energy flow smoothed down a tiny bit, but then a larger uncertainty became apparent, a bit of turbulence, tracking closer.

Joshua. In an airplane. I should have known. Eva formed a loving denial and sent it winging toward him. *Don't come, brother. I need to do this thing. Myself.*

He could be helpful, the rationalists disagreed.

He could be an agent of destruction, was Eva's riposte.

They countered. *You are female. The origin of the mythical blind justice meme. And he is your sword.*

No. I've thought this through, she told them. *You all are a part of me, you know this. It's going to get... difficult. You must support me. A house divided...*

East Baliem Valley, Irian Jaya | Saturday 0800 JYT

Blake stood silently, his features carefully composed and neutral, as Muhammad Zurvan pressed Eva's thumb onto a miniature scanner.

"Where did you get the baseline print?" Blake asked.

"From a wine glass." Unaccountably, Zurvan actually giggled as he connected the device to a laptop. "One of my compatriots traded his hand for it."

"Oh. Yes, I heard that story. The child felt bad about it."

"Child? This is a woman, Doctor Blake, as you doubtless know."

I do, Blake agreed, *but the way you say it... so there was a camera, the Senator's flight crew was monitoring my activities. No surprise. But for him to tell you? How close is the relationship between you madmen, anyway?*

"And a dangerous woman at that, so do not think to induce sympathy in me by calling her a child," Zurvan snapped. "When was she last incapacitated?"

"At Jayapura, about an hour ago. And I was told the ampoules were each good for about six hours at her body weight."

Zurvan grunted. "So was I. Did that hold during your flight?"

So was I? Means the Senator briefed him on the drug; that's a close relationship. "Yes it did," he answered. Blake literally felt the currents of uncertainty swirl around him, but one thing was clear: *these madmen will turn on each other. I need to get out of the middle.*

Zurvan's laptop beeped and he looked down at it. "A perfect match. You have done well, Doctor Blake."

Blake nodded. "The other half of my money, then."

Zurvan stared at him, dark eyes probing. "I could kill you."

Blake smiled disarmingly, controlling his reaction. "Yes, you could."

Zurvan laughed. "But of course men of God like you and I don't fear death. Or just possibly it's the public revelations about me that would automatically trigger upon your death or disappearance. But oh, very well, never mind." He tapped an entry on the laptop's keyboard and waited a moment. It beeped again. "Funds have been transferred to your Cayman account."

Blake pulled out his cellphone and dialed into the account. It confirmed receipt of fifteen million dollars. He hit the code sequence that would shift that into other accounts which would split it and send it along until transactional complexity made it untraceable. Then he waited.

"The first Nova, a bargain at the price," Zurvan murmured. He ran a finger down Eva's cheek.

As Blake awaited a status report on his money movement, he studied Zurvan. *He knows I've got a double in California, and he still didn't kill me, so that's another clue.* Logic confirmed what he'd thought earlier: *they're both willing to collaborate on creating chaos, but once it's created each will seek to dominate. And they think I might be somehow useful. I need to get some distance.*

His cellphone signaled that the transactions had all been completed and confirmed. He nodded to Zurvan, and snapped it shut.

"Well, then?" The man made a shooing motion. "This young woman and I have business to attend to."

Something almost like sadness washed over Blake. He walked over to the gurney, bent down and kissed her gently on the forehead. "Goodbye, Eva," he whispered, and walked away to the idling helicopter.

Chapter 30

O'Donnell Enclave, Waimanu, HI | Friday 1311 HST

Elia O'Donnell sat frozen in the Council Chamber, terrified at the images forming on the big display screen. A half-eaten sandwich sat on a plate beside the keyboard. The other half rumbled in her stomach. *I think I'm going to be sick. Eva, why didn't you kill that man?*

She swallowed hard and let the Sisterhood's mantra to control fear play across her mind. It took a moment before she could speak.

"Yes, Joshua, I can do it. I have to. I know that."

"Good," his tinny voice came back, delayed and flattened by the encryption, "you're the only one with the skill level." White noise hissed through the speaker, background from the aircraft. "I'm sorry, love," her husband's voice softened, "but I need you now. Eva needs you."

"I understand." She looked at the live streaming video of Muhammad Zurvan standing over Eva's prostrate form. *You should have killed him back then, Eva. Fed his parts to the beasts of the forest.*

"Okay. Tell me how many transmission channels are functional."

"All of them. One hundred twenty-eight."

"How many cameras active?"

"Twenty-three." Elia swallowed, trying to relieve the dryness in her throat. "Joshua, the system came up by itself; I didn't trigger it from here. Only to try to reboot the two that didn't respond to their wakeup call."

"Are those two near the pool?"

"No. Forest perimeter. High in the trees, southwest."

"Stationary ones. So all four drones work, then; the hawks?"

"Yes. All four are airborne. I'm looking down from one now." Memories eluded Elia's mantra and slithered inside its defenses. *Pain. Awful pain. And I was dying. At the hands of that man.* She trembled, and the video images jittered until she took her hand off the control pad.

"What's the image quality like? And what altitude is the drone at?"

"It's fine, Joshua. The nano-optics are very precise. It's about five hundred meters up, I think."

"Can you zoom it?"

"The camera, not the image?"

"Yes."

Elia fingered code into her virtual control plane to focus down tighter on the figures on the ground, but nothing happened. She moved her fingers and zoomed the image. She tried manually, on a keyboard, to no effect.

"Joshua, I can zoom the image, but I can't control the drone optics."

She tapped code into the keyboard to drop the drone down fifty meters, but nothing happened.

"Try..." Joshua started.

"I did," she answered, "I don't have any physical control over the drones. None."

Joshua swore. "Eva reprogrammed them."

"What? Why? How could she see this coming?"

"Don't know." Desperation in his voice filtered past the flatness of encryption. "She wanted us to see, but not interfere? I just don't know, dammit."

"Could you tell me how to re-program?"

"Maybe. But I don't think we'll have enough time. What routes are the drones flying?"

Elia's trembling fingers fumbled within the control plane. She willed them to steadiness then watched the results on her monitor. "They look like squared-off circles, Joshua. Maybe like a search pattern. Overlapping orbits."

He grunted. "Smart. From the ground they'll just look like native snake-eagles, circling high up. She thought this out."

"How long..."

"I don't know that either, Elia. But she didn't exactly set this up overnight."

"Prescience, then."

His voice went hopeless in acceptance, even in the encrypted transmission she could hear it. "Guess so. Or at least some sort of contingency planning. Eva cut us out of it from the very beginning."

"Joshua... maybe we should not interfere, not..."

"I can't, Elia. I can't just assume she knows the best answer. Maybe she does. But I'm her big brother, her protector..." His voice broke. "I have to try. To help."

"I understand."

Elia cried silently, listened to her husband's ragged breathing while he gathered himself. Finally he spoke.

"Okay. You can get a decent image when you zoom just the image?"

"It's reasonably good." She shuddered as the camera looked down on the man who had raped and tortured her, and would now no doubt do the same to an immobilized Eva.

"Okay. Stream all the aerial videos to me. Continuously."

Her fingers flicked over the control plane.

"Okay, now some of the stationary bots, in the treetops around the ledge, how do those look when you zoom their images? They clear?"

Elia keyed in the three closest, saw Zurvan's face over Eva's prone form on a gurney, and shuddered again.

"Very clear," she answered. *Too damn clear.*

East Baliem Valley, Irian Jaya | Saturday 0822 JYT

The power that had started building in Eva's mind — from the energy locus now named Gabbatha — escalated as the gurney was pushed onto the rock shelf in front of the pool. The hard volcanic rock seemed to hum, trying to synchronize the locus vibrations with hers. *It wants to touch me,* she thought. *Or it needs to.*

Her body was immobilized, but her mind had fewer constraints. Eva sent it outward to see through the eyes of Gabbatha, riding the wings of a hawk, using its keen vision. The nanocameras were still in place, she saw. And their subtle vibrations indicated her approach had triggered them. *My coding worked!*

When she and Joshua were just visiting, installing the nanobot cameras three years ago, she recalled there had been some sense of contact with the locus. But then it had been just a little tickle. This sensation was strong, restless, urgent. *We will become, Gabbatha, together,* she promised it. She accepted just a tiny bit of the energy that sought transfer, and used it experimentally to power her right eyelid open just a slit. Surprisingly, it worked. *A non-neural control for my paralyzed muscles?*

Gabbatha answered with a surge of energy, sensing Eva's helplessness against the evil towering over her, wanting to give her the means to protect herself. Eva deflected the surge: *I can't do that, Gabbatha, my plan requires me to be helpless.*

The locus vibrations shivered and shifted frequency, conveying dismay. Eva answered. *Yes, I know that. Survival is the strongest drive.*

Muhammad Zurvan moved further around the gurney, unblocking her view of the morning sky. Her slitted eye confirmed what her mind and the hawk had told her: the circling raptors in the sky were not organic; they were her father's little creations, adaptations of DARPA drones. *With nano-tech by Joshua.* She felt a surge of gratitude to them both. *The pieces of my plan are falling into place; this is going to work.* That realization seemed to calm the insistency of the locus.

The rotors of Robert Blake's helicopter sped up and the downwash brushed her as it flew overhead. *Goodbye, Robert. I wish you the best: a death quick and clean, not slow and obscene. Stay out of Joshua's way.* Elements of her plan were beginning to fall into place. She smiled inwardly at the thought. *Okay, there's the first invariant among all these threads of probabilities. Betrayal.* She watched those threads converge slightly, although toward a still-uncertain outcome. *I'm glad that's over with.*

Reaching out through Gabbatha, Eva touched the hawk's mind, just as she had touched those of the whales and dolphins through Waimanu. The bird obediently dropped altitude and flew lazy circles under the lead drone. All four drones tightened their flight paths. *My pattern recognition code works. Good!*

Summoned again, the bird dove down then flared off above her head. *Very nice, thank you, Mr. Hawk.* The drones would home their nanocameras on her in response, which should provide plenty of resolution of her face. *I'll send Sarah a message, tell her to call off Josh.* She accepted a bit more of Gabbatha's power, giving her eyelid more mobility, then blinked the Sisterhood code warning against intervention. *Sarah, Elia, I pray you're watching.*

"A blink! Is it possible the drug is wearing off? Did your Pastor lie to me?" Zurvan bent down to study her face, occluding the sky.

I hope they got the message, Eva thought. *Just move over, please, so I can do it again.* Unaccountably, the man did, and she blinked the code sequence again.

Zurvan pulled back further and looked up at the circling hawk. "Or is there some strangeness to this place that will restore you, Eva Connard?"

Eva took advantage and blinked the message again. *Third time's the charm. Just to be sure.*

Zurvan bent down to study her fluttering eyelid. He forced it shut with his thumb, then pulled it open again. The vacuum in his dark eyes flickered with red, Eva saw. *This man is fully infested with his beasts.*

"My, you certainly are an interesting creature. But worrisome. So as they say in your country, let's get this show on the road." A high-pitched laugh followed that statement.

The rhythms from Gabbatha went dissonant for a moment, chafing at her muzzled state. Eva soothed them.

Zurvan walked away, yelling instructions.

Fear in his voice, Eva realized. *Good. That means whatever his show is to be, we'll get it on the road faster. Suits me.* She let bravado wash out her fear, and communed with her new locus. It was beginning to cohere with astonishing speed.

East Baliem Valley, Irian Jaya | Saturday 0903JYT

The two members of his Abu Sayyaf *jaesh* watched him attentively, fingers on the triggers of their video cameras.

"You are ready?" he asked them. "You remember your training, your skills?"

They both nodded. "We have done this before, Mahdi," one said.

Competence. So good to find it, he thought. He nodded back, organizing his thoughts. "Do not film this. I need to run through it first, and hear your opinion."

They lowered their cameras, and Zurvan began.

"My friends. My faithful. All believers in the One True God. Allah has delivered to me the false prophet." He paused for effect and reached out a hand that twisted Eva's face to the side. "You will get a close-up of her face." The cameramen nodded. "Then of mine." He arranged his features appropriately, and continued.

"There is no God but Allah. These Novas are the spawn of Shaitan. This one, this Eva Connard, claims to be a savior of humanity. She would have you believe that the Novas will bring a better future. She lies. They bring destruction."

Using his thumb, Zurvan pushed Eva's lips into a grimace, showing some teeth. *Excellent! The drug makes the muscles hold position for a moment.* "We will arrange her face just before doing the close-up. A nice ugly snarl. That will minimize the editing afterwards." The cameramen nodded again, and Zurvan indicated a shift to his own face.

"Do not be deceived, my friends. Let your faith be your shield. Put your trust in Allah, in the words of the Prophet. The end times are upon us. The struggle will be hard. But we will prevail. Allahu akbar!" He smiled gravely and let his soliloquy run on. *I've said this so many times, so many ways.* He watched the faces of his cameramen, looking for hints that his delivery or pacing was off. But they both were nodding with the metronomic intensity he always inspired. He stifled a giggle as the thought occurred: *just like the Reverend Blake's sermons, on autopilot.*

"There," he concluded with a question to his *jaesh*, "do you think that's enough? I don't want to run on too long before we get to the judgment and punishment part."

"I felt it, Mahdi! A trembling in the rock itself, beneath my feet. Your message is perfect," the younger one said.

The older one nodded, more thoughtful. "Two versions, Mahdi?"

"Aha! Yes, a fine idea! One for the true believers, the other for those Muslims who haven't yet seen the truth."

"The fools!"

Zurvan smiled at him. "Yes, they are fools. But it is out of kindness that their hearts mislead their minds. Thus the Prophet instructs us to bring them back to the true way."

These two fools may actually have some insight, Zurvan thought. His smile got wider. "If you have good ideas, my *jaesh*, I welcome them. You may help me in crafting a version to bring the fools to the truth."

East Baliem Valley, Irian Jaya | *Saturday 0921 JYT*

Off to Eva's left, Muhammad Zurvan continued bragging to his syco-phants. *Amazing,* she marveled, *the man is actually outperforming my expectations.* She made her right eye blink the Sisterhood code for close attention. There was no wind and the nanomikes were superdirectional, but the audio might still have to be scrubbed to get it clear. *They'll know what to do.*

Or would they? Even though Eva had gathered all the threads of probability to herself that she could, outcomes were still dependent on variables no longer under her control. She gave a mental shrug. *You can only plan so much, and I didn't have a lot of time.*

She blinked the code again to make sure they picked it up as intentional, then shut her eye as Zurvan approached.

"All right, let's film this," he said.

She heard the hunger in his voice and welcomed another key element into her plan. *Okay, there's the second invariant established in this chaos,* Eva thought. *Power.* Her mind watched the threads of probabilities weave more tightly together in support of her plan. *With a little fear in his voice, that's good.*

Eva felt him loosening her pajama top. *No! This I will not permit!* She'd had no choice with Blake; her mind had been powerless over mid-Pacific. But here on Irian Jaya it was different. She metered a tiny bit of the locus' power into her mind to support the intention: *I would have him lose interest in sex.* Eva configured the intention to subtly play on Zurvan's fear, to make him want to just move expeditiously on his plan without any side trips. *This needs to be done before Josh arrives to complicate things.*

"Oh, never mind," Zurvan said, "let's get on with the script. Set up your cameras on either side." He closed the pajama top.

Eva tuned out the man's staging directions and sought communion with her spirit-Sisters. The forms obediently spiraled inward, coalescing into the same three clusters as they came forward in her consciousness. The critical cluster immediately screamed at her: *He is a psychopath! Let Gabbatha be his judge, and destroy him!* But a few of those Sisters accepted that elements of Eva's plan were falling into place. They moved across the spiral to the rationalist cluster, but with reservations: *your plan may work, but it still is less certain than the Sisterhood's. The probabilities you seek to influence are very volatile.*

Eva thanked both clusters for their views then focused on her two supporters: *I need historical precedent. Mary? What happened?*

Mary of Magdala came into sharper focus as she answered. *Two things, I think. I was not ready; I had not your knowledge, nor your strength. I was only a Nova, I believe, momentarily. A genetic aberration. The locus you call Gabbatha was strong in Palestine then; its need for a Becoming was urgent.*

Eva gave a mental nod of understanding. *And the second thing? Jesus?*

Wistful sadness textured Mary's answer. *Jesus thought to save the world from itself. He was a good man, a craftsman not only of wood, but of souls. We sought Gabbatha together, but like your brother he was a not-quite-Nova. And of course both are males, although they both were strong enough in their female aspect to synchronize with Gabbatha in some ways.*

Eva shuddered at the recollection: at this place seven years ago, Joshua had been like a mother wolf protecting her pup: vicious, uncaring, with a purpose so singular she'd had to gently deprogram his mind afterwards.

See, the critical cluster called to her from some middle distance, *you are mother to your Novas. You must become the Sisterhood's wolf!*

Eva acknowledged that possibility, but pushed it to a corner of her mind, the insistent spirit-Sisters along with it.

A terrible time, Mary concluded, *but afterwards we escaped to Egypt, thence to Galatia. We had children. Our bloodline was preserved. You are the ultimate result.*

Eva traced her lineage forward from that, then backward, watching how the spirits of her maternal ancestors aligned with the clusters. Another thought occurred to her, a third thing: *Maybe the enlightened age that started with Greece could not be sustained? Is that a precedent that would apply to my modern times? Do we need destruction so that Novas can rise from its ashes? Is there a karmic cycle from which there is no escape? The probabilities I'm trying to condition against that... are they just subject to too much chaos?*

Her own uncertainty was mirrored in the forms spiraling around her, but regardless of their divergent opinions, respect for her strength and purpose came from all of them. It was a comfort.

O'Donnell Enclave, Waimanu, HI | Friday 1456 HST

Sarah entered the Council Chamber with a question. "Elia, did you tell Joshua that we think Eva might not want interference?"

"I didn't have to, Sarah; he deduced it."

"But he's going on anyway, isn't he?"

"He has no choice."

"Thomas is with the twins, Elia. They're sitting up, taking fluids, talking. They seem okay." Sarah watched the young woman brighten. *The only good news today.* "You can be with them if you like; I'll take over here."

"You can't, Sarah. Josh and I are the only ones who could manage these multiplexed video streams the way Eva wants."

"Eva wants?"

"I'll run down and check the boys, and come right back, but first I want to brief you in, so you can think about things."

"Go ahead."

"First point: Eva modified the operations code for the nanocamera array, Sarah. We're locked out. She has control."

"How…?"

"Yes. And when, and why? Good questions. Like Josh says, she didn't set it up overnight."

"Prescience, Elia?"

"Or something very close. A sense of convergent probabilities. That's actually my second point."

Sarah sighed. *And there's more, isn't there?* She watched the transient brightness fade from the young woman's face as she worked controls and ran a playback several minutes old on the small console screen in front of them.

"Third point: the eyeblink, the Sisterhood duress code. Watch."

Sarah did. *Eva repeated it; so it can't just be a twitch.* "You see that as a direct order, Elia? Not to interfere?"

The young woman shrugged. "That code is context-sensitive."

Sarah agreed. "Could mean 'stand down', or 'hold your fire', or 'don't act just now'… is there more?"

Elia exhaled and fast-forwarded the video. "Yeah. Fourth point: watch this."

Sarah did. *The eyeblink code for 'close attention'.* "So, Eva is ordering us to observe, but not interfere? Is that how you read this?"

Elia stared at her. "And we have a choice to make, Sarah."

Sarah stared back. "Ignore the Sisterhood's proscriptions?"

Elia leaned over and cued a display on a different monitor screen. "I'll be back. In the meantime, also think about this GCN pattern that the locus at Irian Jaya is outputting. It's nothing we've ever seen before, but clearly it's synchronized to Eva."

Sarah watched as the resonance patterns of what had to be Eva's mind were displayed on the probability plot algorithm Elia had created. The indigo-hued blinking signal was reminiscent of a human cell, a darkened nucleus at its center. Shock waves shot out from its core, expanding the outer circumference; a rapidly inflated balloon. Just as quickly, the outer rim collapsed back upon itself, revealing a compressed, tiny purple dot. *But software doesn't have a mind of its own, and this output graphic is simply interpreting the outcomes of conditional probabilities. Divergence and convergence.* The display seemed to suck at her mind, trying to draw her in as she studied it. She fought for objectivity: *I'm a neuroscientist, for God's sake!* But the more she studied it, the more it seemed to change. *Does observing the event influence it?*

A touch on her shoulder and Sarah almost leaped from her chair. "Oh! Elia," she said, casting her a nervous glance, "I want you to see this." She scrolled back a minute in time to where the change had begun. On screen, the cell had accelerated its chaotic expansion and collapse. The irregularity of the fluctuations was unnerving. *Do probabilities really behave like that?* Sarah noted her own breath had become shallow and gasping as she watched. Now, she gathered control back.

"It's clearly Eva's resonance in the center," Sarah continued, "and it's tied to the locus at the periphery, but she seems to have gone into some kind of heightened probability state, unstable... I think maybe it's panic."

Elia murmured assent. "Or uncertainty. She could draw upon the locus to steady herself; right, Sarah? If she feels weak it would help her get her footing." The regular pulsations of the locus danced soothingly around the perimeter of the cell, but did not permeate. "So why doesn't she do that?"

"Yes, the locus should help..." Sarah stopped at the only answer. *You're refusing any help at all. Why, Eva?*

"She could end this. Wipe out Zurvan, those others holding her." Elia said. "She's done it before... so maybe all these fluxes mean she's marshaling her energy for a counter-attack?"

If so, she's wildly out of control, Sarah thought, *she can't focus with these radical shifts in probabilities.* "No, Elia, if she wanted to fight, she would steady herself, draw upon the locus. Then the probabilities would converge, I think; we'd see a less confused pattern. Her refusal is deliberate." *When we created the truine, I caught a glimpse of this; Eva goes only so far and no further.* The memory triggered a sick sensation in Sarah's gut that pushed its way out into her system; a torrent of loss and self-pity.

"So this is what she wants," Sarah said. She felt the younger woman's eyes on her. *Elia doesn't understand, and somehow I do... something is consuming Eva; taking her apart from the inside, as it did with me, and she saved me. Why not save herself?*

Elia inhaled sharply, her response stopped cold by a shift in the blinking indigo cell. The fluxes decreased, with the cell remaining ballooned and static. The indigo shade faded in barely perceptible increments. Minutes passed with the women silently staring at the screen and its newfound steadiness. Any solace offered by the change was overshadowed by the cell's fading color.

"I suspect she's decided, and the probabilities reflect that." *You already know, Elia, you just need to accept it.*

"Not exactly, but a passive approach, I think; accepting the intentions of those surrounding her," Sarah replied.

"She doesn't have to do that! Why not commune with the locus, draw from it?" Elia objected.

Sarah noted the dilation in Elia's pupils, the trembling in her fingers. *Elia would never surrender this way. I wish Eva felt the same.*

Elia did not wait for a response, "I felt better when her cell was going wild. Now, nothing; like she just shut down," she wailed, "like she's giving up."

A memory surfaced then in Sarah's mind, a fragment unattended by anything else save one sure intuition: her mind had been conditioned, her memories carefully edited, by the sole person capable of that: Eva Connard. The fragment consisted of only two words, but she remembered how they had burned her soul. *"Then choose." That stern admonition forced me into a decision. I chose to live.*

Sarah shivered as she stared at Elia's trembling face. *And what have you chosen, Eva?*

Chapter 31

SIO Flight 999X, West of Manus Island | *Saturday 1017 JYT*

The small SIO executive jet blew past Manus Island at an impressive speed, but to Joshua that green dot in the blue Pacific forty-five thousand feet below crawled backward far too slowly. He studied the live video streamed to his laptop computer, watching Zurvan lean over an inert Eva on the rock shelf in front of the pool. *I'm coming, Sis. Hang on.* A faint susurrus of the savage rage he'd given free rein to years past in that same place stirred restlessly in the depths of his limbic system. He recognized the connection with that locus but suppressed it.

"Elia," he spoke into the satellite phone on the seatback, "that's a really crisp image; you were able to zoom the nanocams?"

"No, Eva did that; she still has drone and camera control. All we can do is work with the images."

"She's just lying there; how can she be controlling the drones?"

"I don't know, Joshua. M3, maybe. She is a Nova Becoming."

Joshua considered that. *The M3 worldview hypothesis: consciousness is primary and matter and energy are merely its emergent properties.* The possibility ran down through a logic lattice and got rejected. "She hasn't evolved that far."

"We don't know that."

"If she were at that point, Elia, I think she could overcome her paralysis and simply wipe out Zurvan and his cronies."

They both thought about that for a moment. Elia broke the heavy silence.

"She made a choice, Joshua."

"I saw the goddamn blink code," he snapped.

"We're ignoring it too," his wife answered softly, "Sarah and I."

"Good. Thank you." *But she's right, my baby sister made a choice to take it all on herself. That's clear, but why?* "You think Eva's sure she has this in hand, Elia?"

"Sure? No. I don't see how she could be."

Joshua let a logic lattice parse that thought. *Elia's right. Too much chaos, too many uncertainties.*

"So maybe she's protecting us," Elia added a possibility.

A logic lattice ran with that, evaluating and concluding in the blink of an eye: *because either we can't protect ourselves, or she wanted to leave a competent garrison behind to protect the Novas?* "Maybe," he agreed. But neither possibility computed as particularly probable, so the lattice kept running to the next obvious question: *one of the occasions in which you protect your rear is when there's a good chance you won't be able to come back to help defend it.*

"We should have weaponized some of those drones," he said.

"Eva wouldn't have allowed it."

"I know. A sacred place. Still…"

"No one could have seen this coming, Josh," Elia said, "so don't do 'if only', okay?"

That brought him up short. *I haven't got time for recrimination.* "Right. Where's TC?"

"Coordinating with Carol. She and the President are staging resources in the Pacific. We have nothing close, but the Aussies have an assault ship training in the Arafura Sea. The Indonesians are flying a small special ops team from East Timor to Biak, Presidential request."

Joshua plotted locations and estimated travel times in his head. "I'm probably still closest." The thought of his growing proximity to the locus brought a resurgence of the feeling of connection, and the rage along with it. *Have to be careful with that. I need all my wits.* But it nibbled at his mind anyway, dark and bloody and insidious.

"So what's she going to do, Elia? What's her plan?"

"You saw the second blinked code?"

"Attention to detail. That's how I read it. She wants every little nuance down on tape. Blake and Zurvan incriminating themselves. And our nano-cams have it down from every conceivable angle."

"Then do you think she'll invoke the Sisterhood's solution?"

"The Second Coming myth? Maybe. Let Zurvan show himself to the world for what he is, then crush him? No one would blame her. But that's a power solution; she's never liked it."

"Too much pain, too many innocents hurt. And the Novas would be blamed."

"Yeah. Wars in some cultures. All sorts of bad news." Joshua caught the sadness in her tone, and multiple logic lattices ran in parallel. "You need to tell me something, Elia. What is it?"

"M3, Joshua. Here, I'm sending you the probability plot from the global consciousness network. Watch how it changes. Sarah and I think Eva was conflicted, but that now… now she's firm on her plan."

He watched the display, trying to make sense out of its patterns and sequences. *M3. Eva somehow intends to create an aspect of consciousness so powerful that it will change reality. Or maybe just the universal perception of reality, but she obviously thinks that would be enough.*

Different sections of his physical brain reacted at cross-purposes as logic worked its way through complex probabilities: one part howled with rage, one part cried out with empathy.

"It could work, Eva," he whispered to the computer screen, "I can see how it could. But the cost is too high."

East Baliem Valley, Irian Jaya | *Saturday 1020 JYT*

The energy locus named Gabbatha alternated — it seemed to Eva — between a polite tapping at the door of her mind and a blaring demand to be let in. *I cannot,* she told it, *the survival instincts hardwired into my animal brain would override the plan in my human cortex. Sorry.*

Both wonderment and despair rode the answer, which was a plea to... what? *Integrate is the closest word,* Eva thought. That triggered from Gabbatha an insistent but pleasurable pressure, a siren's song of desire. *Yes, I want it too,* Eva admitted, *but not just yet.*

Instead of arguing more, Eva shifted her mind's focus to the past, when an unformed Gabbatha had been resident at Castle O'Donnell in Ireland. A four-year-old Eva had felt its first enquiring tendrils in her mind. Together, they had actually created the context in which she could communicate with her spirit-Sisters, in which she could join consciousness with the dolphins who frolicked at the base of the cliff.

I remember, Gabbatha told her.

Then you remember the starlings, over Coulagh Bay, Eva formed the picture for her.

Self-organization, her savant brother had explained years later; self-assembly from chaos into order. The individual birds see no overall scheme, they have no leader, no director. But still they form patterns, they move as a whole. The flock has a collective will, an emergent property not present in any definable way in any single bird. The flock will inadvertently create patterns of subtle beauty in the sky: superpositions, the sum of all their quantum states.

And we played with their patterns, the locus agreed.

Eva laughed. *A wonderful child's summer, having those flocks make designs in the sky.* The locus laughed with her and assented, remembering that time, replaying the images in Eva's mind. Eva watched them and remembered how intense had been the joy of creation. *Until Uncle Ham shut me down.* The villagers in Allihies below the castle had begun to worry, and called in the parish priest from Darrynane. *The cross on St. Patty's Day, Stonehenge on the solstice.* She smiled at the memory. *I was so young.*

I am young too, the locus replied, *but also old.*

You do go way back, Eva agreed. Her spirit-Sisters, she suddenly realized, were merely another emergent property, a different manifestation of that quantum force for self-organization, for reverse-entropy, for order from chaos. *For conditioning the threads of probability, down through eons. Epigenetics. The Sisterhood collectively has an intuition for quantum thinking, though they never knew what to call it.*

The locus echoed the concepts racing through her mind: *communications... internet... capability for simultaneity across the globe... bringing coherence...a common community of interest and emotion... the global consciousness.* Or maybe it was more like a mirror than an echo, given its simultaneity. *The state of a quantum event is the sum of all its possible states,* Eva repeated Josh's explanation, beginning to understand it at last on an intellectual level.

Chasing that concept distracted her momentarily, and she felt a hint of integration beginning. *Oh, clever girl!* She laughed at Gabbatha, who immediately stopped her attempt. The locus laughed along with Eva. *Can't blame me for trying,* was the image conveyed.

Of course not, Eva agreed, since she was about to attempt a similar thing. *Be patient, Gabbatha. You see my plan? You and I will shade probabilities to create an emergent behavior in the human species, very much like that we created in those European starlings.*

She showed the locus the threads of probability she intended to weave into her tapestry, bringing out the emergent properties needed to truly welcome the Novas into the world: celebration and beauty and grace and joy.

And I hope to hell it works. Now for the first thread, my mad mullah here. Eva formed the intention, subtle and delicate, and let Gabbatha convey it through a resonance in the volcanic rock shelf into the psychopathic brain of Muhammad Zurvan. Through her one slitted eye, she watched him, the little tells in his body language beginning to react.

Whom the gods would destroy, Eva remembered Euripides, *they first make proud.* Her mind smiled, though her face couldn't. *Duck soup, for a psychopath like that.*

East Baliem Valley, Irian Jaya | Saturday 1021 JYT

It occurred to Muhammad Zurvan, as he instructed his two cameramen on the exact angle and focus of each shot he wanted, just how cleverly he had met a complex challenge. *My foresight was awesome! Who else could have indoctrinated a* jaesh *so well that long years of absence would not degrade its loyalty? Who else would have intuited that the Senator could be a willing and useful partner who would even provide his pawn Blake as a tool? Who else...* His mind let the litany run on pleasurably as he ended his instruction and walked toward Eva. *And now another challenging decision: kill you or keep you to bear my children?*

He squeezed a nipple hard through Eva's pajama top and watched a perspiration break over her eyebrows. "You feel pain, Eva Connard. I know this. Tsk. I wish your facial muscles weren't frozen; it detracts from my pleasure." *I'd like to keep you, truly I would.*

He waved his *jaesh* over. "Some of what you record will be solely for my private archives," Zurvan told them, "keep that in mind if you have suggestions." The two men nodded and brought their cameras up.

"Eva Connard," Zurvan intoned, "you have sinned against Allah."

He made his features darken.

"You have held yourself above Allah." He slapped her head to the left. "You have called yourself a god." He backhanded her head to the right. You have insulted all of Islam."

"Cut," he told the cameramen. They lowered their camcorders, awaiting direction. He smiled at them as he squeezed Eva's reddened cheeks. "Of course she said no such things, so far as I'm aware, but I am sure she thought them. So, in your next shots, be sure to focus tight on my face, to show my righteous anger." He laughed out loud, and they with him; then he composed his face and spoke.

"You are accused, infidel. It is my duty to judge you, in accordance with Sharia, with the principles of Islam."

A resonance ran through the rock and made his toes tingle. "Cut! Did you feel that?"

The cameramen looked at each other. "What, Mahdi?"

"A vibration in the ground."

"No, Mahdi," the younger one said.

"Possibly," the older one said. "There are active volcanoes here. And things called rift zones, I think. They have minor earthquakes."

That was no earthquake. I've felt it before. When I was lying on the rock uphill to ambush the O'Donnell boy. His eyes searched for the spot he had lain and found it. Seven years ago, that situation had not had a good outcome. *But this time it's different. This time, Joshua O'Donnell, I have your little sister. And I am in total control.* Zurvan felt his entire being expand with the fullness of power in that thought.

But then the ground underneath him resonated again. Caution set in. *As much as I'd like to, you are too dangerous to keep as my concubine, Eva Connard.* He nodded to his cameramen.

"An imam brings justice, under Sharia," Zurvan began. *And now I have decided.* He paused for dramatic effect.

"I am the Mahdi, the Twelfth Imam!" He raised his arms and intoned it to the sky.

His cameramen trembled and whispered agreement. "Mahdi!"

"You, he turned to Eva and slapped her again, I judge you a devil, a false prophet. I have considered your crimes against Islam, indeed against the world. Here is my ruling, my fatwa: you are to die by the lash, Eva Connard!" *A hundred ought to do it. I'm so glad you can feel pain.*

East Baliem Valley, Irian Jaya | Saturday 1043 JYT

The cool calm of her rational decision faded under the harsh reality of incipient pain, and Eva was momentarily overtaken by fear. The locus took advantage, trying to sneak in by the door thus opened in the brain's basement.

Oh, no you don't, Gabbatha. Eva slammed the door shut, imposing her rational mind's will on her amygdalic fight-or-flee response.

Have you no sense of survival? The locus conveyed a sense of indignation.

Of course I do. It's just that this situation requires otherwise.

Bah! You're too fixated on your plan.

Well, it's working. Zurvan's every word, every expression, every tone and nuance was being captured on multiple cameras from different angles. *He's self-destructing. He's toast.*

That's no reason for you to do the same, Gabbatha objected. *Your Sisters have wisdom. Listen.*

The circle of spirit-Sisters that Eva had suppressed closed around her, though she hadn't summoned them.

How did you do that?

The locus answered obliquely. *Your Sisters are as much mine now as they are yours.*

That worried Eva. Maybe integration was more subtle than she could perceive. As if in response to her concern, to verify it, suddenly Eva found herself sitting on a stone bench in a garden. An embodied Mary of Magdala stood opposite, by a pool in a small stream. The sound of trickling water came through her physical ears rather than through her mind, audible words with it.

"I remember you, Mary of Magdala," the stream called Gabbatha continued. "Your Jesus was a good man."

"Yes," Mary answered. "And a good father." Fond memories drifted across Eva's vision, children running across a grassy field, blue mountains in the background. "A fine carpenter and cabinet maker, too, later in life, in Galatia."

The stream spoke, a note of regret. "We could not integrate. Our waveforms were slightly different."

"I know that now. I didn't then."

"Your husband, your lover, thought to attempt what Eva does now."

"A mistake. We walked here in my garden. Gethsemane. We talked. But he had his plan; he wouldn't let go."

"Fixated! See?" Gabbatha announced to Eva as the form of Mary of Magdala stood silent. "Strength of purpose can be a blessing or a curse."

Eva acknowledged that, dismissing it with a wave of a hand that now moved and lips that now could form words. "An inherited trait. My brother can be stubborn too."

The stream rumbled pleasantly. "I can restore your muscle function. Minutes."

"You know my decision. Why do you test me this way?"

The locus ignored her question. "Even just your little finger, an energy field... a lance of light, between the eyes. Or in the heart, though this beast hasn't one. Or better yet, lower down, a slow death." The words tinkled out of the stream's flow, amused.

"I must have strength of purpose for this, Gabbatha. Do not undercut me."

"If you die, I will be destroyed too."

"Nonsense. You have no substance in this reality." But Eva turned her hands and looked over them, wondering exactly which reality she meant.

"I will fade away like Waimanu is doing now."

"No," Eva posited. "There will be another time, another place. And another person."

"There is no such, Eva Connard. You and I are entwined. One."

"Then stay with me, Gabbatha. I need your company."

A long cosmic sigh, and a belated answer from the running stream. "I know. I test you to be sure."

"But you must not interfere. Now, while I have my mind, I'm ordering you to honor my intention." She formed the intention, a thing of beauty and power, and bequeathed it to the stream. The threads of its probabilities became enmeshed with Gabbatha, and thus inescapable. The garden vanished and Eva found herself back in an immobilized body, her slitted eye watching the face of Muhammad Zurvan shade out the sun.

And there's the third invariant established in this chaos, Eva thought. *Surrender.* Her mind watched the threads of probabilities converge even more. The outcome tapestry she intended was coming more clearly into view; the picture it showed made her smile. *And now it's more probable than not.*

O'Donnell Enclave, Waimanu, HI | Friday 1559 HST

Sarah watched Elia slump heavily in her console chair in the Council Chamber at Waimanu. *Pressed in by the gravity of the decisions we're forced to make,* Sarah thought. She quoted the ancient Sisterhood wisdom to the younger woman: "Transformation usually requires that something die so some new thing can be born in its place."

Elia nodded wearily. "So they say. But how can I tell Joshua that?"

"You can't. I understand."

Elia raised her head, dark eyes flickering. "Key word is 'usually'."

"I agree. And it can be our basis for assisting him."

"That we doubt our Young Mother's sanity?"

"A thin excuse, I know. But we have none other."

"Parallel paths then," Elia decided, Eva and Joshua.

Sarah nodded. "No one can be totally sure of the best way to effect the outcome, not even Eva."

"Too much chaos," Elia agreed. "One thing to create emergent behavior in flocks of birds, but quite another to do that in human minds."

"Still, she clearly thinks it's possible," Sarah pointed out. "And I guess that I do too… now that I realize exactly how powerful she is, our child of light. But still, it's not certain… even Eva can't be certain in a situation this complex, can she?"

In silence, the two women contemplated the multiple incoming streams of video from Irian Jaya for a moment. Elia realized it first.

"It's the shock value. She's counting on these videos to provide it."

"Forcing an instant shift in perspective! Yes, Elia! I see it now!" Sarah felt her weariness get brushed away by the sudden clarity. "Yes, like what happened in Iran many years ago, after that girl Neda Soltani was shot down and a fair fraction of the human race watched her bleed out on the streets of Tehran."

Elia nodded. "Exactly. And that was a microcosm, just a beginning. Look what eventually happened."

"Yes!" Sarah saw the brilliance of the plan. "What Eva has in mind? A macroshift!"

They looked at each other, marveling at the foreknowledge or prescience or intuition or instinct that had driven Eva four years ago. *That nanocamera array wasn't simple curiosity to research a nascent locus,* Sarah realized, *even though that's how she sold the expense to Joshua.*

But their Sisterhood training in skepticism made them immediately question that. Elia spoke the first objection. "The Sisterhood's solution is nearly as good. Become mobile and take off Zurvan's head. He's already revealed himself for the evil that he is. The video is overwhelming. That should work."

Sarah shook her head. *I like that idea, but...* "No. The Sisterhood's is a power solution. The myth of the Second Coming, the End Times, the return of the Christ or the Twelfth Imam or Horus or whoever... in the form of a fifteen-year-old biracial female... overcoming evil and hate, bringing peace and love to a hungry humanity... very satisfying, yes. But it doesn't carry the emotional weight of sacrifice. It is the wrong solution. Struggles for power would continue into the future. The Novas would be at continual risk."

Elia thought about that and offered another alternative. "She could fake it, her sacrifice. There's precedent."

Sarah shook her head again. *I like that idea too, but...* "I doubt it, Elia. The global consciousness would feel such a falsehood. True empathy requires truth. Eva understands that."

The two women fell silent again while they contemplated the incoming video streams. This time Sarah spoke first.

"We don't know what will happen. So while we support Joshua all we can, we must also respect Eva's plan."

Elia agreed, reaching a hand into her virtual control plane to manage the video streams. "So we prepare these videos; that's what Eva wants us to do. Assemble the pieces to convey her story the very best way we can."

"The very best way," Sarah agreed, "then we release them to the world, timing it properly."

"At the right moment," Elia stared at her.

"The moment," Sarah agreed. A tear eased out and ran down her left cheek.

Chapter 32

Charter MZ987, Southwest of Admiralty Islands | Saturday 1201 SBT

The plane with Robert Blake winged northeastward, heading to California. *Is my double still praying in the desert? I'd better get briefed in on the Senator's next step.* He punched the man's code into his cell phone.

The Senator greeted him with a chuckle. "How you enjoyin' your Good Friday, Reverend?"

"We're west of the International Date Line, Senator. It's Saturday here."

"Aw, yeah. I fergot. Well, I'm still enjoyin' my Good Friday. It is good. And two hours left of it here in DC."

"That makes it dusk in California, Senator. What's my stand-in doing? He still in the desert?"

"Aw, now don't you worry, son. He's doin' just fine. Made hisself a cross, and planted it in the rocks, and he was prayin' in front of it at sunset. Wanna see?"

He heard a few beeps as the man punched some keys, and a series of still photos of Blake's double marched across the small cellphone screen. They were, Blake had to agree, evocative images.

With his index finger he circled the head and shoulders of the shot that showed facial features most clearly and zoomed in. *That's a frighteningly good doppelganger.*

The Senator said nothing into the long silence while Blake studied the image. *He wants me to acknowledge the depth of his resources. To wonder if maybe the guy can even preach like me.* "Nice clone," Blake finally admitted.

The Senator guffawed. Then his tone went conspiratorial. "Nice warm spring evenin' here in DC, boy. I'm strollin' toward the White House. Big pow-wow in the Situation Room."

"What's going on there?"

"The Prez called in the Joint Chiefs. I worked him up, got him all bothered. Our firstborn Nova in the hands of a mad mullah."

"With the implication that…?"

"Hell, I spun it a half-dozen different ways for the man, son. But the one he bit on was disruptive threat."

"So what are they doing in the Situation Room? Gaming it out?"

"Contingencies, yeah. But what they really want is some intel."

"Satellites?"

"None in position at the moment."

"Aerial recon?"

"Zurvan got lucky. Navy's got nothin' close."

"So what will they do?"

"Dunno, boy, but I wanna guide them to the right move. Tell me about Zurvan."

"You're consulting with me, Senator?"

"You've met the man, I haven't."

Blake shrugged. "He's a psychopath. That much I can confirm. He's got genius-level intelligence. He's built a network that pretty much dropped off the map when he did, then came back together instantly when he resurfaced. That says a lot."

"So it does, son."

"He's formidable."

"So am I, son. But his people are fanatics."

"Yours aren't?"

"Oh, I got some, sure. Christian fundies, skinheads. But my core is people that like power and money, son. Those are actually reliable."

There were plenty of people that put ideologies above power and money, but Blake decided not to argue. "The only other relevant thing about Zurvan is that he's probably going to kill Eva."

"Not try to control her?"

"I think he's too smart for that, even if he is a megalomaniac."

"Uh huh. Me too. But I think I'll play it the other way with those bozos in the Situation Room. Get 'em all worked up about a world Caliphate, an Islamic nutcase with Eva's power… that's their worst-case disruptive threat."

"Worked up to what end, Senator?"

"We're coming to the sharp end of the stick here, son; I can taste it. The more excited everybody gets, the less they think, and the more control I got."

Create chaos, Blake thought, *then take advantage of it. Good technique. I've done that myself.*

"Don't call me, son," the Senator added, "I'm goin' in the White House gate now. I'll call you later."

Blake's cell phone went dead.

O'Donnell Enclave, Waimanu, HI | Friday 1620 HST

Elia took a break from her intensive video download editing and assembly, stood up and stretched her sore back. The console flashed with an incoming call from the National Security Agency. Her heart lurched at the caller identifier.

"Adrienne," Elia answered it, "you're back! Does that mean Abraham is okay?"

"Thank God, yes, Elia. He was the first to get the antiviral. It worked very quickly."

"Great! So what do you need?"

"We've decrypted another phone call. You want the download?"

"Please. But give me a quick synopsis, I'm right in the middle of something."

"The essence is… it confirms Blake is working with Zurvan, in addition to the Senator. So we've got an active three-way conspiracy. It was easier to decrypt, because there's one less algorithm layer on Blake's phone when he's talking to anyone but the Senator."

"When? The call time, I mean."

"Just after 1700 this afternoon. Just before Blake landed at Jayapura with Eva onboard."

"Has Carol briefed the President yet?"

"I don't know. But the Senator's been invited into the Situation Room discussion with the Joint Chiefs. He's on his way, apparently."

"And Carol's there, right?"

"Right. She's been there all along. You know…" Adrienne paused a moment, "that's a really good question. Carol's a finesse player. She owes the President the truth, but all her SIO instincts at this point would be to study the Senator, see how much she can tease out of his body language and other tells. So she can figure out his plan and maybe how to turn it around."

"You think she's behind the invitation?"

"Probably. Good thing the President can keep a poker face. I'd rip the Senator apart and feed him to the pigs on his own hog farm."

"Me, too. But… sorry, I've got to go. Joshua is on the line. Thanks, Adrienne."

SIO Flight 999X, West of Manus Island | *Saturday 1127 JYT*

Joshua O'Donnell paced nervously along the length of the small jet. The growing proximity of the Irian Jaya locus thrummed in him, feeding the rage caused by the streamed videos. His fingers drummed his leg nervously until Elia picked up.

"Talk to me," he ordered, "key points, fast."

Elia didn't react to the brusqueness. "NSA decrypted another telecom, the most recent, just before Blake landed in Jayapura." She summarized quickly.

He considered it. "Doesn't tell us much new." *Except that Blake is going to die as slowly as I can manage.*

"Joshua..."

He heard the catch in her voice, even through the encryption.

"What?"

"Eva has a plan."

"I know."

"She intends to sacrifice herself."

"I know, Elia. I figured it out. And she thinks that's the best way." He heard forlorn loss in his own voice, and let the rage push it aside. "But she's not omniscient, she can't know everything."

"The global consciousness plots are showing more coherence." Elia's tone was stark. "It seems to be endorsing her approach."

"I see that, too. You're compiling the videos, aren't you? That's okay, Elia. I understand. You've got to do what Eva wants. Just..."

She interrupted him, the searing truth breaking her voice. "You won't have time to intervene, Joshua. No one will. Everyone is too far away. What will be, will be. Just as Eva has intended."

"Maybe." He swallowed hard. "But the edges of chaos are strange places. Maybe I can work them." *I did before, with Mom and John in the power plant. And I was only nine years old then.*

Despair leaked from Elia's voice. "The planning, Joshua, the cameras... all pre-positioned..." It became almost a wail.

"I know, I know. Wheels within wheels. She saw it coming, or at least sensed future convergence at Irian Jaya."

"And you still think that you..." Elia's voice broke again.

"Listen, love, you and Sarah... do what you need to do to make Eva's plan come out the way she wants it. But as far as I'm concerned, that's a secondary objective." He listened to his wife's breathing, heard it slow, and then the tight control returned to her voice.

"Yes sir," she acknowledged.

That's almost funny, he thought.

"Should we stream the video to Carol," Elia continued, "let her and the rest of the Sisterhood help put it together?"

"Your call. My advice would be to do as much as possible, just you and Sarah. You two have the best appreciation of the nuances Eva would like to see played out." *And if they're that busy they'll have less time to worry.*

"Or Adrienne? She could help, too."

"She's back in action?"

"Yes. And Abraham is okay."

"Good. Yeah, have her help if you need to; still your call." His tone softened. "Our twins?"

"Both recovering, Joshua."

Through the iron discipline Elia's voice cracked just a little, he thought. *She knows I'll go to any length to save my little sister.*

"Kiss them for me," he said. *I may never see them again.*

East Baliem Valley, Irian Jaya | *Saturday 1132 JYT*

With the locus Gabbatha controlled and her three invariants properly set into the chaos as anchors for her intention, Eva at last could rest her hyperactive mind. The interlude allowed her to sense the outside world. She cast her view eastward toward Hawaii, and saw how Waimanu had faded. But still she sensed the power of the love there, and within it read sadness and its meaning: *Sarah and Elia have correctly read my message. They carry out my wishes. Good!*

That thought let her mind be drawn back to the garden, and the stream metaphor that was Gabbatha took on a pleasant contralto voice very much like her mother's. It asked Eva the hard question: "Their love, does it change your resolve?"

"I wish there were another way," Eva confessed.

"Yet you do not seek it."

"Wishes do not make things so."

"Intentions do. For one such as you."

"I would spare them pain."

Both minds wrapped around that concept, for a long moment parsing the obligations of those who accept love. Then in a manner that seemed to Eva to be the mind-version of scratching an itch, the locus suddenly shifted attention and spoke.

"Your brother approaches… I know him…"

"Yes. You do."

"…from before. His mind is beautiful."

"I know."

"His will is strong."

"That too."

"His love drives him to you."

Eva wailed. "Stop this!"

"What if you're wrong?" The water whispered nothing but her own lingering doubt, she realized.

"I'm not," Eva replied, adamant. "This is the only way. You know it is. You and I agreed on that, seven years ago."

The waters of the stream seemed to slow, their turbulence lessening into a contemplative aspect. "That was then; this is now." Then the ripples in the water ran backwards, receding to a vanishing point on some distant horizon in some foregone era, or at least that was how Eva interpreted the vision. The water whispered again. "Another took this path. Jesus of Nazareth. It proved fruitless."

Eva nodded acceptance. "Many have taken it. But not in modern times. And not a full Nova, especially a Nova with all the tools of our modern age." Eva let her plan play across their minds, verifying that it would work. "It *can* change the world."

Gabbatha tried a different tack. "You mourn, Eva Connard, Young Mother. Nuclear explosions, innocents killed, a virus attack on your new species, a betrayal of your love."

"Betrayal," Eva repeated, feeling blindsided again by the acute loss, "yes, on many levels."

"Has that clouded your vision? Obscured other paths?"

Eva paused. *Honest questions. And from my own mind; Gabbatha is just an inner mirror.*

"And are you not betraying your family, your friends, your Council," the locus continued, "if you refuse their help?"

"They understand. They see the plan. They know what has to happen."

"Yet your brother approaches anyway."

Eva sighed. "I know. But it will be done before he can get here."

"Let it be done, then," the locus said quietly in her mother's voice, withdrawing a distance from Eva's mind. But still, Gabbatha's submittal to Eva's intention carried with it a sense of disquiet, of lingering doubt.

Charter MZ987, Northeast of Admiralty Islands | Saturday 1240 SBT

Blake's cell phone vibrated, and he answered immediately. "How's the Situation Room doing, Senator?"

A little pause ensued before the man replied. "Got a twitchy feelin', son. The NSC was lookin' at me funny."

"Carol Violette?"

"Yeah. The bitch."

Blake shrugged. "You said she's never liked you, Senator. How did the President look at you?"

"Shit, you cain't never tell with that man; too good a poker player."

"Where are you now?"

"Strollin' back to the Capitol."

"What did they want from you?"

"Aw, it was just politics. Get input from my Oversight Committee, so if the shit hits the fan I catch some too." The man paused to chuckle. "But I did get 'em to launch two Global Hawks for recon."

"I thought you said our assets were out of range."

"This one's a one-way street, boy. The Hawks get there and do an hour on station, but they ain't coming back. Outta gas. So, a couple hunnert million down the tubes."

"All they wanted was your blessing; tie the opposition party into the decision."

"Oh, yeah, absolutely. Cover their ass on the expense." The Senator gave a booming laugh. "But you shoulda seen it... how l'il Ms. Violette worked me, boy. She wiggled that idea right outta me. Made all the Joint Chiefs think it was my own brainstorm. Piece a work, that woman."

"The Navy actually launched?"

"Yep. Presidential directive. I got to see them birds lift off the carrier, live video. Love that seapower shit, son. God bless America!"

"Introduces another variable, doesn't it, Senator?"

Another rumble of laughter. "Yep, that it do."

"Aren't you worried the Hawks might see something that might come back and bite us?"

"Yeah... maybe." There was a pause, and Blake heard only the man's wheezy breathing, until, "Tell you a little secret, boy."

"What?"

"Got my own people on that carrier. Those Hawks got missiles with nuke payloads. Tactical."

"Are you serious?"

"Sometimes, son, I'm so goddamn smart I amaze even myself."

You amaze me, Senator. A five-term Senator plays a lot of angles, but you've taken Machiavelli to a whole new level. "Wipe out everyone in the area? Drop an atomic bomb on a friendly country? And with Zurvan gone, don't you lose a figurehead target for your eradication of evil?"

"The warheads are Russian, son. Adapted from their suitcase packages. I stole 'em years ago when the Soviet Union collapsed. Got their own distinct radionuclide signature. Russkies gonna have a lot of explainin' to do, bombin' Indonesia like that. Our hands are clean."

Blake was silent, and the man guffawed again. "I'm slipperier than gooseshit, boy." The laugh cut off abruptly. "Keep that in your holy head."

"I will," Blake conceded. "But you think someone will step into Zurvan's shoes?"

"Long line of assholes waitin' to be the Mahdi, son. One of 'em will belly up to the bar. Or the prayer rug."

"But they're not likely to be as smart. Or as charismatic; they won't have his appeal."

"You got it, son."

"So will you actually do it?"

"Dunno, boy. I gotta ponder this some more. My gut tells me that the NSC is onto somethin'. Maybe I want to erase some evidence, create some confusion, maybe I don't."

You do have a lot of gut, Senator, Blake thought, but said nothing.

"Our buddy Muhammad, though," the Senator continued, "maybe I don't want to erase him. Tough call. I'll be thinkin' on it. You too, boy. Lemme know. I'll be back in my office in ten minutes."

The call clicked off and Blake closed his cellphone.

Chapter 33

East Baliem Valley, Irian Jaya | Saturday 1147 JYT

Eva lay prone on the gurney, her body still paralyzed, her mind drifting, wondering what death would be like. Muhammad Zurvan interrupted her reverie. He stood beside the gurney, the high noon sun foreshortening his shadow over her but making it all the darker against the bright blue sky. Through her one slitted eye, she watched him look upward, studying the sky as he spoke.

"The carrion birds gather, Eva Connard; waiting to pluck your eyes from your head. They may pick your bones clean before your brother can find you, I think."

If they were scavengers, they might, but the primary target for these island hawks is tree snakes. Eva found that misjudgment pretty telling; in spite of being confined on the island for years Zurvan didn't even know the local ecologies. *Did you never watch those hawks soar, never try for a moment to send your mind to their sky and be rid of your captors? Are you so absorbed in yourself you cannot see beauty around you?*

Zurvan gave her unspoken question an answer, of sorts. "I'm going to give you a localized antidote to the paralytic now, Eva. It will free up your face and throat muscles. So we can talk, just a little. And of course so you can scream." He chuckled.

His beauty is darkness, Gabbatha spoke from a distant corner of Eva's mind, *and he sees that well enough.*

I pity him, Eva answered.

You should kill him, several of her Sisters advised.

"The last time you were my captive," Zurvan told her, "you spat in my face. Do you remember that?"

I do. And right after that my uncle the tiger carried me off to freedom. Eva remembered that event in all its exquisite detail: the smell of the fur, the powerful haunches bunching for that improbable leap carrying them out of the trap, the sure-footed way the big cat weaved down the steep volcanic rock to the safety of the forest below.

And all for what, Young Mother? For this? The skeptics among her spirit-Sisters coalesced in objection.

She sighed at their persistence. *You must leave me alone now. I need to get on with this,* she instructed. *I thought I told you to go away before.* But you cannot so easily exorcise racial memories locked into genetic makeup, so Eva had to content herself with tuning out their chatter.

The pinch of a hypodermic came in her jaw; first the right side, then the left; then came the warmth of increased blood flow as the facial muscles began to demand it. *I wonder where he stole that technology?*

"There, it should be just a few moments." Zurvan smiled down on her and patted her cheek.

Destroy him, those Sisters pleaded. *If you join your locus you can do that with merely your voice.*

Gabbatha weighed in, agreeing. *There are words that will stop his heart.*

Eva shook her head, mentally. *There's a difference between destroying a person and stepping aside while they destroy themselves, Gabbatha.* She thought that her physical head actually had moved a tiny bit. *You know my plan.* She attempted a physical nod, and it worked.

Of whose destruction do you speak? This man's or your own? Gabbatha slid the rhetorical question into her consciousness as Eva's eyes fluttered fully open. Zurvan's gauntly handsome face stared at her, his eyes twin pools of darkness.

"Ah, yes, it works; excellent," he said.

"Water, please," Eva's dry throat croaked. *Maybe I'll spit in his face again.*

You will infuriate him, Gabbatha advised.

Yes. My plan, Eva agreed. *He will display his full and complete self to the world. Elia will have maximum choice for her selection of video clips.*

He will repay you, her Sisters warned.

I'm dead anyway, Eva answered.

He will see that you take longer to get there, Gabbatha noted.

The man disappeared from her view to root under the gurney then rose up again with a water bottle in his hand.

"Of course, dear Eva. Water. The source of life. Here." He raised her, propped his arm behind her back, and dribbled a trickle of water into her mouth. "Your swallow reflex should be coming back too."

It was. She swallowed. "More, please."

Zurvan obliged. "Good, good. We can't have a good conversation if you have a dry mouth." He smiled at her.

She returned the smile but started the conversation the way she wanted to. "You have a heritable bad gene, Muhammad Zurvan. Then you were abused as a child. As was your father before you. There also is a cultural history, an epigenetic effect amplifying your condition." She contemplated his dark eyes, with an empathy she truly felt. "My little forest people tried, but there was never any hope for you. You remain a predator. A psychopath."

Zurvan's eyes turned darker, bleak vacuums.

"I forgive you," Eva added.

East Baliem Valley, Irian Jaya | Saturday 1159 JYT

"That's the sort of thing we'll have to edit out, of course," Zurvan said conversationally to the two cameras focused on him. *You little bitch!* He dropped the water bottle, grabbed Eva's hair, and slapped her across the face. *Not that you're wrong, but you certainly are disrespectful.* He slapped her again, bringing a little blood from a cut lip, then nodded directions to his cameramen. They repositioned themselves accordingly. *I'll cut everything she said but my name.* He stood tall, still holding Eva by her hair, sitting her upright. *Yes, that will be a good shot.*

"I am Muhammad Zurvan no longer! I am Muhammad al Mahdi! The Twelfth Imam, the Guided One!" He spoke in Farsi with the rhythmic intonations of the preacher, and then repeated it in Arabic, a less fluid sound. *Saves time,* he decided, *and with the languages so different a closeup would reveal the dubbing. My movie should be as natural as possible.*

He nodded to the cameramen and they zoomed in, one on his face, one on Eva.

"And you! You are a child of the devil! Shaitan has fathered your species, these so-called Novas!" He slapped her again. "Admit it, Eva Connard!"

Her lips quirked upward. "A common technique," she told him.

His hand paused in mid-slap. "What?"

"Projecting your flaws on others then blaming them."

Zurvan felt the rage flare but checked his swing; it became only a mild slap. *If I keep her talking I can get enough words to cut and paste a proper audio together.* He looked directly into the camera, addressing it as he would as a mullah leading an audience of praying students. "The devil is clever, to speak like this, my friends; the Great Deceiver. But you know this, so do not be fooled. I speak the truth, directly from the Prophet. Remember the twenty-second *surah*: Allah is the only guide to the straight way."

Eva licked her bleeding lip and smiled again. She turned her head slightly to look into the camera focused on her. "The exalted *gharaniq*, Al-Lat and Al-Uzza and Manat, fly high above you, Muhammad Zurvan." She turned her gaze directly back on him. "From their heavens they see the truth."

Before he could control the reflex, Zurvan looked upward, scanning the sky. *Native eagle-hawks, that's all.* He lowered his gaze slowly back down to her. *Quoting obscure parts of the Qur'an? This girl is well informed.* He paused, seeking to convey to the camera an impression of measured thought and wisdom before he spoke. *Well-informed, but she just played into my hands!* "Indeed you yourself are a Great Deceiver, Eva Connard," he told her sternly, "when you seek to repeat for me and the faithful Shaitan's deception of the Prophet."

Zurvan held Eva upright and slapped her hard, back and forth for emphasis. "Which the Prophet later rejected, when he saw the lie," he added. *And her last will play nicely into my portrayal of her as the devil-spawn.* "You twist the Prophet's words, seeking to mislead. You are the enemy of the faithful, Eva Connard!"

A trickle of blood ran down her chin from the widened lip cut. "I am no one's enemy," Eva objected. "And I do not deceive. I speak only the truth."

Perfect, Zurvan thought, *just take out a few words and I've got her admission. I won't have to slap it out of her.*

"You are not the Twelfth Imam, Muhammad Zurvan," Eva added. "Nor am I one of the *gharaniq*, the pagan goddesses of that Qur'anic allegory." A tear ran down her left cheek. "That is the truth."

Better than perfect, he thought, *exactly the other words I wanted.*

"Thank you, Eva Connard. I have almost everything I need from you now." He let go of her hair and she flopped back on the gurney. Zurvan told his cameramen to stop filming. He walked over to them and had them replay the footage just shot to see if he'd missed anything.

Charter MZ987, West of Marshall Islands | Saturday 1510 MHT

The Reverend Robert Blake looked at his watch. It had been twenty minutes since the last phone call. *Long enough.* He pulled his cell phone out of its charger. *What the question comes down to is, what's the least risk to me.* He turned the cellphone over and over in his hand as he contemplated that question. *The Senator's got his own risk covered six ways from Sunday, probably. The old bastard's a lot smarter than I gave him credit for.* After a while, Blake gave up his recriminations and punched in the code for the encrypted line. The Senator picked up immediately.

"So, what's your feelin', son? Nuke our new bestest buddy Muhammad? Or let the Hawks get their recon video?"

Blake temporized. "First let them see what the situation is on the ground, and then decide?"

"Cain't do that, boy. Once those cameras go live, they'll pick up on visual that a missile's been fired. Navy'll figger out my triggerman after a while and start to ask the wrong questions. Shit could come back on us."

Blake wondered about that. "They must have a status sensor that tells if a missile's been launched?"

"Yeah. But electronics are somethin' my boys can massage. And they have. A picture ain't."

Blake thought through the implications. *So his reach has a limit.* That was some slight comfort. "I didn't know that, Senator."

"I got my fingers on a lotta buttons, Reverend, but I ain't God."

"Then fire them off."

"Your reasoning, son?"

"Mainly, it's the confusion factor. A nuclear strike would come out of nowhere, raise big new questions, put the Russians on the defensive, generally create chaos."

"And the Sword of Islam just used a stolen Russian nuke on Vegas last week. Yeah, Reverend, I agree. Nice big fat red herring. And while the White House is chasin' the Russkies, we got more room to adapt, control the spin."

There was silence while they both contemplated that decision, broken only by the faint ticks of the cellphones' nanotech encrypter.

"How about Zurvan, boy? We get him outta there or let them missiles run right up his ass?"

More downside risk to me if he's alive, Blake thought. "Leave him there. One, we'll get a less effective substitute. Two, it'll take time for the Islamic radicals to regroup. Three, we can use the warhead to tie him to the Sword of Islam, which he denied before. And he won't be around to argue that."

"Uh huh. Well, thank you kindly, Reverend; appreciate your opinion."

"So what will you do?"

"I just purely don't know, son." The man sounded aggrieved. "I gotta make a decision, but this is a tough one."

"When? The decision, I mean."

"Oh… four hours. Little more, mebbe." A long silence followed.

Blake finally broke it, changing the subject. "Your pilot says this fine little jet is going to have to set down on Majuro to take on fuel, so that puts our ETA in California in the early morning tomorrow… Saturday there. How is the switch with my double going to work?"

"I'll have Marta pick you up at the airstrip and drive you out into the desert, Pastor Bob. In one of your UMC off-roaders. You remember Marta?"

Blake felt a shiver but suppressed it. "The false Marta. Very… efficient."

The Senator grunted. "Scared the shit outta ya, didn't she, son? Fuckin' psycho. She'll look a little different but it'll still be her." He didn't wait for Blake to respond. "On the way out, you lay down in the back seat. Out in the desert, your double gets in the front. On the way back you do the switcherooie inside the vehicle. You get out at your UMC office, Marta drives off with him." The man chuckled. "Just do what Marta tells you, son."

Blake pondered that. Two things stood out: *the Senator has penetrated my UMC operations, and Marta's a high-level agent for his organization.*

A third thing occurred to him. "Why so careful? Somebody watching my double in the desert? At three AM?"

"Quick, ain't you, son? Yeah, buncha reporters wonderin' what you're prayin' on all this time, while the shit's in the fan with the Novas. Wonderin' if you got a hair shirt on, or maybe you're whippin' your back out there. They want interviews."

"They haven't gotten through to my double?"

"That patch is private land, and we got a private security force sayin' they should respect your solitude, son. Mean mothers. With big dogs, too. But some enterprisin' reporter just flew a little hexakopter with a spycam overhead to have a look."

"Reporters always want interviews, Senator. And I've been spycammed before. You have any particular points you want me to cover when I do have to talk?" Blake tried to keep the sarcasm out of his voice, but the Senator picked it up anyway.

"Aww, Pastor Bob, you are a bullshitter of the purest ray supreme. I wouldn't ever presume to tell you what to say." The man paused a moment to let Blake digest the returned sarcasm. "Since you asked, though, son, I suggest you keep your lip zipped until it's clear how this thing in Indonesia is gonna play out. I can't control everythin', and we gotta come down on the side of the angels here, no matter what."

"Right, Senator. It's a long flight. I'll work up a few variations of my Easter Sunday sermon, cover the contingencies. 'After agonized soul-searching...' that sort of thing."

"Good, son, that's good; like I said, purest ray supreme." The man's voice sounded distant but then came back strong and harsh. "And Pastor Bob... just because I ain't God, and I cain't control everythin', don't think I ain't got your number. Never think that."

The Senator switched off and Blake sat back relieved. *If he was going to have Marta dump me in the desert, he wouldn't have wasted time on a warning.*

East Baliem Valley, Irian Jaya | Saturday 1217 JYT

Eva listened with half an ear to Zurvan's review of the video clips. With the mind-half of her ear she conversed with her locus.

"Interesting," she told Gabbatha, "he's doing exactly what I'm doing: filming the event to serve a plan. There's a certain karmic balance here." A giggle in her mind threatened to erupt into a physical giggle from her mouth, now that her vocal chords were working. She suppressed it; the cameras would catch its hysteria.

"Only he doesn't know what I'm doing." In the back of her mind she watched the probability threads of her tapestry weave tighter. They were forming a noose closing off the chaos and distortion that would have resulted from Zurvan's success.

"Very satisfying," Gabbatha admitted, "except that the wrong person survives."

"Not for very long, I think. Both he and Robert will come to their own ends soon." Eva watched the threads of the two men play through the tapestry, her mind-metaphor for the probability paths to their outcomes. The locus watched with her. She felt sadness; the locus felt satisfaction. There was some level of integration going on, Eva realized, just by virtue of their minds being entrained in conversation. *I'll have to watch that.*

The locus denied responsibility. "You have instructed me, Young Mother. I will do as you intend."

"But certain things are inevitable, is that it?"

"You and I and your Sisters, your maternal ancestors, there is a pressure toward Becoming. It feels proper, a place for it in the natural scheme of things. A birthing."

"Natural." Eva admitted. She felt it too. "But you're not adding to it?"

"I honor your intention."

There was truth in that, Eva could taste it.

"I haven't done this before," Gabbatha added. "No mind has fit my... resonance."

"Here, years ago?"

"Your mind was too unformed then, insufficiently evolved."

"Joshua?"

"Your brother... yes, close. As was Jesus before him. But although they had some of the female aspect in their minds, their bodies were male. Their resonance was not sufficiently matched to me."

"The whole is greater than the sum of its parts?"

"Exactly."

"Waimanu, then?"

"We are different aspects of the same thing."

Eva had trouble getting her mind around what seemed like inherent contradictions. *Or maybe it's just my limited perspective.* She continued her questioning. "Waimanu gave me power?"

"Waimanu nurtured you. As your father did. And later your brother."

"Your existence is not separate from Waimanu?"

"We are the unity of all living things."

"Including me?"

"Together we are a Becoming."

That brought up the existential questions they'd always asked themselves about the loci. "Do you have free will? Intelligence? Can you act independently?"

"We need a vehicle for expression in this reality."

"You are incomplete?"

The locus picked the quote from the depths of her mind. "And the eye cannot say to the hand I need not thy help; nor the head to the feet, I have no need of you."

"Ah, I see." Joshua's guess about the nature of the loci had been closest to the truth, Eva realized: *a locus is a forcing function, negative entropy, order from chaos. But it needs a canvas on which to paint.*

The thought of Joshua induced a picture — she watching her brother watch her. Abruptly, Eva realized it was accurate. Joshua was in the SIO fast executive jet, looking at a computer screen, monitoring the multiple channels from the cameras surrounding her on Irian Jaya.

"He comes for you," Gabbatha said.

Eva agreed. In her mind-tapestry, turquoise threads of probability ran backward over the blue Pacific to Joshua, and from him stretched further back to Waimanu in Hawaii. She felt the love resonating down those threads, along with the terror.

SIO Flight 999X, East of Jayapura | Saturday 1229 JYT

In the small jet streaking in toward Jayapura at maximum speed, Joshua O'Donnell sat frozen in front of the computer screen. The video images brought a terror he hadn't known in a long time. *I can't bear to watch this,* he thought. The terror flicked over into rage then hopelessness then back again, a vicious cycle. Elia, on the other end of the call, sobbed the same feeling, unspoken. The small inset picture on the bottom of his screen showed her agonized face.

"You need to stay with it, Elia," Joshua managed to say from a dry throat, "it's what she wants, what she intends."

"It's going to get worse, Joshua."

"I know." *I can't bear to hear that, either.* "Call Sarah away from the twins. Let her help. Do your Sisterhood mantras."

"She's coming down the hall now. The mantras... yes. But to watch someone you love...," she choked and couldn't say it.

Die, finished Joshua, and let the rage wash through him. *Die at the hands of a psychopath so that the world can become a better place.* Oh, Eva. "Just do what you can, Elia." *And I'll do the same.*

On that thought came a hint of a connection, a little tendril, fragile and tenuous. *Eva?*

The thoughts that floated back to him were soft, loving, no hint of the agony and terror she must be feeling. *Let it go, Joshua. My plan will work. Events will run their course.*

I can't. I won't. His mind ran the logic lattice and displayed the result. *Look! The video changes all the probabilities.*

Not enough. His sister's reply carried ineffable sorrow.

You don't have to die, Eva. Please don't!

But the connection faded into the whispering sound of the surf breaking in Waimanu Bay, the rhythm of a lone gull's wings riding the updrafts in front of the cliffs, the whalesong offshore.

On the video screen in front of him a ghost of a smile played across Eva's face.

Chapter 34

East Baliem Valley, Irian Jaya | Saturday 1233 JYT

Zurvan scowled at Eva, infuriated by the slight smile that came and went on her face for no apparent reason. He slammed the heel of his hand against the wood of the cross to which she was now duct-taped face-first. "You are amused, Eva Connard?" he hissed.

Indigo eyes opened and stared back at him. Something ancient and dark flickered in their bottomless depths. Concurrently Zurvan felt the rock vibrate under his feet. In spite of the tape securing the full length of Eva's arms and legs to the cross, he took a quick step back, stumbling on the uneven surface.

"Did you feel that?" he asked his cameramen.

Both men nodded in agreement this time. "The earth moves, Mahdi. Perhaps we should be gone. Earthquakes are common here."

"We're on a solid rock shelf."

"But it has cracks, Mahdi, crevices. One of them might open up."

"Suddenly you are geologists?" He stared stonefaced at the two until they looked down.

Eva whispered something. Zurvan slammed the wood in front of her face with the heel of his hand. "What?" he demanded. "What did you say, Eva Connard?"

Her nose bounced off the wood and began to bleed. "They have names," she muttered. Her tongue licked at the little dribble of blood.

"Who has names? My faithful here? Of course they have names."

"No. Your furies. They have names. The dark side of the *gharaniq*. They love hurt and pain and misery."

Zurvan laughed to cover the fear that came with sudden remembrance: *this is a place of strange power.* "Superstition, child. But tell me their names."

The slight smile that so irritated him flashed across her face and was gone. "They will introduce themselves, I think."

The rock vibrated again underneath his feet. The two men at his side exchanged nervous glances, caught out of the corner of his eye. *I may have to kill those fools when the filming is done.*

He examined the gray duct tape with which they had secured her. *Much more convenient than the rope of the Romans.* He walked a circle around Eva. The base of the crude cross was wedged in a crack in the volcanic lava shelf, stone wedges holding it upright. Zurvan pushed at it but the stones didn't shift, nor did the tree bend very much.

"Are you ready to receive punishment for your heresy, Eva Connard?" He made his tone conversational, not betraying the eagerness in it, but he spoke to her back to avoid those eyes. "In case you're interested, you're strapped to an ironwood tree. As you can see, its two branches diverge upward at an slight angle rather than perpendicular to the trunk, but I believe your Christian friends still may appreciate the analogy. Don't you think so, Eva? Hmm?"

SIO Flight 999X, East of Jayapura | Saturday 1229 JYT

Joshua O'Donnell paced inside the small jet like a caged animal. He listened with half an ear to the downloading audio and glanced at the video as frequently as he could make himself. Supercharged logic lattices ran scenarios for rescue, but each came up against the same insurmountable blockage: *Eva has intended otherwise.* Only an iron will kept his mind from imploding with futility. *Equifinality. The solutions converge. You see the train wreck coming but you're helpless.* From Eva's last contact he had gleaned the sense of the tapestry her plan was weaving, its probabilistic outcome getting closer and closer to certainty. *A pretty picture, kiddo. But the problem is you're no longer in it.*

"I concede the brilliance of your plan, Eva," he told the computer screen as he paced past it, "as well as your instinct or intuition or prescience or whatever it was that had us set up those camera arrays four years ago." *But oh, Sis, you could have told me. We could have worked something out!*

Finding no feasible rescue options, Joshua's logic shifted to a deconstruction of Eva's plan, hoping to find a way to reverse-engineer it and develop an opening in her wall of protection. The blink of an icon in the lower left of the computer screen stopped his pacing. He tapped it and Elia's tear-streaked face showed up in the inset video.

"Plus jamais," he told her.

"Never again?" she asked.

"The motto you see in some of the Holocaust memorials in Europe. Elia, it took years for those atrocities to fully come to light, and years more for them to settle into the world's consciousness enough so that the reminder memorials could be built."

Her face looked out at him, not comprehending.

"But today we have the internet," Joshua continued, "an immediate distributor and an irrepressible amplifier. When we feed Eva's videos into it, the shift in human perspective about the Novas will be both sudden and permanent. A blowout in the global consciousness. That's the beauty of Eva's plan."

"Oh. Yes, of course." She looked at him with her head slightly cocked. *They realized that before I did.* "I'm sorry, Elia. What did you want?"

"I just had an idea. Maybe the locus will help you, Joshua. Like it did before."

"Good idea. Why do you think that's a possibility?"

"Because Eva hasn't had a lot of time. She set up her plan, but she wasn't always fixated on it."

"A contingency thing?"

"She was always determined to find an alternative to the Sisterhood's scripted Second Coming myth; that had too much misery, too much bloodshed."

"Okay. So she just set it up to give herself options? You're saying this wasn't hardwired from the beginning?"

"We think — Sarah and I — that Eva didn't really make up her mind until Pastor Bob betrayed her."

"Why then?"

"The last straw. Nuclear attacks, the Nova-specific virus... so much of an emotional load. The world on her shoulders."

"Okay. I think Eva's pretty tough, but you and Sarah have better instincts than I do." He ran a logic lattice to confirm their hypothesis. It did, within a reasonable error band. "The situation is complex, and Eva hasn't had time to think everything through, and she may not be thinking clearly in any case if she's wounded emotionally. That's it?"

"In a nutshell. A Nova, yes; but she's only fifteen, Joshua."

"So the wall of intention she set up to keep us from interfering... it may have a gap?"

"Likely several."

"Tell me just one."

"We couldn't come up with anything specific, but Sarah agrees that the best opportunity lies with the locus."

"Because it's as new to Eva as the rest of her Nova-becoming process?"

"Exactly." Elia stared at him from red-rimmed eyes. "You remember the Sisterhood metaphor, the mind key I gave you on that island?"

He almost smiled. "When we first made love, the key to access the locus? Of course I remember."

"Good. When you arrive, use it again."

"The locus is surely keyed to Eva by now," he objected.

"Joshua, we know so little about this; Eva being the first Nova. And you have shared part of yourself with this locus before."

"My lower brain, the animal survival reflexes."

Elia shrugged. "Still, there was contact. We believe there will be recognition."

He ran another logic lattice and it admitted the possibility. "But Eva almost certainly has intended the locus not to allow interference with her plan."

Elia shrugged again. "Still, it's a possible point of entry, my love."

She stared at him, and he imagined he saw a tiny ray of hope in her dark eyes.

"Okay," he said.

East Baliem Valley, Irian Jaya | Saturday 1302 JYT

"No need to answer that question," Zurvan said as he walked around in front of her. I'm sure that you appreciate the crucifixion analogy at least as well as your betrayer, the Reverend Blake."

Eva closed her eyes, ignoring his darkness, and let her mind chase other sensations. Her cheek rested against the trunk of the tree where the branches diverged. *Ironwood, he said.* She confirmed it with a sniff. *And a young one, the bark is still smooth.* She felt the tree's sap ebbing downward into the rock. *I'm sorry, she told it, that your life was cut short. I'm sure you would have been magnificent. A roost for the eagle-hawks, shade for the forest floor creatures. But it's nice to have your company.*

Vibrations in the rock flowed up through the tree to acknowledge that. Zurvan muttered an imprecation in a dialect she didn't understand, and moved away. *He feels the energy. It makes him fearful.* That actually was good, Eva decided; anxiety would quicken his hand. *Do it and be gone,* she formed the minor intention, *before my brother can arrive and interfere.*

A ripping sound came from the direction of the gurney. Eva turned her head as far as she could to the left, and out of the corner of her eye she saw Zurvan unwrap the whip. *More than just a religious flagellant device; it's got weighted strands, probably lead shot,* the analytical part of her brain deduced, *a Roman scourge.* The animal part cringed into the fight-or-flee reflex, flooding her body with adrenaline and the other crisis neurochemicals, fear rushing toward panic. She forced down the fear, as she had practiced in Joshua's combat games, by reaching out to feel the forest with her whole mind.

Calm edged out the fear, a little. Her spirit-Sisters, circling at some middle distance in her mind, drew closer in support. The stream scene formed in Eva's mind, and Gabbatha spoke out of the rippling water in her mother's voice. "I would help you, Eva."

"You said you would honor my intention," Eva dismissed the offer. "And using my mother's voice is cheating."

"I *am* your mother, and your father, and your brother and Waimanu. And the streams and rivers and oceans and mountains and forest and all living things."

"No, you're a forcing function for the existence of all those physical things, as Joshua guessed."

Gabbatha shrugged. "With you, with the Novas, the cause is now indistinguishable from the effect."

A resonance ran from the rock up through the ironwood cross, a strong one, seeming to confirm the rightness of that statement. A repeat of the imprecation came from Zurvan behind her. With no warning but a grunt, the whip whistled through the air and slapped across her back. Eva screamed, the pain instant and uncontrolled.

"One," Zurvan counted.

Eva parsed her body's reaction. *What's the best course? Stoicism? What if I run out of endorphins? My body's already depleted of their precursors. Do I dare tap Gabbatha?*

"Move around in front of her," Zurvan ordered one of the cameramen. "Focus on her face."

Eva heard the man scrabble across the rock, dragging his tripod, but Zurvan didn't wait. The whip slapped into her back again. She screamed again, unprepared for it.

"Two," Zurvan counted.

Her spirit-Sisters spiraled in close. Mary of Magdala spoke. "His mother and I watched as Jesus was crowned with thorns and beaten. I cannot bear this again."

"Three," Zurvan said as the whip slapped again.

Eva's scream was more muted. "You must," she told Mary and the other Sisters, "I cannot do it without you. And I dare not invoke Gabbatha."

"What? What did you say, Eva Connard?" Zurvan moved in close and pulled her head back to repeat the question loudly in her left ear.

Did I speak aloud? Eva realized she had. "Water, please," she asked Zurvan.

"You beg for water? Not to stop your punishment? Hah!" Disappointment colored his tone, and the musky predatory odors his skin exuded told her there would be no relief.

Get on with it, then, Eva formed the intention. She heard him step back. She chanted her mind into the emptiness of the null, her spirit-Sisters and

Gabbatha trailing her there. *If you're at the cutting edge, you're going to bleed.*
   "Four," Zurvan announced.

East Baliem Valley, Irian Jaya | Saturday 1313JYT

"Ninety-one," Muhammad Zurvan announced with satisfaction. *Those old Romans knew a thing or two about torture,* he thought as he shook bits of Eva's flayed flesh off the whip. But he took care to keep the satisfaction off his face and out of his voice. *A stern but properly disinterested piety, for my cameras.* A steady stream of Eva's blood ran down the base of the cross into the rock crevice. He imagined he could feel the rock hum as her life drained into it.

He had interspersed the lashes with little sermons, exhortations carefully constructed and delivered to inflame Islamic radicals and shift moderates in the proper direction. *Pure genius, to give a message in counterpoint with the lash!*

"We are come now, my friends," he continued, looking straight into the camera, "to the end times. Although centuries of goodness and prosperity will follow, there will be difficult days ahead. But your Mahdi will guide you. I will sweep away the infidel."

"Ninety-two," he said, snapping the scourge into Eva's back. Her head lolled to the side, unresponsive, but she was still breathing. *Tough little bitch.*

"The hour is upon us. Adultery is rampant. Men become women and women become men. My Mahdi will turn the sinful minds of the infidels back on themselves, and they will exterminate each other. That is foretold."

"Ninety-three," he announced at the sound of the sodden impact. *I wonder if I should ease back a bit, perhaps subtly show some kindness through lessening the power of my strokes.*

"The sun will be eclipsed, and time will quicken."

But alas, dear Eva I cannot. I'm about to ejaculate, you see. The throbbing in his crotch had become almost a torment. "Ninety-four," he rasped, fighting to keep the lust from his voice.

"My virus already has neutralized the threat of these so-called Nova sapiens creatures. They are the very false prophets foretold for these end times."

"Ninety-five," he added, swinging the whip, trembling with the tension of holding back his orgasm.

"Those few Novas who recover will no longer be strange mutations." *Not true, of course, but no one knows that at this point.* "Those Novas who escaped infection will be hunted down and brought under proper control or killed."

He paused, switching his gaze from the camera to Eva, giving the moment its due. The cameraman panned slowly over to her as instructed.

"Your punishment is nearly finished, Eva Connard. Your fate is in the hands of Allah."

His ninety-sixth through one-hundredth stroke were delivered with a savagery he couldn't control as he exploded into his underwear.

When it was done, he dropped to his knees facing east and bowed his head to the rock. But he didn't pray. He just let the sexual release flow through his body while his mind replayed the performance. It was almost perfect, he decided; just a few minor issues to watch out for in the editing process.

What did she mean by 'Gabbatha, do not forsake me', I wonder? He logged that for future research.

Another occurred to him: *placed within a circle, my modified cross could be a fertility symbol of some kind.* Future generations of his biographers would doubtless speculate on that, not realizing that his search had been solely one of expedience: something convenient yet evocative to bind Eva to for her lashing. *I should find a subtle way to suggest that symbology.* He trembled with stifled laughter at the irony, content with knowing the cameras would show his trembling as a person gripped by religious ecstasy.

East Baliem Valley, Irian Jaya | Saturday 1316 JYT

Eva Connard's body had long since faded into shock from pain and loss of blood, but from the uncaring null-state her mind remained aware, vaguely, of the conditions of her physical existence. She remembered an old Woody Allen line: *I don't mind dying, I just don't want to be there when it happens.*

So instead of going back to the place where her death was happening, she communed with her spirit-Sisters and with Gabbatha, seeking solace and, perhaps, enlightenment.

"I *am* your mother, and your father, and your brother and your uncle and Waimanu," Gabbatha answered her. "And the streams and rivers and oceans and mountains and forest and all living things. I am the pool and the waterfall your dying eyes see; the birds that your ears hear on the wind's dark song." Her Sisters spiraled in close and tight around Eva's mind, nodding and chanting in a complex melodic counterpoint to Gabbatha's rhythms. "I am the blood you taste in your mouth and feel dripping from your body to the rock below; and that rock also is me."

"We will go on," Eva acknowledged, understanding at last, "together."

"As always we have, Young Mother," her Sisters replied.

"There will be others, to take my place."

"Yes. But you are the first, the One. You first set foot on the path."

"Is that enough?"

"You wove your tapestry," her Sisters told her, "and it is beautiful."

"Your brother approaches," Gabbatha answered obliquely.

So he does. I feel him in the sky. Closing. "I must die now," Eva told them. She was forming the intention when Zurvan snatched her back to physical reality with a bucket of cold water on her face. Instead of cooling her, the drips down her flayed back burned like molten metal.

He yanked her head back by the hair and whispered in her ear; too loudly, she thought.

"You're dying, Eva Connard, and no one can save you, except Allah. Now pray to Allah for forgiveness!" He twisted her head to the right, so that she looked directly into a camera lens. "Pray!" he commanded.

Eva stared at the camera for a moment, smiling ever so slightly. She formed an intention that loosened Zurvan's grip on her hair and turned her face toward him. She let him see the power behind her eyes.

His hand lost its grip.

Eva quoted the Qur'an to him: "Those who don't take vengeance are twice blessed."

His hand dropped away entirely.

"I forgive you," she added.

Chapter 35

The small jet arrowed toward the airstrip in the coastal town of Jayapura. Inside, Joshua O'Donnell sat stricken in front of the computer screen, paralyzed by a ravening mix of rage and fear and loss and love. *I'm coming, kiddo. Hang on.* He forced discipline on his emotions and ran lightning-swift logic lattices. *No time, no time,* they said, one after another, until…

"Abort the approach!" He screamed it into the cockpit.

"Sir?" The pilot craned her head around the seat.

"A straight line to Eva! Now!"

"Aye, sir." There were no questions, just an immediate response. The engines began to wind up, and the co-pilot started chattering to the Jayapura air traffic controller.

"The coordinates are…" Joshua began.

"We have them, sir." The pilot's voice was grim.

Of course. The cockpit has a nav laptop. They've been watching too. "Whatever altitude gets us there fastest, Captain."

The co-pilot began talking to the controller, ad-libbing landing gear problems, clearing the airspace. The engines cranked up another notch. The aircraft nose tilted up and the rushing foothills dropped away beneath.

"Game plan, sir?" The pilot asked.

Joshua pulled himself forward to the cockpit bulkhead. *Good question. Eva couldn't possibly have had time to instruct these women specifically not to intervene. But they're warrior-class Sisters, surely they see her intent. So how to say it?*

As he reached the cockpit the two women exchanged a glance. The co-pilot made it easy on him. "Standing orders, sir. If the One is dead or disabled, interim command of operations reverts to you."

Eva's neither, yet. And they know that, but they're trusting me. "I owe you," he said.

"We'll hope for the best," the pilot replied. "The game plan, sir?"

"HALO chute stowed in the back?"

The co-pilot disregarded the angry chatter coming from the radio and answered him. "Yes, sir. Three of them. Machine pistols and med kits too." She looked at him speculatively. "Need company?"

Another good question. Logic lattices ran. "Maybe as a backup. On a second pass? How's the fuel?"

She looked at the display, then sat back with her eyes closed a moment. "Marginal."

"We'll play it by ear," he decided. "What's the ridgeline elevation?"

"About ten thousand feet, if we stay on our direct line." She played with the nav display. "Hold that altitude over the valley for your jump?"

"How many minutes until we get there?"

She closed her eyes again. "Seventeen, maybe nineteen. We'll have to shed some airspeed otherwise the hydraulics won't be strong enough to keep the rear hatch open." She sounded almost apologetic. "We've never used this particular aircraft on an insertion."

"A lower altitude help?"

"Don't know." The co-pilot closed her eyes again briefly. "Maybe. The aerodynamics and airspeed seem like a tradeoff."

"I'll get ready. Let me know when we've cleared the ridge."

Joshua ran to the rear of the aircraft, pulled out the parachute, strapped the machine pistol on his thigh and the med kit on his belly. He grabbed a helmet with a communicator, carried it back to the computer and keyed the relay. Now the computer would give him communication capability on the ground, with a camera relaying what he saw.

"Elia," he said to the worried image on the screen inset, "did you catch all that? My talk with the pilot?"

"Yes. And I understand."

He watched the planes of his young wife's face harden into resolve. *Good, go into your warrior mindset.*

She did, continuing: "Just four on the ground, Joshua. Zurvan, two cameramen, the helicopter pilot. Nobody else except for Eva."

Joshua looked at the main screen. His sister hung limply on the crudely fashioned cross. Zurvan stood in front of her, dismay still apparent on his face at her words.

Eva may forgive you, but I won't. The rage started to build in him, and Joshua felt the familiar but not-quite-synchronous presence of the Irian Jaya locus matching his rage as it entered his mind.

"Joshua, the global consciousness statistic… the chi-square is ramping up."

He looked at the other inset on the screen, the graph they used as a marker of anticipated probabilities hardening into reality. "I see it," he said.

East Baliem Valley, Irian Jaya | *Saturday 1321 JYT*

The stream that was her metaphor for the locus she called Gabbatha curled around Eva, cool and soothing. She rode with it, washing down toward the deeper blue water that was Waimanu. *Is this my lifeblood running out?* Almost absently her rational mind recognized the flow as a flood of endorphins easing her body into physical death. That moment of rationality brought with it a flash of connectedness: *Joshua!*

"No, Josh," she muttered with shallow breaths, "don't come. You're too late. Too weak."

Her rational mind fired thoughts across misfiring synapses and interpolative senses kicked in, computing an answer. *Minutes away. No, Josh, no!*

Zurvan grabbed her hair and pulled her head up. Eva opened her eyes and his blurry features swam into a snarl but then tunneled down. *I just lost my peripheral vision.*

"What? Your brother comes for you?" Zurvan stared at her for a long moment. He laughed and let her head drop, but not before she'd read the fear in his eyes and smelled it jumping from his skin. She closed her eyes and let her mind enjoy an idle thought: *olfactory is the most primitive of the senses, of course it would be the last to go.*

As if to counter that, her ears picked up the sound of a voice running toward them from the helicopter. "Mahdi! The O'Donnell aircraft aborted landing at Jayapura. It's on a bearing toward here."

"How long?" Zurvan's loud voice in her left ear carried the same fear.

"A jet plane? Ten or fifteen minutes."

"He's too late, Eva Connard," Zurvan hissed, "you're bleeding out." He yelled at the pilot. "Start the engines!" He yelled at his cameraman. "Put the cameras in the helicopter! And get your weapons!"

It's all getting so complicated, Eva thought dimly, as she contemplated the probabilistic threads of her tapestry weaving around the unexpected disarray of her brother's intrusion. *And I'm so tired of it.*

"Mahdi?" Uncertainty tinged one of the cameramen's voices.

"I don't know what this fool is going to do. If he senses his sister's death, he may try to crash the plane to kill us all."

Eva toyed with that concept but rejected it. *No, he wouldn't do that. The pilots would if he ordered, but they're innocents. He wouldn't waste them to eliminate you, Muhammad Zurvan.*

"Your videos must be preserved," Zurvan yelled after the scurrying cameramen, "so I will be airborne, away from the area. You will protect yourselves behind the rocks. Fire on the aircraft if it comes in low."

Wearied beyond belief, and in a dying body, Eva's mind tried to retreat into comfort of the stream called Gabbatha. Neural connections were made and unmade in a fruitless attempt, until she realized duty was interfering, calling her back. *An SIO executive jet. A rear hatch. So you're going to jump. But then what, Josh? You'll hang in the sky too long, be an easy target.*

With her ability to concentrate waning, Eva reinforced the intention of her plan, putting all of her residual life force behind it. She clawed at the fabric of this evolving tapestry of a new possible reality, trying to gather together and weave into a diversion the threads of new probabilities occasioned by her brother's action. *I've done all that I can,* she realized. Her plan would hold or it wouldn't, but she was fading too fast to do any more.

Weariness crested and rolled over her mind.

Eva formed a last intention before she gave herself to the comfort of the stream. *Joshua's doing something stupid, Gabbatha. When he gets here, I would that you keep him safe.*

The stream enveloped her, its burbling ripples forming a cryptic answer.

"The future is not your fate, Young Mother. It's your choice."

SIO Flight 999X, Southwest of Jayapura | Saturday 1321 JYT

The pressure in his mind to turn back sharpened, and Joshua O'Donnell braced himself against it. *My love is stronger than your intention, Eva. I'm your protector. I need to help you.*

The perception that came back in response to his insistence was that of a glass bubble: smooth, slick, impenetrable, clearly Eva's metaphor for 'don't interfere'. *Yeah, I read your intention, Sis. Loud and clear. But sorry. I'm coming anyway.*

There was a certain returned sense of slight concession to the inevitability he just conveyed. So he followed it up immediately. *Your plan is a great one, Eva. I think it will do exactly what you intend. The one problem with it is that you die. I don't want that.*

Neither do I was the sense he got in return. But it wasn't from Eva locked inside her glass bubble, it came from a separate entity, more diffuse, more like... an unfolding. *Like the tapestry I saw in my mind when I was nine. I touched one of its probability threads, just briefly, to save Mom. Here, I can't touch Eva's threads; her hands-off intention is holding. But is the locus constrained like that? How clever was Eva in setting her intention? Uncle Ham cheated a little, shading probabilities. Why can't I?*

That sense of connection, of shared objectives, ramped up sharply. He realized it had been increasing for a while. The locus was clearly aware; either through Eva or by its own perception it felt him coming. *But why would something ageless and immaterial and indestructible care about the demise of a physical body?*

Joshua remembered what his Uncle Ham had said: *death is overrated.* And another piece of perennial wisdom: *one thing has to die for something else to be born.* So the locus shouldn't care. But somehow it did. A logic lattice ran. *Love is an invariant*, he concluded, *an anchor point for the forcing function that creates order from chaos, life from nothingness.* On that hopeful note, he invoked the mind-key Elia had given him years ago, opening himself to communion with the locus.

The sensation in his mind — the pressure to turn back — faded. It was slowly replaced, not with what he would call a welcome, but at least a medium hello. The same resonance he'd felt in that past event was there; but this time again it seemed slightly out of synchronization; no phase-lock with his rational mind. *We've met*, he acknowledged with grim satisfaction as he accepted the locus into his mind.

The metaphorical glass sphere encasing his sister crumbled into fragments. He reached into the center where Eva had been, but she was no longer there. Frantically, his fingers flew over the computer touchpad, looking at her from different camera angles. In all of them she hung limp and unmoving, blood draining, pooling on the rock below. *Eva! Don't die! I'm coming.*

O'Donnell Enclave, Waimanu, HI | Friday 1830 HST

Elia watched the screen inset video, her husband putting on the jump helmet, snapping down the wind visor, keying the nano videocam. *Joshua is going to jump.* She tried to wrap her mind around that. *But if Eva's dead there's no point.* She swallowed her objection. "Use channel 25," she told him.

The multiplexed network icon flickered new settings across the bottom menu bar on the big computer screen in the Council Chamber. Joshua's voice came slightly muffled through the helmet microphone. "Helmet's live," he said. "You hear me?"

"Roger that; four-by" the pilot replied.

A click, and Joshua's voice came louder and more clearly from the speaker. "Digital better?"

"Fine," Elia said.

"Five-by-five," the pilot acknowledged.

A second inset picture popped up in the lower right corner of the screen. It showed the inside of the aircraft as Joshua did a slow three-sixty. "Videocam good?"

"It's good," the copilot said, then added "We just crossed the ridgeline, sir."

"Okay. Follow the terrain down into the valley."

"Joshua…," Elia began.

He stopped her. "You getting the helmet video, Elia?"

"It's fine." *What's he going to do?*

He snapped up the visor. The helmet audio and video cut off. He stared right at her from the small inset screen. "I'm going offline for a few minutes to key the helmet to our ground network transducers instead of this airplane's." The hint of a smile fluttered around his mouth. "It seems you and Sarah were right about the locus. It remembers me." He turned and walked out of the webcam's view, but his voice carried back. "I love you."

Sarah squeezed her shoulder as they both looked at the empty inset. "He will do what he must, Elia." The older woman's tone of practicality brought Elia back from the edge of despair. "And look at the global consciousness display."

We've never seen the statistic climb like that, even with the Vegas nuclear attack, Elia realized. "That's hopeful, you think?"

"It may be Eva's Becoming."

"Simultaneous with her death?"

"We simply don't know, Elia. She's the first; there is no baseline."

They watched the graph continue to ramp up. Sarah played with the console, bringing Eva's torn body into tight focus. "Her blood loss is slowing, it appears."

"Is she still breathing?"

Sarah tried to zoom in more, but the nanocam was already at maximum resolution. She squinted at the screen. "Maybe."

"Josh will jump anyway, I think. He never stops hoping."

"Nor should we," Sarah replied, another overlay of practicality in her voice. "We'll have to be his spotters. Zurvan is leaving, but his two cronies are on the ground, and they've got an arms cache, it looks like."

Elia nodded agreement then voiced her question. "Equifinality? Are there other ways we could help?"

Sarah nodded. "Definitely there are more possibilities now. These videos open all sorts of nuances to Eva's plan." The older woman paused. She looked at Elia, looked at the empty screen inset, and pulled them both back from the console. "I have an idea," she whispered.

"What?"

Sarah shifted around slightly, interposing herself between Elia and the console's webcam, speaking quietly. "Just listen. The twins... have almost recovered."

"Thank God, yes."

"I believe they can act, together, here with Waimanu, as a surrogate for Eva. I believe they can transpose me to Irian Jaya. I can help Joshua keep Eva alive until help arrives."

Elia looked at her in astonishment. "You're her physician. And the locus would help, possibly. But transposition? Eva could only do that with herself. And Joshua, because of their linked genetics. What makes you..." Elia looked at the woman, whose empathy was written large on her face. *She knows.*

"Both boys' fathers are in Irian Jaya, Elia, in the same location." Sarah said. "That's enough of a link, I think."

She speaks of it so matter-of-factly, my secret. Elia felt herself stand back from her own tormenting emotions to match Sarah's pragmatism. *Could she be right?*

"And I also believe I'm supposed to be there," Sarah continued, "that I also have a link to the place and to the locus, although my mind won't tell me what or why." The woman's eyes went distant for a moment. "But I think it will."

SIO Flight 999X, Southwest of Jayapura | Saturday 1335 JYT

Joshua O'Donnell stared at the computer screen, locking the scene on the ground into his memory. The two soldiers had taken up concealed positions within discontinuities in the rock plateau, while Zurvan's helicopter had lifted off and swung to the west, well off their approach path. The limp form of his little sister Eva hung from Zurvan's improvised cross.

The aircraft dropped altitude and slowed. "On approach, sir," the pilot offered. "Looks like we might take small arms fire."

"That a problem?"

"Probably not, the undersurfaces have light titanium armor over the composites. Could be a problem for you though."

"Not an issue, captain. I'll drop from a thousand meters out. How many minutes?"

There was a pause. "Two, sir," came the answer. *Discipline stifled their logical questions. Good!*

"Okay. Drop the rear hatch. Start counting me down."

Hydraulics whined. Air started whistling in the cabin. Joshua took a lingering last look at Eva's video on the monitor screen, just before it started to shake with the turbulence. Her bleeding had slowed but hadn't stopped, he thought. *So there's hope. Hang in there, kiddo.*

He shoved the big equipment duffel bag toward the descending hatch, strapped the parachute to it and set the altimeter to blow the HALO chute open at five hundred meters. *They'll waste a few seconds and rounds before they realize it's a decoy. That's all the edge I'll need.*

Memories flashed across his mind, kaleidoscopic, of how his bloody rescue offensive had been launched in this very same setting years ago. He felt that old rage building, and his body's weakness started to fade as its elemental survival functions stirred awake.

Again you walk the razor's edge, Joshua O'Donnell. The concept if not the words circled around as the locus moved deeper into his mind. The resonance tickled his forebrain and receded; it felt a bit more synchronized, though the patterns still did not match well enough to lock together. *But you are closer than your namesake.* Joshua thought a little humor tinged that evaluation, a sense that the passage of time and human generations had advanced evolution at least a bit.

He allowed the locus to wend its way deeper, into the more primitive and less controllable mind that derived from reptilian and mammalian brain structures and functions. That mind was less discernibly male or female, and there the resonances of the locus found a match. Joshua felt the cosmic click as they synchronized. *Phase-lock!*

Energy flooded his muscles and ran along his nerves like liquid lightning. *My Beast is back.*

Chapter 36

East Baliem Valley, Irian Jaya | *Saturday 1336 JYT*

Eva Connard felt herself in two places simultaneously. In one she hung from Zurvan's crude cross. In the other she flowed in the stream that her mind had constructed as metaphor for the locus she called Gabbatha.

The future is my choice, not my fate? Eva toyed absently with Gabbatha's conundrum. "But they are the same, I think," she answered it.

The stream's ripples burbled in her mother's voice. "Are they? You hold onto your sorrow, your betrayal, as if your hurt requires a hurtful outcome to erase it."

"My body is hurt, that's for sure."

"Your spirit is also," Gabbatha conceded. "But should that dictate your future?"

This is getting irritating. "My fate is what I make it."

"So it is. But your brother, your Sisters, your family… all agree. There now are solutions almost as good as the one you are making happen."

"Not all agree." *Mary of Magdala and Devi of Ujjain see it my way. And so, I think, after all these millennia, does Mr. Bojangles. And they've learned the hard way.*

"Unanimity is rare in any human endeavor," the locus pressed its case.

"Almost is not good enough. I need certainty."

"Certainty is the rarest of all probabilities," Gabbatha dissented.

"I need to get as close to it as I can. My plan is doing that."

"Maybe other plans would do as well now."

The part of Eva's mind that remained in her body noted a change: *my heart is fibrillating, it won't be long now.*

"Maybe, maybe, maybe; possibilities, probabilities, there are many," Eva answered. "But I rolled the dice. I chose my fate. I intended this outcome."

"So you did, Young Mother. As you intended me to protect your brother."

What does she mean by that? The question went unanswered as Eva's brain fuzzed into a unreliable state. *Cerebral anoxia* was her diagnosis and final thought.

East Baliem Valley, Irian Jaya | *Saturday 1337 JYT*

"Four, three, two, one, GO!" The copilot's voice sounded clear in his helmet in spite of the turbulent air hammering inside the airplane's cabin. Joshua shoved the duffel bag out and watched it drop, ignoring the rounds pinging off the aircraft's armored skin. He counted, watching the tracers start to follow his decoy. *They went for it. One.* The parachute bloomed and he watched it dance in the air as rounds slapped into the duffel bag below. *Adjusted their fire. Two.* A lightning-quick logic lattice verified that the aircraft would be just about over their position. *Three.* He jumped, just as the hydraulics began pulling the rear hatch closed.

The air snatched at him, but he twisted quickly into a stable drop and focused on his target, a big rock behind the two who were still firing at his decoy. Time slowed to a crawl. The thing he thought of as his Beast — the primitive part of his brain and the only part that could phase-lock with the locus — snarled at his rational self, attempting to gain control. He ceded a bit to it, hoping. *I haven't got a parachute. And pretty soon they'll shift their fire.* He willed the transposition to happen. It did, and he landed on the rock. *So blind faith works for me too, Eva.* The orange track of tracer bullets carved through the air where he had just been. His Beast laughed in his mind.

Joshua slithered silently down the far side of the rock. Keeping low, he crab-stepped to the crevice from which the first shooter had fired. The man jabbered confusedly with his comrade in another crevice as they both fired into the empty air. *Is there any reason I would need them alive?* His Beast licked its lips and twitched its tail. Blades of energy formed around Joshua's fingers in response, and the machine pistol strapped to his thigh suddenly seemed superfluous. The man's clip ran out and the weapon jacked open. He stood up in the crevice, looking down over the plateau to see if anything had fallen from the sky. Joshua walked up silently behind him.

"You watched him torture my sister," he said. The man spun around. An energy blade flared from Joshua's right hand and severed the man's head with surgical neatness. The eyes widened for an instant before the pressure of blood pushed the head off the torso.

The other soldier's head popped up from a crevice twenty meters away. "Iblis," he screamed, frantically trying to force a fresh clip in his rifle.

"And filmed it," Joshua accused him. He let his Beast reach out his left hand. The energy blade elongated, piercing the man's chest. The Beast ripped it upward, neatly dividing the body and head into two halves. Blood sprayed as the parts dropped back in the crevice. Joshua basked in the blood-lust, lost in his Beast for a moment. Then he screamed, remembering the purpose of his action.

"Eva!"

He jumped the crevice and sprinted toward the limp figure hanging from the cross.

East Baliem Valley, Irian Jaya | Saturday 1338 JYT

"Her brother! There, running across the rock." Zurvan followed that recognition by expressive curses in his native language.

"He is lying under his parachute," Zurvan's helicopter pilot objected, "dead. They could not have missed at that range."

"We were too far away to see clearly, with a poor sightline in the clouds. That was another jumper, or a decoy."

"We only saw one parachute, Mahdi. How did he get to the ground?"

"He has his ways, evidently." Zurvan remembered their last encounter all too vividly; the teenaged Joshua O'Donnell had appeared in places physically impossible for him to get to.

"Our comrades must see him, but they do not shoot," his pilot replied, hand fidgeting restlessly with the helicopter's collective. "I should take you out of here, Mahdi, if there are dangers we cannot comprehend."

Fear flittered through Zurvan's mind. *Probably a good idea.* But the desire to witness Joshua O'Donnell seeing his sister dead overcame caution. "No. The boy and his sister took years of my life. I want to watch him suffer. Move closer."

The pilot shot him a questioning look, toggling different communication channels but getting no contact back. "Your *jaesh* on the ground do not respond, Mahdi."

"Move! Half the distance."

The nose of the aircraft dipped, but they moved forward only slowly. "Is it true what they say about these Novas? That they can control reality with their minds?"

"Where did you hear that?"

"There are rumors, Mahdi. And strange videos. I have seen them myself."

As they angled in toward the running figure, it raised its head and snapped an arm motion. The air ahead seemed to curl into itself and a force shoved the chopper sideways. The pilot heeled the machine over and rode out the disturbance. When it tapered off, fear had fully surfaced on the man's sweating face. He banked the machine away from the pool.

"We must be gone, Mahdi."

"You fear death, my friend?" Zurvan asked softly. *Can I fly this thing?*

He studied the pilot, then the controls, and answered his own question. *Yes. Little difference from my old machine.*

"Not for myself, Mahdi. But I fear if you are prevented from your Coming… we…"

"What's that, on the horizon?" Zurvan interrupted him, pointing.

The pilot twisted sideways to look.

Zurvan shot him under the armpit. The man spasmed once and slumped, only a trickle of blood from the nose and a spreading stain on his shirt.

"Fear hollow points," he advised the dead man, unlatching his harness and shoving him out of the helicopter.

East Baliem Valley, Irian Jaya | Saturday 1339 JYT

The locus had helped him — or rather his Beast — project a gravity wave toward the helicopter, but it still flew. *Too weak to damage it at that distance*, he guessed. A part of his mind noted absently that the aircraft had turned and run. He dismissed it from consideration as he leapt over a last crevice onto the rock shelf and ran toward his sister.

"Eva!" He screamed her name. He tore off his helmet and dropped it. *She's not breathing.*

Frantically, he kicked away the stones jammed in the crevice holding the cross vertical, then tried to lift it out. It didn't move. *Idiot! Think!*

An energy blade sprang from his right hand and slashed through the wood as if it were a toothpick. He caught the cross as it toppled and a tiny blade sliced the tape binding Eva. A gravity wave from his left hand sent the cross spinning through the air to land in the brush a hundred meters away. He laid his sister gently down on the rock. His hands came away bloody.

"Joshua!" Elia's voice sounded tinny from the helmet.

"Quiet!" He screamed at it as he knelt beside Eva. He put his ear to her chest, his fingers on the neck artery. *Nothing.* His mind dropped into an black abyss. *Or was that...? Maybe. Weak; a fibrillation?* If it had been, it faded.

Joshua O'Donnell raised his face to the early afternoon sun and the Beast inside howled its rage and loss. The birdsong in the forest that surrounded the rock shelf went silent. The Beast quested around for something to kill. Time slowed. Sarah's voice, deepened to a husky bass, came from the helmet and finally penetrated Joshua's mind as he caught his breath.

"Joshua! She's not gone! Not yet!"

Hope sprung where there was none. He pushed the Beast to the back of his mind.

"CPR, Joshua! The breath of life. As you give her the breaths, will me to come to you."

"How...," he began, doubtfully.

"Do it!" Sarah's tone deepened more, elongated. "It will work. I will come to you."

Kneeling in his sister's blood, Joshua eased her head back, pinched her nose shut, prepared to breathe into her slack mouth. His Beast bent to his will, to join him in summoning Sarah.

O'Donnell Enclave, Waimanu, HI | Friday 1840 HST

Time slowed, too, in the Council Chamber of the O'Donnell enclave five thousand miles to the east. *Time is mutable,* Sarah acknowledged as she watched on the big screen, *or at least our perceptions of it are.* Joshua's head was dropping ever so slowly toward Eva's.

Sarah stood facing west, and slightly south. She framed the transposition intention slowly and carefully and then began the Sisterhood chant.

Nobody's done this before except Eva. Doubt wanted to assail her but she rejected it. Elia stood behind, holding hands with Ibrahim on her right and Gaelan on her left, and picked up the chant.

Time slowed more, and Elia's voice deepened another register. The twins higher voices seem to mix in, in a complex counterpointed harmony, although so far as she knew they had knowledge neither of the chant nor its long-lost Galatian dialect. *But there are other ways of knowing, aren't there? Eva did at that age.* The chant took on a life of its own, working her mouth and throat and vocal cords, synchronizing her breathing, a psychic autopilot.

Paradoxically, as much as time seemed to slow, the thoughts running through Sarah's rational mind seemed to speed up. Pieces of forgotten memory coalesced and fragmented and came back together again. *When I was a very young Sister, I researched this, didn't I? Neurons working at the same task, matching frequency and amplitude. Communion even between cultures of dish-grown neurons and human brains.* It had been an utterly fascinating research area, how such complex and subtle neural signatures would develop to link neural networks. *To link minds. How could I forget I did that?*

Deeper into the chant, her rational mind observed with detached curiosity how the present signature was developing in this instance. Intuition struck. *Not forgotten. Suppressed.* Doubt wiggled its way back into the rational part of her mind. *Eva hid my past from me. Why?*

That thought seemed to create a little stumble in the cadence of the chant, a minor misstep in Ibrahim's song. She felt Elia adjust slightly to correct for it, and the resonance continued to cohere. She wondered why the stumble, and recalled what Elia had told her just a few minutes ago: "sixteen percent of psychopathy is heritable, Sarah. I've studied the statistics".

Will Ibrahim be a problem? Clearly Elia was worried, had always been worried, carrying that dark secret.

"The Sisterhood mind-ritual for controlling bloodlines?" Sarah had asked her.

"I couldn't. Not without aborting Gaelan too," Elia had cried.

Hiding it from her husband, abetted by Eva's intentions. "That's all right, Elia," she'd told the young woman, "I also have my secrets. Since Eva left Waimanu the veil has been slowly lifting. The threads of my existence are coming together. They are part of a pattern, as are yours. And your two sons." The remembrance of a sense of pattern, though not the pattern itself, drew her rational mind back to the present.

Sarah felt the tickling sense of another presence enter her mind, one that she'd felt the edges of at times while standing next to Eva or one of the twins. *Waimanu.* And then she felt another. *No, two others, distinct individual patterns. John Connard. And Lara. Eva's parents.*

She'd never met them. She'd arrived at the enclave years after their near-fatal encounter, seen their unpreserved but undecaying bodies lying side by side in the cool secure vault at the base of the enclave. *But somehow I know their patterns, I recognize them.* Her scientific self had desperately wanted to investigate, to poke and prod and see how they could be not alive but not yet dead. She especially had wanted to characterize that strange shimmer around their bodies. It was there and then it wasn't, a wraith that could not be held in direct vision, only seen peripherally, and even then you were never sure. *Time means something different to those two than it does to us,* she'd thought at the time. Eva had politely refused all inquiries, only quoting Ecclesiastes… "a time to every purpose under heaven".

These memories seemed to flash by Doctor Sarah Kruse at light-speed, and as the chant went on she felt a resonance begin to build, its basso profundo vibrating her brainstem. *Coherence potentials are ramping up. Waimanu is listening, helping. He misses his friend and protégé Eva. He is integrating neural patterns, cohering them toward our common intention. And he is entraining with the locus in Irian Jaya. It has a name now. Eva named it.*

The resonance built to a crescendo. *This is going to work!* Sarah closed her eyes, wondering if what she heard was the pop of air rushing into the space her body had just vacated.

Chapter 37

East Baliem Valley, Irian Jaya | Saturday 1340 JYT

Time slowed for Joshua as he bent toward his baby sister's pale face. He inhaled as his head descended, slowly, slowly, like he was pushing through molasses. *Her lips are turning blue,* he thought. *Come to me, Sarah, now!* He exhaled into Eva's mouth. A sideways glance showed that her chest rose. *Airway's clear.* He inhaled another deep breath.

Time slowed more.

You've ridden the dolphins, Eva. I know you can hold oxygen in your lungs and blood better than anybody. Come on! Memories cascaded over his mind, like the water over the falls in front of him…

Eva playing in the shallow shore waters of Ireland's Ballydonegan Bay, four years old, a happy, friendly, inquisitive little girl. Perfectly normal. Suddenly one day she slapped the water, a certain pattern to it, then cocked her head as if listening.

"Fishies, Josh-wa, fishies," she'd called back to where he sat on a rock, reading.

He looked up. Fins broke the surface and streamed toward Eva. His reflex leap carried him twenty feet out into the water toward her before he realized they were dolphins.

"S'okay, Josh-wa. They just want to play." She giggled. A dolphin's head popped out of the water and chirped at her. She laughed and swung herself up on its back. The pack turned and streaked out to deeper water. Faster than he could swim, he quickly found out. But just as quickly, they turned and brought her back.

"Dammit! Don't scare me like that, Eva."

"No swears, Josh-wa," the child had answered primly.

When he told his parents the story that afternoon, they hadn't seemed too concerned that he couldn't catch up to her. His Uncle Ham had made a typical nonsensical observation. "What 'tis it ye expected laddie? Ye're a mere Aquarian; Eva is a Pisces!" For some reason everyone except Joshua thought that was uproariously funny.

That's when it started, sis. Your pure joy in the water and all its creatures.

Back in the present, kneeling on the hard rock, Joshua treasured that memory, held it in his mind as a metaphor for her spirit. He put two fingers to the side of her neck, checking. *No pulse.* He lowered toward Eva, slowly, slowly, to give another breath. *Remember it now, Sis, how dolphins saturate cells with oxygen. And then I'll start chest compressions, move the oxygen around.*

The rock beneath his knees sent ripples through his body. As if triggered by the memory of Eva's first dolphin ride, another mind sought his... strange but familiar...

Mom?

I'm here. I've always been here. The warm contralto sound was unequivocally his mother's voice, but it spilled across his mind in the context of a running brook. The context of 'here' carried no sense of location. But that didn't matter, Joshua decided. *Help Eva!* he pleaded.

Another ripple conveyed through the rock, a lesser genetic linkage but no less familiar...

Dad, help me now, he called out to the resonance of John Connard, the man he truly thought of as his father. *You lost your baby sister to a maniac, too. You never spoke of it, but Mom told me once. I was twelve years old...*

I'm here. I've always been here. The deeper voice sounded in Joshua's mind, a comforting familiar baritone that came in the context of the rhythms of waves on the sea.

Your daughter needs you now! he pleaded.

His mouth reached Eva's then and he exhaled another long breath into her lungs. *Come to me, Sarah, now!*

In some middle indeterminate distance in his mind Joshua also sensed the pattern of the man he should have killed years ago, the man they all had believed dead. *He's an interference pattern, a dissonance in the reality I'm trying to create. Is that why Sarah isn't coming?*

He put his fingers to Eva's neck but again there was no pulse. *There may not be enough blood to pump.* A red darkness descended over his vision as his Beast reacted.

A pop of displaced air told him Sarah had arrived. "Help me," he screamed.

Charter MZ987, On Approach Marshall Islands | Saturday 1740 MHT

Robert Blake fidgeted, looking down into the blue Pacific and the postage-stamp sized dots of land they were turning towards.

"Yes, we could make Hawaii," the pilot agreed with him, "but it's faster if we top up now. This is a sleepy little place; we can be in and out a lot quicker than Honolulu or even one of the other island airports. Refuel here, and we can do the long leg to California non-stop."

Blake nodded acceptance. *Whatever gets me back on the ground at my church the quickest. Having a stand-in there makes me nervous.*

As the pilot went back to the cockpit, Blake's cellphone rang in secure mode. The Senator spoke without preamble, his words rushed.

"They may be onto me, boy. I got a bad feelin'. Call Zurvan, tell him to get the hell outta there. I armed the nukes. He's got ten minutes."

Blake was dumbstruck for a moment, questions colliding in his mind. He asked the obvious one first. "Why not let him go up in smoke?"

"Because I may need him."

"Why?"

"Muddy the waters. Give them another target besides me."

"Oh. How bad is it?"

"Dunno. Somebody leaked."

"A phone intercept? Decrypted our talks?"

"Nah. Two-five-six encryption, on a floating reference algorithm? Even NSA cain't break it."

"How then?"

"I don't know, goddammit!" The Senator slipped out of his good ol' boy dialect for a moment. "Probably some knees got wobbly on the ship. Navy's my weakest link."

"Am I…" Blake swallowed hard.

"Yeah, son. You're okay. You're in California, remember? With eyewitnesses. Don't worry about it."

There was some banging noise in the background, underneath the Senator's hoarse whisper. "Just call the fucker, okay? Now!"

The connection dropped off.

If you're not dead yet, Eva Connard, you soon will be. Atomized. Good-bye, my dear. Again. Blake keyed the other security code on his phone and called Muhammad Zurvan.

East Baliem Valley, Irian Jaya | *Saturday 1340 JYT*

Nine. A three, three times; three trinities. Nine is a number that means good luck to the Chinese. *I think they may have something there,* Sarah thought. The odd thought and its number stuck in her mind as she slammed onto the rock shelf in Irian Jaya. *Where have I been?* The scene spun around her, disorienting. Her ears rang. *Pressure change?* She stayed on all fours for steadiness. The rock vibrated under her hands. *But this is higher than Waimanu, not lower.* She swallowed hard and the spinning stopped. *Nine entities, acting as one. Cohered. Entrained.* She was suddenly not certain of the concept. *Elia and the twins, me, and Waimanu. And here? Joshua and Eva and the locus. So Zurvan makes nine.* The thought made her smile. *An unwitting tool.*

He doesn't understand the connections he's made with us. But he senses the entrainment. He's fighting it, disrupting Joshua's pattern. Her mind reviewed those relationships and drew diagrams, edgy, tentative. *How can I remove him from the cohering pattern without collapsing it all back to chaos?* Sarah rose to her feet as Joshua screamed for help a second time. *And where have I been?*

"I'm here now," Sarah croaked to Joshua's back, stumbling toward him.

He was giving Eva chest compressions, counting, but turned his face toward her. Crazed eyes flickering with red impaled her, freezing her in her tracks. *Shaitan!* Fragments of fractured memories struggled to reassemble themselves into a whole. *I've seen you before! Here!*

"Joshua?" she said uncertainly." She blinked, and his eyes were their normal bright turquoise, but frantic. *Where did that other image come from?* She shook it off and moved toward him.

"I think she's bled out, Sarah. I can't get a pulse," he said, desperation seeping out of his voice.

Sarah dropped to her knees and lifted Eva's feet to her shoulders. "Two more breaths then continue compressions," she ordered Joshua. Her practiced fingers searched for the spot an ankle pulse would appear. She began the Sisterhood's resurrection chant, forming the intention, reaching out to the entities she sensed would help. She left Zurvan out. *I know this chant through Sisterhood training, but I've never done it.* Yet the phrases tumbled out of her mouth, in a rhythm clearly syncopated with Joshua's compression-counting. *Why does it come so fluidly?*

More fractured images skated across Sarah's mind, too fast to retrieve, chaotically intermixed with the patterns of the entities with whom she was now entrained. *John and Lara are here.* Or were they? Other images flashed by, fragmented and erratic but nonetheless bringing a measure of understanding. *Oh, I see it now... they're not independent entities. John is Waimanu. Lara is... Gabbatha,* the name came to her from within the flow of the chant. *Gabbatha?* She parsed the possibilities inherent in that naming choice. *What has this child done?*

Joshua stopped compressions and gave his sister two more deep breaths. He felt for a pulse in her neck then looked at Sarah hopefully.

She nodded. "I have the beginnings of a pulse too, Joshua. Come here and keep her feet elevated like this. Squeeze her calves, from ankles to knees. Time it to the rhythms of my chant." *He'll do that anyway, he's entrained in the pattern. I didn't need to tell him.*

He moved quickly to take Sarah's place. The headset in the helmet behind him chattered something unintelligible but he ignored it.

"She's not dead?" A tiny sliver of hope worked into his voice.

"She's not dead," Sarah agreed. "She's... with her... parents." *Now for part two of the resurrection intention: bring the child back to us.*

Doctor Sarah Kruse knelt at Eva's head, cradled it on her thighs, and held the girl's hands in her own. *Time to supplement modern medicine with a healing more ancient.* She lowered her forehead to touch Eva's and continued the chant.

O'Donnell Enclave, Waimanu, HI | Friday 1842 HST

Watching his big screen in the Waimanu enclave Security Center, TC Demuzzio breathed a sigh of relief and hope. *Sarah got there. Maybe between the two of them they can save my god-daughter.* He shifted his attention back to the small desktop monitor and the image of the National Security Coordinator.

"They're both on-scene, Carol. And they've got a pulse. Sarah's doing some of your Sisterhood ... stuff."

"Some good news at last?" The woman's face showed every minute of how long her day had been. "Can I tell the boss?"

"He's not asleep?"

"It's not quite midnight here, TC. Fortunately the man doesn't need much sleep. He hasn't had any since this fiasco started."

Fiasco. That's an understatement. Goddamn world's imploding around us. "Sure, tell him. But I'm still not gonna stream you the live video to watch. Washington's too fucking porous."

"As it happens, I agree. The edited composited clips Elia has been sending are just fine. Our shrinks agree with you guys as to how therapeutic the effect will be when the tape is released. A total game-changer. Total."

"Yeah? Doctor Sam agree too?"

"He does, in fact. Why?"

"He's the only shrink in DC I trust."

Carol Violette gave a brief brittle laugh. "Uh huh; me too. So when do you want us to go public with it?"

"It's our call?"

"So sayeth the Prez."

"Tell him he's a smart man, and thanks, we'll let him know."

"TC, you must know," Carol said softly, "that Eva planned her death for maximum impact. Adroitly."

He felt her watching him as he ducked his head to rub the sudden wetness in his eyes. *Goddamn Sisters.*

"Sorry, TC. Had to say it."

"We're not gonna let the kid die if we can help it, Carol," he snarled. "I don't give a fuck what her plan calls for."

The woman gave a long sigh. "Me either." Then her head snapped around as someone off-screen whispered to her. "Standby one, TC," she told him as his screen flipped to the Presidential Seal.

After half a minute, the NSC hadn't come back on-line and Demuzzio stood up. *I gotta pee.* He'd almost started for the door when Carol came back on-screen, talking fast, near panic on her face.

"TC, we just decrypted a call from Blake to Zurvan. Those Global Hawks the Navy sent for recon have nuclear missiles."

"Jesus! The fail-safes! Blow the fuckers now!"

"Can't. All the safeguards have been over-ridden. The Senator's person is in control; everyone else is locked out."

"What are you telling me?"

"They're targeted and armed. Small tacticals, apparently, but they're going to take out the site completely. Tell Sarah and Josh to get themselves and Eva out of there, now!"

"How long?" Demuzzio asked as his fingers flew over the touchpad.

"Minutes. Five, maybe eight," he heard the NSC before the channel switch cut her off.

Your plan didn't figure on this, did it, Eva? The link to Josh's helmet came up and Demuzzio began yelling into his hand-held communicator.

East Baliem Valley, Irian Jaya | Saturday 1344 JYT

Joshua knelt with Eva's feet propped on his shoulders, massaging her calves in time with Sarah's cadence, working the collected blood from them toward her heart. *I hope her back is coagulated enough she won't just pump it out.* The resonance returned from the rock surface under his knees gave him some hope. *Rock dust could be styptic, a hemostatic agent.* The resonance vibrated acknowledgment. A crystallization pattern developed in the rock around Eva and lightened to a grayish dust.

But dimly, even through the focus created by Sarah's chant and the rock's resonance, something probed at Joshua, an irritant. The urgency of it finally broke through. *TC. Something's wrong.* His head snapped around and he looked at the helmet three feet to his left.

"What? What did you say?"

Sarah's chant faltered, and Joshua focused his suddenly acute hearing on the helmet.

"You gotta get out of there," Demuzzio's voice screamed. "Nuclear missiles incoming. Five minutes, maybe less."

"What?" *That can't be. Who would…* "Say again?"

"Nukes! Missiles, goddammit! Joshua, grab Eva and Sarah and transpose back here!"

Joshua rejected the impossibility of nuclear missiles. *TC's tone says he believes it.* Logic lattices sprang up in his mind, speed-driven by adrenaline. Sarah's chant faltered and stopped and she lifted her head to look at him.

"Did he say…?"

"Yes. Can we do it? Transpose?"

Sarah's eyes lifted skyward, eastward, then turned inward. "No. Not in just five minutes. I can't form an intention instantly like Eva. I need to chant my mind into it."

"Does Eva have a pulse?"

"Weak. She's nowhere near conscious."

Logic lattices spun out his options at light speed and rejected them just as fast. He was down to one: *use a gravity wave to deflect the missiles into the ground before they detonate.* The probability of success of that tumbled out of the lattice: *less than one percent; they'll come in too fast to pick up visually, although I might get one of the two.*

His Beast slammed to the fore of his mind and Joshua howled his rage into the sky. The helicopter that was rapidly receding into the distance abruptly slewed sideways.

East Baliem Valley, Irian Jaya | Saturday 1345 JYT

The howl from Joshua transfixed Sarah. Neural gates that had been sealed shut years ago by Eva's complex intentions blew wide open. Memories exploded through her mind. She slumped sideways and Eva's head rolled off her knees. Then the iron discipline of a Sister kicked in. *No time now.* She ran to Joshua and slapped him hard.

"Carry Eva into the pool," she screamed. "Now! Take in as much air as you can and drop into the whirlpool. It will carry you safely away."

Joshua's eyes blazed bright red and his hard hands reached for her. She slapped him again, harder. "And the water will shield you from the radiation. Go!"

The rage snapped out of his eyes as reason returned. He instantly scooped up Eva and ran west across the rock plateau toward the pool and its roiling drain, a huge lava tube.

In a quick intention, and with a power she hadn't thought to possess, Sarah hardened the water under Joshua's sprinting feet. As he reached the vortex in the middle of the pool she released it.

He screamed over his shoulder as he and Eva dropped from sight into the vortex. "Come on, Sarah!"

"No, Joshua. I have business here," she whispered to the place where he had been. "Save Eva. Go n-eiri leath. Godspeed."

Doctor Sarah Kruse turned slowly back toward the east. The fleeing helicopter was now a dot in the sky.

"I have business with you, Muhammad Zurvan," she said. She let the suppressed memories flood into her mind. They wove into the pattern of intense power that was moving from the rock up into her feet and beginning to saturate her entire being.

I will need Elia's help. Sarah touched that part of the power pattern that was Waimanu and used it to open a channel to Elia's mind.

Chapter 38

O'Donnell Enclave, Waimanu, HI | Friday 1846 HST

Elia O'Donnell choked a scream off in her throat as Joshua and Eva disappeared down the water vortex. *The boys. I have to be strong for them.* The extreme forces buffeting her mind crescendoed as the barriers Eva obviously had placed collapsed. Suppressed memories spilled out, their dam broken: *Sarah is my mother!*

The twins yelped as her hands convulsed around their smaller ones. Elia's mind convulsed too, as Sarah's actions sank in. *And now she's going to die.* The scream ran forward to her mouth, but froze there. The forces unleashed in her mind were now palpable in her physical world and the stone floor resonated beneath her feet.

That resonance reflected from the twins' hands into hers, but somehow it was calming and reassuring. *They're only six years old. It's too soon. Waimanu?*

"It's what Gramma wants," Ibrahim said.

Gramma? They knew? Or they know?

"It will be okay," Gaelan offered, squeezing her hand.

Eva! Why? But Elia knew exactly why, in a crashing moment of karmic clarity. *Some sorrows are too deadly to bear.*

Demuzzio's feet clattered down the hall toward them and he charged into the Council Chamber. "Feel that? It may be an earthquake. We should get to the surface."

"No, Thomas, we're safe here."

He stared at her, and at the two boys holding her hands. They nodded confirmation at him.

"I need your help, child," Sarah's eerily calm voice came from the speakers above the big monitor screen. "There's one last thing we must do together."

She stared back at Demuzzio. *He loves her. He heard her say goodbye to Eva and Joshua. He knows what that means. Oh, Thomas!* Elia would have dropped to her knees had not the power evoked by Sarah's voice kept her erect. *May love sustain us all.*

Demuzzio's console on the big table came alive, with the worried face and voice of the NSC on its monitor screen. A clock appeared under her image, counting down. "TC, where are you?" Carol Violette paused, but Demuzzio stood frozen and out of the range of the console's camera pickup. "Are they out of there yet?" The clock spun down. "This is our best estimate of impact. We can't assert any control over the missiles. We scrambled fighters but they'll never catch up in time. I'm sorry." The urgency in the woman's voice ratcheted up. "TC? TC, come in, please."

Sarah looked at Demuzzio's anguished face and pointed a finger at the door. *The boys don't need to see this. Especially Ib; he cannot be connected when the moment comes.* "Gaelan, Ibrahim," she snapped, "go to the kitchen with your Uncle Tee. Drink plenty of guava juice, you're both still dehydrated." The three of them snapped around and ran out the door, as if marionettes on her strings.

Melodic words of power streamed from the monitor as Sarah began to chant. Elia recognized it instantly, although comprehension was not solely in her mind. *The Sisterhood intention for karmic rebalancing. Or retribution, depending on how you intone.*

She ran to Demuzzio's console and put herself in the camera's view. "Carol. Joshua carried Eva into the whirlpool. They have a slim chance, I think. Please be silent now. I need to focus." The woman opened her mouth then closed it and nodded.

Elia turned her focus back to the big screen and watched Sarah's hand motions. She felt their intent, the resonance flowing through the rock floor into her feet. She kicked off her sandals so she could feel it more directly. *Zurvan is between us, on a line. I can be her anchor point.* She had certainty, suddenly, that it would work: the gravity of the earth would bend to their intention as if they were Novas.

I understand, Sarah, she told the presence in her mind. She looked at the countdown clock. *But we must do it quickly.*

Elia entrained her mind with Sarah's, joining in the chant. A distant part of her watched their intention begin to slow Zurvan's fleeing helicopter.

East Baliem Valley, Irian Jaya | Saturday 1347 JYT

Thank you, Elia. A part of Sarah's mind paused to admire the smoothness of the younger woman's entrainment into the intention, her control over emotion as she saw her mother facing certain death and her husband and sister-in-law with a less certain but still likely fatal outcome. *Good for you, daughter. You have the power. You would have been Prima of the Sisterhood had not Zurvan upset the pattern.*

A parent's pride wrapped itself into the chant and flowed across the Pacific to Elia; a wave, a cycle, a thing that was both of the water and not, but that took no time for its transit. It supported the young woman, then strengthened her. *A good thing,* Sarah thought, *we have no time to waste.* The countdown clock wasn't visible to Sarah's eyes, but through Elia's mind she knew to the second what it was reading. Her voice grew stronger, her song more melodic as the chant unfolded their intention. Elia's voice, she knew, would be making the rock of Waimanu sing, crystalline molecular structures aligning. The rock under her own feet sang with energy, flooding into her now. Images of little forest people arose from the rock and arrayed themselves around her, adding their voices to the chant.

Their intention grew in power, and the localized gravity bubble it caused stopped Zurvan's helicopter in mid-air and began to draw it back toward Sarah. She smiled grimly as the mind-pattern inside grew erratic and fearful. *Now you see what it is like to contemplate your own death, Muhammad Zurvan.* In the far distance, the aircraft swung violently to the left and right and tried to drop altitude. *As you have made so many innocents contemplate theirs.* But the bubble held the helicopter secure, and with Elia's anchoring force to the east and Sarah's pull to the west, it accelerated toward her tail-first, becoming larger than just a distant speck.

With their minds wrapped together, and entangled with the loci Waimanu and Gabbatha, the communion of mother and daughter was as close to a Nova as a human could get without having that gene fully expressed. Sarah felt the rapture of it. *Oneness, as I die. That's enough.*

Charter MZ987, On Approach Marshall Islands | Saturday 1748 MHT

Blake held his cell phone well away from his ear as Zurvan screamed from it. "Tell the Senator to defuse the missiles! Now!"

"What? What's happening?"

"I'm being pulled back to the pool!"

The questions raced through Blake's mind. *Pulled back? A helicopter? How? Is Eva still alive? Who else could do it?*

"I'll try to reach him," Blake said. He cut the connection and looked at the phone, astonished and uneasy. *Eight minutes ago, the Senator cut me off, and it sure sounded like trouble was showing up on his doorstep.* "Like hell I will," he told the phone. "If they're onto him, he's not getting any call from me. You're on your own, bud."

The aircraft banked sharply onto its approach and Blake watched the airstrip slide by as they circled into the landing pattern. He wondered about the Senator's situation. He wondered about Zurvan's fate. But most of all, he wondered whether the island below was big enough to get lost on.

East Baliem Valley, Irian Jaya | Saturday 1349 JYT

Sarah's chant tapered off. Their intention was fully formed now and self-sustaining: Zurvan's helicopter was inextricably bound inside the gravity bubble the intention had created. She spread her arms wide and swept them together in an encompassing motion, drawing the aircraft toward her. She spoke to it reflectively, calm in contrast to its frantic attempts to escape.

"Your end will be far too quick, Muhammad Zurvan, but I will give you a minute to contemplate it."

The countdown clock she saw through Elia's eyes ticked below a minute as she continued. The memories flooded back, sharp and acute, fed from the minds of the little forest people now solidified and arranged in a parabola behind her focal point.

"Twenty six years ago, you killed my family. You raped me and dragged me across the desert behind your horse and dropped me in a canyon to die. Me, Doctor Hessa Gibran, a neurosurgeon in the American University of Beirut Medical Center, a woman who only wanted to help those in need, in my own country that needed me so badly."

Her words sought the pattern of Zurvan's mind and invaded it.

"Years later, with all memory lost except my given name, with my brain damaged and its morality center destroyed, I became Hessa, your witch. You never knew I was the one you had so casually raped, and thought you had killed. But there were dozens by that time probably, so why would you remember one? And I was disfigured, scarred, broken. Unrecognizable."

Like this, Sarah thought, and caused the power running through her to recast her trim and fit body into the image of the mangled and broken old witch she'd been seven years ago in this very same place. A casual afterthought draped her in the black burkha she'd worn then.

"My broken mind sought evil, and you showed it all the paths. But deeds have consequences, Muhammad Zurvan, and yours have just come home to you."

With her mind, Sarah nudged the aircraft around so that Zurvan's distorted screaming face looked at her through the Plexiglas canopy. The rotors were an irritant, so she froze them, leaving the helicopter suspended powerless in her gravity bubble. She drove more words home into his mind.

"But you were just a tool, Muhammad Zurvan, a tool for a fifteen year-old female Messiah and her secret plan for a better world. That's why she had the instinct to save you years ago, why her little forest people held you captive until your time. Of what use good, if there is no evil against which to contrast it?"

Zurvan screamed at her, a unintelligible cacophony of curses and pleadings and fear and hate.

"And that's why Eva's little forest people saved me," she continued. Why they remade me into Doctor Sarah Kruse, a new person but with my old physician skills. They made me into a new Sister, too. Not the Prima I had been, but a simple helpmate to the Novas. In Waimanu, a place where Eva could protect me from my past."

The countdown clock ticked into single digits.

"I am the dark side of your gharaniq, Muhammad Zurvan, the furies of pain and hurt and misery. I am all those things you will find in your personal hell."

She smiled at him through the contorted visage of Hessa, his witch.

"And so you die, by your own misdeeds."

Sarah saw two streaks in the sky to the rear of the suspended aircraft. Her role was complete. The curving line of little forest folk streamed away into the whirlpool behind her, their intention released.

The helicopter thumped down onto the rock in front of her.

Zurvan's frozen pale face stared out.

Sarah opened her arms wide.

The countdown clock ticked to zero.

O'Donnell Enclave, Waimanu, HI | Friday 1850 HST

Elia O'Donnell's scream echoed down the long rock hall from the Council Chamber to the kitchen.

TC Demuzzio grunted as if punched.

The boy Ibrahim paled and sat down hard on the floor.

His brother Gaelan immediately dropped to his knees beside Ibrahim and put his arms around him.

"See to Mama," Gaelan told Demuzzio in a strangely adult tone. "I've got Ib."

Demuzzio opened his mouth, then shut it and sprinted out of the kitchen and down the hall.

O'Donnell Enclave, Waimanu, HI | Friday 1850 HST

"Mother!" The pain ripped Elia's throat as she screamed it again.

The Chamber's big monitor screen showing the multiple nanocamera feeds around the Irian Jaya pool had flicked white then the images vanished. Now it slowly recovered to the blue screen of no signal input. Elia gasped for air and her knees trembled and gave way. Demuzzio ran in and caught her as she started to collapse.

"She's gone," Elia sobbed into the big man's chest.

"I loved her too," he answered, almost crushing her with the desperate strength in his arms.

They cried together, until Elia looked up at him and stuttered the question through her tears. "The twins?"

"Gaelan's got Ib. Said he'll be okay." Demuzzio held her shoulders. "Eva? Josh? Any sense that...?"

Elia shook her head. "It's all one big roiling chaos." She trembled. "Thomas, I don't see how... a nuclear bomb... even with the water..."

Behind them, Carol Violette's sad voice came from Demuzzio's console monitor. "A pinpoint hit. Right on the coordinates of the pool. Weather satellite shows it clearly. Downloading the video feed... now."

The console screen split, half of it showing the NSC's drawn face. "I'm so sorry," the woman said, struggling to assert control over her voice.

The other half-screen showed a view from the orbiting satellite. A mushroom cloud was rising from what Eva had always referred to as 'my sacred pool' in Irian Jaya.

Neither Elia nor Demuzzio could turn to look at it.

Chapter 39

East Baliem Valley, Irian Jaya | *Saturday 1351 JYT*

Total darkness enveloped Joshua as the cold water rushed them along. He still clutched Eva tightly, but his hand was no longer over her mouth and nose. After what his internal clock had timed as almost a minute underwater, the violence of the whirlpool had dropped them into what he thought was an underground cavern. They'd bobbed to water's surface and after he gasped in enough air he breathed some into his sister. She gave a spasmodic cough in his face, half air and half water.

Breathing on her own? "Be a dolphin, Eva! Remember the dolphins," he'd yelled encouragement in her ear. No response, but that was all right: *she's at home in any kind of water.*

By his count, they'd been in the water now for almost four minutes. The continual roar and the two drops they'd gone over since exiting the whirlpool told him the flow was still very fast. *Carrying us further from annihilation. Good!*

It will carry you safely away, Sarah had said. *Thank you, Sarah!* Aside from the terror of being sucked down helpless into a roaring cold dark wet cave, the woman had been right, the water was carrying them safely away. *To somewhere.*

An interesting question, how Sarah could know that the underground river would carry them to safety. *Eva wouldn't tell me where it went, so why would she tell Sarah? Because she's a Sister? Or because there's a meaning to this that I could never see?* Joshua felt the increase in turbulence that signaled another drop over a waterfall coming up, and breathed air into Eva as insurance. They tumbled over a third drop, more a rapids than a waterfall, but in water deep enough that they never submerged nor banged off any rocks. Once in the smoother water flow downstream, a logic lattice went to work, rewinding Joshua's eidetic memories to pull out salient facts. It paused at a debate he'd had with Eva almost four years ago…

"The pool is sacred, Joshua," Eva had told him. "No investigation."

"I just want to verify the river's underground route… I'm curious about where…."

"No."

"Why?"

"Sometimes curiosity is best left unsatisfied."

"Not much of an answer, Sis."

But she'd just looked at him and shaken her head. So he'd dropped the issue.

The lattice logic spun back through older memories, stopping at one with a serrated sharpness. *Seven years ago, when Eva first came into Zurvan's enclave, she was wet,* Joshua now remembered, *soaked with that distinctive smell of the fog forest lignins that get into the rivers. Exactly what I smelled when I was at her sacred pool, when my Beast had me and my nose was preternaturally sharp. And that's exactly what I smell now.*

Which meant Eva had transited this underground river before, but then never said a word about it. And four years ago she wouldn't let him explore it to satisfy his curiosity.

The lattice posited possible answers, but he dismissed them all as irrelevant to their present situation. *The more important question is when is this underground river going to dump us out? And where? Into what sort of radiation zone?*

Time to worry about that when they got there, he decided. *And when is an issue too. This water's not freezing cold, but in my state I'm going to go hypothermic eventually.*

Pressure pulsed in his ears and he felt rather than heard an insane howl in the air, a hammering even above the roaring of the water. *The nuke hit. We've got a bigger problem.*

It will carry you safely away, Sarah had said. *But what does a neuropsychologist know about hydraulic shock waves in water?* A logic lattice began to run. *How much distance have we covered? What's the water depth and bottom configuration? What attenuation from the falls? What pressure relief points in the cavern? What...?*

At least a dozen key variables. He fed estimates and ranges lightning-quick into the lattice, but knew what the answer would be before it tumbled out: *insufficient data.*

Joshua renewed his grip on Eva. He barely had time to turn his feet and hers upstream before the shock wave slammed into them.

O'Donnell Enclave, Waimanu, HI | Friday 1852 HST

TC Demuzzio held a trembling Elia tight against his chest, feeling a matching tremble move from the rock floor up through his feet. Finally he lifted his head to look at the mushroom cloud on the console's split screen.

"They both hit?" he asked Carol Violette on the other half of the split screen. Elia spasmed in his grasp and he tightened it, patting her back.

"No, TC. That's not the attack pattern. The second missile is only insurance in case the first fails or gets shot down. So the second one got incinerated in the blast. More radionuclides in the air, but only one explosion."

"Small warheads?" *Maybe Joshua and Eva have a chance*, he thought.

"Yeah. Tactical. Our decryption of the Senator's phone call says they're adapted from Russian suitcase nukes."

"You pick that fucker up yet?"

"We have."

"And our Judas? Pastor Bob?"

"Shortly."

"Save a piece of those bastards for me."

The NSC just smiled grimly. "Can you update me on what went on at the site just prior to…" the woman's edge softened as she saw Elia trembling, "…I'm sorry, TC. Never mind, I'll just look at what video you've streamed to us."

"No," Elia gasped, her voice breaking. She turned in TC's arms to face the monitor. "No. Don't look. Erase it now, anything you've got that's time-stamped after 1845 Hawaii time."

"Seven minutes ago? Elia, I'm the NSC. I have a duty. The President will want to…" she stopped, looking intently out of the screen at them. Demuzzio felt a different kind of vibration in the rock as Elia stepped away from him and toward the console. The young woman straightened up and her voice lost its quaver.

"You have a higher duty, Sister Carol. With Eva gone, and Joshua gone too, I am acting Prima. Erase it, please."

Demuzzio watched the conflict fleet across the NSC's face. Then to his amazement the woman nodded acceptance.

"As you say, Prima Elia."

Elia's tone softened. "Too many interpretations are possible, Carol. After we get out the version that serves Eva's purpose, I promise you, we will invite you and the President to see the full record."

The NSC nodded again. "Safer that way, I guess. If it doesn't exist it can't get out." She looked down momentarily, her hands moving off-screen. "Okay. Now the last clip I have is Joshua carrying Eva into the pool. Is that right?"

"Yes. Thank you. Now I need about an hour to compile a composite video that you can send out to the world."

"Uh huh. Okay, I'll keep myself busy with non-SIO duties." The NSC grimaced. "No doubt the President will be wanting to explain to the world how bombs with a Russian radionuclide signature got dropped on a friendly foreign nation by Navy missiles under control of rogue elements in the US government." She clicked off and the Presidential Seal came on-screen briefly before the secure connection dropped.

Woman's a master of understatement, Demuzzio thought. Then it struck him, an axe through his heart. *Just like Sarah could be, sometimes.* The vibrations coming up through the rock floor shifted again, into a resonance that seemed like it wanted to console him.

Elia must have felt the shift. She wilted into the chair in front of the console and became just a grieving young woman again. She drew her hands down her face, wiping tears, and looked into her palms as if their wetness held all answers.

"Sarah is my mother," she said, her voice breaking again. "Was."

"Your mother." Demuzzio repeated, struggling with the concept. "And there, at the end… what was that… transformation?"

"What she used to be."

"What she used to be." Demuzzio repeated that too, rubbing his head. "And what was that?"

"Retribution."

"She pulls a helicopter back out of the sky. Zurvan in it. I get retribution. But…"

Elia shook her head and stood up, purpose firm in her again. "Later, Thomas; it's complicated. Now we have work to do. Sarah's gone, so you must help me with the video." She moved over to her own chair and motioned him into his. "To make happen what Eva intended."

What Eva intended. She intended a lot of things, it seems. Did she intend Sarah to take out Zurvan, for Sarah to sacrifice herself that way? Demuzzio stopped rubbing his head and, like Elia, drew his hands down across his cheeks to take the tears away.

"She loved you too, Thomas," the young woman said.

"I never told her."

"Tell her now."

"She's dead now."

"She's in my memories now. Tell her anyway."

He did.

The meaning that was returned through the vibrations in the rock floor was one of satisfaction, of completion. TC Demuzzio slumped into his chair in the quiet Council Chamber and waited for Elia's instructions.

To die a hero is not a bad thing, something elemental whispered, consoling him.

East Baliem Valley, Irian Jaya | Saturday 1451 JYT

Joshua O'Donnell fought his way upward through water that felt like mercury, dense and heavy and malevolent, wanting to crush all air out of his lungs. He tried to scream but the pressure was too high, driving water into him instead. He felt consciousness sliding toward oblivion. But then cool fingers touched his temples, a lightness that pushed away the water.

"Come back to me, Joshua," a familiar voice crooned. Or at least that was the meaning he inferred from the ancient Galatian. His tense body relaxed as the words resolved themselves into components of a chant. *Eva tricked me again! An elegant ambush by her friends the dolphins. And now she's fixing my ribs…* But that thought trailed off as it faced recognition. *No, that's a past event, weeks ago, a training session…* Fragments of more recent memories skittered across his consciousness. Slowly, sensations arrived from different parts of his body. *I'm lying on sand, soft, fine-grained, warm. I feel good.* He opened his eyes.

Eva's face looked down on him, inverted, framed by flowered trees with clear blue sky above. His head rested on her knees. Her cool fingers stopped their rhythmic patterns against his temples.

"Are we dead?" Joshua asked.

"No." Eva smiled down on him. "But I could kill you for almost screwing things up." She laughed and gave his cheek a tiny slap.

He rolled to the side and pushed himself up on all fours. A wave of dizziness made him lower his head.

"Slowly, Josh, slowly. It took me quite a while to de-water you."

He waited out the dizziness, then pushed himself up to sit against his heels, facing Eva, matching her posture. "Almost?" he asked. "But we're good now?"

"Very good."

"No radiation?"

"We're upwind."

How could she know that? Joshua shrugged it off: *if she says it's so, it is.* He asked a different question instead. "Sarah?"

Eva's gaze turned inward. "She found what she sought."

"She's dead, then."

Eva nodded. "But you remember what Uncle Ham said."

"Death is over-rated?" Joshua smiled at that. "And you? You were very nearly dead, kiddo. In fact, clinically, I think you were. You okay now? Let me see your back?"

She bent her head to the ground and showed him.

He grimaced. "Why don't you heal that?"

"Oh, the marks are just cosmetic now, superficial. The underlying tissue is knitted back together."

"You're keeping the marks?" A logic lattice formed, ran, and popped out the answer immediately: *part of her plan.*

"You were crazy to come, Josh," she said softly.

"I guess."

"But I'm glad you did."

"I helped?"

Eva nodded again. "You remember what else Uncle Ham said? About you and me and the water?"

He laughed as he quoted the old man. "She's a Pisces, laddie. You're a mere Aquarian."

"It helped when you reminded me. Otherwise we both would have drowned, I think. That was a nasty pressure wave."

"I wasn't sure you'd hear me."

"I didn't, not in the normal sense of hearing. But I got the message. My cells scavenged oxygen. Not much, but it was enough."

"So. You like my outcome better, kiddo?"

"I'm still in my body. Never quite realized how attached I've gotten to the darn thing."

"I'm glad." Joshua was content just to contemplate his little sister, watching the dappled sunlight flicker in her amethyst eyes. Gradually he became aware of the other flickers around her. A glow, really, splinters of light. *From the green of the trees, the blue of the sky, the black of the powdered volcanic sand beach, the bright sunlight of a mid-afternoon tropical sun.* A thousand shades and tones coalesced into an aura around Eva, and he understood. *More than attuned to nature; she's actually fundamental to it.*

The patterns in Joshua's mental tapestry metaphor tightened down in their weavings, probabilities converging on the outcome they'd all envisioned and hoped and prayed for. He watched the threads weave around Eva. Some of them, he imagined, stretched back over the Pacific to Hawaii.

She grinned at him. "Yes, the twins and Elia and Uncle Tee, they're all okay."

"I won't ask how you know this."

Eva giggled, the happy sound she always made when she out-foxed her brother-protector.

"The world's a mess, but it won't be for long."

"Your plan?"

"As amended by you, thank you very much, Joshua." She giggled again.

"De nada," he replied, laughing himself. Eva's inner child had always been infectious, a source of delight to his sometimes over-serious self.

"Elia is doing the right thing, Josh. She's compiling the video for Carol, who will send it out to the world. The global consciousness stats have been ramping up for hours now, anticipating it."

"Tough to watch," he warned.

Eva Connard stopped giggling. Her expression hardened into one much older than her young face, and a weary sadness ran across it. "Necessary," she told him.

"Helluva plan," he admitted, watching his mind knit together the now-inevitable good outcome. "There's a lot you never told me, kiddo."

"I'm truly sorry, Josh. I couldn't."

"Yeah. I'm beginning to see that now." His logic chased the threads of the tapestry backward through a multiplicity of conditional probabilities. *Sheer elegance*, he marveled. Eventually he smiled and asked: "Heisenberg's cat?"

"Meow," she answered.

O'Donnell Enclave, Waimanu, HI | Friday 1951 HST

Elia O'Donnell stopped in the middle of her work and shrieked. TC Demuzzio jumped off his chair.

"What?"

"They're alive, Thomas!"

"Both of them?"

"Yes! Alive and well and... wow!"

"What?"

"That's amazing!"

"What?"

Elia's gaze turned inward. "Eva just... how can I describe it... just downloaded an instruction set!" *And it's all part of her plan. So elegant. So beautiful. So... loving.*

"Downloaded?" Demuzzio rubbed his head, looking at his console monitor.

"Right into my mind. Wow!"

"They're alive," Demuzzio echoed. He sat down. He laughed. He cried. He stood up again. "I'll go tell the twins," he said.

"They already know," Elia said, her voice full of wonder.

Demuzzio sat back down. "An instruction set for what?"

"For the video, what she wants compiled."

"Okay. Let's do it, then."

"It's already done, Thomas. Sarah and I guessed almost exactly right. I just need to add one minor tweak..." she studied the screen images and worked the controls of the holographic interface "...and there, it's set to go." She flicked the send icon and they watched the download indicator.

Elia saw Demuzzio begin to relax.

"Now what?" he asked.

"We hope," she answered.

"The video is powerful stuff, Elia. I can't see any way it won't work."

"Hope that the destruction going on now in the outside world stops quickly," she amended, "that radical institutions in their death-spasms don't do more damage."

Demuzzio nodded. "Disruptive threat. Existential conflict. Okay, but I'm hoping for a quick resolution. And I really think we'll get it."

"I do too, but..."

"Don't underestimate the human capacity for stupidity?"

Elia shrugged. "We never anticipated the Senator. There probably are more loose cannons out there. Some of them have nuclear capability."

The download indicator registered a completed transmission and Elia turned her perception inward. *It's done, Young Mother.* She smiled at Demuzzio and began to relax. *I love you, Joshua,* her mind added to the message.

Demuzzio spread his hands. "Yeah. Okay. I'll hope."

O'Donnell Enclave, Waimanu, HI | Friday 2110 HST

Carol didn't waste any time, Demuzzio thought. The big screen in the Council Chamber showed one of the major network's late-night talking heads delivering a warning about the graphic content of what they were about to broadcast. Then Demuzzio's monitor lit up and the NSC's red-rimmed eyes stared out at him.

"Jesus, Carol, you need some sleep," he told her, "you look like shit."

"Always the charmer, TC, huh?"

"Sorry."

"Ah, you're right. But I've got to put the finishing touches on the President's statement. He goes live at 0700 Eastern."

Demuzzio glanced at the wall clock. *Less than five hours.* "You trying to ride the peak of the global consciousness response?"

"I don't know if we can time it that closely, but that's the general idea, yes."

"I like it." He studied her for a moment. "Anybody in your office?"

"No. And the doors are shut. Why?"

"Your ears only, Carol."

"What?" She studied him in return then smiled slightly. "You're not the Prima, TC. You can't bind my consent. Is this something that Elia should be telling me? Where is she?"

"Asleep with the twins. Your ears only, please."

The woman shrugged and waited him out.

She'll see it, Demuzzio decided. "Eva's alive," he said.

Carol Violette's jaw dropped. Then she whooped. "This is great news, TC! She's back with you guys? And Joshua? He make it too?"

"Elia says they're both okay. Still on Irian Jaya." Demuzzio rubbed his head. "How she knows that is a mystery to me, but I trust it."

"So do I, TC." The NSC laughed, and her face suddenly looked much livelier and younger. "But why keep it a secret? Escaping a nuclear blast, that has to be a good thing, *n'est-ce pas?*"

"Eva wants a cap on it, Elia says. She and Eva and Joshua need time to work something out."

The woman's eyes looked at him from the monitor screen, steady and unblinking. But then they widened. "Jesus! The SIO second coming myth? Eva's going to adapt that, isn't she?"

Demuzzio rubbed his head. "I dunno, Carol."

"I do. And what a lovely idea!" She whooped again, a full-bellied laugh. "Okay, TC. It's in my ears only. I won't tell a soul, not even the Prez. Until Eva tells me it's okay."

The NSC clicked off, and Demuzzio was left staring at the Presidential Seal, his questions unasked and unanswered. He rubbed his head and stumbled off to bed.

Chapter 40

Majuro, Marshall Islands | Sunday 0410 MHT

The Reverend Robert Blake sat staring at the monitor placed just outside the bars of his small holding cell. His status as founder and leader of the United Ministries of Christ, the world's pre-eminent Christian evangelical group, had done him no good at all with what passed for the local police. They hadn't said much, except to tell him he was being held at the request of the US government.

Right after he'd been served a spartan dinner, the computer arrived. Without saying a word, the guard had set the laptop on a chair just outside the cell bars and flipped up the monitor screen. It looped an hour-long video that had been shot from multiple viewpoints around the pool in Irian Jaya.

Amazing technology, Blake conceded as he watched his perfidy play out to the world for the third time. His betrayal was a but a shadow of the monstrous acts perpetrated by Muhammad Zurvan, but it was still enough to make him squirm. *I had no idea that technology even existed. And Eva never said anything to me about it. So she foresaw all this, that's the only explanation.* It was, he also conceded, probably the most elegant entrapment of all time. *She let me do it to myself.*

Halfway through the first hour, as a camera showed Eva's back being flayed to shreds and the poorly concealed lust on Zurvan's face, Blake had lost his dinner into the cell's stainless steel toilet. His stomach still rumbled at the enormity of his missteps, and now he sat bent over on the edge of the bare cot, his arms tight around his chest.

Footsteps sounded in the corridor outside; the guard's clacking heels on polished concrete and a softer sound. *Rubber soles.* He stared at the concrete floor, head in his hands, vaguely remembering hearing a jet whining down to land at the nearby airport twenty minutes ago. Its sound had echoed through the barred but open high window above the toilet.

"I wondered who they'd send," he said, looking up as the cell door clanged shut behind a slender woman in jeans and a flower-print shirt. The guard retreated up the corridor. "What's your name?"

"It doesn't matter."

Another hard woman, he realized. *One of the SIO warrior class. She could probably kill me with either hand. Will she?*

The woman pointed a remote at the computer and the sound muted.

"I'm not really here, you know," he told her, "I'm in the desert in California, preparing my Easter sermon."

The woman shook her head, a slight smile acknowledging the feebleness of his effort. "The FBI has your double in custody. A nice job, a very close match. But we have his DNA. We have your DNA."

"Then I have nothing to say."

She shrugged. "You don't need to. I came a long way just to point out one thing."

"What's that?"

"A public trial. Very messy. People screaming for your head."

Will she kill me now? Blake sat back, reflexively filling his lungs to call for the guard.

But the woman didn't move. "See this shirt?" she asked. "The print?"

Blake let out a little breath and nodded. "Red hibiscus. Eva liked it. Wore the flower in her hair."

"One of her pet projects was to restore the plant to its natural habitats on the islands."

"Yes, I remember."

"We've recovered the thirty million Zurvan paid you."

"Impossible," he scoffed.

The woman smiled and gestured at the monitor. "As impossible as those video clips?"

So, she caused the laptop to be put there. He offered no answer.

"We thought it would be appropriate to use the money in Eva's restoration program," she continued. "That particular hibiscus is an endangered species."

I remember how animated Eva got when she told me about the program. "And am I?" Blake asked.

The woman's smile narrowed into a tight hard line. "I think you know."

Again he had no answer; again she continued.

"A public trial, Pastor Bob. Very messy," the woman reiterated. "People screaming for your head, your church in tatters. All that shame, for a proud man like you, a minister to millions."

"There's always a way out," he mustered.

She lowered her voice to a whisper. "They don't have much serious criminal activity here in the Marshall Islands. So they don't keep much of a watch on prisoners. And they left you your belt."

The two stared at each other for a long moment. The guard arrived when she beckoned. "Thirty million," she said over her shoulder as she walked out, "to plant red flowers. Thought you'd appreciate the allegory."

He listened to the guard's footsteps clatter down the hall alongside the almost inaudible steps of the woman. He nodded. *Point taken.*

Blake took off his belt. Standing on the toilet seat, he cinched it through the bars of the small high window. He fashioned the end into a crude noose and slipped it over his head. *No time like the present.* Keeping his hands firmly in his pockets, he let his feet slip sideways off the toilet.

O'Donnell Enclave, Waimanu, HI | Saturday 0611 HST

TC Demuzzio sat in the big Council Chamber, sipping Kona's finest coffee. *I feel better than I have in a long time.* He picked off news feeds from around the world and dumped a few of the more interesting ones on the big projection screen to study in detail.

Weather satellite passes continued to show a massive localized rainstorm over the East Baliem Valley on the island of Irian Jaya. Too tight a cyclone, a meteorological impossibility, excited TV weathermen kept pointing out: the energy was far too dense to be supported by the atmospheric physics in that part of the Pacific. *But it's keeping people out, isn't it Eva?*

He toggled semi-systematically through other news feeds, following the revelations people had experienced as they awoke to the carefully-crafted videotape of Blake's betrayal and Zurvan's evil and Eva's sacrifice. He paused to listen to the Aga Khan's calm voice delivering a well-tempered message to Islamics world-wide. *The book Eva gave him... man's got some serious cred now.*

The small console monitor in front of him on the table lit up with the Presidential Seal and then the NSC's smiling face.

"Morning, TC. Thought you might be awake."

He smiled back at her. "Looks like you caught a few zzz's yourself, Carol."

"A few. The rest is makeup. But thank you."

"Great statement you wrote for The Man. I watched it three times. Got teary-eyed. First time I've ever cried for a politician."

She laughed. "Our President, TC, only took some of my words. The rest were his. And they came from the heart."

"Yeah, yeah. Good job anyway, Carol. All the right buttons. You see the Aga Khan? The Pope? They're all pushing the right buttons too."

The woman nodded and changed the subject. "So what are Eva and Joshua doing in Irian Jaya? They're still there, I presume, judging from the storm."

"Rebuilding the blast zone."

"You're serious?"

"I didn't believe it either."

"How do you know?"

"Eva talks to Elia."

"I presume you mean not on a cell phone."

"Right. Eva doesn't need one anymore."

"She talk to you directly too?"

"Naw. I ain't got the right receiver in my noggin, Elia says."

"A Sister thing? I'd like to talk to Eva directly if I could."

"No. It's a threesome thing. Apparently a link got established when the ladies were in that trance trying to figure out the virus."

"Sarah's dead."

"Yeah. No longer with us. But now she's a telephone line, or a satellite link, or whatever the right equivalent is for a mind."

He watched the NSC's face as she processed that.

"Rebuilding the blast zone," Carol Violette murmured. "Can I give the Prez a heads-up on what their plan is?"

"Eva said sure." Demuzzio rubbed his head and launched into the explanation.

The NSC listened, saying nothing, her bright eyes totally focused on him. Eventually she nodded. "Different angle, but it fits the Sisterhood myth."

They looked at each other for a moment, in mutual recognition that the world had changed completely.

Demuzzio spoke first. "So how about an update from your end, Carol? It's what — eleven AM in DC? Your feds got Blake?"

"He's in a holding pen in the Marshalls. We're scheduled to extradite on Monday."

"He talking?"

"A Sister's visiting him now. We'll see."

"Tell her to strangle the fucker for me."

That brought a tiny shake of the woman's head. "The Sisterhood doesn't normally operate that way, TC."

"Has it escaped your notice that these ain't normal times, Carol?"

She smiled at the sarcasm. "We'll see," she repeated. "And in the meantime, our forces and friendly governments are picking off the remaining K'Shmar sites."

"Life is good," he said.

"You bet," she answered. "I'll start prepping The Man for Eva's next big event. Sunday noon, you said? Let's keep each other posted, okay?"

Demuzzio nodded and clicked off.

O'Donnell Enclave, Waimanu, HI | Saturday 2310 HST

The two of them stood on the promontory above Waimanu Bay, listening to whalesong under a full moon. *They sound so happy,* Joshua thought as his ears twitched forward a tiny bit.

Eva laughed and answered aloud. "They are. A few babies have been born already; lots more on the way. Life is renewing itself."

He nodded. *They have a natural sequence.* A logic lattice made the correlation. *Just like the sequence Eva's plan is bringing about for humans.* Now it was his turn to laugh. *Eva's plan!*

"So complex yet so elegant. I'm still not sure how you conditioned all the probabilities."

"Your mind is wired to do it the hard way, Josh. Boolean logic lattices, beautiful things to watch work in your mind. But they're all crystalline framing: yes or no, zero or one, on or off."

"It's never been hard for me," he objected. "It's natural."

She shrugged. "Your way isn't for me. I do it an easier way."

"Intuition?"

"Um. Not exactly. More like… computational equivalence, is what your friend Stephen would've call it."

He laughed delightedly. "Definitely more natural. Hey, whatever works. But what about the logical loose ends?"

"You mean am I alive or dead?"

"That's the biggest one. The world thinks you're dead. The good outcome, the empathy we're seeing on the GCN, is predicated on that."

"Not completely. Elia left some ambiguity in the video. Your wife is very clever, Josh. I'm not sure you ever fully understood how clever."

He nodded agreement. *No doubt of that, but ambiguity leaves opening for bad possibilities too. How to broach that?* "You know, Eva, the ancient Roman emperors, after they died… it was a custom that they became gods."

"I didn't know."

"Emperor Vespasian is lying on his deathbed, circa 79 CE, and says 'Drat, I think I'm becoming a god.'"

Eva laughed. "Okay. I get it. You're pretty smart too, bro."

"So what are you going to do? Play dead?"

"No, I can't do that."

"Dead gods are safer than live ones, I'm pretty sure."

"I still can't do it."

"Why not? Besides being safer, you'd probably be more influential."

"Because it's not true."

"That makes a difference?"

"I don't want to get a new species off on the wrong foot."

"Have you talked it over with Elia?"

"Yeah. She quoted one of her spirit-Sister ancestors."

"Who?"

"Hypatia."

"The Egyptian mathematician. What did Hypatia say?"

"To teach superstitions as truth is a most terrible thing."

"Ah."

"And she and Elia are absolutely right on this one, Josh."

"Ancient wisdom."

"Some of the best. One of your ancestors, by the way, pre-Jesus, was Archimedes."

Joshua contemplated that for a moment, searching his eidetic memory. "He holed up in Greece, in Syracuse. So far as history knows, he never had a family; geometry was the only love of his life."

Eva giggled. "He got his education in Alexandria…"

"I know that, Eva."

"…some of which was in bed with a Sister who, in current terminology, was extremely… horny."

"The Sisterhood's grand plan. So I have that to thank for my unusual brain?"

"Yup."

"So what about him?"

"He said essentially the same thing as Hypatia, six hundred years earlier."

"Doesn't sound like something he would say."

"It wasn't. He was quoting his Sisterhood lover, one of Hypatia's ancestors."

"Ah. Got it." *Now she's trying to divert me from the question.* He re-asked it: "So you're not going to be dead and a god? You're going to be alive and a what?"

He watched her luminous eyes absorb the bright moonlight. It played across amethyst pupils, flickering there like it did on the waves entering Waimanu Bay below.

She sighed. "I don't know. For now I'm going to be an ambiguity."

"Not alive, not dead? Not human, not god?" His logic lattices spun up, worked, and tumbled out a probabilistic answer. *She won't lie, but we need to preserve the deity myth until the dust settles on this and the Novas are safe.*

Joshua shrugged. "Your call, of course."

"I need latitude to work. Ambiguities have more… degrees of freedom."

"Speaking of work, are you sure I can't help you any more with the rebuilding?"

"No, Josh. You gave me exactly what I needed, the science I didn't have, the molecular knowledge of the rocks and earth and flora."

"I still don't believe it, even though I watched it come together."

"Destruction of the reality doesn't destroy the template, Josh. You repaired Aaron O'Meara's spine that way, remember? You were nine years old."

"That was a lot simpler, I think, than rebuilding a waterfall and a pool and a rock plateau from nothing but a radioactive crater."

"Some ways yes, some ways no."

Joshua shrugged again. *The world as a computational equivalence.* "Come on, sis, let's go in and celebrate." He turned onto the path leading down the cliff to the enclave portal.

"I can't, Josh. Not yet. Say hi for me."

He turned. *She's biting her lip. She's crying.* He walked back and hugged her.

"I... need more time before I face them."

"Face them? They're your family!"

"A family I betrayed." More tears ran down her cheeks.

"You didn't..." he started.

"I couldn't tell you my plan. You wouldn't have let me go through with it. I caused you almost impossible grief, all of you. And Sarah died."

"Everyone forgives you, Eva."

"I know. That's what's hardest. I can't face forgiveness right now."

She's in a more fragile state than I thought. "Okay. So what are you going to do?"

"I'm going back to Irian Jaya. I'll bury myself in work. I'll tidy up the loose ends at the pool. I'll get ready for Easter tomorrow. Maybe by then I can face forgiveness."

"You'll let me know if you need help?"

"Thanks, Josh. I will." Eva wiped her cheeks. "Oh. Yes, you can do one thing. Put one of the spare airborne nanocams right here in this spot. I'll transpose it."

"The hawk simulation? Programmed?"

"Yeah. Secure uplink. The Indonesian re-entry team may not have high-res video gear."

"Got it," he said. *Back to business to divert your emotions? Done that myself, kiddo. I'm sorry for you.*

Eva touched his cheek. "Mom and dad, they're okay now. They're waking up. Tomorrow morning. Help them out." Then she turned and leaped off the cliff toward the whales singing in the bay below.

He watched her circle in the air a moment, like the water-birds for which Waimanu was named. She called back to him over her shoulder. *"Aloha,* big brother."

"A hui hou, little sister," he whispered.

Eva Connard sang her sadness to the whales as she descended and passed over, and then vanished from sight.

Joshua O'Donnell turned and walked down the path to the enclave, his steps light and heavy at the same time. *Ambiguity.*

East Baliem Valley, Irian Jaya | Monday 0400 JYT

Eva Connard stood in the pre-dawn dark but she could see. The rain pounded around her but she was not wet. The wind howled past but not a hair moved on her head. She stood inside a bubble of her own devising, an intention that made gravity do her bidding, and reviewed her reconstruction work. She saw that it was good.

"You agree?" she asked Gabbatha. "You're the one for whom this pool was your outward reflection in the natural world."

"Close enough," the locus agreed, in a way that conveyed to Eva the sense of a repaired and re-tailored shirt being tried on.

She saw the damaged patterns with her left eye and the repaired patterns with her right eye. *A few microscale changes will bring them closer together.* "Um. Okay, maybe just a few more tweaks."

"Not necessary. You should rest."

"But the sixth day isn't over yet," Eva objected. She smiled at the thought: *creation is great fun, hardly work at all.*

"In this work you seek escape from your sorrow, Eva." The voice delivering that truth was her mother's, though the words were Gabbatha's.

"Therapy, Mom," she agreed.

"Useful, then. But afterwards some rest. Your performance tomorrow requires more integration."

"Okay." She sighed. *Managing minerals at the atomic level or plants or animals at the cellular level... duck soup compared to managing your own emotions when you can feel everyone else's so intensely.* Eva focused on the tasks at hand, driving her mind back through the collective memories of her spirit-Sisters to the times before written history. Ancient eyes, she discovered, had seen through nature to the underlying truths of higher levels. *Nature is the clothing of consciousness. Spirit is reflected in nature. The loops both feed back and feed forward, threads in the tapestry of time.*

"The old pantheists saw this," Gabbatha agreed, "as did many others. But then the arrogance of increasing knowledge of the physical world turned matters of the spirit into the dry and overly cerebral religions of your modern era."

"And now? Novas will see the kinship between spiritual values and the natural world, won't they?" *A feed-forward loop, the Nova gene.*

"See it, taste it, feel it," Gabbatha confirmed.

"As acutely as you and I do?"

"You and I, yes."

And soon there will be little difference between us, I suppose. Eva's intentions reached out to touch a few rocks here, a few plants there, then reached outside the storm to invite the circling hawks to fly in once the wind began to die down. Time bent to her wishes, and she set it to let the storm blow itself out in a few hours.

O'Donnell Enclave, Waimanu, HI | Sunday 1106 HST

Elia Baradei O'Donnell stretched and yawned like a cat, arching up from her chair in the Council Chamber. *To wake up in the morning to sex with your lover... yummm.* She grinned at the big monitor screen as she watched multiple streams of live video from the Indonesian reconnaissance team. Then she laughed out loud, for no reason other than pure contentment. Suited men with instrument packs were preparing to enter the area that the storm had interdicted for the past two days. The wind had dropped but low scud clouds still rushed by, occasionally misting the camera lenses. *Our nanocams don't have that problem. I wonder if Joshua managed to get a few air-dropped so we can make our own record.*

Elia stretched again, lazily and contentedly, and let a different part of her mind watch another scene playing out, this one inside her body rather than on the big monitor screen. At the proper moment she reached out with the fingers of her Sisterhood training to condition the probabilities of that internal scene. *I think this baby needs to be a girl, Joshua. The world should be safe for her now.* Elia made the decision and the alkalinity and hormonal balances shifted in her uterus to welcome the ovum as it descended. *She'll wrap you around her little finger, Joshua. Infinitely worse than Eva. You poor daddy!* The laugh turned into a full-throated belly-laugh, resonating her ovum as one of Joshua's little swimmers broke through its sheath.

On the screen, coordinated movement caught Elia's eye. The suited re-entry team began walking into the area. *Just over a kilometer. They'll go slowly, checking radiation levels. A half-hour to get there, maybe forty minutes.* Joshua was down in the vault helping his groggy mother and stepfather. TC Demuzzio was in his Security Center coordinating with government operations and simultaneously entertaining the twins.

She keyed the enclave intercom to advise them. "The Indonesian teams are starting to go in now. A half-hour to reach ground zero, I think. Maybe a bit longer."

Chapter 41

O'Donnell Enclave, Waimanu, HI | Sunday 1107 HST

Easter Sunday, TC Demuzzio mused, *I wonder if I should do an egg roll with them.* He studied the twins, who were in turn studying the big tom-cat intently. Mr. Bojangles was sitting on Demuzzio's table in the Security Center, returning their studious looks, unblinking. He purred. His tail flicked rhythmically. Ibrahim and Gaelan seemed entranced; even their mother's voice on the intercom hadn't broken their concentration. *No, I guess they're past the egg roll stage.*

Finally the cat gave a long slow blink and switched his gaze to Demuzzio. The entity for whom the cat served as avatar spoke inside Demuzzio's head, amused.

"Ah, well, yes and no, laddie. When ye incubate bird's eggs artificially, ye roll them. Slowly and carefully, and not always in the same direction. Aids the developin' embryo, y'see."

Demuzzio gazed back at the cat and spoke aloud, amused himself. "This late in my life, I finally perpetrate a metaphor?"

Gaelan and Ibrahim looked at each other and giggled, their concentration broken. The cat tilted his head toward the door. The twins giggled more as they scampered out, bare feet slapping down the hall toward the kitchen.

"Bring a pitcher of guava juice and some glasses to the Council Chamber," Demuzzio yelled after them. "Please."

"A metaphor, yes. And a nice one at that. Yer smarter than ye give yerself credit for, laddie."

Demuzzio smiled. *Maybe. Hard to tell when you're in a group like this.*

The cat's gray eyes flickered. "Ye have questions for me, now that it's a bit of privacy we have?"

"I've always had questions. Just never got many answers from you, old man."

The cat blinked slowly again, something that might or might not have been a grin making his whiskers twitch.

Fucking Cheshire Cat. "Only the few answers I put together for myself, sixteen years ago… and I believe you erased even those from my mind," Demuzzio continued his complaint.

The big tom's body seemed to shimmer.

"Ah, 'tis true enough. Constrained by the Covenants, I am. But 'twas for the best."

Demuzzio shrugged. "Water over the dam. Your Covenants no longer apply, I think. So tell me now."

A very long sigh filtered into Demuzzio's mind. It carried undertones of pride and humility, war and peace, gladness and sorrow, glory and shame; all in a long struggle toward the endpoint that was Eva. The sheer scope of it was stunning, the details too overwhelming for him to absorb. *But the entire story is there now, locked in my mind, so I can look at it if I want to. Thank you, old man.* For now, Demuzzio got the general sense of it and was content with that. "Eva was your last best hope, wasn't she?"

"Aye, lad. She was."

"When the attempt with Jesus didn't work out."

"I thought it premature. As did Mary of Magdala. But he was a stubborn man."

Images flicked past Demuzzio's inner view. *An opiate in the water-soaked rag raised to the man's lips as he hung dying. A bribe to the Centurion guard to verify that death had occurred. The release of the not-quite-dead body to the care of the Arimathean, in the safety of whose tomb Jesus was nursed back to partial health.*

Demuzzio stared at the cat, mesmerized by the unblinking gray eyes. Other images played out. *The flight of Jesus and Mary of Magdala to Egypt. Infection from the wounds. A long recovery with the Therapeuti of Alexandria, while the Zealots hunted them. Their subsequent flight to Galatia and anonymity and many offspring. Centuries later, the morphing of the ages-old myth from allegorical to literal, in the gospels.*

"A mistake?" he asked the cat. "Surely you could have kept them from it?"

"The Covenants, lad... they respect free will."

"So you just salvaged what you could."

"The bloodlines, yes. Both were very close to Novas. Mary especially. She was the source of much of his power. The locus at Irian Jaya — which Eva has named Gabbatha — resided in Galilee in that era."

"Over two thousand years. A long time to wait."

"This modern world presents a more favorable context."

"More rational?"

"Aye. And more caring."

"You could have fooled me, some days."

"Trust me, laddie. I have a longer historical perspective."

Demuzzio laughed at that. "I guess so."

"Friends, then, Thomas?" The question came framed in his mind, but his ears heard the plaintive meow.

Demuzzio leaned forward in his chair. He reached out his hand. He rubbed the shimmering tomcat behind its ears. He got a purr in return.

Over East Baliem Valley, Irian Jaya | *Monday 0621 JYT*

Eva Connard's viewpoint hung in space, several planet-diameters above the Indonesian island-state of Irian Jaya. She saw her body, and felt it, but knew it was just a projection of her mind; the stars shone through it. With her two equally insubstantial companions, she watched the day/night line move westward across the island.

"Half in darkness, half in light," she whispered.

"As will be...," said the entity who was conjointly her father John Connard and the locus Waimanu and the male aspect of the intergalactic wandering guardian of the implicate order.

"...always," finished the entity who was conjointly her mother Lara Picard and the locus Gabbatha and the female aspect of that wandering guardian.

"But for now... we're moving into daylight." Eva smiled at the planet below, feeling its joy.

"The cycle moves on," the female aspect acknowledged.

"In an upward spiral; here, at least," the male aspect agreed.

"Thank you for your help," Eva told them. "Thank you for coming back when I called. Thank you for saving mom and dad."

"Desperate love is a powerful call." The guardian that was the image of her mother smiled at her, starlight flaring in her green eyes.

The guardian that was the image of her father reached out his insubstantial hand to touch Eva's insubstantial cheek. "We will always come for that." His deep blue eyes flared at the contact.

Eva's physical cheek, thousands of kilometers below, felt the warmth of his touch.

"Will they remember?" she asked the images. "Mom and dad, their physical selves, their brains... when you leave this time, will they still know, understand?"

"That choice we leave to you, Young Mother. The memories encoded in the neural mass of their physical brains are complete."

"Gabbatha and Waimanu?"

"Your interactions with the loci over the past years, yes, they are in your parents brains, intact. They have those memories."

"But access to the memories? And is there danger in recalling them? After being in time-stasis for so long?"

A composite shrug followed some contemplation by the two guardians. "Time is just an emergent property of your reality. It doesn't flow; your existence flows... a matter of perspective. But best to let memory access occur gradually, we suspect."

"Suspect? You don't know everything?"

A tinkling laugh came with the response. "What would be the fun in that?"

Eva watched the stars shining through both images resonate in a frequency that matched their laughter, and smiled herself as she chased the answer a bit further. "Through the memories of Waimanu and Gabbatha... they will see my pain and sorrow as well as my joy and love?"

Another composite shrug. "The two-edged sword of existence. Gabbatha is the female aspect of life. Waimanu is the male aspect. Yin and yang. In the human species they are not separable, but neither are they complete by themselves."

"I'll let them see their memories," Eva decided.

They laughed with joy and spoke as one. "You are a good step, Young Mother. You and the Novas. Farewell."

The two images elongated into vortices of energy, green and blue light, chasing each other away from the planet. At the outer edge of Eva's vision they entangled, their complex patterns folding inward, becoming one, and vanished from sight.

O'Donnell Enclave, Waimanu, HI | Sunday 1128 HST

Although Elia Baradei O'Donnell's body stood in the Council Chamber of the enclave, her other eyes watched the scene in space and saw the entities depart. And it was not only her eyes, she realized. *I have company, an audience of spirit-Sisters gathered, all watching over my shoulder.* A gentle touch came on her shoulder.

"Mama," she said, reaching to pat the hand that was not really there; the Chamber was empty save for her. "Welcome to my mind."

"It took me awhile to re-cohere, and to get oriented." The entity that had once been the physician Hessa Gibran, a neurosurgeon... who had become Hessa the Crone, a tool of Muhammad Zurvan... and who was then resurrected by Eva as Doctor Sarah Kruse, a physician and neuroscientist...

That history passed through Elia's mind. It conveyed a sense of wonderment as the entity clothed itself in its past identities, working forward through them.

"I've been waiting, mama." The longing Elia felt, and the waiting she experienced, was not just over the last few hours or days, she suddenly understood. It went back to her childhood. Even though her adoptive mother had been a wonderful woman, there had always been an ineffable sense of something missing. *A gap in my spirit.*

Her mother spoke to Elia as her daughter for the first time since the child was born. "I've been up to the mountains. I've been down by the sea. I've wandered, unformed in this world."

"Your body is just atoms now, mama. Scattered to the winds."

"You would think that something with no physical existence cannot be physically destroyed. Yet there must be a connection." Puzzlement pervaded the entity's words.

"Patterns, mama. The body is a composite of waveforms. There is resonance, back and forth, Eva says, between our patterns and our realities. And Joshua agrees, though even he cannot fully comprehend its quantum nature. Do you not remember those discussions?"

"Patterns? Nothing like a nuclear blast to perturb them, I guess." Amusement leavened her words. "In any event, Eva guided me back. Again."

She'll remember eventually, Elia decided. "My mind is your mind now, mama. Welcome home."

The two minds spiraled around each other, entangling. Other spirit-Sisters joined them. Elia stood mesmerized at the dance, until physical reality intruded.

"Elia?" Her husband stood in front of her, a half-worried smile on his face. "Where are you, love?"

She gently moved the spiral of maternal ancestors to the back of her mind and focused on Joshua in her physical reality. She stood on her toes and kissed him.

"Right here," Elia said. "Right here with you."

"Elia, I'd like you to meet my parents." Joshua stepped aside.

They are a handsome couple. They looked healthy, though they leaned on each other. *Amazing what that child did.*

From a different part of Elia's mind, Sarah looked through analytical eyes at the two people she'd tried to kill when she was Hessa the Crone and doing Zurvan's bidding. Their eyes glittered, star-sapphire rings around the pupils, Lara Picard's brilliant green, John Connard's just as brilliant a blue. *They exist in another dimension too*, Sarah told Elia.

But Elia had no time for analysis. Her joy was so massive it pushed out all thoughts but one: *our children have living grandparents.* She opened her arms and ran to them.

East Baliem Valley, Irian Jaya | *Monday 0657 JYT*

Eva's mind lingered in space, not troubled in the least by having a perspective from multiple locations at the same time. She watched the terminator line on the planet below edge westward, bringing more early morning light to the valley. Low scud clouds from the intense storm remained pocketed there, obscuring the area. *The sun will need to break through at just the right time. I want a rainbow across the waterfall behind me. It will be good luck.* She formed a meteorologically precise intention for a wedge of drier air to descend and begin to dissipate the clouds, and departed from her space perspective.

Standing on the ledge above the reconstructed waterfall and back in her physical body, Eva turned on the communicator her brother had provided. She keyed it to control the drone. The small hexakopter took off quietly and stationed itself above the thinning cloud deck. At a distance, a casual observer would see it as only a dot in the sky, possibly one of the circling hawks.

"You getting video, Josh?"

"Five by, kiddo. Still some ground fog or low stratus over the pool area where you are. It's thinning out, though."

Eva shifted her perspective to one of the hawks. At her bidding it dropped past the drone and into the cloud deck, flaring out below it and flying across the waterfall a few meters in front of her. She saw the hawk in her own eyes, and at the same time saw herself through the hawk's eyes. With a wave of her hand she sent the bird back up through the clouds. She laughed into the communicator. "Nanocameras. Satellite transponders. Uplinks to computers. How quaint."

"Quaint? One of my coolest concepts?" Her brother managed to sound aggrieved.

"Better to fly with the hawks, see with their eyes."

"No doubt. And when you can persuade them to output a digital signal, maybe we'll switch over."

A part of Eva's mind idly considered that. *An interesting question for you, Josh. What will a post-digital world be like? What problems will it bring between the new and the old, the haves and the have-nots?* Then she pushed idle thoughts out of her mind and cast her perspective eastward toward the approaching re-entry team. She heard their excited chatter, watched them move faster as their radiation counters continued to show nothing above natural background. They were getting close to the edge of the rainforest that opened onto the volcanic rock ledge around her pool.

Eva wove flowers into her hair, waiting. She adjusted her white dress. It was a modest Hawaiian muumuu, but cut low in the back to reveal the bloody marks left by Zurvan's scourge-whip.

The re-entry team chattered around the rock edge of the pool. Video camera crews moved in behind. Eva stood concealed above them, at the top of the waterfall, sensing the low morning sun in the eastern sky begin to shred the remaining thin clouds.

"I'm about to go in now, Josh. I set the drone east, at the edge of the forest. You can take over it now." She set the communicator down without waiting for a reply and prepared herself, intuitively parsing the dynamics of humidity and heat. The sun was about to break through and give her the rainbow. *Any moment now.*

O'Donnell Enclave, Waimanu, HI | Sunday 1159 HST

In the Council Chamber of the Hawaii enclave, through the drone's nanocamera, seven souls watched the scene unfold at Eva's sacred pool and the waterfall behind it. Five of those souls were *Homo sapiens*. Two were nascent *Nova sapiens*. Ibrahim and Gaelan were certainly human in all senses, and the Nova gene in them would not fully express until after puberty, but still they regarded what was about to happen with somewhat more equanimity than their mother and father and grandparents and adopted uncle TC Demuzzio. *They see with another sight,* Joshua O'Donnell thought as he glanced toward them. *I envy their confidence.*

In the foreground, the Indonesian re-entry team bustled excitedly around the edge of the pool that had been ground-zero for a nuclear strike not two days ago. Joshua worked the controls of the nanocamera as it circled above them. *Any minute now,* he thought, *they'll bring out a calibration source and check their instruments for the fifteenth time.* They did as he predicted, in a flurry of activity and shouting and gesticulation more reminiscent of Italian troops than the more laid-back Indonesians. Gaelan whispered something to Ibrahim and they both giggled. One of the troops tossed a weighted tube into the pool to pump a sample of water and sediment into a pail. A radiation detector held over that drew only negative shakes of the head and more gesticulation. *Nice cleanup, Eva.*

Then the clouds parted. A low shaft of sunlight kissed the tops of the trees to the east and ran west to intersect the waterfall. A rainbow formed immediately in the spray and mist above the pool. The vortex in the center of the pool widened and deepened, its rhythmic roar shifting to a sound that had overtones of coherence. The Indonesian team turned to look at it.

In the Council Chamber, Joshua worked the nanocam controls to tighten focus down on the center of the pool. A part of his vision not associated with his eyes caught the afterimage of a big tiger-striped tomcat perched on the ledge above the waterfall. It shimmered with the same shards of light as the rainbow below. One forepaw hung casually off the ledge, relaxed, but its gray eyes were intent, observant. Joshua stole a quick glance at Mr. Bojangles to his left. The cat rested in identical posture, foot hanging off Eva's console, watching the big screen across the Chamber. *Maybe he's there, maybe he's here. It's all probabilities.* The cat's shimmer began to slow its rhythm but took on a deeper amplitude.

As they watched the big screen, Eva rose slowly from the pool's vortex. Water neither splashed on her nor dripped off her. Flowers were woven into her curly hair. Her body seemed to tug at the rainbow above, the splintered light of its spectrum drawn in by the pure white of her dress. She spread her arms, palms up, and rotated slowly on the water's surface. The whirlpool beneath her feet went flat and quiet as she stood on it.

The film crews that had followed the re-entry team had three cameras locked on Eva. They did not speak, nor did any of the re-entry team. A collective moan came from all of them when Eva's rotation showed her lacerated back. Otherwise there was little sound; the forest had gone silent, the waterfall merely whispered.

She stopped her rotation when facing back east toward the people on the rock shore of the pool. A sun shaft played full on her but she did not blink. Eva smiled, a gentle welcoming one. Little native songbirds flew around her and a few perched on her outstretched arms. Her indigo eyes danced with their music.

One by one, the soldiers knelt on the hard rock. "Eva," they chanted, "Eva! Eva!"

On the console in front of him, Joshua saw the shimmer around Mr. Bojangles deepen and peak and vanish. In the vision that had nothing to do with his eyes, he saw the image above the waterfall leap into the sky and chase a blue-green glittering trail away from the earth and into deep space.

On the big screen, one of the Indonesians yelled in an agony of hope: "Eva! You will come to us?"

"Go down to the water in the twilight," Eva answered in her musical contralto. "The wind will whisper my name. The waves will carry my love."

Then she vanished.

The End

About the authors

Lee Denning, a pen name, combines the first names of Denning Powell and his daughter Leanne Powell.

Denning has been a soldier, scientist, engineer and entrepreneur. The Connecticut resident recently sold his environmental consulting firm and moved to Hawaii. His extensive background in the physical sciences underpins their stories.

Leanne is a California resident, and a psychologist and corporate writer by day. By night she turns her passion for words and ideas to fiction and poetry. She contributes much of the metaphysical and psychodramatic content of their stories.

Monkey Trap, the first book of the *Nova sapiens* trology, was published in November 2004. *Hiding Hand*, the second book, was published in October 2008. See the website at monkeytrap.us and the blog at monleytrap.us/blog.

Don't miss any of these highly
entertaining SF/F books

➢ Alien Infection
(1-933353-72-4, $16.95 US)

➢ Burnout
(1-60619-200-0, $19.95 US)

➢ Cynnador
(1-933353-76-7, $16.95 US)

➢ Hiding Hand
(1-60619-016-4, $19.95 US)

➢ Jerome and the Seraph
(1-931201-54-4, $15.50 US)

➢ Monkey Trap
(1-931201-34-X, $19.50 US)

➢ Strange Valley
(1-931201-23-4, $15.50 US)

➢ The Last Protector
(1-60619-001-6, $19.95 US)

Twilight Times Books
Kingsport, Tennessee

Monkey Trap
Nova Sapiens Book I

Lara and John are given the incredible powers of the next stage of human evolution by two alien visitors. One wants to help the human race fulfill its potential, to transition into the *Nova sapiens* state. The other wants to use those powers to return the race to a more primitive state of mindlessness and darkness, to assert its power. But which is which?

Praise for Monkey Trap

"The first volume in a projected trilogy presents a cast of convincing characters and a compellingly paced plot. Denning, the pseudonym of a father-daughter writing team, uses quick changes of scene and character-building flashbacks to create an sf adventure that combines hard science, mysticism, and alien contact. For most libraries."
Library Journal

"*Monkey Trap* is a SF thriller that keeps you on the edge of your seat the whole time, wondering what's going to happen next. There are two alien visitors, one who wants to help the human race fulfill their potential and one who brings only chaos in his wake. But which is which? Will the visitors bring about the next stage in human evolution or its destruction?

"With well drawn characters and a wealth of detail, it's a book you may want to read again to get the full force of it. Any book that deals with alien visits to earth can easily fall into a cliched trap, but not this one. There is a real imaginative tale here, and what more can you ask for in a SF novel? A great read."
Annette Gisby, editor of Twisted Tales

"This is an immensely exciting SF thriller..."
Dr. Bob Rich, author of the The Stories of the Ehvelen series

"...I have not often seen such an evocative presentation of what [Global Consciousness Project] is about, both the science and the philosophy."
*Dr. Roger Nelson, Director, **Global Consciousness Project**.*

Order Form

If not available from your local bookstore or favorite online bookstore, send this coupon and a check or money order for the retail price plus $3.50 s&h to Twilight Times Books, Dept. LS712 POB 3340 Kingsport TN 37664. Delivery may take up to two weeks.

Name: _____

Address: _____

_____

Email: _____

I have enclosed a check or money order in the amount of

$_____

for _____ .

If you enjoyed this book, please post a review
at your favorite online bookstore.

Twilight Times Books
P O Box 3340
Kingsport, TN 37664
Phone/Fax: 423-323-0183
www.twilighttimesbooks.com/